Betty Burton has won a
Women of No Accoun
stories, *Women are L*
several awards for her
Festival Theatre Awa
televi

Born in Romsey, Hampshire, Betty Burton now lives in
Southsea with her husband, Russ, and is working on her
fifth novel.

By the same author

Women are Bloody Marvellous!
Jude
Jaen
Women of No Account

BETTY BURTON

Hard Loves, Easy Riches

GRAFTON BOOKS

A Division of the Collins Publishing Group

LONDON GLASGOW
TORONTO SYDNEY AUCKLAND

Grafton Books
A Division of the Collins Publishing Group
8 Grafton Street, London W1X 3LA

Published in paperback by Grafton Books 1990

First published in Great Britain by Grafton Books 1989

Copyright © Betty Burton 1989

ISBN 0-586-20182-3

Printed and bound in Great Britain by
Collins, Glasgow

Set in Garamond

FOR MY WOMEN FRIENDS

THANKS FOR YOUR HELP

To Elizabeth Murray for Menken and Nevada.
To Christa Worthington for Boston.
To Bill Jones for Mister Slope and other clergymen.
To JRB for the railway navvy idea.

June 1850

HAMPSHIRE

SAINT BARNABAS' DAY. Hedgerows in the June lanes are fat and heavy. The lacy caps of guelder rose, entwined with woodbine and red-clawed, pink-bowled briars, glisten like snowflakes at the tops of the hedgerows. Foxgloves and cranesbill, clover and potentilla exhibit glorious genitalia for bumble-bees and brown butterflies, who hardly know which ready blossom to visit next.

Along one such lane, in Hampshire, half-way through the nineteenth century, walks a young man in his early twenties. Slim and pale. The slimness is thin and the pallor is not pink-tinged but dull, as though he lived on the edge of fatigue. But this does not diminish the handsomeness of his face, which derives from good bone structure – an oval shape, straight nose and wholesome teeth.

His name is Peter. Peter Warren. Not long ordained, he is, to be correct, the Reverend Peter Warren, which, in view of the casual state of his dress, his masculine good looks and a commonplace image of the solemn clergymen, is surprising. He has not the look of a cleric who spends much time in the company of dainty teacups and small cakes.

He leaves the lane of sweet-smelling hedgerows and takes a side-turning which is no more than an arbitrarily worn track leading over the turf to some chalky workings which look like a round-barrow in the making, high up on the downs. As he does so, he sees three figures a hundred feet below and for a moment halts his stride and raises his hand.

He calls, 'Hello there!'

But the warm breeze rushing upwards over the downs

carries his voice away from them, and they are looking carefully at where they are going, so he walks on towards the 'barrow', losing sight of them as they pick their way along a raw white cutting in the green downland.

Although they have never met, the young clergyman knows who these three are, and something about them. Their family has lived in these parts probably as long as his own, and in rural communities such as this is and always has been any bit of news is immediately communicated – from market-place to village, to hamlet, to inn and even the most isolated farm – by carrier, carter and packman.

So Peter Warren already knows that the young man of the group is Auryn Tylee, who at twenty-one is the same age as himself. The young woman is Ruth Tylee who is tall, flaming-haired and twenty; the third figure is Caroline, ten or so years younger than the other two, who has a severe skin disease.

He knows also something of their history, gleaned from the kind of gossip that would naturally surround anyone recently arrived, after a voyage of many months, from Australia. He knows that they are of local ancestry and that their father, who led a rebellion, is exiled for life and that their mother, who has brought them to England, is soon to return home, leaving these eldest three of her five children in the care of an aunt.

Gossip has it too that the reason for the three of them returning to the home of their ancestors is that Caroline cannot hope to be cured of her disease unless she lives away from the drying climate of her homeland.

Gossip also has it that Ruth Tylee is a rare beauty. Gossip often gets such things wrong but, being red-blooded and twenty-one, the Reverend Peter Warren wants to see for himself.

The lanes on the lower part of the downs are even more alive with bees than those higher up, and the three young people are taking in the novelty of the exotic fecundity of the county of their ancestors. Of the three, only Caroline was not born in the village a mile or two from where they now walk, so that Auryn and Ruth have ragged bits of memory that they try to stitch together as they walk.

They have passed small red-brick houses, knapped-flint cottages and wattle-and-daub hovels with thatch as unkempt as crows'-nests, on the way to the object of their curiosity – Great Hole Tunnel. The knowledge that they should not be here adds to the thrill of the expedition as they scramble down the embankment. The young girl, arms stiff with bandaging, slips and slides.

Her brother holds out a hand to help. 'Steady, Carly.'

'Don't fuss, Auryn. I'm not a cripple, you know.'

'Take Auryn's hand, Carly,' Ruth Tylee says. Caroline accepts her brother's proffered hand as they enter the place they have come to see.

A vast cavern. Not the glassy bubbles of the Maribars nor the weird, festooned chambers of Wookey. This cave has water-pools on its lumpy floor, smooth chalk walls, shining with moisture and smelling of rusty iron and dead moss. This cavern has not been made by heaving or eroding Nature, it has been made by men.

Beyond where the light reaches – down from a hole in the roof and in at the entrance – is unfathomable blackness.

Forty men could stand shoulder to shoulder at its base, sixty where the walls reach the widest part of its curve, and fifteen tall men, each on the shoulders of the one beneath, to reach the roof.

This cavern is the entrance to Great Hole Tunnel.

Great Hole was made by navvymen who took shovels to the chalkhill and dug one spit . . . then a foot, a yard, a mile and on, on, into one side of the downs and out the other, and then on, on until they had shovelled and burrowed for thousands of miles the length and breadth of Britain, changing trade, society, and customs, upsetting the lives of settled families, enticing away settled women, brawling with settled men.

Fighting, drinking, fornicating, labouring.

Most navvymen were dead before they reached forty.

They built the canals, the dams and the railways of Great Britain.

Ruth Tylee's skin contracts with a creeping shiver as the damp from the walls of chill chalk touches her warm, brown skin. Yet it is not just the drop in the temperature that causes the shiver – it comes from within herself.

For a few moments she is deaf to her sister's chatter.

Strangely, although it is the opposite of the open lands around her old home, this place exhilarates and stimulates her in the way that some parts of Toolagarry have done. There she used to ride her horse out into the bushland until she felt that only herself and the animal existed. There she used to shiver in exultation as she drew in her breath and sang out loudly to the desert, controlling her breath, holding the notes high and long. There she had thought of the sound as being breath from the heavy blue sky. She loved the sound of it. Over the years, as she grew up, the power and range of her voice had grown. In the evenings she often sang her few songs, but none of the family had ever heard her voice as it was when she sang with abandonment to no one but the horse and the sky.

Now, in this vast cave, she wishes that she could be here alone, to hear her voice as she had once heard it echoing in an Australian hill-cave.

Only the cavern at the mouth of the tunnel is visible from where Ruth Tylee stands with her brother and sister. Tentatively she sings out 'Cooo-eee'. It echoes around the chamber.

'Ruth!' her brother says. 'You're worse than Carly.'

Caroline, taking this as a rare compliment, makes a smug face at Ruth.

Now Caroline calls, so that her voice too returns from unfathomable blackness, beyond where the light reaches down from a man-made hole in the roof of Great Hole Tunnel.

'Isn't it *just* like a cathedral, Aury?' Caroline asks.

'Caves of Hell rather,' he answers.

'No, she's right, Aury,' says Ruth. 'It is like a cathedral.'

'And when did Carly see any cathedral?'

'In Ma's Knowledge book, of course,' Caroline says.

'Aury has no imagination.' Ruth, as usual, sides with her sister against the attempted authority of their tall brother.

'I know. And you've got too much. Come on, Carly, Ruth. I shouldn't have agreed to come here, it's no place for you.'

'Oh, *Ruth*, tell him to stop being such an old fuss-bugger.'

Her elders in unison: 'Caroline!'

'Well, *I* think that it looks like a cathedral.'

'It's a work-place, child,' says her silver-haired brother, 'and if we don't get away soon, the navvies will be back.'

'Tell him to stop calling me "child", Ruth.'

'Stop calling her "child", Auryn.' Ruth elbows him, smiling broadly.

'Not until she stops behaving like one. Now come along, this is a dangerous place.'

He begins to walk away, hoping that his unruly sisters will follow his lead.

Walking slowly backwards, out of the mouth of Great Hole, guided by Ruth, Caroline reaches out to take her brother's hand as well. It is to show that she is not in a seriously rebellious mood. She feels sorry for Aury and wishes that he had not taken upon himself the protection of herself and Ruth.

And sorry because he is different from the rest of the family.

Ruth is robust and healthy, and has since childhood felt protective towards him. With his pale complexion and silver hair, he has always seemed to be isolated from the rest of the brothers and sisters, with their colourful red or brown hair and freckled skins.

Just as they reach the mouth of the vast tunnel that has been cut through the Hampshire downs, Ruth halts.

'Look, Aury, isn't that just "The Hole into Heaven" picture in the Book of Knowledge?'

Beaming directly downwards through the opening in the roof of the cavern is a column of sunlight, so bright as to appear gold against the blackness of the unlit tunnel. It lights up the arc of the white walls, shining and glittering upon the running moisture, reflecting off the pools of water on the floor and the surface of the iron railway tracks.

As they take in the extraordinary transformation, something moves in the column of light and begins to descend slowly. It is a kind of large, round wicker basket with a man inside. Caroline's eyes are wide, she holds on tightly to her two protectors.

'Ahoy!' For a moment the basket halts, then moves again as the rider makes a signal to someone above ground. 'Ahoy, there below.'

The basket speeds up the last ten feet or so and lands bumpily. The rider gets out and comes towards where they stand, wary and unsure.

'I saw you along the road. This is by way of being a short cut to catch you up.'

Auryn speaks up. 'Sorry if we are trespassing. But we'd heard that the place was certain to be deserted today because of a funeral. We were just leaving – the child was curious.'

Caroline gives him a warning squeeze.

'Well, to be truthful, we all were – curious, that is. But we'll be off now; I dare say the excavators will soon be back.'

The young man raised his eyebrows and shrugged his shoulders. 'No need to hurry, they will not return for hours yet. They took a large collection for "Old Ragged Crow's" wake, enough for a good six hours' solid drinking. There are navvies who have come from all over the diggings in the South. I've done my part, reading the burial service, nothing to do but to leave them to it.'

He gives a formal bow that Ruth sees as incongruous in the circumstances. 'Peter Warren – preacher and navvyman's missionary.' He laughs, seemingly at his title; when he laughs it is within his entire face. His mouth is as wholesome as her brother's. Ruth cannot see a single gap of a missing tooth nor yet a blackened one, and his lips are mobile and full. She smiles back. The gossip as to his looks is not exaggerated.

'Six hours of randying shows you that I am a poor kind of missionary; I have no success with curbing drunkenness.'

Many things have surprised them since their arrival in England, but none more than a young man, dressed in rusty black with a frayed neck-cloth, descending in a basket and claiming to be a missionary.

'And you are the visitors from the Antipodes come back to their ancestral home.'

They each shake his hand.

'How do you know that?' Caroline asks.

'Why, good Lord, Miss Caroline, from your fame. Auryn, Ruth and Caroline.' At their genuine surprise, his laugh echoes back into Great Hole . . . a big laugh.

Ruth raises her eyebrows at him. 'And what are we supposed to be famous for?'

'Why, for coming home to your birthplace. For having sailed the high seas.' As young men hoping to appear favourable to an older sister are inclined to do, he directs his smiling remarks at the younger one.

Now back in the open, the June midday sun is thin and lukewarm compared to the Australian sun in Toolagarry, where the Tylees have grown up, but Peter Warren squints his eyes and puffs out his cheeks at the sudden blast of warmth.

Caroline looks back at him with the solemnity that her family recognize as the expression that goes with facetiousness. 'That's not why we came here, Mr Warren. Ma brought us because we was just tired of being at the bottom of the world and always going about upside-down on our heads. It is not easy staying on earth if you aren't the right way up, you know.'

'That's enough of that sort of forwardness, Carly,' Auryn says with just enough sharpness for Caroline to know that he means it.

Unnecessarily occupied with tightening the string that is binding her sister's hair, Ruth says, 'That's Carly's idea of a jest – so many people have joshed her about being at the bottom of the world. I'm afraid you will find us a bit rough in our manners, Mr Warren – we don't come from very civilized parts, and we've always been encouraged to speak up for ourselves. Ma said that people here was likely to find us a bit forward, especially Carly. Overseas people . . . I mean English people . . . they don't like children to speak up, do they? We have always been brought up to say what we think between ourselves. We live in quite a remote place . . . we don't ever see many . . .' The sentence trails off and she looks to Auryn for help.

'Toolagarry is a very wild place and . . .'

'I know,' says Mr Warren earnestly. 'One of the penal settlements, isn't it?'

'Yes, it is.' Auryn's chin lifts a couple of inches. 'Our father was a Radical who was sentenced to be hanged for his beliefs, and my mother carried me in her arms in support of the same . . . we are not ashamed, Mr Warren.'

Ruth hears in Auryn's voice their father's rhetorical style, the strong Radical family tradition and the buttress of their parents' marriage. The Tylee children were fed Radicalism with their infant pap.

Suddenly Ruth realizes that Auryn does not really understand what that means, any more than she does herself. They learned the words but not their meaning.

'Nor should you be, Mr Tylee. People in these parts have great regard for those who spoke up for their neighbours at the time of the Riots. The Tylee name is remembered.'

As they take their leave of him, Ruth realizes that this man probably understands what she and Aury do not. Perhaps he has grown up in the embers of the old protest. Perhaps here they still glow. She senses his involvement and feels inadequate and a sham..

PART ONE

New Experiences

I

KITTY FIRE-BUCKET

IN THE RICH, BROAD LIGHT of the June afternoon, Peter
Warren stood atop the 'muck' pile of the railway cutting and
watched as the three figures diminished and eventually
disappeared into the soft, open country.

Good, fat land. Good for grain growing, for root crops,
fruit and the rearing of cattle and sheep. This gash the
railway navvies were cutting through the lush downlands
was like a sabre wound across the breast of a woman. It
would never heal.

He tried to imagine what it would be like in five years
when the muck was carted, the men, horses and wagons
gone. It did not seem possible that any living thing would
ever germinate or take root on the arid chalk and red gravel
of the banks.

The railway company would send its engines to carry
people along the rails, through the Great Hole Tunnel
towards the coast in one direction and to London in the
other. To travel freely, and to carry goods ever more quickly
between the cities and towns of the South, seemed to Peter
Warren not to be adequate compensation for the wounded
breasts of the Southern Downs.

He rolled his trouser bottoms clear of the chalk muck
and began walking towards the shanty-town. If the gang
returned from the burial very drunk, alone he would be of
little use to stop their aggression towards their women or, in
their drunken generosity, the loaning of them out to half the
gang in exchange for beer. A navvy wouldn't lend his shovel
or ask to borrow his mate's, yet the way their women were
exchanged was something the young clergyman had not

been able to come to terms with. He had grown up in a
family of eight children where five of them were girls, so that
he was constantly bothered by the vision of one of his sisters
transposed into the situations of degradation his work led
him into.

Any woman who threw in her lot with a farm-labourer
had little enough to call her own, but usually she had some
security and a little dignity, and lived in a community where
there were grandmothers and cousins and a handed-down
history. But a woman who took up with a man on the tramp
had nothing except transient neighbours. Those who were
married had gone through a navvies' ceremony of 'jumping
the stick', which was literally that, and wasn't the least bit
binding. Most navvy marriages ended with the man
suddenly leaving and going off on the tramp without fear of
consequences from Parish or Law.

The one bit of good luck that a navvy woman left in
destitution might have was if her man had held the tenancy
of a hut or a shanty. Although a woman could not herself
hold a tenancy, she could transfer that of her lost man to a
new man of her choice. Consequently, a woman with a
tenancy in her gift was sought after for the dossing-down
rents it brought.

To visit just such a woman was the purpose of Peter
Warren's visit to Great Hole shanty-town.

Whatever name she had before she arrived on the diggings,
Kitty 'Fire-Bucket' was her name now and was likely to be for
as long as she remained on the diggings, and through however
many men's hands she might pass. As her conventional, more
law-abiding sisters must take the identity of the husband, so
must the navvy woman adopt the anonymity of her man, and
be known only, as were most navvies, by his nickname.
'Cocky Fire-Bucket' had boasted himself 'a man as good as
they come – thirty gallons of ale a month'. Like his wandering
fellow navvies, he had dressed like a dandy.

Cocky, having got in bad with police for having knocked a local farmer senseless in a drunken brawl, had sloped off on his own. He shared out the spoils of the years of their relationship as fairly as he thought right. He took the skillet, the blanket, the candles and the balance of his last earnings. He left Kitty with her share – a toddling child, a babe at the breast and, in her gift, his tenant's rights to a sod hut at the edge of Great Hole shanty-town. Being unable to take over the tenancy herself, Kitty and the two small Fire-Buckets were now on offer to any man who promised to be good to them – and, failing that, any man at all.

'Well, Kitty, have you thought over what I said? It's a rare good offer. It'd mean a roof over your head and a bit more stability for the children so that they could attend school when the time comes. It would be only rough cleaning work, but that's what you're doing at present.'

'I know what you said was kindly meant, but I should be fair lost stoppen in one place. I an't never known nowhere except the cuttens and the shanties.' She had a soft West Hampshire accent mixed with something from even further west, in which certain words, coming at the end of a sentence, rose on the last syllable as though questioning its correctness. This gave an impression of shyness. The Reverend Warren liked Kitty Fire-Bucket and had hopes of 'saving' her. He had persuaded a good Christian farm-wife to give Kitty a roof over her head in return for rough work.

'That's no reason why you shouldn't learn to live somewhere better.'

'I wouldn't have no friends nor nobody. I know everybody on the diggens. They're a set of buggers, but I belong to them.'

'You don't belong here, Kitty. You're different from most of them. Your mother was teaching you something. Learning your numbers, learning to read.'

'I can read all right. I still got one book.'

'There you are then. If you took this position, you could have other books, the place is full of them.'

'Well, I don't know that I should want that many, the one I got is pretty good, and that takes me months enough to get through.' Her pretty young face became serious. 'My Mam give it to me when she died. She said she brought it with her when she run away from home with the Ole Man. She said she couldn't abide the thought of parten with him.' She laughed. 'Parten with the book I mean, not parten with the Ole Man. Though she did say that when she first went away with him, she would have run off the edge of the earth with him, she was that taken by him. I never liked him. I always thought he was a dirty ole sod, even though he was my father.'

'Kitty, you know I keep telling you that such words as those aren't good.'

'I can't help it, Vicar-dear. It's being with Cocky for so long. I don't hear myself saying it, so I couldn't stop even if I tried, and he *was* a dirty ole sod, anyway.'

They were standing outside the rough turf-roofed hut upon which nodding grasses and coltsfoot bloomed; the whitewashed board walls within indicated the pride that Kitty had taken to make something of the place. Peter Warren nodded at the high bank behind the hut. 'Do you remember how the water came down there last winter?'

Kitty laughed. 'Ah, it was a bit like a river of milk runnen across the floor. Fire-Bucket said he was going to get us a few bits of planking before the next bad weather starts . . . and now the bugger's been and gone off on the slope. He was always the same Fire-Bucket – say he'd do a thing then do summet else.' She prodded the straining toddler who had made a puddle at their feet, 'Round the side and do it.' The child moved a few feet off and squatted in the approved place, a yard or so from the doorway.

'Have you got a man in mind for the tenancy yet?'

'Dutch and Ollie.'

'Both?'

'I thought Dutch'd be all right, but of course Dutch won't come without his brother, and it seems to me it'd be better to have two men that gets on with each other than two that fights.'

'Dutch and Ollie fight like dogs.'

'Not *mean* fighten. They just squares up to each other when they're in drink, or when they got an argument to settle.'

'How old are you, Kitty?'

'I don't know. Sixteen or maybe seventeen or summet like that.'

Peter Warren compared her to his own sister at home, wearing decent aprons and print frocks, this very moment learning jelly-making under their mother's instruction.

'Well, Kitty, if you can't be persuaded to take the place you've been offered, at least promise that you'll come down to the Mission again.'

'Listen, Vicar-dear, it an't no use me promisen. Fer a start Dutch an't a man that'd be very pleased at a woman of his doing that kind of thing . . .' The baby gave a whimpering cry and Kitty drew aside her bodice, squeezing and inspecting her milk-rigid white breast before she put the baby to it. The clergyman flushed at the unexpectedness of her exposure and tried to force his wayward thoughts into the realms of Madonnas in blue robes, and wondered, as he did frequently, whether he was the man for the work he had chosen. She continued as though there had been no break, '. . . not when he's sloggen at the diggens, he wouldn't like me randying off up the Mission.'

'But the Mission needs good young women like you, Kitty.'

'Why, love you, Vicar-dear, there an't many men that called me "good" – not in that way. And I got to be straight with you. When I came down there a few times, it was because I felt sorry for you. You work that hard. But honest, Vicar, it an't a very exciting thought to sit in a old hut and sing hymns.'

'There's more than that goes on, you know it does. The letter-writing and . . .'

'And nothen else.' The babe slept. She removed her beautiful breast from its mouth and stood uncovered for a moment. His eyes could not leave the perfect shape and he suddenly experienced a stab of sharp anger as he imagined the calloused hands of the two braggart brothers having possession of it. He watched her hitch her bodice in place and lifted his eyes to find her watching him. For a second she touched the side of his face, much as a mother does to comfort a child. 'Vicar-dear, 'tis time you got yourself a nice little wife. You're too sweet a man to be wasted.'

2

SUSPICION

CROUD CANTLE FARM, the 'ancestral home' to which the
Reverend Warren had referred that day in June, was set in
the village of Cantle. And the village of Cantle was set safely
in a Hampshire valley protected by four arms of the
Southern Downs. The cottage was very old and, along with
its few acres of land, had belonged to the family for a
hundred years and more. When their mother used to sit with
them in the insect-ridden Toolagarry evenings and tell them
true stories, or when her long, clear memory caught her
arm-deep in suds, she filled the children with their history.

So it was that when Ruth saw Croud Cantle for the first
time after years away, she could have gone immediately and
without guidance to the well, the old dairy, the pig-pen or
into any of the rooms and any of the plots, so familiar was it.

On the morning last April, when her mother was ready
to start out on her return journey to Toolagarry, they had
stood together with Aunt Selena and looked across the
Cantle Valley.

'You'll miss all this green, Ma.'

But her Ma had shaken her head.

'I shall miss you, child, and Aury and Carly, but this
valley has grown too small now . . . not only the valley, the
whole country seems shrunken and closed in.'

'I like it here, Ma.'

For answer her mother had simply patted her on the arm,
and Aunt Sel began all over again her assurance that Lidia
could go back to her other children in Toolagarry, knowing
that these three would be well cared for.

'You understand, Sel, if all or any of them pines to come

back, then there's enough left to pay their passage home. Just look how much better Caroline is in just these few months. If she stays on with you another year, I reckon her skin'll be cured.'

A surgeon from a ship visiting the colony where the Tylee family had settled, had said that he had seen such a condition before – always on red-haired children with delicate complexion. In his opinion the skin had no defence against the sun or the dryness and heat of the region. The only cure, he declared, 'is for the bairn to be sent to live in Scotland. Aye, she'll bathe her poor wee arms and legs in soft water and the dews and mists will moisturize and stop the cracking. Why, woman, did anyone ever see the soil of Edinburgh open up from baking under the sun, as it does in this place? 'Tis no wonder the poor lassie canna bear her breeks upon her.'

England was settled upon as second best. Ruth wanted to return to England where she was born, and, with Auryn, would help Aunt Selena to run Croud Cantle, the little farm which their mother had inherited long ago.

And last April, Ruth had seen the muscles at her mother's temples working as she tried to chew back her emotion when it was time to return to Pa and the two young ones, and her new farm in Australia, the one she had not inherited but had gained by putting her faith and what money she had into the new country. Pa, by reason of being a convicted man transported there for life, had no choice.

'She'll be all right, Ma . . . she will.'

'Of course she will. I wouldn't be leaving her if I didn't think that. I'm happy to see how changed she is already – just the stopping of the itching alone makes her easier.' A short silence had fallen as they watched Caroline racing around, playing games with the old farm dog, so different from the child who had since birth been tormented by her cracked and bleeding skin. 'Oh dear God, Ruthie, how shall

I keep going without you all?' Tight vocal cords made her voice waver but she did not cry.

'Lord, Ma, anybody'd think we wasn't ever going to see each other again.' She tried to compensate for the lack of conviction in her tone by smiling, but that was equally unconvincing.

'You know that I can't come back, Ruthie . . . not until Adam don't need me any more.'

At the mention of her exiled brother's name, Selena had turned away and gone back to the house.

'Poor Sel, after all this time she still misses Adam as much as ever.'

'I don't think I could bear it, to know that Aury had gone for ever,' Ruth said. Ruth had another brother, young Barney, but it was the thought of losing Aury with the finality with which Aunt Selena had lost Pa that made Ruth understanding.

'I reckon it's knowing that he's alive and well even though he's at the bottom of the world. In a way death is easier to come to terms with. Everybody has that to face up to,' Ma had said.

'And poor Pa. You stop with him, and take on that new land you were offered, and you'll get rich, and we shall come and see you, even though I shall be seasick for six weeks and Aury will pretend he's not terrified of falling overboard. Carly will look after us.'

'Ah, yes, wasn't she a good child to us when we all thought we should die of misery?'

'A little sea-going nurse. I think she revelled in it.'

'And when you get back, just think, you'll probably have time to spare growing your old lilies, now that there's three lots of baking and washing less.'

For the first and last time, Ruth saw her mother weep.

That was seven months ago, so that by now she ought to be nearing the end of the long sea voyage.

* * *

It was now late November, and as Ruth came up from the bottom field with field-mud weighing down her boots, she looked at the lopsided old cottage and was glad to be here. She felt a sense of belonging, being part of the chalkhills, of the junipers, reeds and flowers, of the stone and flint of the walls and of the chalk downlands that sloped away behind the cottage. Years ago, the aunt who had left the place to Ma had kept a book in which she had written down anything that came to mind. Now Ma had brought it back to the house. In the book, Ruth had come upon a paragraph which pondered on the idea that, because she was nourished by the food that grew upon the soil of the Cantle Valley, and drank the water that ran through the chalk of the downs, then she was made of their same substance. Ruth understood what had prompted her ancestor to write that.

Late in the day, the winter sun had dropped below the Western Downs, leaving the sky with a warning red glow. She took her implements into the outhouse where Auryn was sweating at sawing a long length of timber.

'God above, Ruth, it's a wonder this place didn't fall down.'

'Well, what can you expect? It's a marvel that Auntie Sel has kept it going as well as she has since Uncle Robby died.'

'I'm not complaining. Just stating a fact.'

'Well, just don't refer to it in front of her.'

'God's nails, Ruth! I'm not a fool.'

She scraped the mud from her implements much more vigorously than was necessary, so that the metal rang. 'Only when you speak like that!'

'You'd rather I sounded like the Cantle lumpkins?'

'Who's a bigger lumpkin than someone who looks down on another for being the villager that he is?'

'Stow it, Ruth, if it's not Pa's words you're spouting, then it's your lover's.'

Ruth's cheeks flared as red as her hair as she flung down

the scraper, and it sparked off the flints underfoot. Angrier than she might have been had she not recently been swallowing his jibes.

'He's not my lover. And what would I want with spouting *any* man's words? Do you think I haven't got intelligence enough to spout my own? And in any case, I do at least spout them – not simply glower at people.'

'Who glowers?'

'All the time. You've become a glowerer and a misery.'

'Pot calls the kettle black.'

'Oh, tit-for-tat – don't be such a *child*. If you are going to say something, at least be original.'

'And don't you start another of your paddy-rows, Ruth.'

'Me? Start a . . .'

'Yes, these days you start up three paddy-rows a week.'

'Well then, how about a real row – one with some lump behind it.' With the word 'lump' she whacked him hard across the backside with the cane she was using to pick out the mud from the tines of a fork.

The blow could not have been very stinging through his hard corduroy breeches, but it was unexpected so that when he swung round he was still holding the sawn-off end of timber, which hit her a blow that sent her flying. His pale face blenched even whiter and for a moment the shock of what had happened caused both of them to go immobile and stare at one another. Then he rushed to his sister, raised her up and, throwing his arms about her, rocked her comfortingly. 'Oh, Ruthie, Ruthie, I'm sorry. I didn't mean to hit you. Did it catch you hard? Are you hurt? Let me see.'

One way or another it had been coming for some time. Suddenly, Auryn burst out crying like a child and put his arms about her. 'It's just the not knowing if Ma's arrived back safe.'

This was not the true reason. Being the young man that

he was, he did not understand that his own nature was the enemy of an easy state of mind. He laid down standards of behaviour, made rules for himself and expected others to live by those same standards. If they did not, then he felt that they had let him down.

Perhaps it was that he had inherited from his mother the sensual nature of her family. A nature which must shrivel and harden if it is restricted and made unexuberant when crossed with a strongly conflicting nature. Perhaps this conflicting nature, inherited from his real father, Luce Draper, was not best nurtured by his step-father, Adam Tylee, who had been imbued with a sense of conscience that had nothing to do with any idea of 'sin'.

Perhaps it was that whereas his mother and step-father would never acknowledge the concept of 'sinfulness', Auryn had a keen, albeit unaware, sense of its meaning. More than that, his misery was self-inflicted, for he drew on the idea of 'sin' whilst rejecting his parents' ideals.

Thus it was impossible for him to know what to do about the sometimes overwhelming love he felt for Ruth. Because it frightened him, he made himself stiff and judgemental and too often as condemnatory of any wildness in her as he was in himself.

If this is the explanation of the tight emotional bonds in which Auryn held himself, then it helps an understanding of Ruth who inherited not only her mother's sensual nature, but her father's passionate one. If Auryn was unconsciously afraid of his 'sinful' tendency, then so was Ruth of hers – the difference was that Ruth did not admit of 'sin' any more than did her parents. It did not make her free, quite the reverse. Because she wanted Auryn's affection, love and, above all, his approval, she was always aware of her own actions in his presence.

Distressed at seeing him so emotional, she too let go of her pent-up tears, and in the chill, lamp-lit outhouse, she clung to him as she used to do in their mutual misery twelve years ago, in that strange, empty, uncomfortable land, where their mother had taken them to join her husband, Luce Draper, only to find that he had died before they had even set sail.

In those early days they resented him for dying and spoiling everything by making Ma unhappy. Their mother had not known how unhappy they were, so they had comforted each other.

Ruth wiped her face on one corner of her rough apron and offered her brother the other. 'We could do with Pa here,' she said.

They both loved Pa and could not now imagine him without Ma, or she without him. They could not remember when it happened, but suddenly their name was Tylee and Adam Tylee became 'Pa'.

'He'd soon settle us.' He put his arm protectively about her.

She relaxed into the warmth of his armpit and breast, breathing the reassuring smell of Auryn. Although she had always felt herself to be the protector, it was always from within a set of rules that established her own subservience to him. She knew that he could not have borne it had she hinted at what they both knew – which was that he relied upon her strength. She sensed that he would tighten his arm and kiss her hair before releasing her. Had he not done it, she felt that she would have wailed aloud for need of that comfort. Unsure of how he would react, she gave a brief kiss on his downy stubble as she pulled away from him.

'Poor Pa. I think that it is worrying about him that makes me so fidgety about Ma.'

'I know, I can't think what he would do there without her.'

'Organize the native people,' she said. The relief of

having cried, and spoken her unsaid fears, caused her to giggle and then lead him too into unwarranted laughter.

His guard now down, he did not stiffen as they stood leaning against one another until they regained their composure, then were silent for a minute.

'Talk to Carly, Aury.'

'What about?'

'Her bad dreams.'

'Poor little Carly. I've been a real fussbugger, only concerned with my own feelings.'

'When she gets a bad one, Aunt Sel takes her into her bed.'

They resumed their work, Ruth rubbing an oily rag over the implements, Auryn marking off measurements.

'I think she's the kindest person I've ever met. Don't you think she's kind, Aury?'

'She is that. If it wasn't for your red hair, you could be her daughter, have you noticed that? Once or twice when you've both been working together and you've got bonnets on so that your mop is covered up, you look more alike than you and Ma.'

Ruth made no reply, and he went on: 'Same height, same chin and nose, same cheekbones . . . only your hair is like Ma's.'

Ruth had noticed, and having noticed, had looked more closely at her aunt, and seen that she was indeed a younger version of Selena. It had at first puzzled, and then when she came to the only possible conclusion, concerned her.

Auryn turned suddenly and caught his sister, brows drawn, gazing at him. 'What's the matter, Ru? You should be flattered – Aunt Sel's a handsome woman for her age.'

'Oh hush, Aury, haven't you worked it out for yourself?'

He frowned. 'Worked what out?'

'I don't even want to say it.'

Still he looked puzzled. 'I'm never very clever at the end of a long day. Just say it.'

She drew in her breath. 'We call her "Auntie" because she's Pa's sister . . . so really she's not supposed to be related to you and me at all. So . . . if we are Pa's *adopted* children . . . then why should I resemble the Tylees?'

In the glim of the oil-lamp, she glanced up to catch his expression. 'And I do, don't I? Even our hands are the same.'

She paused, wondering whether to tell him how her suspicion had been aroused.

He stood stock still, looking at nothing except the thoughts springing up inside his own head.

'Ruth!'

'What other explanation is there?' She could have told him how her suspicion was almost confirmed by a single entry in the Family Book but she wanted him to come to the inevitable conclusion for himself. The entry, one of the last written in that hand, read: '*I believe that she is within a hair's breadth of finding herself enmeshed in such passion that it will break all their hearts. She was made for him and he for her. Domesticity ill suits her. They should be equals in leading this uprising. It seems inevitable that they will become lovers. It is as though nothing else can be the outcome.*' The protagonists un-named, it was the most enigmatic of all the hundreds of entries made over half a century. Ruth was certain of its meaning.

'I don't want to think it, Ru.'

'You *have* to, Aury, unless you can explain it any other way.'

'It would mean that . . . No, I won't believe that of Ma.'

'She would only have been a girl. Such things happen, Aury.'

'It would mean that you would be only my half-sister. No, Ru, no, I won't have that.'

'Nothing wrong with it – Carly and the twins are only half to us, and we love them, don't we?'

'Right! But not to *us*!' He paused, his eyes searching the walls but seeing only the consequences of his thoughts. 'If what you are suggesting is the truth, then you are Carly's *sister*, and I am only half-brother to *all* of you.'

'That makes no difference. When have we ever even given a thought about it till now? We're all Tylees . . . all of us.'

'No, then I am alone as a Draper – not a Tylee like the rest of you. That's why you are all so red and brown, and I have none of the features of the rest of you.'

'If it comes to being a "Draper", then so rightly am I – Ma never had our names changed, so I'm Ruth Draper if you like, and you're Auryn Draper. Does that make it any better? We can easily return to our old names if you like.'

'It's not the names. You are right. It's all so obvious. It makes me alone, Ru . . . me and the four of you.'

'Aury, don't *say* such a thing.' Suddenly, she felt panic-stricken, she had not expected him to make so much of it. It was getting out of hand. Her tone became placating. 'And it's probably not even true, lots of people look like other people – just coincidence.'

'I don't belong.'

'Don't say such things. Of course you belong. Even if it did turn out to be true, it wouldn't make any difference to me that we had different fathers. Now stop. We're behaving just like we used to, when we frightened ourselves with the willywinds and had to run indoors and put our heads under a blanket.'

'God's nails, Ru! It's some willywind when it seems as though your father cuckooed my father with our mother. That's a terrible thing. Adultery.'

'Auryn, don't! Let it be. I wish I had never started this. It's no better than trying Ma and Pa in their absence with no evidence, then passing sentence.'

Suddenly he took her face quite roughly between his hands looking wildly at her, and for a moment when he drew his face close she thought that he was about to kiss her fiercely upon the mouth, like a lover. 'No evidence, Ru? It's here! Solid enough evidence – you are a Tylee. No wonder they would never speak about *him* – Luce Draper – my father. She didn't really mean it when she said "Let the dead rest" when any of us asked about Luce Draper. She was ashamed . . . they were ashamed. And so they should be.'

He stood still and rigid, his hands held slightly away from his sides making fists of his hands, his head forward.

Ruth tried to take his hand but he held the fist. 'Listen, Aury, if we are not careful this will do something that can't be mended. Auntie Sel will notice there's something between us and she will worry . . . and what would we say? That we believe that her beloved Adam was a . . . ?'

He finished it for her. 'A seducer.'

He heaved a sigh, moved a step and relaxed his tense muscles.

'Let us never mention it again. If we are not blood brother and sister, it will never matter to me . . . in a way it makes me love you more . . . it makes you and me special to one another.'

He turned sharply and was about to say something, but then simply shook his head.

'Promise not to mention it again, Aury.'

'I can't make such an open promise as that – who knows what could happen? It might need to be spoken of one day.'

'Then say that you will never mention it to Auntie Sel or ask her anything that might make her . . .'

'Might make her open up a can of worms, too?'

'Not a can of worms, Aury. If you think about it, even if it *is* true, it did no harm to your father, he thought he had a son and a daughter, and he was dead of fever before he ever saw me.'

'How do we know that? Perhaps he died knowing that they had done wrong. Perhaps he didn't even die of fever . . .'

It took a moment for his suggestion to register with her. 'Aury! No, no. Don't start thinking such vile things.'

'Oh . . .' With little fingers at the bridge of his nose and palms cupping his face, he looked at her. 'No . . . I don't really think such a thing. I just say it because I feel so bloody angry at them. Very well. If it is ever mentioned, it shall not come first from me. Auntie Sel has had years' enough worry about him as it is.'

He put out the oil-lamp, and they walked slowly back to the house. The sky was dark now, with stars large and clear in the ink-blue dome that fitted over the valley. Yard-mud crackled beneath their feet.

'Frost tonight.' Conversational tone, normality returned.

He, too, seemed to have douted his emotion, his anguish, his passion, with the douting of the lamp. 'You sound as though you've lived here all your life, Ru.'

Ruth drew breath heavily, releasing the tension that had strapped her chest.

'I feel that I have – it's where I was born.'

'I know what you mean.'

At the porch, Ruth held him back. 'It's probably not true, Aury. Don't even think about it.'

'Right.'

'We're on edge just now. It will all be normal again when we get a letter from Ma to say that she's arrived.'

'Right.'

But it was not right, and would not be again.

That night, Ruth had the first experience of a nightmare that was to terrify her for years. The terror was not in the content of the dream, in which she was back in the empty landscape of Toolagarry. That night she was alone in her dream, riding a white horse; later on there were sometimes two or three horses, but they were not hers although they rode beside the white one. As she rode, it was always an extraordinary free and wild experience which she knew was not only for herself, but for the horse also. Gradually she became aware of herself becoming the horse, and vice versa, ecstatic and free. Then suddenly, as she was about to meld with the animal, in a sweating terror she leapt awake and, in waking, saw herself at the edge of a precipitous drop, so high that there was only blackness below. The image of the precipice and the drop remained in her vision for minutes after.

3

December 1850

IN THE BLEAK MID-WINTER

THE EVENTUAL ARRIVAL of a letter from Mrs Tylee, written soon after she set out on her homeward voyage, did act as balm on the household. They were surprised to learn that, as well as being the legal owner of Croud Cantle, their mother had deposited 'a sum of money with a solicitor, which is to be used by you for such items for your betterment or education'. She charged Auryn and Ruth with 'helping Selena run the farm to support yourselves by your own labour' and Caroline with attending to 'your cure and your learning'.

Although at fifty their aunt, Selena Netherfield, still had the tall, upright physique of many of her family, her brother's trial, his death sentence and its eventual commutation to transportation for life, had left her emotionally bowed. Her own marriage and widowhood had scarcely touched her; it was the twenty years' absence of her idolized brother Adam that had both filled and emptied her life. And now, unexpectedly, she had been given charge of three of his children.

A charge she took with delight and seriousness, and about which she wrote long letters, telling him of her joy at their 'coming like sparkling lights into my life' and of the decisions she had made about them.

To have Auryn working about the place took her back to when Adam was the same age, and in the two girls she saw so many of their father's mannerisms. Twenty years of unexpressed love for her brother was now given outlet.

As well as the joy there was the responsibility. When the Reverend Peter Warren took to calling ever more frequently, she reported that 'It is, of course, Ruth who is the attraction, but I do not think that it is mutual', and that 'Auryn has a scheme to visit the Great Exhibition at the Crystal Palace in the coming year. It is likely to be very informative and to the benefit of their education, but even if it were not so worthy I might still have agreed that they should go there as a reward. They have, during the year that they have been living here, worked their fingers to the bone.'

Inevitably, the quarrel between Auryn and Ruth, although apparently resolved, slowly bubbled to the surface and showed itself to their aunt. In Selena's own mind, there was no doubt that Adam had been Lidia's lover whilst her husband was alive, and that Ruth was the result of the affair. Ruth had tried casualness and subtlety in probing about that period of her parents' life, and eventually asked her aunt, 'If my real father did not die until I was about six, and I am only adopted by Pa, then why do I look so much like you? Auryn doesn't – he looks exactly like the little portrait Ma has of her first husband.'

''Tis not for me to speculate on things like that, Ruth. If there is anything to tell, then it is your Ma and Pa's business and not mine.' But she made it her business and wrote, 'Addy, I think that you must write to Ruth and Auryn. I do not want to interfere, but my guardianship of the children insists that I do. To be blunt, Ruth and Auryn believe that she is your true daughter and not adopted. They are both, I believe, very confused in their emotions.'

The despatch of Selena's letter, even though they did not know its contents, seemed to act as a balm upon the young people – or perhaps it was the celebration of Christmas, into which Selena put a great deal of preparation. She had bought a magazine in which there was an illustration of a bedecked fir tree, which was said to portray that which Queen

Caroline had once ordered to be produced for a children's party, and drew Carly into her plans to bring back the old tradition of the farmhouse and bedeck its walls with leaves and berries.

For a week, as soon as she was released from her lessons, Carly would rush up the lane to finish her chores and start on the great garland she was making in the barn – holly, laurel, old-man's-beard, teasel and cow-parsley heads, woven into a long string which was strung between beams awaiting the proper time to be brought into the house.

On Christmas Eve, Ruth cut holly-boughs from the hedgerow, and Auryn dragged huge lumps of applewood, all in the early hours by storm lantern because Selena had extra orders for eggs and poultry and pork-roll to take to market and she and Ruth had to be on the road long before the sky was light. The two women returned flushed, from the pleasure of having sold well, as well as from the cups of hot, spiced ale exchanged between stallholders. Quickly, they consumed bowls of Carly's soup, then went out to get ahead with as much of the next day's work as they were able.

It was tradition grown out of the necessity of their occupations, caring for beasts, poultry and horses, that brought Cantle people to the church just before midnight, rather than the easier morning service attended by their betters. In St Peter's Church, carols and amens were visibly white on the chill midnight air, but in the yellow candlelight – the colour of June afternoons – the congregation of labourers' and estate-workers' families did not look as frozen to the marrow as they were. Children were wrapped around with any length of cloth that might be put to use to keep out the night air, and as they moved, the smell of goose-grease plaisters and wintergreen vapour overpowered the common odours of body and clothes.

To see such a great number of seats filled, the new vicar might have persuaded himself that he had a congregation of good Christians, but he understood the good people of Cantle, and knew that they were not 'his', though he believed – or hoped – fervently that, all in good time, they would be. Most of them still adhered to the old ways, practised charms, and rites and spells. In Cantle there was a firm belief that at midnight on Christmas Eve all the animals in barns and stables would kneel, and many a stockman arrived late for the service from looking in on his beasts.

Adherence to the old ways did not preclude them from taking what they wanted from the new, and, in any case, much of what they enjoyed about a 'good service' had derived from the older practices – the singing, the flames, burning aromatic herbs, carved wooden figures and priestly robes that transformed mortal man into a god's go-between. And what matter if a few ancient symbols, such as mistletoe, were banned from the church? A sprig of it might easily be worn beneath a shawl or tucked into a waistcoat pocket. A small congregation of counterfeit good Christians. Very small in these times, since a change in farming practices had bled Cantle of its young people.

Such gatherings as the three young Tylees attended with their aunt now served the purpose of the labouring villagers to reinforce the knowledge that some sort of village did still exist in spite of the evidence of ruined hovels, of corn growing where a row of cottages once existed or of footpaths overgrown for want of tramping work-boots.

Caroline was excited. Selena not being 'much of one for all that sort of nonsense', she was seldom inside a church like St Peter's. 'We haven't got any place like this at Toolagarry. Isn't it wonderful! You see, Aury, I told you that Great Hole place was like a cathedral.'

Auryn smiled. 'If we go to London, I'll take you to a cathedral – then you'll see.'

In the gallery there was as much the sound of ale being poured as there was of fiddle tuning, but the trio of village

musicians, even had they been too far gone in drink to
remain upright, could have played the old carols – as in fact
they had proved on many occasions. This new vicar was
young and not so tolerant as the old one, and had made it
known that he was soon to modernize St Peter's with a small
wind-blown organ. The musicians, therefore, knew that
their days of importance in the village were numbered, so
they had nothing to lose if they enjoyed the last of their good
times.

The service ran its familiar course of prayers and carols,
until Reverend Howard announced the number of a hymn
that was outside the traditional repertoire of the congregation. The musicians and the vicar, however, had practised it,
for, as part of his plan for change, the vicar had been
determined that there should be a different carol this year.

The congregation rose, no shuffling of hymn books as
there would be at the morning service, only the rustle of
coarse cloth and the shuffle of hobnails on the stone floor.

The fiddler drew a clear, sad note, and the vicar started to
sing. On the fifth word he faltered slightly at the surprise of
hearing a soprano voice as clear and pure as meltwater. As
unobtrusively and solemnly as he could, Reverend Howard
scanned the rows. A few mouths opening and closing in an
attempt to do something with this new strange carol . . .
then his eyes alighted upon the only two singing in time to
the musicians. They were the young woman and the girl
who had come to work at Widow Netherfield's place.

A strange woman, the widow, polite yet intimidating.
On the one occasion that the Reverend Howard had paid a
call to the cottage, upon the death of the husband, he had
been taken aback both by the large numbers of books on the
kitchen shelves and by the woman's fine accent and good
pronunciation. A strange woman, who had made it clear
that, whilst he was welcome as a neighbour, as a representative of the Church he was only tolerated, and on just this one

occasion because her husband was dead. 'He was baptized and left no instruction as to how he should be buried, so you must do what is necessary,' she had said, 'but I may as well tell you now, you are not to say any twaddling nonsense over me when my turn comes.'

Faces turned in the direction of the carollers, some necks being bent or stretched to satisfy curiosity as to who it was singing out in church as though the place was a barn and this was a harvest supper. They saw a young woman with hair like flames licking the nape of her neck, and an equally bright-headed girl. The elder of the two's cheeks blushed brighter and brighter as she realized attention was centred upon them, but her voice did not falter.

''Tis that gel up Miz Netherfield's . . . well, if she an't a proper nightin'gale.'

Of all the congregation, it was perhaps Selena who was most surprised.

At the door, the vicar did not linger as long as he would on Christmas morning, when the agent and keepers from the estate and the tenant families attended St Peter's, but he made a point of greeting the two singers and giving the family 'God's blessing on this day'.

'You were quite a celebrity, Ruth,' Selena said as they walked Howgaite Path, the narrow track that led to Croud Cantle.

'It was a carol that Ma taught us – we used to sing it back home.'

'I never knew you had a voice. It sounds quite trained.'

'I could have died when I realized we were the only ones singing.'

'Ma used to make us all practise,' Caroline said, 'but only Ruthie can do it properly.'

Ruth began to protest.

'You've got a good voice and it will get better – that's if you'd stop being so almighty conscious of people listening.'

The light, bantering tone that had been missing from Auryn's voice for the past few weeks had returned, and they all felt better for that and smiled to themselves in the dark.

Ruth said, 'It's not that I mind people listening . . . I get so flustered when they *look*. Ma always said singing was the most civilizing thing a person could do in the place where we lived.'

Lived – past tense. Recently, the three young visitors often tended to speak as though they had put Toolagarry behind them. Even Caroline, who had been born there and therefore, unlike Auryn and Ruth, had not spent part of a childhood in the village, unconsciously referred to Cantle as her home, rather than as the place she was visiting.

'I wish I had known, I would have asked your Uncle Jack to bring his fiddle tomorrow and we could have done a bit of civilizing of our place.'

Auryn said, 'Aunt Sel, compared with Toolagarry, Cantle is as civilized as ancient Greece.'

'Why, child, you do come out with some surprising things. Whoever taught you anything about ancient Greece?'

Wideawake now after their walk in the freezing air of early morning, they took indoors the holly-boughs and mistletoe, and Auryn and Caroline with a great deal of ceremony carried in Caroline's long garland, which they draped along one wall.

'Why, Carly, it's lovely. I never knew you had it in you to stick at anything so long,' Ruth remarked. 'It's much better than the ones we used to make.'

'Do you think Vinia and Jo will help Ma to make one?'

'Of course they will,' Ruth said, drawing her young sister to sit beside her. 'It wouldn't be like Christmas without a garland on the porch.'

'You hang it on the porch?' Selena asked.

'Why for sure,' Auryn replied. 'It's where Ma used to put the table for Christmas day – it's the coolest place.'

The girl and the two women sat together on the ingle bench and watched Auryn tying the holly-boughs to the beams.

'What do you think they are doing this exact minute, Ruth?'

'Probably fast asleep, which we should be.'

'No,' Caroline said. 'I think Vinia is saying to Ma, "What do you think Carly's doing this exact minute, Ma?"'

Suddenly the reality of the divided family was foremost in all their minds; tears ran down Caroline's cheeks, and Ruth's eyes brimmed.

Auryn knelt down by his young sister. 'You promised you would own up if you got sad and wanted to go back.'

She wiped her cheeks and nose on her sleeve. 'Oh Aury, can't you tell the difference between "sad" and . . . and, well . . . remembering people? "Sad" is if they were dead. They aren't *dead*.'

'But do you want to go back?'

'No!' Her young voice was firm. 'But I wish that they would all come here.'

'Well, you know that they can't, Carly, so you might as well face up to it.'

'Oh, *why* did Pa have to do all those things so that they won't let him live here with us?'

Her anger and frustration at the insoluble situation might have brought on more tears; instead, she kicked out at the smouldering log which rolled out onto the pegged rug, and, in the rush to prevent a house fire, the emotion of that moment was dissipated.

'Come and let me take your skirt off.' Selena would have done anything so that the people dearest to her, these children and Addy, could have lived the lives they wished to. Caroline allowed herself to be petted a little and went upstairs to bed in her flannel petticoat and knitted stockings. 'Get in my bed tonight, lovey. We'll keep ourselves warm together.'

Above their head, Selena's old bed creaked as Caroline gave herself a few bounces upon it.

'Ah, well,' Ruth said. 'It sounds as though she's soon over it.'

'I dare say she misses . . . everything. I think you all must. Sit down, Auryn, perhaps this is not a bad time to spend a few minutes talking about . . . the future.' Auryn, ducking his head to avoid the beams, took the chair before the hearth.

'We've talked about it, Aunt Sel. Ruth and I want our future to be here. That's right, isn't it, Ru?'

Selena's neck flushed bright red at the words she had never dared hope to hear, but she said nothing.

'We feel that we belong here,' Ruth said. 'It is as though the twelve years' childhood in New South Wales has been the visit – not this.'

Right from the start, Selena had not let herself think otherwise than that eventually Caroline would grow out of her ailment, and that they would return to Toolagarry.

It was more than twenty hours since Selena last slept, and she was suddenly dead tired.

4

VOICES

ON CHRISTMAS MORNING, early, Ruth went out onto the hillside that rose behind Croud Cantle Farm. Tradden Raike is the gentlest of the four downland arms which surround the Cantle Valley, so she chose to climb it the steepest, untracked way.

There were times when she had a gloomy restlessness that she could not rid herself of for days. Back in Toolagarry, her cure was to take a horse and ride bareback and fast as though to outride and lose her hag, and, having outridden it, often she would sing to the deserted land. But, in this small landscape there was no distance, no far horizon to ride towards. So she climbed.

At the summit she stood, heaving white breath into the cold air and looked down upon the place where she was born, and now the place she had decided to remain in.

But for what?

Certainly not to become the wife of some estate worker or farm-hand. Since girlhood she had felt herself to be empty – perhaps not empty – rather, unfilled. Gradually, she had come to believe that she would do something special with her life: Ma and Pa were convinced of it, yet she could not remember a spoken word that indicated their belief in her ability.

What ability?

True, as she had come to realize since arriving back here, she had received an unusual education, much of it directly from the many books that Ma and Pa somehow seemed to have acquired. But what could a twenty-year-old girl do with a good knowledge of poetry and geometry, simple mathematics, history, the Greek heroes, and an untrained voice? When she was twelve or thirteen, she had tried to ask her mother whether her own feelings had been the same. '*I can't believe that there was a time when you said to yourself, "If I had a man and five children to feed and keep washed, then I should want nothing more."* '

The expression of sadness that came to her Ma's eyes was something Ruth had never seen before nor would ever forget. '*Ah, girl, womanhood is creeping up on you.*' She had laid her hand gently on Ruth's belly. '*Because women are born with this handful of emptiness, nature conspires to make us fill it, even if it isn't in our own nature to do so. Perhaps you will be the kind of woman who, when the emptiness is filled and you're all swelling with a child, will find that fulfilment enough. People will approve of you. I used to be told that my mother was like that – "a good little wife and mother", they always called her.*'

With Ruth's own first qualms about the inevitability for herself of a role of wife and mother, she caught in her mother's tone a hint of resentment or anger. She had laughed wryly. '*They can't say that of me, Ruthie.*'

When these restless and gloomy moods came upon her, Ruth seldom knew from what source they originated, but this time she did know. The phrase '*This one minds me of her*'. She had felt her mood grow from a small sand-grain of unease to a slab of stone beneath her breastbone. Late last night, she had been writing up the diary Ma had persuaded her to keep from childhood, when the phrase led her to open one of the musty old books that her mother had left in her keeping.

There were several volumes which collectively were 'The Family Book'. Their pages were brittle and foxed from age and the various changes of climate they had been taken through. It had been in one that she had found the enigmatic reference that had started the rift between herself and Aury.

Ma had left the books on a high shelf, still in their leather and oilskin wrapping. *'Don't bother with them until you are ready to ... well ... listen to the past.'*

At the time, Ruth could not imagine ever being ready to open such uninviting covers. *'Don't read till you have a feeling for the place. One day you will want to know ... I mean really want to know, then's the time to read your history.'* She had tousled her daughter's hair and smiled. *'But don't expect there to be angels in these books. Most it's about the women of the family, women who tried to get something more out of life than they were expected to want. And when you come to read them, you'll see you've nothing to be ashamed of in your forebears – they didn't win much, but – by it all – they tried.'* Ruth had looked at her mother's pretty fading ringlets escaping from her cap, and tried to imagine her when she was twenty and as bright red as herself, but she could not. Then yesterday, walking through the village after the midnight service, she had heard voices in the darkness, enough of a conversation to make her curious.

'Who's she then? She don't look nothing like none of the Netherfields.'

'Why, you must know who she is, you only got to look at the hair for that – she's a Nugent.'

'Ah, I do recognize the likeness, now you come to say. I remember the day the old lady died – well ... must be fifteen year ago now. This one minds me of her, now I come to think.'

'That'd be the grandmother.'

'No, no, she passed on donkey's years before. The old lady I mean ... never got married.'

'This one minds me of her.' The phrase had aroused Ruth's curiosity. Their mother had talked a lot about the old days. Ruth knew that they had been a rebellious lot, but it was only now that she was living in their home valley, in the old house, amongst people who were no longer names in

Ma's stories, that Ruth felt herself to be part of an unfolding story. It would have been natural for people to say that she looked like her Ma, but unexpected that she should bring to mind an old lady born in the last century. So, she had burnt the lamp-oil into the early hours of Christmas morning reading the neat, fading words of an old lady born more than eighty years ago, and who died imprisoned for her views, an old lady of whom a gossip was 'minded' when she saw Ruth.

Until recently, she had been incurious about her ancestry, but now her own conception of her likeness to Aunt Selena on the one hand, and strangers being 'minded' of the old lady Nugent on the other, perturbed her – as did the sudden possibility of a change in her relationship to Aury.

On Tradden Raike she let the voice, which she had found trapped between the musty covers, speak to her. The voice which talked with tenderness and love for 'my beloved valley', and described with authority the growth-cycle of the bee orchid, or pondered upon poverty, government, and upon education for poor people, and how she had tried to rectify its lack in Cantle, and how she had failed in her ambition.

This morning, Ruth looked about her through new eyes, or rather through those of the old woman of the journal – her eyes had looked with such passion from this summit. Ruth had walked over Tradden Raike dozens of times in the past year, treading the same paths and sheep-tracks that the other girl had walked half a century before, yet Ruth had never noticed the *'elegant stature of cow-parsley tipped with frost'* or been aware of *'the scent of the juniper tips when pinched'*, or seen how *'Cantle valley is a cake divided by the River Dunnock and the roads into six slices, five of which are for gobbling by the Estate, and the sixth by the Church, leaving the crumbs of a bit of common land for the rest of the inhabitants.'*

That girl's voice had spoken tenderly about nature, compassionately about the lives of working people, and with great anger about the want of justice and compassion in the rich and powerful. She had revealed her most raw feelings about jealousy and desire. The passionate nature of the girl, and later the woman, was in the faded words on almost every page that Ruth had turned to. Yet it had been one of the shortest entries that Ruth had found most affecting, and which had sent her out this morning. Dated 'Christmas Day 1788' – when, Ruth had calculated, the young 'J. Nugent' whose neat signature was put to each entry would have been but a few months older than she herself was now ... *'My virginity has gone. Well! Four words, seven syllables. Gone. Between one second and the next. Gone. On Tradden's bones, beneath matted brambles with their clots of abandoned nests – gone in a moment of exquisite quenching of desire. Ah, Will, you will never know how much I love you. I love you. Love you, Will.*

'The Old Ones on Tradden were wild today, I gathered a holly-bough. They would see me bound to Will for ever, but they shall never make me Corn Queen to join them in their never-ending seasons of genesis. Will did not take my maidenhood, I gave it to him with love and passion. Yet, that Song of Solomon must be the beginning and end of all physical love between us. We both have too much work to do to indulge our consuming lusts which will inevitably lead to the same dragging domesticity as those girls I once danced the maypole with. Will would call it passion, but I know my own nature. The Old Ones know me and I know them, we are of a kind. Their lustful blood is in the blood of this family. We have to guard against its destructive force.'

It had been this passage that had been the source of Ruth's melancholy. She had felt that she knew the child who had written the first entry in the journal in a shaky hand, knew the girl who gave herself to her lover on a long-past

Christmas Day, recognized the woman that she herself would become.

Although she was almost afraid to read it, she had not been able to resist turning to the last entry in the journal, in her own Ma's hand: *'Judith Nugent of Croud Cantle Farm, Cantle, in the County of Hampshire, died from the effects of tainted food in Winchester Prison 25th November 1830 where she had been held for an act of rebellion against the established order which she held passionately to be wrong. Buried in Winchester in an unmarked grave.'*

Why had this woman denied herself the physical love that she evidently burned for? What did she achieve in all those years of working, fighting, striving to make a better life for her neighbours? A woman who held beliefs so passionately that she could die in prison for them when she was over sixty years of age.

She lived the way she chose for herself.

Ruth's answer seemed to come from the air around, and from deep within her, dissolving the stone of foreboding. *She made the decision for herself.* If the story of that life told in the old journal did not have a satisfactory conclusion . . . it didn't matter! What mattered was her independence. Unprivileged, poor, labouring from dawn to dusk, yet she lived a life that was worth living.

But . . . what would happen if all women denied the next generation that warm, chaotic scramble which had been her own childhood? It must be possible for a woman to find something between the two. Men did. It would be thought usual for a man like Peter Warren to carry on his mission as well as have the pleasure of being a parent.

Peter Warren. She was beginning to like him, but only 'like'. He was good company, lively and funny. And he was such a transparently romantic young man, and so earnest about his 'mission'. What was the mission? What did he actually do? He had talked, but she had never really listened.

Shame – it was so obvious that he felt tenderly towards her, she must be kinder to him.

Now smiling to herself, Ruth sat in the frosty air on her bundled-up shawl and looked about for the *'matted brambles with their clots of abandoned nests'*, and let the words from the past go through her mind again and again. When that girl had sat down to write on that distant Christmas Day, she had known that there would come a day when it would be read, indeed, had intended that it should be. A plate pasted on the frontispiece read *'For those in the next century who desire to know of our lives'*. How courageous of her to write her most intimate thoughts.

Now that she had spent several hours listening to that extraordinary woman's voice, Ruth wanted to see her own surroundings afresh. She squatted and looked closely at the crimson stalks and seedheads of a clump of dock and saw that it was indeed *'something quite beautiful in its colour and form, catching the low December sun more alive in death than when it was in full seed'*.

Suddenly Ruth wanted to grasp a handful of the garnet stems and rush down to Auryn and tell him about the old book, so that he could share what she had discovered, but something held her back. She knew he would not understand the nature of the girl who believed in the presence of ancient deities. She imagined his disdainful expression, his masculine hauteur, his voice. 'For goodness' sake, Ruth, I know you're reckoned to be a bit fanciful, but it beats cockfighting to get excited about a bunch of old weeds.'

Poor Aury, who would probably never understand what the girl had meant about *'The Old Ones'* who had *'existed throughout time on Tradden'*.

As she walked back down the slope she knew that she could have made no other decision than to live here in this valley and was sure that nothing would ever woo her away from it. Her female forebears had farmed here as mistresses of their own land, her Ma had run it alone. Ruth saw herself as the next in the family line. *'Croud Cantle is a women's land, masters do not thrive here.'*

The farm would one day be hers alone, when Aury went back to Toolagarry, which she was convinced he eventually would. He was already growing away from her. At times she could not bring herself to think of the time when they would not be together, but she had come to realize that it would be for the best. It must come, when some other woman would lay claim to him, know his dreams and fears, rub his back with wintergreen, cut his silver hair, comfort him with her arms. Could she bear this to happen?

As she reached the path at Raike Bottom, she saw the little 'Baker' Toose delivery trap carrying her Uncle Jack and Auntie Ginnie up Howgaite Path towards Croud Cantle for the Christmas dinner Auntie Sel had taken so much trouble to arrange. She hitched up her skirts and raced like a ten-year-old to catch them up, and arrived with them, red-cheeked, breathless and laughing at nothing but her own light-heartedness.

5

CHRISTMAS DINNER AT CROUD CANTLE

'WELL, MIZ NETHERFIELD, that was a proper blow-out, and no mistake.' Mrs 'Baker' Toose slapped the sides of her belly and puffed her cheeks, red veined from years of taking loaves and cakes from the hot bread oven of their little bakery. A strange coarse face that appeared at first to belong to one who is simple-minded, perhaps because she was given to a kind of perpetual smiling. A forty-year-old face that did not look forty any more than it did any other age. A rough face that was beautiful to Jack Toose, because he had never seen it except as a blur – what he saw was the Ginny who lay beneath its surface.

Selena nodded her thanks. 'Though credit for treats must go first to your game-pie, Ginny.'

'Along with the Croud Cantle goose,' Jack Toose said. 'The best-baked bird I ever tasted, and we always used to have a good goose at Croud Cantle as I remember.' His memory served him false, but it did not matter – his memories of past Christmases here were good ones.

'Uncle Jack!' said Caroline. 'I thought you all lived on nothing but "b'iled turnips" in the old days.'

It was impossible to get any idea of expression from what one saw of Jack Toose's eyes through the great magnification of his spectacles, but the way he held his head to one side, looking towards the ceiling, indicated a moment of stepping back into his childhood and into other Christmases in this same room, around this same table.

'Somehow we always managed a bit of a meal at Christmas.' He lowered his spectacles and squinnied at Caroline and smiled. 'But we had a great filling of turnips first.'

Jack Toose's eyesight was so poor that the only way he could see any word of a book or newspaper was to hold his face a few inches from the page and peer through the spyglass which he always kept in a skin bag in his pocket.

People who had known his father said 'old John all over again', and knowing in what high regard his father was held, Jack Toose took it as a compliment even though he knew that he would never make the go of his little bakery shop that his father had once made of a plantsman's business. Jack Toose had married a girl who had once been thrown upon society's dust-heap, loved her passionately and found her to be a great wonder. Ask at large within ten miles of Blackbrook, where they lived, 'Which is the happiest and most loving couple you have ever encountered?', Jack and Ginny Toose might not have immediately sprung to mind – because people will so often equate such things as happiness and love with beauty and grace, neither of which the Toose couple had – but at the mention of Jack and Ginny Toose, people would be bound to smile, and nod, and agree that they could not think of any couple who were half so content with one another and so loving after a dozen or so years of marriage.

'I can't say I relish them much these days – what say you, Ginn? You had turnips enough in your time.'

'There's plenty of folk in Blackbrook graveyard as'd change places with any of us for a dish of turnips this Christmas Day, Jack Toose,' she replied in her coarse, broad Hampshire.

'I vote the plum-pudding my favourite,' Auryn said.

'That's because he found the wishing-stone in it,' Caroline said.

Ruth raised her hand. 'A vote for the raisins-set-on-fire candidate. What about you, Mr Warren?'

'I shall be the diplomat.' Peter Warren rose to his feet, spilling his wine. 'Oh. But that says my piece better than I

. . . look – "My cup runneth over"!' Cheerful laughter as he raised his glass. 'Dear friends who have taken me into the warmth of your family . . . good Hampshire wine, fine Hampshire food prepared by skilled Hampshire women, and the very best of Hampshire companions –' jokily, he leaned conspiratorially towards Caroline, who sat beside him – 'in spite of one of our number who was born upside-down in a place where they walk on their heads – I offer you the old country toast of Hampshiremen . . . "To Hampshire Hogs".'

'Hampshire Hogs.'

Caroline's voice dropped into the little silence made by the sipping of the toast, 'And Hampshire *women* as well, Mr Warren.'

'Of course, Miss – that was implied.'

'Then you should say it.'

'Yes, Ma'am. Of course, Ma'am. "Hampshire women and their daughters." '

Caroline Tylee grinned up at Peter Warren. 'Now you've made a toast to *me*.'

'Well, Miss, if it's a toast of your own that you wish . . . Ladies and gentlemen, please raise your glasses to an exceptional young woman. Unequalled in courage, without parallel in intelligence, unrivalled in beauty, and most certainly matchless in *forwardness* – I give you "Caroline Tylee".'

His mood was infectious, heightened as Auryn called, 'We don't want her.'

'And you shan't get me, Auryn Tylee. Anyhow you're my brother and you an't handsome enough. I shall give myself, and marry you, Mr Peter Warren.'

'Lord, my cup runneth even more over. I had not even thought to marry a creature so far above me. A wife with twenty inches of bright red hair, ah 'tis my dream.'

Only Jack and Caroline herself missed the glance in

Ruth's direction that Peter Warren could not restrain. Ruth did not give any sign that the glance meant anything at all.

Within fifteen minutes of finishing the meal, the table was cleared and the dishes being cleaned and stacked by Selena, Ruth and Ginny, whose lives were so filled with well-organized working hours that each job was done at a clip. Auryn and Peter Warren lit pipes and went to throw swill to the pig and water the horses, whilst Jack said that he would help Caroline to finger a flute that he had brought her as a present.

It was still not yet two o'clock, so that when they reassembled, they felt great satisfaction that even the chores had not nibbled much at their rare holiday.

'Now it's time for music,' Caroline announced. 'I will play the tune that Uncle Jack has taught me.' It was halting and unrhythmic, but it pleased them all to see the young girl wrestling and determined to play the little piece correctly.

'Well done, lovey,' said Ginny Toose. 'You got the Tooses' ear fer music. Did you know that there was a Toose that played a march before the King hisself?'

'Was it Uncle Jack?'

'God forbid that I should ever waste good strings and resin on *them*. No, your Auntie Ginn must mean one of the lesser-talented of the Tooses who's only fit to play before kings and princes.'

'Then *that's* where Ruth gets her voice from – the Toose family,' Selena said, with a meaningful nod to indicate what she had discovered.

Jack Toose leaned forward towards the higher of the two red blurs. 'Can you sing then, gel?'

'Only like anybody else, Uncle Jack.'

'Oh, Ruth!' Auryn exclaimed. 'Stop being so damned modest. I don't see why people have to be modest about the talents they were born with.'

'Of course it isn't like anybody else,' Caroline said to an

annoying accompaniment of breaths into her new and fascinating flute. 'Ruthie sings like a corncrake with a bad cough.'

'Well,' said Selena, 'my knowledge of musical things don't make me the best judge, but I can't say that I ever heard a prettier voice than sung at St Peter's at the midnight service not more than fourteen hours since.'

'Easily settled if you sing for us now, Ruth,' said Peter Warren. The 'Ruth' was out before he realized it. First names between unmarried rural people were used as a matter of course, but not by such a one as Peter Warren, who was town-bred and had been a daily student to Blackbrook Grammar School and Winchester College. She did not retract it, and so established that they were on first-name terms, which meant nothing to anybody except himself.

'Come on, gel. Tell me what it shall be and I'll accompany you.'

'On yer vi'lin.' Ginny beamed at the company. 'It's a new vi'lin. Go on, show him to them, Jack,' Ginny said proudly. 'I bought him for Jack as a present.'

'Ah, I still says you shouldn't a spent all that money. See, 'tis a proper violin, not just a barn-dance kind of fiddle.' His supple fingers moved across the frets as his bow drew out a few notes.

Ginny, still beaming broadly, said, 'You won't hear sweeter music than that this side of heaven.'

Caroline came to lean against him as he ran a soft rag over the chestnut-red wood.

'I can smell spice-cake in your jacket, Uncle Jack.'

He peered closely at her. 'And I can see a little gel that looks like she might get a lesson or two on the flute if she could bide quiet for five minutes so her sister could sing for us.'

'I don't know what I should sing.'

'A carol, Ruthie, sing a carol,' Caroline demanded. 'And I'll play too.'

'Stow it, Carly, you're putting yourself so forward that we shan't laugh because it's not funny.' It was Auryn's stern voice that she always obeyed, so she contented herself with sitting close to Selena and fingering the notes on her flute without putting it to her lips.

'All right, I'll sing.'

Jack played a lead-in few bars and they all fell silent.

As it had in the church, Ruth's young, sweet, unaffected voice captivated everyone, her uncle especially, so that when she reached for a high note and plucked it with such ease, he drew his brows together and shook his head with the same emotion as when he drew such a note from his violin. Each time she reached the refrain, they all joined in, and burst forth with applause at the end. Peter Warren stood up to emphasize his appreciation, calling 'Splendid, oh splendid!'

After that Jack played some of the popular Harvest Supper jigs and circle dances till their tapping feet could not do other than to follow him as he led them to dance a chain around the kitchen table.

Eventually, Ginny Toose sank into a chair saying, 'Dear Lord, I swear my boot-soles are afire.'

'Then let's hope you've all worn off your dinner, ready to eat a slice of pie,' Selena said, dabbing at her moist forehead and retying her cap-strings.

Again the table was laid out with food, this time meat pies and fruit tarts and the best of Croud Cantle preserves and the largest of the apples from the little orchard. Caroline was flushed with pleasure as she helped assemble the festive table. When they were ready to start, Jack, as though he had suddenly remembered, said, 'Lord! I almost forgot, I brought along a few currant buns of my own baking. I'll fetch them.'

As mulled ale was being passed down the table, Jack returned, carrying a large white box, which he placed before Caroline. 'Here, Miss, I suppose you'd better have the first choice of buns or we shall never hear the last of it.' Carefully, as he always made movements that required co-ordination of eye and hand, he removed the box-lid and lifted out a snow-white mound.

Caroline's eyes flickered over the snowy object. 'Look, Ruthie, Aury, it's us, it's us! Oh look, Uncle Jack has made models of us.' The three little figures were identifiable more from their relative sizes, clothes and most of all from the colouring of the hair.

Jack Toose laughed. 'Ah, that's a kind of fiddling work that's beyond these eyes. It was your Auntie Ginn that made them. They're sugar people, so if you fancy biting one another's heads off, then there you are.'

'No! No! Nobody must ever break them, they are wonderful.' Caroline held her small hands protectively above the figures. 'Auntie Ginn, you're the cleverest person in the world to be able to make people . . . Goodness, Aury, wouldn't Vinia and Jo think that was a good trick to have a sugar doll of themselves?'

The two older women exchanged understanding glances, neither of them sure how much the exuberant young girl really missed her family. She seemed as much and as little content as any girl of her age, but they could remember stones that they had carried in their heart when they were ten years old.

At seven o'clock Jack and Ginny prepared to leave, offering to take Peter Warren back to Blackbrook with them in their little pony-drawn cart.

'You could take me as far as the path that goes down to the shanty at Great Hole.'

'You're never going down to that place on a dark night like this, Mr Warren,' Ginny said. 'Them wild navvies will knock you down for your bootlaces.'

'They might, but then so might a man who isn't a navvy, Ma'am. How many born-and-bred Blackbrook men have knocked down a man in some alley-way for less reason than to rob him of his bootlaces?'

'Ah well, a fair enough argument, but you can't deny that they're a fearsome and wild bunch of men.'

'I can't deny that there are plenty who are, but some have got wives and children, and I'm accepted as being some sort of a man of God. And as long as He wants me to be going about among them, then I don't reckon that I shall lose my bootlaces.'

'A pity there wasn't a few more clergymen that went about the world like Jesus hisself. You'm the closest I ever seen to that, so come on and we'll take you there.'

Peter Warren blushed, looking both embarrassed and pleased at Mrs 'Baker' Toose's unaffected way of stating what she thought, and tried to catch a glimpse of Ruth's reaction to it, but she appeared to be busy fetching coats and shawls and hats and bonnets.

It took them ten minutes to wrap up against the frosty night, while Auryn went out to make the pony and cart ready. As they stood in the kitchen lighting some lanterns they heard heavy boots and men's voices.

'In here, in here.' It was Auryn. He unlatched the scullery door. 'Auntie Sel, Ruth, there's some men here asking for the Reverend Warren – one of them's hurt.'

6

DEATH AND LIFE

'I DON'T WANT YOU GOING there, Ruth. It's no place for a woman. You stop here and tend to the man.'

'Don't tell me what to do, Aury Tylee, I've tended enough injuries. It don't need three of us to see to one man.'

Ignoring any further protests, and not waiting for his ire to rise at being spoken to dismissively, Ruth hastily tied a shawl about her head, drew the hem of her skirt between her legs and tucked it in at the waistband, and sprang up into Jack Toose's little delivery cart that Ginny was holding ready. Having no option, Auryn drove away with Ruth, Peter Warren and 'Rat-ear Sojerman' – one of the men who had come with the message.

The day had started damp and chill but now, as they rumbled over the bridle-path across the downs, Ruth noticed that the cold easterly that had earlier blown over the downs had cleaned the sky to indigo glass so that even the smallest or most distant stars were visible. On the higher ground, there was still enough wind to clatter the stiff twigs of dogwood and elder, though in the still pockets, frost was already settling. Once they were over the downs, they had to leave the cart and walk.

They hardly spoke as they picked their way by lantern-light along new pathways created by the railway builders. As they trudged along, their steps broke newly frozen surfaces, small pools and puddles tinkled like broken china, their footsteps crunched, their breath was loud and visible in the empty air, and small animals scuttled off through the strawy stems of last summer's grass.

When, back in the spring, Auryn had contradicted

Caroline's 'cathedral' view of the great man-made cavern and called it 'caves of Hell', he had perhaps imagined the place as it was on the December night when they arrived there.

Over the months since they had last been here, the excavation of the cutting had got well under way, its high mounds of chalk 'muck' piled like a snowy mountain-range, marked at intervals by the wooden barrow-runs up which the navvies pushed and hauled heavy loads. But they noticed little of this in the chill December dark. They slithered their way down to the bottom of the cutting.

Where water from the surrounding downs ran constantly into it, and where the drainage work was not finished, they had to squelch through deep, sucking sludge. Had there been enough light, they could have walked along the rails or sleepers, but in the dark it chanced misfooting and turning their ankles. Knowing that it would be a muddy walk, Ruth had brought pattens, but the glutinous mud was too deep for them, so after they had been sucked off for the third time, she left them where they were and walked in her boots. Before they had gone more than a hundred yards towards the tunnel, her skirt was getting soaked, so she tucked it up even higher, clear of her knees. Noticing, Auryn said, low and sharp, 'Ruth!' She replied in kind: 'Don't be a fool, Aury, would you have me take it off?' and ignored his latent outrage.

Rat-eared Sojerman, who because of his drunken state had now fallen behind them, had not been very coherent in relating what had happened. All that they could ascertain was that there had been a big randy in one of the shants during which a challenge had been made and some of the men had gone to Great Hole with women, who were equally drunk, and people had been injured. Whatever had happened had sobered him up enough to go for help, but he was still well under the influence of a long drinking bout.

'Another fight, Sojer?' Peter Warren asked in a hard, steady voice, quite different from that in which he had made his 'runneth over' toast.

'Ach well, y'know what we're like when there's a randy inside us. There's no remembering what we intended doing. A test of strength mebbe. I reckon it was to do with hauling the women up in the basket. I think there was an explosion.'

'Dear God, there's times when you're no better than a pack of wild schoolboys.'

'We are that, Padre.'

'And you hold the gift of life cheap. How many are injured?'

'All of them, and the two women. Only m'sel' and "Gloucester Charlie" was able to move to come for you.'

'How did you know where to come?'

'I heard you telling that you'd be going to some jollification in the village after the service. And "London" once saw you going to that farm. It was a gamble that it was the right one.'

'You should have gone for a doctor.'

'And d'ye reckon he would have come? To the cutting – on Christmas night? Ach, Padre, y'know better than that. Let the drunken bastards sort it out – only good navvy is a dead navvy – isn't that what they say?'

'There's a lady here!'

Now, hurrying ahead as well as they were able, they heard the navvy bringing up the rear, stumbling over the sleepers and cursing his feet.

Then they heard the cries. Before they were within sight of the tunnel – high, wailing cries.

'That sounds bad,' Auryn said.

Peter said, 'You don't have to come any further. You've done enough to get me here.'

'We've seen injuries before today,' Auryn replied. 'Now that she's come, Ruth might as well do what she can, too.'

She felt a familiar flush of anger at his accepted authority over her, especially as of the two she was the less likely to be squeamish, but her pique was soon quelled by the frustration of trying to hurry in the awful quagmire.

On several occasions their home in Toolagarry had become a makeshift hospital for injured convicts who in many cases received poor treatment or none at all other than what Ma and Pa organized – once, when a small arsenal at the fort had exploded and there was nowhere for the injured convicts, and another time when a wall had collapsed upon the men building it.

Now that they were close, it was obvious that the cries were those of a woman. Shrieks of fear and panic interspersed with a long stream of curses and threats. 'God blast your eyes, you stinking Irish bastard, if I could find you I'd cut it off with a blunt knife . . . Sweet Jesus save me . . . Get this off me, I can't move . . . let me up.' Then a shriek, and 'Ah, I can stop it. Get that Irish bugger who did it . . . I'll gut you like a rabbit . . . Holy Mary Mother of God, forgive me . . . Don't let me die. You bastards, come back, have you left me here to die? Oh Mother, Father.' Then a shriek. Then silence.

At the mouth of the tunnel, Peter Warren banged up the lid of a long box and took out a tar-flare, lighted it from the lantern and lit two more flares, which he handed to Ruth and Auryn.

Inside the Great Hole Tunnel, he set light to an empty tar barrel, so that the flames turned the white chalk of the tunnel walls to restless redness. Black smoke billowed upwards, but the beginning of the tunnel was lit well enough for them to see several bodies strewn around. There was a strong smell of gunpowder that pinched the nostrils.

'Over here . . . oh . . . oh . . . his skull's smashed. He's dead.'

'And here . . . look, a woman. It looks as though her neck's broken, doesn't it?'

'Where are the others? I thought Sojerman said there were six. Where's the woman who was screaming?' Peter Warren raised his voice and shouted: 'Is there anybody can hear me?' No sound came back.

'There's another woman here. Oh dear God, Ruthie, come quick . . . I think she's . . .' Auryn's face was faint.

The figure lay upon a tangled heap of what appeared to be the basket, rope and gear. She was a tangled heap herself, her arm a twisted bloodied mess and her body arched in an unnatural position. It was difficult to tell whether she had been wearing a skirt when the accident happened, for all that covered her now were some strips and tatters of a bloodied petticoat.

'Let me,' Ruth said, kneeling beside the twisted figure. 'Get this light propped up. You see to the others.'

The woman was breathing faintly, but she was not conscious – whether from the drink or her injuries it was difficult to tell. The smell of vomited gin and beer was powerful. She was giving birth: the baby's head had appeared, but the birth contractions seemed to have stopped.

For a moment Ruth was panic-stricken, not knowing whether to try to drag the baby out, or to try to revive the mother in the hope that she would be able to expel her trapped child. No! Hopeless – the mother was near to death, if not already dead. The baby might die. The baby. Stop. Think. The baby won't be able to take breath like that. Try to move the baby. She had helped Ma birth Vinia, and had got enough animals into the world. She thrust her sleeves back, and, holding the baby's small slippery head, began trying to ease it gently out. It would not move. She tried again, but could not get any leverage on the frail head. She pressed the woman's abdomen and felt a slight movement.

'Both of you come here. Quickly, or this baby won't survive.' The two men stumbled towards her.

'Lift her up, one each side, beneath the arms.'

When the unconscious woman was supported by the two men, Ruth, squatting beween her legs, and holding her skirt stretched wide over her knees to catch the baby, manipulated the woman's abdomen. There was a mild contraction. She tried again, this time forcing her fingers into the birth canal. The baby moved, freeing its neck. Now, Ruth could ease the baby's shoulders. She pressed again. The baby slithered out and Ruth caught it.

For a moment, the three young people stood looking down at the prize Ruth held in her hands. At once he gave a loud-vowelled cry into the red gloom of the cavern and on, atrophying in the darkness of the tunnel. She held him to herself whilst Peter cut the cord and freed him from his mother. 'You poor little man. What a welcome into the world.'

Without thinking, she ordered Auryn to take off his coat to cover the woman, and Peter Warren to pull off her own petticoat so that she might wrap the child in it.

Auryn seemed unable to move, holding the mother like some rag doll. Now they all looked at her, the mother whose child they had just seen safely into the world. She was not a woman – a tiny thing, hardly bigger than Caroline and probably not much older. A child giving birth to a child.

In the market, Ruth had heard tales about the use of very young girls amongst the navvy population, but it had been hard for her to believe them. She could not imagine a grown man violating such a frail body as this. It was not uncommon in a rural community for girls of sixteen to become wives, but they were usually buxom and womanly. Hard to comprehend the full meaning of child prostitution, until now. But now she had heard the young girl's oaths and curses, and had seen her immature body expel its great burden.

'I think she's gone,' said Auryn, his face wet with sweat

and tears. 'Hell's teeth, Ruth, she's gone and died. Look at her, she should be in a classroom learning her letters.'

'I believe her back was broken,' Peter said.

'Sit and hold the child, Aury.' Her voice was thick with sadness and anger. 'I'll help Peter with the others.'

But the others were dead. It was impossible to tell why they had died; only how – from an explosion.

'You can do nothing here,' Peter Warren said. 'Shall you take the child back to the house for now? I should be grateful if you would, and I will take it to the women in the morning. I will stop here and straighten up these poor souls.'

'Poor souls? They are animals!' Ruth said fiercely. 'No . . . that's not fair to animals, there's none that would behave so depraved.'

'I know it seems so. It is easy for us to judge from our positions of privilege.'

'Privilege?'

'Yes, you and I have the privilege of choosing *not* to live as girls like this do.' He was now helping Ruth to lay down the body of the child-mother, with some kind of dignity, beneath his own topcoat. 'I doubt that she had any choice. The gin was to obliterate the misery of it all. And the fear. We can't even say that we forgive her her sins – they are not hers. They are ours.'

'Oh, I can forgive *her*, it's the degraded beast who did . . .' She choked on her emotion.

'Theirs is a different world – and we are the beneficiaries of it.'

Ruth did not know what to say to him. Inside the jolly companion, the romantic lover, the grateful guest, was this other man. Compassionate, practical and good. Quite by chance, back in the summer months, in this great cavern, they had met a good man. Following her moment of climactic emotion, Ruth thought that she understood the story of the anointing of feet with precious oil. She did not understand what he meant by the sins not being the girl's, but suddenly she felt that he was surely right.

'Will you be all right, Peter?' Auryn asked.

'Of course. If you meet Sojer, tell him to fetch the overseer.'

'I'll go myself when I've taken Ruth and the baby back.'

'Ah, better if you would. If you could care for the baby until tomorrow, I believe I know a woman who will wet-nurse it. I dare say Sojer will have gone back to the shanty or you'll find him sleeping it off in the cutting. The sooner the overseer knows, the better. We need to get the bodies out.'

'Let me have him a moment.' He held out his hands for the baby. 'Do you think that "Michael" will be all right for him?' He smiled wryly. 'I think from his mother's curses that the father was Irish. Michael is a good Irish name.'

'Then that is the last choice the girl would make, if you ask me,' Ruth said sharply.

'Then you choose. At this moment he's more yours than anyone's.'

'Then let him be Simeon.'

The young clergyman dipped his finger in a pool of water and made the Christian mark on the child's forehead. 'In the name of the one true God, you shall be Simeon.'

7

THE GREAT EXHIBITION

'"Geefs, of Antwerp, contributes a group depicting the beautiful legend of Genevieve; who, wrongfully accused of infidelity, is driven by her lord into the wilds of the forest, where she and her infant are succoured by a fawn until her innocence is established and she is again sought by her husband. The group, as composed by the artist, is touchingly and simply told,"' Peter Warren read aloud.

The little group of Auryn, Ruth, Caroline, and Susanna and Miss Dorothy Warren, the Reverend Peter's youngest and eldest sisters, stood in a close circle around the young clergyman and a statue of a naked woman holding a naked child. One of scores of naked women, on display for the classic edification of well-crinolined and high-bodiced viewers of new sculpture. And for the secret delectation of their tight-trewed and heroic-breasted escorts, those sly viewers of voluptuous, wanton artists' models depicted in marble.

'Ugh, succoured by a fawn!' the young Susanna said.

Miss Warren said, 'Hush, Su,' as she had done a dozen times since they had started their inspection of some works of art.

Susanna and Caroline were much of an age, and whilst Caroline's comments were equally direct and condemnatory, Ruth was not so embarrassed by them as was Dorothy Warren. The two young men were either amused, or could not be bothered with two girls whilst there were pretty young women to attend to. And for all her airs and graces, Auryn was apparently enthralled by the elegant Miss Warren.

'There's nothing "ugh" about that,' said Caroline. 'Most people are succoured by cows and goats. I don't mind fawns, but I think the woman was silly. Look how she's gazing up, Aury – her baby will fall from her lap at any moment if she doesn't look to it.' She giggled and whispered to Susanna, 'And he would soon tell me and Ruthie off if we went and sat in the woods without our bodices on.'

'Caroline, behave sensibly and learn something,' Auryn said in the pompous manner the pretty Miss Warren would approve. 'She's probably thinking of her lord and her home.'

'Then she must be *very* silly. If somebody wrongfully accused me of infidelity, I wouldn't go home again for *anything*,' said Caroline in her clear, high voice. People turned in their direction.

Now it was Ruth who said, 'Hush.'

'Well, I wouldn't. He drove her to the wilds of the forest and she hadn't done nothing wrong, and then when he finds out that she was wrongfully accused of infidelity, he says "Oh, it's all right now, you can come home," and then she goes. I wouldn't! Would you, Susanna?'

'Caroline!' Auryn's voice held a warning note. 'You might think your opinions worth shouting to the world, but not everybody wants to listen. So *bide qui-et*!'

Whilst neither of the girls' voices had caused many heads to turn, the raised voices and broad vowels did so. Dorothy Warren tried to walk casually from the exhibition hall, quickening her step so as to distance herself from these friends of Peter's. Once or twice since they had set out, she had thrown her brother a glance which probably meant, 'If I were not a properly brought-up and sophisticated young woman from a good Blackbrook family, then I should leave you this instant. But as it is, I know my manners and I shall make allowances for people whose bad fortune it is to have lived amongst convicts for much of their lives.'

Until not much over a year ago, the Tylees had never experienced trends or style in either clothes or furniture. Tables were for eating from, chairs were for resting upon. Clothes were for protection – from hot sun, rain, dust and insects. Lately, Ruth and Auryn had learned something of the meaning of fashion, but nothing of its nuances. Often, Ruth was confused into thinking that because a woman wore a frock with lace, petals and flounces, she must be a lady of rank, whilst fine, plain grey wool with hand-stitched tucks denoted a much lower order of society . . . *for goodness' sake, why should a girl wear anything except made of lace and flowers if it was possible?*

It was not until she was introduced to Dorothy Warren on Winchester railway station, that she realized that she ought to have taken more notice of Aunt Selena when she asked if Ruth would like to have a new skirt for the occasion. 'No, Auntie Sel, it would be a waste if we are travelling by railway and then walking about all day – the dirt and dust would spoil it. Just a change or two of bodice to carry me over a couple nights there.' And Auryn had added his weight by saying, 'Lord, Auntie Sel, she's got a basket full already, don't encourage her or she'll prepare a travelling saddle-pack.'

At Winchester railway station, Ruth had almost felt the shrivelling of the neat Miss Warren as she extended a flounce-wristed hand. 'How wise of you, Miss Tylee, not to wear your best for the journey. But where is your travelling case?'

'Goodness, Dolly, what would Ruth want with a travelling case for a couple of nights?' Peter Warren jumped in, seeing Ruth's confusion. 'She's not an idle miss like you, to spend days on end flitting around London.' Trying to smooth over Dolly's fault of snobbishness. 'Dolly is staying in Town for a fortnight with our brother.'

Had Ruth not been so overawed by the great hissing engines, and the noise and steam, she might well have blurted out 'Oh this is my best,' and made matters worse by explaining that she carried fresh bodices for herself and Carly and a shirt for Auryn, contained in the cane basket, and that she would sleep in her shift.

Auryn did not seem to notice or, if he did, to mind that whilst every other young man was dressed in checked or striped trews with a nipped-in waisted coat, he wore breeches and leather gaiters and a thick cord jacket. Neither did he appear to mind that most of his kindly gallantry was rejected by Miss Warren. The Reverend Peter Warren's good humour, no doubt at the presence of Ruth Tylee, smoothed away any awkwardness.

No others of the Warren family had Dorothy's manners, which had been learned from the columns of magazines for young ladies; she was an avid reader of the advice given within their pages. If the advice was that the second button at the wrist of a glove should remain undone to denote the more casual air of morning attire, then it would remain undone until she had eaten breakfast – unless, of course, breakfast was taken later than noon, when it ought rightly to be referred to as 'luncheon' by anyone in the fashionable set, 'nuncheon' being now at least six months outmoded. Her family teased her: 'If *Ladies' World* was to say it was the thing to do to paint a blue ring round her nose, then Dolly would do it.' But Peter said that it was a passing phase and that she would come to her senses when she realized that she was a nice enough girl without such nonsense.

His purpose in suggesting that she come on the trip was to reveal to her the dignity and beauty of simplicity such as Ruth Tylee's. The reason given to her was that he wished to take Susanna as company for Caroline, but would not be able to manage her alone. He was sure that no woman could be in Ruth's company for long without seeing her perfection and wishing to emulate it. It never occurred to him that the reverse might be the case.

Ever since the efficient and calm way she had dealt with the crisis at Great Hole, Peter Warren had been head over heels in love with her and, as he confided to his brother, who lived in London, as soon as the time was right, he would ask her to marry him – or rather wait for him, until he found a way to provide them with some sort of a home.

When she saw Dorothy Warren trying to keep the balance of politeness by not abandoning them, yet walking at just sufficient distance so that people might not believe that they were of the same party, Ruth felt sorry that the Tylees were such insensitive creatures. The more she looked around her, the more she saw how unsuitable was their dress for such a grand occasion and such a magnificent place. Three rural bumpkins demeaned the great spans of glass, glittering over fully-grown trees, by walking there in market-day clothes. Ruth could see that it embarrassed Dorothy Warren to be in a group without style.

Hurrying ahead, she caught up with Dorothy Warren. One thing Peter Warren was right about – Ruth's simplicity could be disarming.

'Miss Warren. I hardly like to ask you, but you are turned out with that much perfection that I don't know who else better I could ask.'

Dorothy Warren raised her secretly-combed and lightly-oiled eyebrows, and the corners of her mouth. '"Dorothy"', she said. 'After all, you are on first-name terms with my brother, and we are much the same age.'

'Well, it is probably our fault that we call him Peter; it's our country ways to use first names without thinking.'

'Is your old home in the country?'

The image of the long empty shoreline, endless unin-habited miles, vacant blue skies and the isolation of the Toolagarry Station could never be conveyed to a young woman who had never known what it was to travel a thousand miles of unpopulated land.

'Very much so. It's a tiny garrison and a trading station.
Blackbrook is a huge city in comparison.'

Dorothy Warren smiled with uncomprehending politeness. 'How interesting. What is it you were going to ask?'

'I was going to ask whether it is possible for me to buy
some more suitable clothes than these. I have my best
market skirt and a new bodice, but . . .'

Dorothy Warren was delighted at the other's deference.

'Would you mind a made-up dress?'

'I shouldn't mind anything.'

'Many dressmakers these days keep near-finished
garments and bonnets. If you shouldn't mind wearing such a
thing?'

'How soon could it be done?'

'Oh, this morning easily.'

'Dear Lord, Dorothy, then let us do it at once.'

Dorothy Warren's face lit up. 'Oh, that would be the
most jolly thing to do.'

Leaving the young men in charge of the girls and
somewhat taken aback at the sudden intimacy and secrets of
their sisters, Ruth and Dorothy left the Great Exhibition
with an imperious assurance by the *Ladies' World*-trained
young woman that they were not children, and that she was
perfectly capable of 'popping about' in London.

Within an hour Ruth was in a ladies'-dress establishment
in which a partly-made garment could be finished, by the
combined effort of a dozen young girls working together,
within an hour.

'The deep burnt-orange tan colour! Oh yes, such a
wildly exciting thing for a red-haired woman to wear,'
exclaimed Dorothy. 'I could never wear it, but on you it is
absolutely *the* thing. And if you were to have a net overskirt
in black it would easily double for a dinner occasion.'

The bell-skirted frock, nipped at the waist and cut
demurely at the neck, was exactly the same colour as Ruth's

hair, which was of such a brightness that it often seemed to steal colour from anything that came close to it. With this frock, the hues of fabric and hair were patted back and forth between the two, neither draining the other.

While the frock was being finished, the two young women were provided with a small fitting room with a mirror. Dorothy Warren removed her hat and jacket and proceeded with pins and combs to create a simple abundant chignon of Ruth's hair, upon which to sit a tiny curl-brimmed replica of a billycock hat. When the dressmaker fitted the burnt orange sash around the frock, the transformation was made.

Ruth turned this way and that to see in the long mirror.

'Oh, Dorothy, you're a real wonder. Doesn't she look beautiful? Nothing like she did when we came in. I like her . . . oh yes, I *do* like her.'

Dorothy Warren was delighted at what she had created. 'She's the *real* you, Ruth.'

'No, she isn't. She's somebody called Miss Tylee, whom I've just met through you. I'm not beautiful – but *she* is. Oh, come, Dorothy, let's take her back to the exhibition. I can't wait for Aury to meet her.'

Dorothy, quite intoxicated by her own cleverness, was already creating the amusing story that she would relate to her Blackbrook friends.

They arrived back at the south entrance in a public conveyance, Ruth in haste to introduce her alter ego to the others.

'Slowly, Ruth.' Dorothy lightly restrained Ruth's eager-ness. 'Let the skirt swing.' Strolling, they walked to the South Transept where they had arranged to meet the others. Inside, Ruth looked along the long paved aisle of indoor gardens, huge trees and palms, spurting water, and magnifi-cent statuary. Suddenly she felt to be taking part in something, such as in a performance she had once seen in

Blackbrook when she was a small child. Then, princesses and kings in silken clothes and high wigs sang to one another as, lit by a row of flaring lamps, they sauntered about the stage.

Whilst Ruth Tylee would find it difficult to saunter, the new young woman wearing the burnt-orange frock was able to do so with ease and grace.

'Wait, Ruth. Don't say anything. Wait till I go round the other side of that little garden where I can see them through the shrubs. I want to see their faces when they realize who it is. Just go and sit beside them.'

Auryn and Peter Warren were seated on a back-to-back bench close to a complicated fountain whose jets fell splashing from a height of twenty or thirty feet, whilst Caroline and Susanna, in the careless charge of their brothers, darted about in the spray.

From the waving of their arms, one could tell that the young men were deep in conversation with another man a few years older than they, apparently on the subject of a twice-life-size equestrian sculpture of yet another woman who was free to ride out with nothing covering her generous breasts and only gossamer about her thighs.

Only the stranger was facing Ruth as she walked in their direction. Had it been Ruth, and not Miss Tylee, who received the frank and excessively appreciative stare, she would have faltered and called out Auryn's name to cover her shyness. As it was, she returned the stare, even dipped her head a fraction to one side in acknowledgement as he leapt up and swept an empty place beside him with a murmured 'Allow me.'

At this, Auryn and Peter turned curiously from the statue. Peter Warren flushed like a schoolboy when he realized that it was Ruth who was seated beside them. Auryn jumped up, exclaiming, 'Ruthie!'

Standing up and taking a step away, Ruth said, 'Well?

Haven't you anything to say except "Ruthie"? Isn't Dorothy a blessed wonder? I feel quite different.'

Auryn was saved from knowing what to say by Caroline and Susanna rushing up, dewy from their enjoyment of the water-spray. Caroline's high voice rose higher. 'Ruthie! You've turned into a lady. Look, Susanna. Oh, Aury, let me have a special dress too.' Wheedling.

'I should think not. I reckon Ruth must have broken the bank as it is.'

Ruth was about to defend the frock when Dorothy came up and threw her arms about the neck of the stranger who had said 'Allow me' and who, since, had been viewing the little performance by the Tylees with smiling interest.

To Ruth's surprise, Dorothy kissed him on both cheeks and said, 'Teddy, Teddy. Where did you spring from? I thought you were in Birmingham till Friday.'

The man hugged her in return and said, 'Up to your tricks again, Dolly.' At which she pretended the naughty child and hung her head; then she held his hand and drew him forward. 'Ruth, may I present my brother, Edward Warren of Bloomsbury. Teddy, this is Miss Ruth Tylee of Toony-something or other . . . well, she has come from the bottom of the globe.'

'Toolagarry in Australia,' Ruth said, 'but now from Cantle.'

Taking Ruth's hand formally, he said, 'So your brother has told me. Dolly never was a great one for geography.' His voice was cultured and gentlemanly, and showed no broad trace of his Hampshire origins, which were still detectable in the three others of his family. His manner was easy, yet courtly, giving the impression that he offered his full attention to whomever his eye lighted upon. Had she been wearing her Ruth clothes, she would have felt the full disadvantage of her childhood away from civilization.

'What use geography, Teddy, now that we have the

railway and one may travel from Blackbrook to London in a straight line in hours?'

They spent the rest of the evening in Edward Warren's company. He was older than Peter by something like ten years and, although there was a remarkable family resemblance in their wide brows, fine straight noses and generous mouths, these features became more elegant in maturity so that one might say that Teddy was ten years more handsome than his pale, work-worn brother.

Since the night of the tragedy, Ruth's admiration for Peter had grown. But the admiration was more akin to that for a fictional selfless hero. Only equally selfless heroines fell into the arms of such men, and Ruth was beginning to recognize something of her own nature and that of the passionate and emotionally unstable bloodline she sprang from.

Almost daily she expected Peter to ask her to 'throw in her lot with his' or to make some similar declaration – meaning wedlock, of course. But since the two cathartic experiences of last December, she was determined that she would find a better way of living her life than as a wife.

Once or twice, ideas had entered her head, but reticence and a lack of confidence in her ability stopped her taking them any further than to wonder whether they were possible. It was all very well having a Ma and Pa who brought you up to believe that you had special qualities, but it was something else to discover what they were and how to go about fulfilling the promise.

Today she imagined herself grown in stature. She felt that she belonged in this splendid glass palace filled with the achievements of great scientists, works by the cream of European artists, and the crafts of British furniture-makers, silversmiths and leather-workers. She felt too, that, whatever it was she was going to do with her life, it must be to do something perfect, something to which people would pay the same kind of homage as they were paying here.

The Tylees had only three days for their expedition. Ruth and Susanna had wanted to go back and see some of the exhibitions which had intrigued them yesterday, but Auryn wanted to look at a scientific exhibition. He had been in a fit of pique that Ruth should not have consulted him before she went off like a flibberty-gibbet, spending money without asking him, and at the resoluteness in her reply that it was her own and she could please herself. She hated them to be in a state of irritation with one another so, as she usually did, she placated him by giving in entirely to his desire.

They met the Warrens in the public dining rooms to eat breakfast, and whilst they were there a messenger came with a note for Peter from his brother.

'Listen,' he said. 'Teddy wants us all to dine with him this evening.'

Ruth felt an unexpected moment of excitement at the invitation. 'Invited to dine' was a phrase which before this she had only encountered in novels.

'Shall you come?'

Susanna and Caroline settled it for them by setting up a clamouring to go that only agreement would quell.

Edward Warren lived in a large gloomy-looking house in Coram Street, but to Ruth its gloom only added to its splendour. She had never entered a house with columned doors. She and Auryn caught one another's eyes and raised eyebrows at each other.

'Is your brother rich?' Caroline asked Susanna clearly.

'I don't think so. He only sells fodder.'

'Sells fodder? You mean like Carter Jepp in Cantle?'

'Hush, Carly,' Auryn said. 'It's not good manners to ask questions like that.'

'I don't see why not. If I was rich, I wouldn't mind people knowing.'

'Well, you're not, and you are to be on your very best

behaviour. I'll bet there aren't half a dozen more girls in the whole of London this evening allowed to sit at the dining table with adults. *Don't spoil it and get taken home.*'

Caroline knew how far she could go, and knew that this was it.

The gloom of the exterior was dispelled by the light and colour within the house. Edward Warren came out into the hall to greet them.

'I have a suggestion. If you would care to eat at once, I could take you afterwards on a little jaunt to Pimlico to see my new project.'

'What project's this one?' Peter asked, with the kind of indulgence in his tone that would have been more appropriate from the elder to the younger man.

'You'll see. You'll see. It's settled then?'

The young people were in a mood for any extra bit of fun before returning to their workaday lives.

The dinner was very informal, with simple food served. Ruth sat poker-backed in her dark-orange finery, watching Dorothy's movements, and felt almost at ease with the crystal glass and shining cutlery. Caroline, for once overawed and unsure, allowed Auryn to guide her into some sort of mannerly behaviour.

When it was over Dorothy said, 'Now, Teddy, what's this jaunt? Where is it to be?'

'Don't get all excited, Dolly – it's not an entertainment, it's just something that I'm involved in that I thought you might like to see. Get your things on, we're going to Pimlico.'

They crammed all together in a cab, the two young girls on their brothers' knees. After a drive through the warm evening, the cab drew up before a tall grand-looking building. Five stone steps led up to four separate entrances, each with embellished glass doors. The upper storeys were set back several feet, which created a kind of balcony fronted by six columns with stone pediments, and around the roof was a stone balustrade topped by a fanciful winged being. Painters were at work on the doors.

Dorothy jumped out at once exclaiming, 'Teddy Warren, it *is* an entertainment.'

'Not yet, Dolly, but I think you may find it entertain*ing*.'

He led the way, the painters tipped their caps and stood aside to allow them to pass. Once through the doors, they were in a spacious area with a stone floor, marbled columns and marble steps leading up at either end. A glazier was fixing some beading around a series of beautifully decorated mirrors.

Teddy gave Dorothy and Ruth each a hand and said, 'This way. Mind your skirts, there's a lot of wet paint,' and led them through central double doors.

'Goodness, Teddy. What is it?' Peter asked.

The elder laughed, revealing the family trait of wholesome teeth, obviously pleased with himself. 'It isn't anything yet. But by next week it will be Bounderby's Supper Rooms and Hall of Music.'

'Teddy! Is it yours?' asked Dorothy.

'No, Dolly, I'd have to be pretty rich to own it entirely – but I aim to do so before very long. What do you think, Tylee?' In asking Auryn, Edward Warren glanced at Ruth, obviously pleased with the impression he was making upon all the young people, but wanting the approval of a pretty young woman.

'It's most fine, Mr Warren.'

'Only fine? Shouldn't you say better than that, Miss Tylee?'

'It *is* fine . . . and it's impressive, breathtaking, dazzling and amazing.' She gazed up at two huge unlit crystal chandeliers, sparkling and gleaming even though there was no light other than that which came from a row of lamps on the rostrum, where workmen were painting.

'There! Miss Tylee appreciates the nature of the place. One is not expected to be merely impressed, one should be dazzled, amazed.'

'That's what I am, Teddy,' said Susanna. 'I am dazzled and amazed. I thought you only sold sacks of oats. Isn't it amazing, Dolly?'

'Very amazing. And are we to know what your part is in this dazzling fairyland?'

When he laughed, Ruth knew him to be a man who liked admiration and attention. 'I am to be the lamplighter. I shall set the place ablaze so that all London will want to take supper at Bounderby's and see the very best of entertainers. I am a partner in this venture, I shall be the one to give it style.'

'Does that mean you have to light all those lamps yourself?' Caroline asked seriously.

'Every single one. Do you know how many there are?'

'Yes. The nine wall brackets have seven each – that's sixty-three. The two at each end have twenty each – that's four twenties are eighty. Eighty and sixty-three is one hundred and forty-three. And the huge ones have fifty each on the bottom and twenty more at the top which is . . . a hundred and forty. Just a minute, just a minute.' She closed her eyes. 'Two hundred and eighty-three lamps.'

'Well, the deuce! I've never counted, but I'm prepared to believe her.'

Caroline flushed red with pleasure. 'I am right. I calculated twice to check.'

'I think that deserves a prize. Come with me, you two. No grown-ups, just these two pretty misses.' He held out a hand to each.

A phrase that her mother often used about Pa in his younger days – 'He was a man who could charm an old man or a young child as he chose – charm the birds down from the trees' – the description fitted Edward Warren too.

He took the girls off, leaving the four others to wander around and look in wonderment at the vast supper room. An elegant, colonnaded gallery ran around three sides, its plastered front embellished over almost every inch with raised plaster-work and paintings. At the far end, raised up from the floor, was a wide brass-railed rostrum behind which was a vast work in bas-relief depicting a group of nine bathing nymphs. Everywhere, the flickering lamps caught the glint of crystal, glass, shining brass, white plaster in a pristine state, and an ornate confusion of painted flowers, fruit, cherubs and voluptuous bare-breasted women with gauzy drapes revealing their thighs, and cloven-hooved pipe-players ogling them.

Peter Warren, hands thrust into his pockets in a most unclerical way, looked at everything, shaking his head and saying, 'Well! I never dreamed he had this in mind. Ted always was a dark horse, wasn't he, Dolly?'

'He always likes to make a mystery of everything. You see – he cannot even take the children for a treat without making quite a thing of it.'

'And look at yesterday. He said most definitely that he would be in Birmingham until Friday, and up he pops the other side of a clump of palm trees and says, "Ah, Peter, thought I might find you here." Find you here? A vast place the size of the Great Exhibition and he strolls about looking for us as though it was Blackbrook Market Square.'

'Perhaps then,' Ruth said, 'he will be very good at creating style here. Making such gestures is really very stylish.'

'I think it's a good thing she's going home tomorrow, don't you, Peter?' Auryn said with a half-smile.

'Why so?'

'Because when she starts using phrases like "creating style", I think it is time she got some farmyard mud back on her boots.'

Ruth smiled, but she was not entirely sure that he did not mean it seriously.

He had not said much the entire evening. Ruth suspected that he felt so unsure of himself that he would not chance saying anything that would put him at any more disadvantage than he already felt himself to be, remaining content to listen to the very talkative Warrens, and to watch their town manners and look at the splendid building.

Now he said, 'I don't really understand the nature of this place. What exactly is a "Supper Room"?'

'I take it to be after the style of the Blackbrook Assembly Rooms when they are used for a glee, or a singing concert,' Dorothy Warren said.

Auryn glanced at Ruth and raised one eyebrow a fraction. Ruth shrugged her shoulders almost imperceptibly in answer. Then she said, 'I dare say it seems strange to you, but the only meeting place of any kind in Toolagarry is a wooden sort of a hut used as a chapel and everything else besides. We never heard of a glee in our lives. And since we've been back in England, we've never been to any Assembly Rooms.'

'How stupid of us,' Peter Warren said. 'Dolly, why do we take everybody for granted? We're both as bad.'

'I didn't mean you to apologize,' Ruth said. 'Only to explain what are glees and what goes on in the Assembly Rooms.'

Susanna and Caroline came rushing back, clattering across the floor of chequered tiles, both wanting to tell at once that they had been given some wonderful frozen strawberry frappé, which was being prepared in a special ice pantry.

'The man said that it was the same as he made for the King of Italy –'

'– and the Queen said that he must go to the palace on her birthday and make some more –'

'— and his name is Umberto, and he is the best ice-pudding maker in England.'

'And Italy.'

'Yes, and Italy.'

As Edward Warren took the party on a tour of the grand place, the young girls walked about in great freedom and delight, with their fluted glasses of frappé, which they ate with tiny spoons, making it last — Dorothy Warren saying 'Tut-tut, I don't dare tell Mother', without any real seriousness.

'Here, where we are standing now, here will be tables and chairs where people will be able to order supper to eat whilst the glee is on or an orchestra plays. Not that it will have any resemblance to what Blackbrook would recognize as a glee. It will be altogether a much more extravagant affair than the way it is done in an Assembly Room where the food is always served in a side room. Our clientele will sit at tables with their friends and take as much or as little food and drink as they wish, whilst entertainment is provided constantly. You see there?' Squatting down to be on a level with the children, Edward Warren pointed to brass rings high in the ornate ceiling. 'On the grand opening night, a negro woman black as my boots and pretty as a picture in sparkling jewels and feathers will swing out over the dining tables ... hanging on only by her teeth!'

The vision of that event stopped the visitors. They gazed upwards.

'Lor', Susanna, what if her teeth break!' Caroline's observation started them all into laughter, as much because of their buoyant mood as at her comment.

They had now reached the rostrum upon which was a grand piano covered with a dust-sheet. Edward Warren whisked it off.

'Now, Dolly, when you've calmed down, let us see what good all those music lessons have done you.'

'Not here, Teddy.'

'Of course here. This pianoforte has been imported from Germany, it's not likely you'll lay finger on another as fine unless you marry into the Berol Estate.' He spread his own hands on the keys and pressed out two or three loud and accurate chords. 'Sit down, Dolly, sit down. You know that you are dying to show off your talents.'

She allowed herself to be pushed onto the playing stool. 'I can't think what to play.'

'Play that polka thing you're always rattling off at home,' Peter said. 'I know that you can play it without the score.'

She played a few chords, then plunged into an impressively fast piece of playing, after which she sat rubbing her palms together saying, 'Teddy, I think I could become very attached to this piano,' and immediately rattled her way through another piece.

'You and Peter sing.' The two brothers took no persuading, and Ruth thought of how civil the Warren family must be when all gathered together, and wondered what Peter Warren thought of the times he had sat at their rough table, and of the hearty dancing he had encountered at Croud Cantle last Christmas.

'Do you play, Miss Tylee?' Edward Warren asked.

'Goodness, no. I never laid finger on any piano at all.' Unaffectedly, she spread her broad palms for him to see. 'Farm-girl's hands, I'm afraid. Caroline is the player in the family – she is learning the flute.'

'Ruth sings,' Peter said. 'She has a beautiful voice.'

Although she tried not to, Ruth blushed. 'No, no, it's nothing special.'

'Oh, *Ruth*. People only think you mean the opposite if you say things like that,' Caroline said. 'You do sing nice – why don't you just *sing* and not make a fuss about it.'

Peter Warren stood aside to make room for Ruth at the

piano. 'Tell Dolly what you want – she can usually pick anything up once she's got the key.'

'Everything's gone out of my head.'

'Sing the one you sang at Christmas about Young Lovel and his bride.'

'Oh, it's such a sad song.' She looked at Auryn, hoping for his approval, afraid that she might make a fool of herself. In her mind's ear she heard his comment: 'Oh, Ruth, did you have to make such a poppy-show?' He was sitting quietly on a step beside the rostrum lighting the pipe that he had bought for himself yesterday.

Peter spoke in his sister's ear and she played a few bars of 'The Mistletoe Bough' in different keys. Ruth nodded. Dorothy played a short introduction and Ruth began to sing, keeping her hands clasped and not raising her eyes from Dorothy's hands. When she reached the words 'Spending their Christmas holiday' she realized that the sound filling the air was her own voice.

As she looked up and saw the vast room, Ruth suddenly felt elated. It was as though the place was an empty box that she could fill with her voice, as she used to imagine filling the void of the open brushlands. She took breath deeper into her lungs, as she used to do there, singing against the hot breezes and space of the great openness around Toolagarry. It was impossible to sing like that in a room the size of the one at Croud Cantle. Controlling and manipulating the expiration of her breath gave her a feeling of fulfilment.

She had often visualized the inward breath as a bundle of white, which her lungs, throat and mouth fashioned and coloured, so that when she sent it forth again, it was as multi-coloured ribbons, each note with its own hue.

She sang. Now sending out streamers of pale, sad violet and pink; those of the top notes rippled high against the white ceiling before floating down, while the ribbons of lower notes went like waves towards the back wall. Out into the huge box of space, she sent the music; artlessly, she moved her arms and hands as she told of the tragedy of the bride who hid playfully from her groom in a trunk, was trapped, and died on her wedding day.

As, in the guise of stylish Miss Tylee, she had felt able to be bold at the exhibition, so she could do this – because she was, for the present, not Auryn's younger sister, not Ruthie, nor the farm-girl: she was that woman who had stepped from the mirror in the dressmaker's, the one who could saunter with swinging skirts, and pick up in seconds how to use a table-napkin. The woman in the burnt-orange frock did not, however, obscure the viewpoint of the farm-girl Ruth, who was allowed to see everything through the eyes of her assured alter ego as she acted her part.

As the last, sad note hung clearly in the space of the hall, there was an outburst of hearty clapping. The sound brought Ruth back to reality. The workmen, painters, carpenters, glaziers had halted in their work and gathered in a ragged audience, captured by the sound of the old song. One of them called out in a London voice, 'Now that's what y'call a voice'; another shouted, 'Ay, Miss, sing us another.' Ruth smiled at such plain appreciation and gave an exaggerated curtsey. In doing so, her face came level with Auryn's, and he did not look pleased.

Usually she was a pacifier. There was the side to his nature that she did not like, where he set standards and made rules and expected himself and everyone else to keep them. He liked to have control, and would have laid down the time they got up and the time they retired had he been able. It was that side of him which had put the disapproval on his face yesterday when she had bought the frock. When she stood up to him, he would always come round and admit his pomposity or unreasonableness, and whilst he seemed to enjoy the battling, she thoroughly disliked it.

His solemn face showed that he disapproved of her

making a show of herself. As she straightened up, it came to her that he might be envious. Perhaps that was always the problem. When he said that she was making a show of herself, it was that he wanted to be the one to be noticed. She felt irritation at his childish behaviour, but now was not the time to show it.

Longing for his approval, and knowing that she would not get it, she withdrew her attention from her brother, and raised her eyes to find Edward Warren's gaze fixed upon her, thumbs against his lips, hands in a prayerful attitude.

'Wonderful! Totally wonderful! What are you doing making cheese for Blackbrook burghers who are already too fat? Tylee, you should not keep her hidden away in the back of nowhere.'

Ruth smiled with pleasure and said quietly, 'It is not Auryn who keeps me hidden anywhere. We have a farm to run – it is how we earn our bread.'

'Fiddlesticks to bread, with a voice like that you could live on quails' eggs and champagne.'

'Oh, Teddy,' Susanna said, 'and strawberry frappy.'

'I told her not to make a fuss and go on and sing,' said Caroline.

Dorothy, not happy at the edge of attention, ran her fingers over the keys. Auryn came and stood beside her. 'Will you play something else?' Delighted at her return to centre stage, she smiled her most adorable smile at the only man present worthy of it – wonderfully handsome in spite of leather and tweed.

His action in ignoring her and pointedly favouring her 'rival' was to Ruth like the wrist-twisting 'Chinese Burns' that children give to one another – a permissible small torture denoting a desire to give a greater one. She would have given much had he simply said, 'That was nice, Ru.'

Some compensation came from the Warren brothers. Peter said, 'I should love to hear you singing some arias from grand opera – you have the most wonderful voice I have ever heard.'

'Wonderful? Fiddlesticks, Peter, she is *superb*! Absolutely superb.'

She accepted that Peter might be biased, but the elder of the two was not a gazey lover admiring every small skill. 'Do you really think I have a voice, Mr Warren?'

'Oh, yes, Miss Tylee, you have a voice and a half. You have talent and you have . . .' he took her hand and, raising her arm, turned her a little this way and that, holding his head on one side in consideration . . . 'you have a very wonderful figure. If you would come, I would give you a contract to perform at Bounderby's here and now.'

The last phrase fell into the silence that followed Dorothy's final crescendo.

'I think that it's time we went back to our lodgings, Ruth.' Auryn, stiff with politeness. 'Thank you for showing us your . . . and for the supper.'

That night, and for many nights thereafter, Ruth had her dream of riding to the precipice.

8

QUEEN OF THE MEADOW

THIS WAS TO BE Kitty 'Fire-Bucket's' second wedding ceremony, and although she did not yet know who she was going to jump the stick with, she thought that it would be at least more enjoyable than the one to Cocky three years ago when she wasn't old enough to enjoy a good randy. Now that she was seventeen, gin and beer no longer made her sick, but gave her a glow and a feeling of freedom that nothing else did.

Dutch and Ollie had been bunking at Cocky's old shanty for about a year, when the overseer told Kitty she must get the tenancy settled up and paid. So she decided to make a good do of it and 'jump the stick', which was the favourite – almost the only – form of common marriage in the Great Hole shanty-town.

It was simple: two people held a stick – possibly a broom-handle, anything would do – and the couple joined hands and jumped over. On one side of the stick was the uncoupled state, on the other . . . a kind of commitment. To some couples, jumping the stick was as binding as a service in a church with marriage-lines signed and marked. But to many men it was the easiest way of getting a woman of your own without having to borrow or pay. If you later wanted to 'slope off' – to take your pick, shovel and belongings and climb the sloping sides of the embankment and away, away – then you went. The easiest form of divorce.

Not many women sloped off.

A man who sloped off alone could earn his keep with his pick and shovel. A woman's three or four children with empty bellies tended not to be an asset when it came to liberty and the open road.

Kitty's jumping-the-stick took place in the summer, at about the same time of year as the Croud Cantle family were having their London visit. Kitty washed her face and hands and feet, and those of her children, then she washed her and Maggie's hair, then rinsed it with an infusion of fresh chamomile flowers, and let it dry un-knotted. Few people had seen Kitty with her hair pale, washed and hanging in loose curls. Maggie's stiff little mop was as dark as Cocky's, but the new growth on baby Agnes's was exactly like Kitty's own, loosely curled and the colour of pale ale.

The foundling baby, Simeon, whom the vicar had brought to the shanty hut last Boxing Day and had since paid her a few pence to wet-nurse alongside her own, was now a thriving little thing who looked up from the breast and into her eyes, and whilst still holding the nipple with its tongue, beamed a smile of recognition.

Kitty loved this one.

It had not come to her as had Maggie, by the rape of her thirteen-year-old body; nor as had Agnes when she was fifteen, with a black eye from Cocky for being a frosty bloody bitch who wouldn't move herself to give her husband a bit of fun. The boy baby had come without a belly to make her stagger, without sickness, blood or pain. She always referred to him as the Vicar's Baby. Grinning at her own joke, she would tell people, 'It was the young vicar what give me this baby – one of his names is Peter, after him.'

Peter Warren had heard the joke and didn't mind. His conscience at having asked the girl to take on another child was not kind to him. But to save the child was the thing. Kitty had full enough breasts to feed two babies. He gave her a little money, she could buy a bit of fish or meat for herself and get some bread and farm-milk for the older baby. Kitty was one of the few navvy women he had any confidence in to hand the baby over to – though it was not so much the

women he did not trust, but the men they lived with and the
conditions of the shants.

Washed, and in the only skirt she had that was not
tattered or made from sacking, Kitty took her three babies
into the fields and picked herself flowers – a bunch of St
John's wort and queen of the meadow, whose rank sweetness in the hot, still air was as heady to her as the sweat of a
man's body. Then she searched the hedges for the fresh
herbs she needed to make Bitter-brew. The lore of the
women had it that there was something in the green of the
fresh leaves, compared to the same when dried, which made
the remedy more effective in keeping a woman's belly
empty.

Now that she had been forced to decide on a man to take
on Cocky's tenancy, she would no longer have any say
about the use of her own body. It would not be her own
body. But women do what they can to defend themselves.
Right from the earliest times when they peopled a landmass
which was still undivided, women have taken leaves and
chewed them, picked berries and squeezed their juices,
ground seeds and roots, and tried to defend the womb
against the uninvited child with anything from animal-fat to
fleece.

She sank down onto the long grass, making for herself
something of an occasion by thus sitting down in the middle
of the morning, with her face and hands washed and a great
armful of flowers beside her.

'Don't you go runnen off so I got to find you.'

The small child, Maggie, looked dumbly at her mother,
and ran round in circles, keeping an eye on Kitty. Kitty took
off her shawl and laid the other two babies on it. Baby Agnes
was old enough to crawl but, in the warm sun, she lay
quietly on her back until she went to sleep, her hands above
her head and knees spread wide. Kitty sat, twisting scabious
flowers in her own hair, flicking flies from the babies and

tickling Simeon with a seed-head of grass making him laugh
and sneeze.

'I a tell you summet, my little ole darlin'. If I could find a
lucky stone that still had a wish left I'd make us a bloody good
wish.' The baby laughed its trust in her, and her judgement.
Kitty turned over on to her stomach, pulling grass stems and
sucking off the pale, tender ends, savouring them on the edge
of her teeth as if they were gross grass stems of asparagus. She
nibbled clover heads, and idly tried unsuccessfully to mimic a
bee, by working the tip of her tongue into the hidden parts of
vetch and toadflax for pollen and honeydew.

'Well, bugger me, darlin', look if it isn't a magic four-leaf
clover. What a bit of luck!' She nipped off the leaf and sat
looking at it. 'I heard that there was such things but I never
believed it. Look.' She held it close to the baby's face so that
its eyes crossed at trying to focus.

Kitty giggled. Agnes jerked in her sleep at the sound, and
Maggie came back to sit down. 'Look, Mag, it's a magic
four-leaf clover, and we got one wish.'

The little girl reached out, but Kitty whisked it out of her
reach. 'No, you a only tear the bugger to bits, you have a
look and see if you can find one for yourself.' The child
looked blank as she so often did when Kitty spoke to her.
'You an't deaf. I know you can say somethen when you
wants to. If this magic clover-leaf would work, I could wish
for this mornen to last for ever and ever.'

She twirled the leaf on the end of the baby's nose. He
sneezed. She laughed and tickled him. The little girl got up
and stood watching, then gave Kitty a kick with her small
hard bare foot.

'You'm a real little bugger, Mag, you a grow up to be a
bloody Shifter if you keeps goen like that. Now come and sit
down and be nice, and I a tell you.'

Kitty held out an arm inviting enough for Maggie to flop
into it and sit quietly.

'If we could stop like this you woulden't never have to grow up, Mag, and you wouldn't have no bloody ole man poking you about like you was a bloody ole bit of a carcass . . .

'And my face would go on feelen all nice and fresh and tight, and I should have on this nice cotten skirt instead of me ole prickly one . . .

'Ah . . . and I shoulden't have no bloody ole men poken and feelen me neither . . .

'And I shoulden't have to get no kindlen nor snapwood for a fire, because we shoulden't be cold nor hungry . . . just think, Mag, we should always be nice and warm and dry, and we shoulden't have nothen to worry us.

'And Vicar's Baby and little Agnes would lie side by side as happy as kittens and never have no thought except to get all excited at this here bit of ole waggle-grass.' The baby Simeon drew in his breath and shrieked with the ecstatic thrill of Kitty's smiling face, the fullness of his belly and the playful tickling. He sneezed again.

Along with the delicate sneeze, there came from the distance, the sound of a great coarse cheer. Kitty threw herself onto her back and said, 'Oh sod it, they finished already.' For ten minutes, she gazed up through the shimmering heat, through the shrilling larks, flitting insects, fluttering Red Admirals, flickering damsels; through pollen and dust, and layer upon layer of uncomprehending and incomprehensible life, at the blue July sky, which reflected back into the blue of her own glistening tears.

Then, she pushed herself up on one elbow and gave Maggie a squeeze. 'Ne'mind, Mag. Our turn a come, like my Ma used to say. She used to say, "Men's a lot of rubbish and I don't know how they come to be in charge", and nor don't I. There's times when I look at Dutch and Ollie and I thinks to myself, you don't never think of nothen except diggen the bloody cutten, poken some bloody woman, and drinken your sodden self stupid.'

Maggie looked silently at her mother.

'I wish you'd hurry up and start to talk, Mag, so I know that you understands what I mean. And I shan't let the Vicar's Baby be no navvy neither. I sometimes wonder if I done the right theng turning down the Vicar's offer to go skivvying. But I always gets frightened from my wits when I think about leaving the diggens. When you been in a place ever since you were born, you don't know how to carry on in another place. He can't understand that. I dare say he thinks I'm a bit of a sukey. Ne'mind, one day I shall ask him if he a learn you how to get away from here. I reckon that's my wish. "I wish that Mag and Agnes and the Vicar's Baby get away from navvies".' She kissed the leaf like a relic. 'And me, Kitty Fire-Bucket, too.'

Having used up her wish, she carefully placed the clover-leaf inside her bodice, then she arose, picked up the Vicar's Baby and slung him on her back tied in the shawl, and, with Agnes in one arm and Maggie keeping up with her in fits and starts, Kitty Fire-Bucket took her children up the rise towards the main road along which she had decided to walk to get to the shanty-town by Great Hole and to see who had won the tenancy. As she pulled herself and Maggie up a hump in the hill, she came upon an old market woman, with two great empty baskets beside her, sitting on a bank and gazing down into the valley. Although she was smiling faintly, the woman looked tired.

Oh . . . fancy if you bees as old as that. And nothen to look forward to.

What Kitty had to look forward to she could not have put into words, yet, constantly optimistic, she knew that there was *somethen. There had to be somethen or it wouldn't be worth putten up with everythen. One day it would happen, like finding a magic four-leaf clover. If you could find one of them, anythen might happen.*

The leaf was being pressed flat between Kitty's firm

bosom and her bodice – when she got home she was going to keep it in a bit of white paper in her book.

As they passed by to climb the stile, the market woman said, 'Hello, child.' Maggie looked away. 'Say hello to the lady, Maggie, say hello, nice to her.' Kitty gave the woman a smile, because she was sorry for her being old, and because you could see she must have been quite pretty once, and for having great baskets to lug back from the market.

It was a toss-up whether Kitty Fire-Bucket took Dutch or Ollie. It was an arranged marriage in every sense. Kitty needed a protector to take over Cocky's tenancy to allow her to stay in the shanty, and Dutch and Ollie wanted the hut and the extra money brought in from a couple of lodgers and the sale of beer to them. In the end they decided to settle for it as they settled everything, by wrestling.

9

A FIELD OF SCABIOUS

JULY. ANOTHER MEADOW, not far from the diggings, was blue with scabious which did not last long under the hundreds of heavy boots that now invaded it. Thrushes and blackbirds went prudently to the top of the hawthorns, sparrows stayed and scavenged; at one time there would have been a retreat to the hedge-bottoms of small animals, but since the advent of the navvymen, there was scarcely an edible creature of fur, feather or scale for miles around. Even quills were not safe from a man living rough on the tramp.

Word went round, beer was brought by sellers yoked like milkmaids, and bets made. None of the refinements such as ropes, rules and referees. The two brothers, stripped to the waist, spat upon their hands and went for each other.

There was little to choose between them physically, but to the navvies they represented something to side with, or against. 'Getters' against 'Runners-out'. Dutch was a Getter, Ollie a Runner-out.

Each side backing their own.

Getters thought themselves the kings of the railway navvies – this claim was always disputed by 'Tigers', and concrete fillers, but as the tunnelling was complete and there was no concrete work, the Getters of Great Hole reigned there. Precise and skilled, as they picked and shovelled at the muck-face and cut their way through the chalkhills. To see a good gang of Getters at the face was to see a human machine, a long row of fifty or more backs bent at the same angle, arms lifting in unison as though timed by a metronome, no talking, only each man's grunt as his pick bit into the chalkface and the spoil fell for the Runners-out to shift. A rhythm of work, like Viking long-boat oarsmen, chain-gangs of convicts or slaves, women hoeing or rice-planting. Of all the working teams, only the navvies had no songs. Just the timed grunt.

Ollie's supporters, the Runners-out, although they were not quite so well paid as the Getters, had an arrogance about them. Their back and arm muscles were as full and hard as the Getters' but, unlike them, they had hard leg muscles from running up steep embankments with heavy barrow-loads of spoil. They were essential to the quick progress of the digging – if they didn't move the muck, then the Getters would have to stop their rhythm, which slowed them down and made them irritable so that rows broke out with the overseers. Runners-out worked individually, each servicing a part of the cut. Large, scooping shovels filled wheel-barrows, then the heavy loads had to be pushed along planks, up sides of the embankment, in one unstopping movement, almost at a run. If the barrow tilted, then the Shifter – or Runner-out – must leap away from the load with the agility of an athlete and let the load crash back down into the cutting.

Great numbers of Runners-out ended their working days under such loads with crushed and shattered limbs. But both Dutch and Ollie had reached their early thirties without any grave injuries. So far the only damage done to them was by drink. The natural hazard of any navvyman.

Not that they saw early death as a hazard – many probably did not realize how high were the chances of accidental death in a navvyman's life. Navvymen died in their thousands of 'bad luck'. The reckoning of deaths in the building of the Great Southern was 'one to a mile, thirty to a tunnel' – an estimate on the low side, for it did not take account of those men who had sloped off and died in the Spike, nor of the women and children of no account who died from the poor conditions, bad food and disease rife in the shanty-towns.

Thirty gallons of ale a month was the average navvy-man's consumption of beer, and it was part of their 'bad luck' that such heavy drinkers should work in some of the most dangerous conditions that any engineer might think up.

So, with plenty of ale being sold, the representative of the Getters set about his brother, who was for the Shifters. It was not an uncommon sight to see these two locked in one another's hold. Kitty had told Peter that it was not 'mean fighten' which, by the measure of a really vicious set-to of no-holds-barred wrestling, was true. They did not gouge eyes, knee scrotums, or bite ears, or scratch or kick or knife as would navvies doing drunken battle with local farm workers. Anything else to get the other brother down was allowed. Evenly matched, the contest for Kitty Fire-Bucket's tenancy and body, and more importantly their 'side', it could be anybody's fight, which made it worth the bet.

As for Kitty's place in the bargain, each brother knew that, win or lose, he would get his share of her; they had always been like that with their women. But this was the first time that either of them had been persuaded to jump the stick.

Bets were made. Somebody said, 'Right', and they threw themselves at one another.

Slap of bare breast against bare breast.

A unified grunt as each pair of hands gripped and held the waist of his opponent's breeches.

Their holds had no names, there was no sequence in their moves, or thought given to the outcome.

Charge. Grip. Twist. Hold. Because they were so well matched, there was little movement once the hold had been made until one of them lost his footing . . . then . . .

Thud. Grip. Heave and hook calf with ankle until the other too lost his balance.

Then again, and again the charging and test of muscle.

The contest lasted for the best part of an hour without stop, except to allow a spit of blood or a dash in the face with beer. At last one of them was down, and gave best to his brother.

He held up his hand and a cheer went up. 'Getters! The Getters! Dutch got Ollie this time.'

Having declared the winner, Dutch threw himself upon Ollie where he had fallen. They lay gasping on the crushed scabious in an emotional brotherly embrace. 'Go on then, ye bugger. Go and let Annie scrub down thy sweaty body, and let's get started with the randy – I could drink a bloody gallon non-stop.'

10

RED CLOVER AND MEADOW-SWEET

SELENA NETHERFIELD HAD FINISHED EARLY at Waltham Market that same day. It had been too hot for the butter to last, so she had sold it off cheaply and quickly before it went oily. Most of the other produce went, as it usually did, to people who came to the Croud Cantle stall regularly as had their mothers and grandmothers and great-grandmothers before them. Croud Cantle had the reputation of being reliable. And reasonable. Reasonable meaning that Selena sold good-quality produce at poor-quality prices.

Although she felt fatigued by the long walk in the hot weather, along the Wayfarer's Way back to Cantle, she tried to step it out.

Today the children were coming home . . . *They'll be tired after their long journey on the railway and the walk back from Blackbrook . . . and they'll be hungry – especially Auryn and Caroline.*

A slice of fried ham and eggs apiece, three for Auryn . . . and the vat of fresh elderflower has started working . . . good thing it's set it in the old dairy . . . nice and cold – Ruth loves it cold like that, with a leaf of mint, fizzing, before it settles down to make wine.

In her mind's eye she set the table for them and visualized herself listening to their experiences. It had cost most of what was left of Lidia's money . . . but an experience of a lifetime . . . no regrets when they are older that they did not see the great achievements of the age they were born into. She began to compose the letter that she would write to their father. *Dear Addy* . . . there were times when she ached to see her brother. There were times when she caught a glimpse of him in Ruth's eyes and Caroline's chin and nose. She longed for him now as she had longed for him every day for twenty years. But she had one thing of him – she had his daughters. And they were coming home.

Her legs ached, and she was hungry. A good place to have a bite of bread and onion. She climbed a stile and sat in the shade of a great, old beech, looking down into the downland valleys that lie to the west of Wayfarer's Way where one had a panoramic view of the building of the new railway.

Chewing her bread, crisp-crusted now from the heat of the day, she saw both the shambles and the organization. The engineering was a wonder, the facilities for the people shameful.

Addy would be furious about the conditions. The railway engineers expected working people to live for years in those terrible shanty-towns. Addy . . . exiled from his own country because he protested the degrading way in which his neighbours had been forced to live.

She chewed her bread on her front teeth, the only dozen she had left. In trying to stop the dry crusts cutting her gums, she gave the impression of nibbling daintily.

Further down the hill in the same meadow of red clover as herself, she saw a pretty picture – a young woman with a little child who was skipping about, and two babies lying in the grass. The sound of her voice carried up on the still, hot air. Selena could not hear the words, only the gentle way that she was talking to the children. She did not recognize the girl as local, yet it was not likely that she was a navvy's woman, out there idling around in the middle of the day.

A cheer went up from somewhere distant. Selena strained her eyes in the direction from which the sound came. Then she saw that what she had taken to be a tip of spoil was in fact a gathering of men. Navvies, probably having one of the drinking bouts they were notorious for.

Brutes. She had seen more bruised eyes and broken arms
among the small community of navvy women, than among
all the women in the Four Parishes, who worked with cows,
who wielded sickles, or did any of the heavy farm work of
the area – and farm labourers were not known for great
gentleness to their womenfolk. Addy would have said she
must understand them. *'Brutal lives beget brutal people. It is
easy for a gentleman, with no worries about where the next
mouthful is coming from, to be gallant, just as it is easy for a
mother with a nursery and nursemaid for a flock of children
never to lay a hand on them. You have to try to understand
why it happens, Sel. People aren't born brutal. One day we
shall have a good and gentle society.'* It grieved her that he
should have come to doubt his own beliefs.

*Addy, people need leaders like you again. Another Adam
Tylee to stand in the open fields and preach equality. Such a
lot of young people gone from the land for ever. The rest too
cowed and afraid to start anything again. Twenty years, and
I'm getting too old. They say that Auryn has got his father's
looks – I can see nothing much of his mother's fire. You've
been a good father to him, Addy, but you haven't taught him
how to be righteously angry like you used to be.*

She smiled as Auryn's pale complexion and silvery hair
came into her mind. Handsome. *If he were a woman, they
would say he was beautiful, yet he doesn't know it . . .*

*. . . he could have done with a bit more of Lidia in him.
Caroline has – she's like her mother, all right. There's times
when I could pick her up and hug her to me, poor little thing.*

Suddenly, she noticed that, since she was last here, the
face of the cutting was a mile further advanced, almost out of
sight. *Once the railway's finished, life will never be the same
again. And the only people to get anything out of it will be the
ones that always do.*

Many times since the face of the diggings had first come
into view from the south Selena had stopped and looked

down at the shanty-town. At first there had appeared some long huts, then a few smaller ones, growing haphazardly yet with some kind of order along a roadway until, now, it was a small village.

She had never been near the place; few local people did, except for catchpenny grocers, yoked like milkmaids, who walked up and down the cuttings selling beer at high prices. But she had heard something of what life was like there. It was a wild, unknown, alien place. From time to time a navvy woman would come to Croud Cantle Farm and ask to buy fresh fruit or perhaps a few penceworth of goose-grease for a bronchial child: 'Can you sell us a bit of grease for the bronikal, Missus?'

Respectable women mostly, who did not try to get into the kitchen as gypsies often did, but stood in the porch and waited. Selena, curious enough about their mysterious life to want to get them talking for a few minutes, always offered them a drink of cold fruit juice or hot cordial, which they always accepted. So it was by small, dropped crumbs of information, now supplemented by what Ruth had seen that terrible Christmas night, that Selena had built up a picture of life down there. It must be grim, especially in winter.

Exploitation, Addy. A word you probably haven't heard. It's one that the Radical press uses these days. Not that many people in these parts have the same interests they used to. 'Let the past bide,' they say now. There's yet another set of workers – they call them navvies – they're the ones now who are being exploited . . . the same way our people were, except we were never so degraded as they are.

The young woman and the children were now coming up the hill. Ah, they were such a pretty picture, they raised Selena's spirits. Such a pretty girl, holding in one arm a sheaf of meadow-sweet as though it was a May-queen wreath, whilst in the other she held a baby; a second baby rocked in a slung-shawl on her back. Not mother to all three surely . . .

the child who was walking had none of her pale skin and fair hair . . . yet the girl seemed to be the mother.

When the girl looked directly at her, Selena said, 'Hello, child,' and the young mother thought it was the little girl who was being spoken to. Is she really so young a mother as she looks?

The girl was over the stile and helping the small girl to slide through. Selena tucked away her image of the girl with two babies and a little child, carrying her virgin's sheath of meadow-sweet. She would tell Addy about them. He would understand the significance of her description. They had never needed to explain such episodes to each other.

Addy must have been transported years before the young girl was even conceived – and now she had children of her own.

Twenty years, Addy, and I'm old. Forty-three this year. And you're already fifty.

The brother whose warm, dry hands she longed to hold in her own had never aged beyond thirty. He still came into the yard, making his presence known, sweeping her off her feet and swinging her around, elated from addressing a successful meeting. She needed some time each day to renew her images of him.

Refreshed now, Selena left the main road and went over the downs towards the Cantle Valley to prepare for the return of Adam's children from the Great Exhibition.

11

THE BRIDE

ON HER WAY to her wedding to Dutch, Kitty Fire-Bucket met the Reverend Warren, who had come straight from his expedition to London and, like Selena, he was struck by the picture of the pretty girl with her babies.

He did not at first glance recognize her, then, realizing who it was, felt quite joyous. 'Kitty! What a picture, a treat for sore eyes.' He patted Maggie, looked at Agnes and smiled at Simeon, feeling pleasure and satisfaction at his part in the saving of the child.

'See, Vicar-dear, I'm looking after your baby well enough, ain't I?'

'He looks blooming.'

'So he should, he's a real little bugger. He fair empties me. You should hear him yell when he's hungry. Just like all the men – can't wait five minutes when they wants somethen. He's a nice little bugger, though; I fair loves him.'

Every time he went to visit Kitty, he wondered to himself why it was that he felt so awkward when she spoke in the coarse way of so many of the women who lived close to the railway navvies. It was part of the dialect of her people.

'It's about time I gave you some more money.' He handed her a coin. 'I'm sorry it can't be more.'

'That's all right, Vicar-dear, you can come to my wedden to make up for it.'

'Is that why you're all dressed up? The flowers, etcetera?' She looked fresh, almost virginal with wisps of fair curls blowing gently across her face and falling over her womanly bosom. He did not recognize it as jealousy but, as on the earlier occasion when he had not been able to take his eyes off her bared breast, he felt a momentary stab.

He had seen many men and women in every sort of dress and undress, had sat in a hut comforting a dying man whilst there was coupling taking place a few bunks away. Often he'd had to clear bawds and their clients from the door of his little Mission Hut. Few who lived in the shanty-towns had the privilege of privacy, so that every aspect of life and death went on under the eye of the rest. He took all this as part of the mission he had undertaken. Yet . . . he could not look upon Kitty suckling a child or listen to her speaking coarsely, without feeling that he was blushing to the roots of his hair.

The saints help me! What kind of missionary to Africa would blush at the sight of the naked skin of a black girl?

'The flowers is just idle nonsense, I love the smell of the white stuff.' She held the flowers to his nose. 'But the wedden's why we are all clean and dressed up.'

'Which one? Dutch, or Ollie?'

'I don't know. It don't make no difference. The overseer that come for the rent said I'd better hurry up and put my name to one of them or I should get the shove out of the hut in a week. They just finished fighten, so we'm on our way down to see which one got to have me.'

'Kitty, can't you see how degrading that is? A fight is no way for men to get themselves a wife in a civilized country.'

She laughed. 'Vicar-dear, you been runnen your little church for long enough now to know that the diggens an't no civilized country – not like the one where you lives.'

'No reason to admit defeat.'

'I don't! Look, I'll show you summet.' As she pulled aside her bodice and thrust her fingers in, Peter Warren concentrated on looking at Maggie. 'Look, 'tis a magic four-leaf clover. I bet you never seen one. Careful, I'm going to put it in my book to keep. Vicar-dear, do you reckon that by maken a good wish it's admitten defeat?'

'I suppose that wishing good, can only *be* good. You could let me give you a Christian ceremony.' He wanted the Church to cleanse her of the man Cocky, and had a momentary vision of never again calling to find her in her slatternly working skirts. 'If you could persuade – whoever it is going to be – to marry you in the sight of God, it would do no end of good. Good spreads. If more navvy people would marry properly, then others would follow and the community must surely be better for it.'

'And what good would that have done me if Cocky had church-married? I'd a been joined to him legal and then what when he went and sloped off?'

She pushed up her chin and looked challengingly at him, her face serious.

'You see, you got no answer for that. He wasen't such a bad man as some, but nothen would have kept him here once he made up his mind he wanted to go off on the tramp. Who's to say he wasent married before he took up navvying? And, like as not, he's got some other wife now, and what good would be-en church-married have done me or his new girl? I should a still had to take Dutch or Ollie or *somebody*, shouldn't I? At least I got somethen left if your ole Church don't marry me legal ... I got my*self*. I might have to belong to one of them to keep a roof over our heads, but they don't *own* me. And they don't own my babies neither!'

Her arguments were irrefutable, her questions rhetorical, his answer unsatisfactory. He felt about in his mind for an answer that he was sure should have been there, but it was bare of everything except platitudes. He knew that she could see his falseness.

'God meant us to marry in His sight, not in the sight of a half-drunk crowd.'

Kitty relaxed her serious expression, poked him with her elbow and laughed. 'Lord love you, Vicar-dear, I don't reckon there'll be many who's only *half*-drunk.'

More than anyone, this girl had the capacity to cheer him up.

His London expedition had been both happy and miserable. He had revelled in being with Ruth whilst she was discovering the wonders of the modern world, and had felt dashed and inadequate when he saw how impressed she had been by the wonders of Bounderby's and Teddy's house and style. He had felt her flickering between her natural simplicity and the sophistication that London had tempted her with. The orange dress was understandable. She was young, could probably be as giddy as Dolly at times.

Kitty laughed at her own wit.

He shook his head benignly at her. 'Well, come along, then. I am going down to the Mission Hut to get some letters done. Let's go and see what sort of a prize you've won for yourself.'

With Agnes hitched upon her hip, Maggie buried in her skirt, and the baby slung behind, Kitty Fire-Bucket flung out the arm that held the flowers and made a pose. 'No, no, Vicar-dear, it ain't me that's getten the prize, can't you see 'tis one of they that gets it.'

Picking up Maggie and carrying her on his arm, the young clergyman walked slowly beside Kitty down towards Great Hole town. The phrase 'a prize more precious than . . . ' came to his mind and he puzzled to remember. Whatever it was, either a Getter or a Runner-out had won it. *God works in wondrous ways . . . and I am not clever enough to understand why He must do so.*

Shanty-town weddings were often no more than two people moving their belongings under the same roof. From time to time though, something special happened to make an occasion of it. The two brothers had been cutting their way through Hampshire for years, and although they were both heavy drinkers and had spilt the blood of many a local farm

labourer, the fights with their own kind were not vicious.
They were good workers and never 'near' with their money
– considered a despicable trait in the community of the
navvies. It was natural that when one of them decided to
stop living the single life and jump the stick the community
should make a randy of it.

'It won't be a real randy. It's still another five weeks till
they get next pay-out, but they'll find enough to buy some
beer. Any chance to dress up and drink theirselves silly.'
Kitty wagged her head as though she were talking of
naughty boys up to their tricks.

'I wish you'd promise me something, Kitty,' Peter
Warren said.

'I don't never make promises unless I know first.'

'Don't take to drinking yourself.'

'Love you, Vicar-dear, it's a bit late for that.'

'No, it's not. Gin especially.'

'But it's a lovely feelen when you got a tot or two of
crystal in you. It makes you happy.'

'That's not happiness.'

'Near enough.'

'A person can be happy without gin.'

'I know that, but not very often. I was happy this
mornen in the field with the babies.'

'Well then . . . At least promise me you won't take gin at
your wedding party.'

They had reached the footpath that ran down to the
disorder of ramshackle dwellings, huts and sheds that was
Great Hole shanty-town. Anyone who might have seen
them standing looking down – the pretty girl with her two
babies and the handsome young man in coarse tweeds
carrying the toddler half-asleep on his shoulder – might
easily have mistaken them for a young keeper and his family
coming back from a day at the fair.

'Not as pretty as where you lives, is it, Vicar-dear?'

'You know where I live?'

'Oh no, but I knows it's in Blackbrook, and I been to Blackbrook Fair plenty of times.'

'What about that promise?'

'Well, I tell you what. You come to my wedden, and when they've got theirselves three sheets in the wind, you have a good look at Dutch and Ollie and ask yourself if you'd want either of them crawlen on top of *you* tonight unless you'd had a tot or two of crystal to keep your spirits up.'

Peter Warren looked at her with great trouble in his expression and shook his head hopelessly. As they walked down the footpath, he was deep within himself.

'I'll tell you what, Vicar-dear. I make a bargain with you. If you bring me down a different book from the one I got, I won't take a drop of gin till I read it.'

'And that's a promise?'

'I don't need to make promises. If I says I'll do it, then I will.'

'Right! Then I'd better make it the thickest book I can lay my hands on.'

Kitty laughed. 'Trust you to try and get the better of me, you ole bugger. All right, it can be thick, but it's got to be interesten and exciten.'

'You got the better of me when you said I should look at Dutch and Ollie, so now I'll turn the tables on you. I want you to take a good look at Black Annie – they say that there has never been a prettier woman ever on the building of the Great Southern Railway.'

Now it was Kitty's turn to look preoccupied.

'You didn't imagine she was born a drunken bawd, did you, Kitty?'

12

AT BLACK ANNIE'S

IN HER HUT AT THE GREAT HOLE shanty-town, Black Annie drew off a jar of new ale and held it up to the glim light coming through the open shutter of her hut and cursed the brew for being cloudy. Even so, she drank it down.

Like many shanty queens and navvies' prostitutes, Black Annie was no spring chicken and looked a good ten years older than her true age. This wasn't surprising to anyone who knew something of life on the cuttings.

Twenty years ago, 'Fox-ear Capper', a smooth-tongued navvy, had excited her with his white breeches, fancy waistcoat and silk neckerchief; then bewitched her with talk of the free and easy life of the shanty-towns; then seduced her and stole her away from the farm where she had been a farmer's pink-cheeked young bride.

As a man who enjoyed being unencumbered on the tramp, Capper had soon had enough of the coupled life. Within a year, he had sloped off, Annie had had a child, and was servicing a hut full of single navvies, one of whom was the tenant who held the paper which gave him rights to run it as he thought fit.

No escape then. What farm was going to take on a slut with a brat when there were good girls such as she had been herself? Her new man was avaricious and was not content only with the hut, and the sale of beer, but ran a bawdy-ken on wheels – a wagon which he drove up and down the length of the diggings with half a dozen women and young girls.

Inevitably, in a society where hard-drinking men had short fuses when their money had run out, his greedy nature was his undoing. One day he did not return to the hut. It was said that there had been a fight over money, in which he had been bested and he had gone on the tramp, but there were men and women, including Annie, who knew under which stretch of the Great Southern Railway embankment his bones might be found.

And so Black Annie was passed on to another man . . . and another . . . and another. Soon, she had lived in the shanty-town longer than anyone, she did deals with the tommy-shop, had a good beer trade apart from that in the hut, and still ran Capper's old wagon with the girls. She was good with her fists, and whilst from time to time she took a leathering or a black eye from a man well gone in drink, it was a brave sober man who would cross her – she held too many of the strings that held together the ramshackle society of the Great Hole shanty-town.

If it was not a woman's world, at least Black Annie had got for herself as much as any woman might.

In many ways, the life suited her. She had grown slovenly, and had never got on well under the thumb of her husband's mother who had ruled the house and dairy Annie had run away from. Black Annie liked to be the ruler – not the ruled.

But all that was a lifetime past. Now, her abundant black hair was being taken over by a wiry grey invasion that gave her a wild look. She liked a 'sip of crystal' in the morning, but gin wasn't the drink of navvy women so much as beer. Black Annie, like all the hut queens, brewed the beer which they sold. Black Annie's drink was strong dark ale to which she was so addicted that her belly had taken on the permanent shape of pregnancy.

But, except for that one time, and without the aid of the near-poison of the essential 'Women's Tonic', Black Annie never became pregnant, so that she had always been a popular prostitute who would lay decently without any fuss. A man left her feeling that he had got what he had paid for.

Fox-ear Capper, who had introduced her to the navvy-man's way of life, introduced her also to syphilis. In turn, she had passed it, ring-o-roses, to some of the men who rented the bunks in her hut or ten minutes in the wagon. She was no worse nor better than the rest – syphilis was endemic in every shanty-town the length and breadth of England. Like winter-fever, summer-fever, rats, stinking midden-holes, flood and foul drinking-water, the pox was a fact of life to be treated by whatever was practical or popular at the moment until it reached the stage where it was no longer infectious.

It was calculated by the contractors that the ratio of women to navvymen was about one to twenty. Even so, a queen needed to keep men visiting her and buying beer to pay her way at the tommy-shop if, like Annie, she was trying secretly to bury a bit of silver so that she might fulfil her dream of ending her days in some nice little town lodgings. There were legendary women who were supposed to have made enough out of selling beer to become a madam in town – nobody could say who they were, or where, but the idea warmed a good many chilled female souls.

Over the last year, though, Annie had felt as though she were losing her grip. First, Little Capper, her son, had taken his shovel and gone off on the tramp, as was only natural in a youth of his age. Then Dutch and Ollie both went off together to take over Cocky Fire-Bucket's hut. She had quite missed little Capper coming in, and Dutch – Annie had always had a soft spot for Dutch. He and Ollie had worked with 'Boxer Joe', Annie's present man, for a long time, and it had been Boxer Joe who had brought the two brothers into the hut. 'They're good strong men and they've got a long swallow.' A recommendation. And so they were – hard-working, virile, hungry and thirsty. Annie's bundle of beer-barrel keys and the bedstead had rattled frequently when the brothers were lodging in the hut.

Now they were gone. Not altogether, for they often came back from the diggings with Boxer Joe for a few quarts. And a lend of Annie, because that young Kitty was playing about and refused to allow either of them behind her curtain until the tenancy was settled – so they said, and why shouldn't she believe them?

Criminal – teasing men like that, if it's true. Dangerous too, she's likely to lose some teeth if she don't look out – especially Ollie, he's a right heavy-handed bugger when he wants to be. Just as well that I'm soft with the pair of them. That girl of Cocky's knew she would have to hand over the tenancy sooner or later, it was only because Overseer wouldn't put his foot down with her, and she seemed to have got the Mission Vicar round her little finger. Still, it's an ill wind . . . if Kitty hadn't played them up, then they might have finished with Black Annie's for good and all a year ago when they said they would take over Cocky's shant.

Annie mumbled on to herself until a dozen or so men, including Boxer, trooped into the hut; then she began sorting out the strings that hung over the side of the stew-pot. The black iron cauldron bubbled away almost night and day as Annie cooked for her lodgers. Each man brought his own meat from the tommy-shop – or, if they were broke, did not buy it from an estate or game park. The lumps of meat were tied in linen bags with a certain number of knots in the string to identify the owner of each piece, and left to simmer for hours with whatever vegetables might get thrown into the general liquor. Today, because of the wedding randy, both Dutch and Ollie had meat cooking in Annie's cauldron. Like in the old days before they moved out to the edge of the town. She began to dish out the food. The smell of cooking meat in the hut overpowered every human smell there, of which there were many.

'Buggered if I an't ready for that.'

The other men took their meat to their bunks. Annie

unlocked the beer and drew off a huge jugful which she proceeded to take round the hut, either taking money or 'ticking up' till pay-out day. Then she sat down at her own 'living' end of the hut, eating with Boxer, Dutch and Ollie.

'Ah, Dutch, you should a stopped along with us. What do you and Ollie want with taking on a hut of your own? It an't nothing but trouble, an't that right, Boxer?' Not the kind of question Boxer liked to answer – a fifty-fifty chance of giving the wrong one. 'You should give her what-for. Let her know who's the man. Well, which one is it? Who *is* the man, then?'

Ollie said, 'I lost me footing and Dutch held me down.'

'He's a bloody liar, I beat him fair and square,' Dutch said with brotherly affection.

'*This* time.'

The two men punched one another playfully as they went naked to the water-butt outside the hut, where they soaped themselves and Annie douched them over with a jug of water, ready for Dutch to jump the stick with Kitty and both to drink themselves into a stupor along with the rest.

13

SCENES OF RURAL LIFE

THE YEAR OF THE Great Exhibition slipped into history. Ruth entered long pages of description of the event in the book in an attempt to continue at least some record of life at Croud Cantle Farm, and she wrote letters to Toolagarry, knowing that her news would be months old before they reached there and that yet more months would go by before she received the replies.

There were ups and downs, Auryn and Ruth seeming to swing from closeness to antipathy to one another. Ruth made allowances, knowing that the revelation that he was the 'different' one of the five Tylee children was disturbing to him.

Caroline was growing tall and slim like the Tylees, her skin had now healed and regrown with the translucence that sometimes comes with bright red hair. She had reached the end of what could be taught her at the little school in Cantle, so spent her days working with Selena, Ruth and Auryn, and received a much broader education from Selena and her shelves of books than from the shrivelled teaching doled out in the Church School in the village.

Selena did much of the baking and preparing of their market produce. Croud Cantle could hardly be called a farm when compared to those of the Estate – it was not much more than a small-holding and scarcely enough to provide work during the low months for four of them. Jack and Ginny Toose were generous, finding work for Caroline, and using Auryn's developing joinery skills to do make-or-repair jobs in the bakery and shop, as well as feeding and lodging them whilst they worked, and paying well without patronizing them.

Not many occasions arose when Ruth could take her London frock out of camphor – once, when Mrs Warren invited them to spend the day with her family, and once when Ruth and Auryn were called to see their mother's solicitor – to be told that once his fees had been taken, the money that had been in his keeping for them had gone with the last lots of thatching and repairs to Croud Cantle. As, except for the London visit, they had not relied on it, it made little difference, only that their commitment to live in England was actual, now there was no money left to go back.

Ruth felt that the visit to Mrs Warren's had not been a success. The Warren home was surprisingly well-to-do and fashionable, and Mrs Warren, who had been widowed some time, seemed to lead a very social life. Dorothy had reverted to being snobbishly polite, whilst Susanna seemed to be having some kind of war with her mother who constantly flicked her glances with the message 'Don't you dare, Miss!'

Later, it occurred to Ruth, from an apparently innocent remark by Mrs Warren about her hope for 'Peter to take his proper place in Blackbrook society', that there might have been a family contretemps with herself as its cause, for he now visited Croud Cantle almost daily.

It was not long after that visit, that 'Carrier' Jepp brought to Croud Cantle a letter which might have upset the Widow Warren.

Coram Street, London

Dear Miss Tylee,

I trust that you will not have forgotten the occasion upon your visit to the Great Exhibition, when you visited also my establishment, Bounderby's. I most certainly have not, for you sang – one does not easily forget such a unique voice.

You may not have heard of the fine reputation that Bounderby's has quickly gained, but if you have, then you will know that it is an establishment of the highest reputation and style, with an unsurpassed name for entertainment and good food in the Continental fashion.

At the time, as you may remember, I suggested that if you wished to do so, then I should be pleased to offer you entrée into the world of entertainment. It would be an unforgivable loss if your voice is not heard by a greater public.

It may be that the transition from your rural life to performing in London is too great a leap into the unknown. If you would consider the possibility, I assure you that you would receive the greatest consideration and care from myself and my staff. I have secured the services of the renowned Gustav Braun who has 'made' some of the most famous names in the entertainment world.

Perhaps you would like to discuss this with your guardian. I shall be in Blackbrook within the month, when it might prove convenient for us to take the matter further if you so desire.

May I add that I sincerely hope that you consider my offer favourably.

Your honoured servant,

Edward Warren

Although Ruth was outwardly dismissive of the letter – particularly to Auryn who turned sullen – it threw her into turmoil. Her moods swung from doubt to confidence in her ability. She wondered whether Mr Warren had other motives – singers must be ten a penny in London. But always, somewhere at the back of her mind, lurked a vision of herself singing again at Bounderby's but before a full audience. This vision both thrilled and terrified her.

She replied, thanking him and saying that she would like some time to consider, but on the whole thought that her decision must eventually be to refuse his kind offer.

In the summer Peter Warren asked Ruth if they could be married.

'I have not much more than the clothes I stand up in, Ruth, and a small income, and I can offer you no immediate improvement. It is an impertinence to ask you, and I'm only doing so now because your Aunt Selena mentioned that some young farm labourer had asked for you. I can offer you at least as much as he might. And I love you. I can hardly move without thinking of you.'

The day had been hot and still. He had gone to meet her along the road from Waltham and found her taking a rest at the roadside and chewing on a thick crust, her green-stained hands marking the crumb of the bread. He no longer wore rusty black, but dressed like an estate worker with a loose shirt and an old straw hat, which he had taken off and waved when he had seen her in the distance, before hurrying towards her and sitting beside her.

He had looked more healthy and handsome than she had ever seen him. He said that he had been giving Auryn a hand with some hoeing, and she had said that he should do it more often if it made him so well. His light-heartedness had been boyish.

That night, she lay in the stuffy little bedroom with the windows flung open to what Selena called 'dangerous night humours', and realized how near she had been to accepting him. He had sat beside her in the tall summer grass and looked so handsome and so . . . good. She still thought of him as having goodness in him.

'Bless us, Ruth, how I prayed last night to give me the

courage to ask you. I don't know where the courage came from but I'm asking you, will you marry me? There is not a woman like you in the Four Parishes, not even in the county nor the whole of England. Even if you were not the most beautiful, I should still count it that I had got the prize if you say "yes". Ruth, I love you so much that I can hardly think of anything.'

There, in the dappled shade of a crab-apple tree, with heavy bees harvesting the chalk-valley flowers and hedgerow-blossom, the notes of larks, blackbirds and thrushes spattering everything with showers of music – there, bare-legged and unencumbered, in a skirt cut above the ankles, Ruth felt for a moment that a handsome lover made the day complete.

That night, she again went over the sweet words of his proposal, and wondered how long it had been that she had remained silent. He had taken her hand. Warm and dry, as when they had shaken hands when they first met. She remembered being conscious of that. And of his face so close that she could see each hair where it had been shorn with the razor that morning; his collarless shirt was unbuttoned showing a vee of white skin and coiled masculine hair; she could smell the dampness of the flannel, and the field-dust carried in his clothes. She had never before recognized his maleness as well as his handsomeness.

He had flicked away a crumb from her face, and put his mouth gently in the palm of her hand, part kiss, part caress. Suddenly she was overtaken by a new experience. He had said, 'I love you, Ruth, how I do love you' simply but his voice almost fierce. *I shivered. What did he think of that?* She remembered being conscious of having to think about controlling her breathing so that he would not hear how breathless she was. She remembered her clenched thigh muscles, the dryness of her throat and the moistness in her mouth.

Perhaps it had been her long silence . . . *Was I smiling? probably* . . . and the fact that she had let her hand hold his . . . *Was I touching, feeling the outline of his hand?*

Even now she could feel the shocking, warm softness of the first man to kiss her on the mouth. *Did I return the kiss? Yes, yes . . . of course I kissed him. And held him. Of course, he supposed that I was accepting him.*

Even now, hours later, as she thought about him, desire rose again and was alarming in its power.

'No! I don't love you.'

Yet still higher it rose.

There had been the hardness of his arms – like Pa's.

'*I'm sorry, Peter, I don't want to marry.*'

There had been the scent of his body – like Auryn's and Pa's, yet unlike theirs in its permissiveness.

'*I don't want to marry anybody.*'

And there had been his warm breath, soft mouth and the knowledge of his desire for her.

'*I don't want to be a wife!*'

She threw back the cover and went to the window and opened the bodice of her flannel night-shift to the cool air of the pre-dawn. Breathing hard, she stood with her eyes closed until the turmoil of mind and body was calm.

Was that love? No. It was something else . . . attached to words like sin, weakness and lust. A part of love, but not love. Desire. Strange that one has never understood the true meaning of a common word. For the first time she had 'desired'; not the flickering thrills of girlhood, but a deep and lusty need of the man – not necessarily Peter Warren, but the satisfaction of being loved by him at that moment. *Loved? Oh, that word!*

The night was as beautiful as the summer day that had preceded it, and the one that would follow. From the yard below, the homely and safe smell of dried mud and dung drifted upwards. Beyond that, the old apple tree, where she and Auryn used to swing on ropes before they went to Toolagarry, was a black sketch in India ink against a deep blue background. Along the slope of Howgaite, where the River Dunnock runs, a faint white mist hovered. Far across the valley a little owl called, then a barn owl, and, in the scrubby bushes at the foot of Tradden Raike, a few daybirds were pre-empting the dawn.

Not love. If it was love I felt so strong, then I'd want to marry him and I don't. Poor Peter. Each time she thought of the way she had indulged herself so sensuously for those few minutes, then to refuse him, the weight of guilt became heavier. *Poor Peter, so bewildered. Hurt. Unforgivable to be so cruel.*

The astonishing thing had been the discovery that he could be so ardent.

She made a little sound, part anguish, part unsatisfied need. From below came another sound – 'Oh' – surprised, then a rustle of someone moving.

'Ruth?' Auntie Sel. A low voice, almost a whisper. 'Is that you awake?'

Ruth went quietly downstairs. Selena was sitting on the little bench in the porchway from where one could see across the whole Cantle Valley.

'It's so humid. Can't you sleep neither?'

Ruth sat close and tucked her hand under Selena's warm elbow and said, 'Guilty conscience.' She had meant it to come out jocularly; instead, her voice quavered and she began to weep.

'It's all right, all right.' Selena drew Ruth to her until she had quietly cried herself out. 'Are you pining for your Ma? Auryn's the same, he thinks he doesn't show it, but it's there. I sometimes wish that he would cry. I've always thought it a bad thing that we stop men weeping.'

'Auryn?'

'I think there's times when he misses Lidia and Addy. If

he'd allow himself a weep sometimes, he'd let it out, instead of which it festers and makes him irritable.'

'There's times when you miss him too – Pa. I think you miss him a lot more than we do.'

The older woman was silent for a moment, then said with the utmost heaviness that was almost grief, 'I can't tell you how much, child.' After a pause, she went on, 'Was it something happened today that bothered you? I thought you looked far away when you came back from Waltham.'

'Peter Warren wants us to get wed. I don't know what to do.'

'Oh.' Flatly, unemotional.

'I couldn't sleep.'

'Do you want to get married?'

'Auntie Sel . . . Ma's the only other woman who would say something like that when a girl tells her she's been proposed to –"Do you *want* to get married?" Isn't that all that women are supposed to want? Aren't you supposed to say how lucky I am that he's asked me? Handsome, respectable, not a dung-boot farmer, educated, a Reverend gentleman.'

'You don't think that's enough?'

'No.'

Selena Tylee made no response.

Ruth said, 'When I said I didn't know what to do, I didn't mean about getting wed – I've already told him "no". I like him, he's so handsome and attractive to me, and good and intelligent . . .'

'Then what?'

The light was subtly changing, the sky lost some of its glassy clarity, and a gentle wind blew up from the valley. Dawn was running in like a fast tide from the direction of Kent and Essex, soon it would flood over the downs, across the Cantle Valley and on into Devon and Cornwall.

'It's hard. To put into words . . . When we . . . when he

. . . *Oh!* There was a moment today when he was asking me, when I wanted to give myself to him. Not to marry him – to *give* myself. Oh Lord, Auntie Sel, and I believe for that moment he would have taken me. I've never known anything like it before. If it was love, then I would have said "yes" and been thrilled, and come bouncing into the house, wouldn't I? But it was more like the feeling when you're parched to death. All you want in the world at that moment is a drink. All you want is to have your thirst satisfied. It doesn't matter what about anything . . . you can only think about quenching your thirst. I really took fright that I could feel so . . . out of my depth.'

'I reckon that's about as good a description of it as I've heard. You don't have to be afraid of it, child, but respect it, it's very powerful. If you don't want to get burned, then you have to be very careful with the tinder that's going to set you afire. Rest assured, there's always somebody ready with a spark.' Selena patted Ruth's hand and held it comfortingly, and they talked on in quiet voices.

The telling of what had happened was a relief, and lightened Ruth's mood. She gave a quiet small laugh. 'I don't know who was the more scared of ourselves, me or Peter.'

'I dare say you've both led a bit sheltered lives, you in that place with no proper friends your own age, and him with his missionary work. He's always struck me as an innocent. All that there's as old as the hills, and everybody has to sort it out for themselves. You can see by the size of some of the families round here how many get burnt playing with that fire . . . and from the Harvest-got babies that are birthen round about Easter-time. You an't alone, my gel, there's not many a girl who, when she gives a lad the freedom of her bodice in a moment of idleness, gives a thought that it will all end with a cradle.'

'That is what worries me, I want more in my life than a husband and children.'

Selena laughed softly. 'Dear girl, you should ought be careful who you say that to, for fear that you set them against you.'

'Who against me?'

'Why the men – and women – who have made their mistakes and would pull you down along with them.' There was amusement in her voice. 'Men don't take kindly to us if we can do without them. You only got to read between the lines a bit in some of the old writings right back to the Garden of Eden – Eve was the one with the mind. She was the curious one who wanted to learn about the world she found herself in. Adam was too scared or too lazy . . . but, dear Lord, didn't she get paid out for it.'

Ruth's mood was much lighter now and she smiled in the darkness. 'There's a bit in that old Family Book: she says, "I doubt there would have been much fuss and talk of sin and temptation if Adam had picked the Fruit of Knowledge." '

Selena made a small, amused sound of agreement.

Ruth continued. 'I don't exactly want the Tree of Knowledge instead of a husband, but . . . I want . . . Oh, I want to do things . . . see things. I want to be as free as Auryn to walk away from here tomorrow if I had a mind to.'

'It isn't all that simple for a man, you know, not if he's poor. Auryn wouldn't have an easy time. He'd have to tramp the roads before he found work, perhaps sleep in a haystack . . .'

'I know! I know! But at least he could choose that. And I can't.'

Selena did not reply immediately; then, taking Ruth's hand, she said, 'What is it on your mind, gel? I don't reckon it's only the bit of sparking between you and Peter Warren, nor turning down his proposal to you.'

'No,' Ruth said. 'It's . . . well, Edward Warren's letter.'

Selena did not immediately reply, and they sat in silence.

Then: 'I reckon you have decided . . . you don't need me to tell you.'

'Yes, Auntie Sel, I reckon that I have.'

'Auryn will object.'

'Yes.'

'Don't fall out with your brother, Ruth. It's terrible to be cut off from a brother.'

'I'll not fall out with him, Auntie Sel. I just hope he don't fall out with me.'

They sat quietly, each woman engaged in thoughts of herself and of the other. A cottage window down the valley lighted up, then white smoke went up from a chimney.

'There's Phil Barfoot getting up to see to the horses. Haymaking the big field today,' said Selena.

'It's going to be hot and dry cutting today. Have you decided whether to come?'

'Ah yes, child, they need every pair of hands they can get. There's not many spare hands left in the village these days. And we can do with every extra penny we can get hold of.'

'I should like to take up Mr Warren's offer, Auntie Sel. But there's Carly.'

'Your Ma and Adam gave me charge of Caroline till she's a woman.'

'That will be one of Auryn's objections – he'll say I should be here to bring up Carly.'

'Then we will have to spike his objections.'

'When we were there, he said that Bounderby's was no sort of place for a woman.'

'Wouldn't he have said the same if you had accepted Peter Warren and been involved in his Mission in that awful shanty-town over at Great Hole?'

Ruth laughed wryly. 'Do you know that I remember him saying that about the tunnel itself when we first came here. And I found out later that there were women working there, digging alongside the men. It *is* a terrible place. And perhaps no place for a woman, or anyone else for that matter, but what Aury meant was it was no place for a woman like me, and I don't see that it is for him to decide.'

'Ah, child, you know your brother better than he knows you. He believes he is responsible for you. Addy was the same when I was young. It's what most men believe, in spite of the evidence that they see every day of their lives. They see with their own eyes that women grow up to be adults just as able as they are themselves, yet they will insist they must be responsible for us.'

'Like we were children.'

'You must stick to your ground if you mean to go to London. I'll help you. Auryn must get on with his life and you with yours. We don't get two – at least not in this world.'

'There's something like that too, written in the old book. There's a lot that you and she must have in common; I often hear you say the same things that she wrote.'

'I dare say we were brought up on the same food – Radical pamphlets for meat and Radical talk for pudding. There were a lot of us one time.'

'Like Ma?'

'Your Ma is an exceptional woman. You should be proud of her.'

'I am.'

'Then go to London and be a famous singer if that's what you want. And she'll be proud of you – and so shall I. Not for being famous, but for not being afraid of trying to be what you want to be – it's a trait in the women of your family. It won't be easy.'

'No harder than it would be if I was to marry Peter Warren.'

'You might find it harder in ways you're only just beginning to understand.'

Now the first pink light outlined Old Winchester Hill. A cock crowed, then every cock in the valley feared for its little dunghill and crowed back. Soon more cottage windows glowed softly yellow against the warm purpling dawn.

Within a minute or two of there being silent calm night, dawn, wakefulness, and energy spreads over the hamlet in the valley.

The day of haymaking the big field. The essence of it almost quivers in the air. A day of hard sweated labour, parched throats, aching muscles, shared bread and beer and bawdy jokes, as men and women work side by side. The sweltering closeness of other men's wives and sweethearts. The sidling looks at other women's husbands. The weather has held, and no sign of a break in the good fortune. A good haymaking is essential to the Estate, and thus to the backs that wield the sickles and scythes. A mood of excitement. Next to harvest, this is the great day of the village year.

Cutting the big field. The start of a few days when hedge-bottoms and ditches will rustle with surrender to urgencies, such as Ruth experienced yesterday, reaching a climax of communal satisfaction when the last swathes of hay are scythed down and the animals entrapped there flee for their lives.

Ruth knows that she will not regret it, if she never knows another haymaking in Cantle.

PART TWO

London Life

I

BOUNDERBY'S

BOUNDERBY'S SUPPER ROOMS, on Ruth's second visit, looked very different. Now it was complete, a splendid palace of red brick, polished mahogany and engraved glass.

An astute businessman, Edward Warren had sold most of his fodder-supply business, on the grounds that the horse trade had reached capacity in London and could now only diminish, and had bought himself well into two prospects – Bounderby's, and an omnibus company serving the busiest routes. Not only had he bought himself into Bounderby's, but he now owned the lion's share so that he could have influence on the entertainment world and the whole philosophy of a taste of gracious life and modish enjoyment.

When she arrived at Waterloo Station, and began to walk towards the exit, panic struck Ruth. Had there been a train steamed-up and ready to go, she might have boarded it, and gone back to Auryn and humbled herself. It was the only thing now that would heal their wounds. It was weeks ago that they had had their most wounding row, and since then he had been morose and depressed. This morning, he had gone off to Blackbrook early, so as not to be there when she left home. It had been her most anguishing moment, yet she knew that if she was ever to have any kind of peace of mind, then she must leave him and the farm and come to London.

And now she was here. Ruth Tylee from a remote village that had shrunk to a hamlet. Most of her life spent working with a matchet or hoe in her hand, and she had come to London on the vaguest offer to sing in a theatre. London must be full of girls who could sing. Edward Warren most likely made such offers all the time . . . yet he had assured her in the presence of Selena that she had a unique talent.

When she reached the main concourse, she was surprised to find that he was waiting for her. 'So, you've come to London to make fame and fortune.'

'That makes me appear like a youth setting out with his bundle on a stick – except that youths aren't met by important gentlemen who carry their bundle.'

'I wanted to make sure that you wouldn't turn and flee.'

She laughed nervously. 'I believe I almost did.'

'And . . . I had instructions from brother Peter.' Smiling, charming, man of business.

'I didn't realize Peter knew I was going away. I haven't seen him for . . .'

'He was so insistent that you be taken great care of that I wondered that he entrusted you to *me* at all.' His smiling glance sideways and his sophisticated air were too enigmatic for Ruth to know if Peter had said anything about his feelings for her.

'I have taken lodgings for you. A room in a house where the landlady is familiar with the strange hours that people in the entertainment profession must keep. You will like her. And there are one or two others who are at present engaged at Bounderby's.'

Goodness! The entertainment profession. For a second, Ruth caught her breath, then smiled to herself, imagining the letter she would write to Carly. Carly would be impressed.

Except for some cleaners, the foyer and entrance to Bounderby's was empty. Ruth stopped to look up at a great banner on the façade of the building.

At Bounderby's! Each night.
Annette and Josephine. The Great Waldofo.
Morgason.
Miss Ellie O'Dowd –
'The Flower of Dublin'

'And when shall we see . . . well, certainly not "Ruth Tylee": we must put our minds to who you shall be, and what. Do you like the name "Rosalie"?'

'I haven't ever thought of it.'

He laughed. 'It would suit you.'

Ruth raised her eyebrows, but said nothing. *What* shall I be? Selena's advice to 'bide quiet until you see what's what' seemed sensible; Ruth did not want to appear any more ignorant than she was.

Suddenly he said, 'Sing something.'

'Now?'

'Yes. Anything that comes. Just sing.'

For a moment, she felt the panic of shyness rise. Carly – ever wise and straight at the heart of things – Carly had said shyness is thinking you're important.

So she sang. A new ballad that Jack had bought for her.

Edward Warren shut his eyes and nodded the whole song through, and, when it finished, he sat and looked her up and down. 'Ah, I wasn't mistaken. You can sing!'

'Well enough?'

'Well enough. You've some way to go before you are ready on character and presentation but the voice is wonderful. I have great plans for you. It was whilst I was listening to you sing that first time that the germ of an idea came into my head . . . but that's for later. Now, I have . . .' He looked at a delicately chased silver pocket-watch '. . . just one hour to spare, which is enough to show you what is what and, if he comes, to introduce you to Gustav, who will be your professional tutor and accompanist.'

'Lord alive! I never sang with anybody except Uncle Jack and Caroline.'

'Gustav has played in the best Assembly Rooms of Bath and London. He can be of the utmost help to you. I have discussed my scheme for you with him, and if anyone can make something of you, then it is Gustav Braun.'

'He is foreign?'

'Pronounced "Brown", written B-R-A-U-N. No, he's English as me, but it's better in this business not to be Augustus Brown if one is a pianist.'

Ruth began to wonder what else 'in this business' it was better not to be.

They did not go in through the glazed doors as they had last time. Instead he led her up one of the wide sweeps of marble stairs, along a red-carpeted corridor, in which only one of the many gas-lamps was lit, and then through some wide double-doors of polished redwood.

'Here we are.' He swept a hand across the dimly lit gallery. 'Wait.' He called out to somebody unseen. 'Harry – take the lights up.'

From somewhere came an indistinct reply. He held out a hand. 'Come down.' She went down to the front of the balcony and sat at the table he indicated.

'I always bring people up here first – it gives a better picture of what Bounderby's is for.'

Suddenly the entire place was filled with light, and she found herself looking down the length of the large hall, which when she had last seen it had been empty. Now it was filled with dozens of long narrow tables for seating ten or twelve people, and scores of small round tables. She could see into the aisles behind the tall pillars, where there were little curtained alcoves with plush seats and delicate cast-iron tables. Every table in the place was covered with a white cloth upon which was a low bowl of flowers trailing greenery.

'Where we are now is the gallery for ladies, away from the main dining hall below. Look.'

She looked down into the vast pillared and vaulted hall.

It was not surprising that Edward Warren appeared very proud of the place. It was a fantasy, a daydream in which people who lived in brick houses could make believe that they lived in palaces.

'Well?'

'I feel quite speechless. It is a dazzling . . . magical place. After I was last here, I tried to describe it to my aunt, but I'm not sure that I succeeded . . . I don't know how I should tell her what it's like now it's finished.'

He looked at the place himself as though considering the same thing. 'Well then, the question is could you tell her what Bounderby's is *for?*'

'Down there? That's for pleasure, absolute pleasure and nothing else, and here where we are, too.'

He looked pleased. 'You are the first person to get it right first time; they say "Well, of course, it's a supper room", or "Everybody knows Bounderby's is the place to be seen", some say it's a place for entertainment, or music or food. But you got it right . . . because it's all of those things. Absolute pleasure.' He paused, then said, 'I sensed that when you said "down there?" there was a qualification.'

'Well, I think that for you Bounderby's is not only for pleasure . . . I mean not only. It is perhaps for making your fortune.'

He shot her a glance, then laughed loudly. 'Shrewd, Miss. As well as pretty – we shall get along very well. Anything else?'

'I should think that somewhere, probably hidden well away, Bounderby's is also a terrible lot of work for somebody. Lord, just think of washing all those table covers. And cooking food for so many people and cleaning up after them.'

'Ah, but you won't be doing that. Not that keeping the paying public entertained is easy work . . . oh no, not at all easy. Come along, then, and I will show you the part that works.'

She followed him where he led, over the whole building where, although there were still several hours to go before opening, there were scores of people at work – in the kitchens, sculleries, ice room and boiler room. As they were returning to the front of the house, Ruth asked, 'Do you mind if I ask you something? Why are you taking so much trouble? You're an important man and I am a nobody . . . a country girl, with no experience. Perhaps I have something of a singing voice, but I've got a long way to go if I'm ever going to make a name for myself, yet you are spending your time showing me round the place as though I might buy it.'

He was silent for a moment as he led the way to one of the long tables where he indicated that she should sit.

'It was something that started when I was a young boy at Blackbrook Fair. I was seven, yet I still remember every detail. My brother and I – not "Peter the Church", but John, the medic – we had spent the whole day going round all the open booths, and the monsters and tricksters and we had spent almost all of our few pence. One tent we hadn't bothered with because it was plain and had nothing at all inviting about it to persuade us to spend a single penny on it . . . however, there was music coming from it, so we crawled under.'

As he built up the picture, a smile, that was quite different from the sophisticated jolliness he had previously exuded, softened his expression. He had taken one of the flowers decorating the table and was caressing it delicately. Although he was looking at what he was doing, his gaze was inward, seeing two errant little boys at 'Black' Fair.

He dropped his head back and gazed at the ceiling. 'And I was stunned. I can't tell you how much. Brother John wasn't impressed and tried to make me go back with him, but nothing would make me leave. Well, of course, if we were to see it now, we should see it for what it was – one of those grubby travelling side-shows, all paper flowers, artificial trees and painted scenery, with one or two painted old women and pock-marked old men done up in gaudy. But to me it was like crawling into fairyland.'

He shook his head and laughed wryly. 'I hid there and, when they packed up to leave, tried to run away from home. Seven years old, can you imagine my heartbreak when they wouldn't let me go with them?'

'Well, yes I can. When I was the same age we went on our long voyage, and I wanted nothing in the world except to be one of the boys who climbed the rigging.' He looked at her, up and down for so long that she began to feel embarrassed. 'What happened?' she asked.

'My father was too much of a dreamer to be a good man of business, but he was a good father – he bought me a toy theatre, with card actors. And so, with school and learning the family business between, the little theatre brought me where we are now.'

'That's a lovely story.'

He brought his mind back, looked at his hands fondling the flower, put it back in the bowl and brushed back his moustaches. 'I suppose it is. What on earth started me on all this? I've never told that to another soul.'

'I had asked you why you brought me here?'

'I showed you Bounderby's because I was sure that you were going to understand the place – and you do. I believe that before long you will *be* Bounderby's.'

'Be?'

'Ach! To sing, to sing and give pleasure with that voice of yours each night, so that you and Bounderby's will become associated in the public's mind. We must leave it there for now. I have an appointment, and I want to see that you have a good room. Come! We will leave Gustav till later. With Mrs Cox, you'll be among friends. Annette and Josephine are there. Come here tonight with them.'

'*That* Annette and Josephine?'

'Ah yes. Netty and Jo – the scourge of every theatre manager in London. But they are unique. Excellent artistes. Perfectionists. The most tasteful act of its kind on the entire continent of Europe.'

2

ROOMS AT COX'S

IT WAS FOUR O'CLOCK in the morning before Ruth finally got between the clean, rough sheets of Mrs Cox's 'first-floor back with facilities', having watched Bounderby's at work for the entire evening. The 'facilities' were a small fire – not large enough to heat the room properly, but sufficient for making toast – and a tray with tea-things for three people. Although the room was furnished with an ill-matching assortment of bits and pieces, it was somehow brought together comfortably by an abundance of velvet pillows and cushions of many shapes and sizes.

'I made every one myself, and though I say it who shouldn't, you'd go a long way to find better rouched velvet than that.'

Ruth responded in exactly the best way to get off on the right foot with the landlady: 'I've never been in a room with such beautiful cushions.' Which was true, for she had never been in a room with much in the way of cushions at all.

Edward Warren had proved to be kindly and thoughtful regarding her accommodation. Within minutes of leaving Bounderby's, he had walked her the few hundred yards to Mrs Cox's rooms, ordered that same Harry who had flooded the supper rooms with light to take her bag round, and had left her with a raising of his hat, and an assurance that she would be very comfortable, and that he would see her that evening.

Now, many hours later, lying on her back, with the strange sounds of a live city and the light from street-lights not letting her sleep, her mind was full of the images of her first day. Making some order of her thoughts by writing them down in a letter to Cantle had disposed of some of them.

Carly, how you would like Gustav Braun (said Brown). He wears the very latest fashionable matching jacket with wide lapels and trews that are ankle tight. His waistcoat breast is padded, so that he walks like a pouter-pigeon and in the street he wears a kind of military cap. Oh yes, and the moustache – it is very waxed and fixed in the shape of two letter S's on their side and his hair is cut as short as a schoolboy's. But he does seem to be a most kind person – and *what* a piano player, his fingers go so fast that you can't follow. I don't know what I shall do when I have to sing for him tomorrow.

She would write nothing about Annette and Josephine in her first letter home, except to mention their names. Netty and Jo. She hadn't known what to make of them when they had come into her room.

They had come straight in from their own room across the passage. Netty first, dressed in nothing but a kind of long peignoir, a pair of thick woollen socks and a satin turban hat suitable for a visit to the opera. 'Oh my, Jo,' she called into the passage, 'just look here, Teddy's linnet has come. She's an exceptionally pretty thing. Not a linnet at all, a lovely, sleek red fox.' She closed one eye at Ruth. 'That will speed her up, she *adores* red hair. She once made our hairdresser change the colour of mine, but it was so *wrong* for my complexion.' She stretched her neck so as to look at herself in the mirror. She was dark-eyed, creamy-skinned and black-haired. She was beautiful. Her cheekbones were high and her chin small and dainty as were her hands and wrists, and, for all that she was tall, she appeared fragile enough to drift on a breeze.

After inspecting herself as though she had never seen her face before, she had flung herself down on Ruth's bed ignoring her hat being knocked over one eye. 'Oh, it's so nice to have a girl in here again. Shall you stay? Oh, I hope that you do. Coxy's is *such* a convenient place, it doesn't matter which of the halls you're playing in London. Are you making tea, dearest? Oh, lovely! Me and Jo are always desperate for tea. I'm Netty, if you didn't know. Jo's the other one.'

The landlady had seen to the fire and kettle almost before Ruth had taken off her bonnet, so that by the time Jo had wandered in and was also lounging upon the bed, the tea was brewing. She was equally extraordinarily dressed but differently, in beribboned and frilled pantaloons, a laced bustier which pushed her figure into a high-bosomed exaggerated shape, and an extremely white wig dressed in the style of the classical statues of which Ruth had seen many at the Crystal Palace. Except that Jo was altogether more buxom than Netty, they were very alike. She helped Ruth pour the tea.

'Oh foxy, foxy yes.' The new girl fingered Ruth's hair. 'Wonderful stuff, wish I had it. I absolutely *pine* for foxy hair.' Taking Ruth by surprise she kissed her on the cheek. 'You are "Foxy" from now on, and I'm Jo if she didn't tell you.'

'Why should I?' demanded Netty.

'So that she knows which is me.'

'Are you sisters?'

'God's breeches, no!' Jo exclaimed. 'There's blue blood runs in my veins and butcher's blood in hers.'

'Ha! Listen to the hussy – boasting of it. I should keep quiet if my papa was a poxy old duke.'

'You do look alike,' Ruth said, engaged and amused by the coarse, amicable way they teased each other.

'We need to be alike for the act.'

Jo reached into a side pocket of her pantaloons and drew out a little silver case, extracting from it a thin black cigar which she lighted with a coal which she picked up with the tongs.

'Have one?'

Ruth shook her head and tried not to appear surprised. Selena had said, 'You must be prepared for people who will not live at all like us. Take them as you find them, and hope that they will do the same for you.'

'Don't mind, do you?'

'No, although I don't know that I should want such strong smoke about me all the time.'

'No more do I,' Netty said. 'But I don't get much choice. She smokes like a regular soldier.'

'A sailor, Nett. And if I didn't like a cigar, you'd have to learn to smoke one yourself for the new act.' And she slapped Netty's neat buttock.

Netty rubbed the slap. 'Watch it, Jo, or I shall need two cover-coats tonight.'

'Ah, poor pozzy. Let Josey make it better.' At which she exposed the slapped buttock and proceeded to massage it tenderly whilst they both sipped tea.

'Give us the wig to try, Jo.' Netty pinned up her own dark hair and sat before Ruth's dressing mirror and adjusted the curls of the pure white wig. 'There! What do you say, Foxy?'

'Lovely. Is it for your performance at Bounderby's?'

'It's for a new thing we're planning. Did dear old Teddy tell you about us?'

'I saw your names outside Bounderby's. He said that you were the best there was in the whole of Europe.'

Jo jumped off the bed and pulled Netty to her feet and gave her the wig. 'Only the best for Bounderby's. Come on, Nett, let's show her. Want to see the new act, Foxy?

Nobody's seen it yet.' She turned a chair round and pushed Ruth into it.

'Imagine, imagine,' Jo said, taking the turban hat and winding its scarf about her head, 'that this hat is a wig like that one. This . . .' she opened up an umbrella and hung it over the open door . . . 'is a grove of trees in a garden, and this tray is a cornucopia in the Grecian style . . . and you'll just have to imagine that I have a bow and there's a quiver of arrows hanging on my pozzy.'

Ruth nodded. Then Netty dropped her peignoir whilst Jo kicked off her pantaloons so that, apart from Jo's bustier and Netty's socks, the two girls were quite naked. 'Imagine, imagine,' Jo said, placing a stool, 'that I've taken this off and my buzzies are bare, too.'

There was little at all left for Ruth's imagination to need to work on. The girls' bodies were extremely beautiful, as devoid of hair as their faces, and as finely complexioned.

'Now imagine, imagine that we are entirely painted over in white, our eyes are closed.' They each closed their eyes, took a pose and stood absolutely still, Jo frozen in the act of aiming a bow and arrow, and Netty holding the cornucopia high above her head. There was no sign of either of them breathing, not a flicker of an eyelash nor a twitch of a finger. They had become two lovely pink statues. Still, unapproachable, remote. They stood like that for about two minutes whilst Ruth's mind rushed about trying to make sense out of the casual way that she had suddenly accepted two naked strangers standing in classical poses in her bedroom, beside an open door beneath an umbrella that was supposed to be a grove of trees.

Jo opened one eye and, scarcely moving her lips, said, 'Now . . . in through the gate comes a young man. He's waiting for his lady-love but she's late – he wanders about, sings a bit of a song, then comes and sits on Netty's pedestal. Takes out a cigar and lights it. Then, playing the fool, says to

Netty, "My dear. . ." He looks at the engraving on her pedestal . . . "My dear Miss Juno, a thousand apologies – I forget that the young lady of these fast times likes her cigar." '

Jo closed her eye and Netty took up the story. 'And then I open one eye and wink at him. "Thank you, sir, I do not smoke cigars," I say, "but my friend Diana does."'

The girls were absurd and droll, and Ruth burst out laughing.

The two statues relaxed and became flesh again. 'Oh, Nett, my sweet, the dear Fox likes it.'

'Ah-ha,' Netty said. 'Then I think that you were right, Jo, the act will work.'

'Dearest thing, aren't I always right?'

'Tell her the rest, Jo.'

Side by side they sat on Ruth's bed whilst they put on their bits and pieces of clothes, as unaware of their naked bodies as babies.

'Well, the young man – we always call him Charlie . . .'

'No, wait,' Ruth said. 'Who is the young man – I mean, who acts with you?'

'Oh, any pretty lad, really, it doesn't matter so long as he can learn a few lines. It's we two they all come to see.'

'I can well imagine it. Go on, tell the rest.'

'Charlie offers me a cigar. We both come down from our pedestals, I begin to smoke it, and he tries to make free with us, so we retaliate. And we have quite a frolic. Well, of course, our paint begins to crack and Charlie's clothes get all covered in white. Then we hear the lady-love coming (that's usually one of the line dancers) so we try to brush Charlie down but make matters worse.' They both began to do the actions.

'Then in our haste to get back on our pedestals –' they climbed on to Ruth's bed '– Juno picks up Diana's bow and Diana has the cornucopia. We hear the lady-love getting closer. Diana tries to stretch over to give Juno the cornucopia. Ah . . . she cannot reach her. Charlie tries to help by jumping up to take the cornucopia but he hits his head and knocks himself senseless. So, when lady-love enters the grove, she finds her lover where he has fallen. The curtain comes down on Juno reaching out for her cornucopia and Diana trying to take back her bow – both frozen into a state of shock.' They froze again, in absurd and awkward poses.

Ruth, taken up in the telling of the story, applauded as they bowed low.

'I have never seen anything so amazing and extraordinary and funny.' Ruth had never seen any kind of performance at all except the Cantle mummers and some side-shows at the fair, but she was convinced that these two were the best in Europe – they had seemed to have become statues.

'Shall we show Teddy, then, Nett?'

With the mention of his name, Ruth suddenly realized that the risqué performance that they had put on in her room would in reality be done lit by gas-lamps in full view of hundreds of people eating supper.

'Naked like that, don't you feel . . . well . . . at all embarrassed in front of people? I should die.'

'Be damned if you would!' said Jo. 'Cold sometimes, but not embarrassed – after the first couple of times you wouldn't think about it. Those two hussies who paint their thingummies and show them off, isn't *us*, they're Annette and Josephine. Netty and Jo sit by the fire and toast muffins and save their ha'pence. Nett and I aren't any more real to the Gobblers than the statues they have in their murky little back gardens. We're something they can feed their fantasies on.'

Netty laughed. 'That's how we came by the idea – we used to be line dancers. We were walking in a cemetery looking at the statues, and we came upon a Gobbler feeling a marble angel's buzzy. He didn't know we'd seen him till Jo said, "Don't squeeze too hard or she'll squeal."'

Jo showed her neat white teeth in laughter. 'By God, didn't he just go off, Nett? Just like the start at Ascot Races.' After a few moments, she said seriously, 'I say, Foxy, Teddy says that you are quite new to this lark.'

'Absolutely new.'

'I know it's what he was looking for, somebody untouched and uncontaminated by other theatres ... a Teddy's-own production. Well, I think he's right, he's the best we've ever worked for, willing to try anything new, anything at all that will surprise the Gobblers. If he's going to make you into something, Foxy, then you'll do very well. Teddy has excellent taste. But as for feeling embarrassed, have nothing but contempt for them. If you are willing to paint your buttocks gold and let the Gobblers throw you sovereigns, then do it, just so long as it pleases you – never do it for *them*.'

Ruth didn't know why, but she felt that she was receiving the wisdom of Solomon. The girl's face was sober and intelligent, her partner nodded at each statement.

'Do you know why Nett and I call them Gobblers?'

'Because they sit there gobbling food whilst you entertain them?'

'Not just food ... they gobble *us*. They gobble fresh meat, young, firm and tender, they gobble it all until they are weary of the taste. By that time, we are only bones anyway, so they spit us out and bay for something fresh. So whilst they have the taste for you, Foxy, make them pay, pay, pay.'

Ruth poked the fire to give herself time to try to take in what Jo was saying.

Netty spoke. 'Don't let Jo dampen your spirits before you've even begun. It's different for you, you're a singer, your body isn't so important, you can always bone it or pad it a bit and put on a lovely gown. Jo and I don't have many years to get the little house we are saving for.'

Jo took Netty's hand and kissed the palm. 'We have enough for the house; now we are saving for the furniture and the nest-egg to live on.'

They had left as unceremoniously as they had come. Netty said, 'Be ready in your fancy-rags by nine o'clock. Teddy says you're to come with us.'

Jo had laughed her hard laugh. 'To have your first look at the Gobblers before he feeds you to them.'

'Oh, Jo, don't! That's not fair, Teddy is nice.'

'As theatre managers go . . .'

'No, Jo . . . Teddy is a nice man.'

'Watch it, Nett, or I shall be jealous.' Jo had playfully slapped Netty's buttock again, but this time quite hard.

Of all the images of that day which, at four o'clock in the morning, moved round her mind like beads in a kaleido-scope, it was the gentle kiss Jo had given Netty that disturbed Ruth. A kiss that reminded her of the one which Peter had given her when he declared his love. Had she not seen from their nakedness that they were women, then she could have believed them to be lovers.

That evening, from the side of the stage, she had watched them arrange themselves as representations of marble statues to great applause from the 'Gobblers'.

For a year, Ruth lived almost entirely in the confined world of Bounderby's and Mrs Cox's. Working, practising, learning to read music with Gustav Braun in the morning, sleeping or lounging around with Jo and Netty in the afternoon, and working again at Bounderby's till the small hours, then falling into a dead sleep, waking refreshed to start again. In all that time, she only twice suffered her 'precipice' dream – both times she awoke well away from the edge.

She wrote some letters to Croud Cantle but fewer to Toolagarry. Neither place seemed now to have much connection with her present life. She had expected to fret and be lonely, instead she enjoyed her new friends and new experiences. There was never time to be lonely.

The hours were long and the work exacting, and if the splendid supper rooms were comfortable, spacious and warm, the back-stage area was certainly none of these. Nevertheless, Ruth loved the time she spent there. After the first few days, she saw Edward Warren only in passing. He had called her into his office on the second day and told her what he had planned for her.

'Netty and Jo, Waldofo and Ellie O'Dowd are good performers, and the patrons like them, but I want a performer who will be the very personification of Bounderby's, who will epitomize the ambience of the place . . . the philosophy. I want someone who will perform only at Bounderby's and nowhere else, and who the public will clamour to see, but can see nowhere but at Bounderby's. Must be a woman, for no man could create mystique, or command the loyalty of admirers as a woman may. She must be a singer, for there is no other form of entertainment that will do – no acrobats, or instrumentalists, or amusing acts like Netty and Jo. Do you understand that, Ruth?'

She didn't know how to respond. It seemed obvious that he was referring to her.

'I'm not sure that I do.'

He clasped his hands and looked around him for the right words. 'Do you remember the evening when you all came here with Dolly and brother Peter?'

'Of course, I am never likely to forget.'

'You sang. And for the second time in my life I had that same experience of surprise – revelation – as when brother John and I went crawling into the fairground booth. When you agreed to sing, I expected to hear something like Dolly or her friends perhaps, sweet and charming; I never expected to hear a voice as good even as Ellie O'Dowd's. But you *sang*, not trilling sweetly from the throat, but sang from within. That tragic ballad in a minor key, every word as clear as an ice crystal . . . you sang and your voice reached every corner of the hall. Do you remember what I said?'

'Yes, I do. "You have an exceptionally fine voice, Miss Tylee. If you should like to put it to use, then you must let me know."'

'Something like that. Except that what I wished to say was "Don't go back to Cantle, but stop in London and I will make you famous."'

'Goodness! I should have run a mile.'

'I suspected that you might. And I don't think that your brother or Peter would have been much in favour.' He grinned, very boyishly for his years.

'Auryn is much against me coming.'

'And yet you came.'

'This is my life, not Auryn's.'

He looked at her with curiosity, but said nothing.

She found herself feeling shy again, but pushed herself into saying, 'Twice since I arrived, you have talked about a "plan" . . . that you have an idea that you want to fulfil. Now you have talked about making a performer for Bounderby's – do you mean me to be that performer?'

'Bless your life, Ruth, who else should I mean? There is no one else that it can be. Over the months since you first sang and put the idea into my mind, I have listened to dozens of young singers, dozens. Ach! None of them would do. As each one opened their mouths, I waited expectantly for the voice of Ruth Tylee to emerge. Poor little singers, they could scarcely help it that they did not possess the voice that echoed in my head.'

'What is the idea, the plan? What is it that I am to do?'

'Do everything I have planned for you to do. It will take

months of work. Gustav has worked out a scheme. If you will do it, then you can be the best-known ballad singer in the country. He will not spoil your voice, nor stretch it to reach operatic notes. You shall be a ballad singer – a story-teller in music.'

'How can it be done?'

He got up and came round to the front of his desk. He took her hand in his and laid the other over it. 'Ruth, you really do not know what an exceptional voice you have. I have never heard such power in a female voice. I believe that with the right instruction your voice will be unique. We shall begin by making the whole of London curious to hear you. For weeks prior to your début, you will be seen and not heard, stories will fly about. Mystery. Is she a Russian aristocrat? The runaway daughter of a wealthy industrialist? Or is she a milkmaid?'

Ruth smiled. 'Lord alive, nobody will think that I am a Russian.'

'They'll believe it, if we make them. Whispers, news-papers, rumour. My dear girl, people will believe anything if they want to. London society thrives upon it. Take away their little scandals and mysteries, and you put out the light of their lives. Look at Netty and Jo. All London believes them to be the dual mistresses of royalty.' He laughed. 'London *wants* to believe it. Yet they love no one but each other, and don't try very hard to conceal it.'

The transformation of Ruth into 'Rosalie' took some-thing over a year.

3

TRANSFORMATION

CAROLINE TYLEE SETTLED herself as gracefully as she knew how in a front seat of a curtained compartment of the Ladies' Gallery at Bounderby's Supper Rooms and tried to suppress a nervous laugh. Susanna, with the urban sophistication of a young girl on the verge of womanhood, was more familiar with public places, though this was her first visit to a supper room. Their escort, Peter Warren, signalled to a waiter, but before he could attend, another waiter placed wine and cake before them.

'Sir, Mr Teddy has left instructions that the young ladies are to be served this and you, sir, whatever you wish.' As he poured, the sparkling wine foamed in the glasses. Caroline looked sideways to see what Susanna would do, then raised her glass to sip when Susanna did. Peter Warren settled into a chair behind them.

'I should like to see it at night,' Susanna said.

'You wouldn't like the noise,' Peter replied. 'Imagine all those seats taken by people eating and talking.'

'They don't when Ruth sings,' Caroline said.

'No. So I have heard.' Peter's calm voice and manner belied the disturbance he felt. Since the day that he had proposed marriage, he had never set eyes upon her. Over the months he had put more and more effort into running his Mission, and had tried to put the troublesome passion out of his heart and mind by working himself very hard. Several times, his older brother had suggested that he pay a visit to London, but Peter always found good reasons for having to refuse. This time he could not, for the idea for this special occasion had come from Susanna and there had been no one else available to bring her to London.

'This afternoon is noisy enough,' Susanna said.

Although the main dining room was empty, the balconies and galleries were filling up with young people of about Caroline's age and their parents, uncles or escorts.

'She said you can hear a pin drop.'

An attendant in a red jacket came into their compartment, bowed and presented them each with a large embellished card.

THE PRINCESS AND THE LOST SLIPPER

A Christmas-tide Entertainment

For the raising of funds for the benefit of the founding of a new home for orphans under the patronage of the Seventh Earl of Shaftesbury

GOOD FAERY Rosalie
BAD FAIRIES Misses Annette and Josephine
PRINCESS   Miss Ellie O'Dowd
PRINCE   Mister Cedric Carver
BARON   Mister Edwin Foster
SCULLION   Tommy McCabe
GOOD FAERY'S ATTENDANTS – Bounderby's Dancers

The trembling in Caroline's hands shook the card and she bit her lip so as not to cry at the sight of Ruth's new name. She felt a warm hand cupping her cheek and ear and was grateful to Peter Warren for understanding. She wondered if he still hoped that Ruth would marry him.

'I wish Auntie Sel and Auryn was here to see her.'

'I dare say they'll come one day.'

'Don't you think she is splendid, Mr Warren?'

'Absolutely splendid.'

'Did you see the way the gentlemen bowed to her when we were having our dinner?'

Susanna said, 'Dolly's nose would be put out – she likes to be the one they bow to.'

'Your sister has a gentleman of her own now she's engaged.'

'She would sooner be "Rosalie".' Susanna sighed heavily. 'So would anybody.'

'Rosalie. Rosalie,' Caroline said, smiling to herself. The two girls had used the name on every possible occasion since they had arrived that morning.

'Goodness, Carly,' Ruth had said, laughing, 'people who know me don't call me that. It's just my professional name.'

'Oh no, Ruthie – Rosalie is a wonderful name.'

'I reckon that Auryn don't think so, does he?'

'Aury sulks whenever we talk about you. And if we buy anything new he says, "I suppose that came from London", and Auntie Sel always says, "It came from a great good bit of fortune that came this way, so you might as well enjoy it."'

'Oh, dear.' Ruth ached when she thought of Auryn still bearing his resentment that she had defied him. He had gone so far as to forbid her to leave. That had been the real cause of the rift between them – that and the bitter moment when she had retorted, 'Who are you to forbid me? You're not my guardian, you're not even my brother when it comes to it.' She had not meant to say it, and would have done almost anything to retrieve her words. But they were said, and lay between them like a bed of coals that neither of them had the courage to tread to reach the other.

'I wish that he would accept the inevitable. Life for me is so enjoyable that I don't want any of you to be unhappy.'

'Well, I'm not. Nor is Auntie Sel.'

'He doesn't like your sister to sing in public, does he?' Susanna said.

'Hush, Su, that's not your affair,' Peter reproved her.

'Well, Caroline *said*.'

The balconies and galleries were now almost full. There was an expectant hum of youthful voices and a chink of glasses and plates. Caroline watched as people opened the card and when she saw somebody point and comment, could hardly refrain from going to their table and telling them that 'Rosalie' was her sister.

None of the letters had prepared Caroline for the sudden realization that Ruth had been changed into somebody else.

At the railway station, she had eagerly searched the little crowd of people awaiting passengers, and had not seen Ruth – until the woman in a dark fox-coloured skirt and jacket with high cuffs and wide lapels said quietly, 'Well, Carly, an't you going to say "hello"?' Caroline had been too overawed to speak at first, until Ruth laughed and became Ruth again for a moment. It was as though she had grown six inches taller, and although Caroline had now grown almost to Ruth's height, Ruth seemed to tower above everyone. After she had greeted Peter and Susanna, they walked the concourse of the railway station where every gentleman either looked back at her or raised his hat.

Now Ruth had disappeared to prepare for the performance.

There was a sudden rise in the hubbub as musicians appeared. Then there was music and the flames of the lights lowered.

'Lordy, Su, I shall burst with excitement before it starts.'

Peter Warren sat back in the shadows of the drapes.

The play was a simple adaptation of the traditional story of the princess who lost her slipper at the ball. Any story would have done as a vehicle for Ruth's songs in pretty dresses and for Netty and Jo's appearances in fleshings and tinsel wings.

When Ruth appeared on stage dressed in her pretty rags,

the play stopped for her to acknowledge the outburst of
applause. To this young audience she could only have been
known by her reputation and by the mystery which had, as
Edward Warren had foretold, been woven around her. On
stage, she was graceful, outgoing and exotic. Few people
other than Netty, Jo and her mentors, Edward Warren and
Gustav Braun, knew how sick with apprehension she was
before every performance until she was on stage.

In the early days, it had seemed that her nerves were so
bad that she would never be able to relax her vocal cords
sufficiently to sing before the public at all. Many times at
night, bathed in sweat, she had awoken from a dream in
which she was struck voiceless, rigid and dumb before the
Queen and the Prince who had exchanged glances, then
burst out laughing at her. In practice with Gustav, she sang
with ease; it was only when she tried to sing on the stage at
Bounderby's that her throat seized up.

Netty and Jo had been concerned for her, and spent
hours lounging on her bed giving her advice and teaching her
how to use their special actors' face paints, and how to walk
well and how to breathe so as to loosen the muscles as
Gustav had taught her.

She quickly learned all of this, but none of it – including
the way, at Coxy's, she soon fell in with their half-clothed
informality and ease whilst toasting muffins, talking and
drinking endless tea – none of it could cure her stage fright.
Until one day they had brought into her room a wig of short
hair and a mannish costume.

'We think we've found the cure for you to try, Foxy,'
Netty said excitedly. 'You are to dress in Jo's best breeches,
the ones she once came courting me in for a lark.'

'I *couldn't*!' Ruth protested.

'Oh, Foxy!' said Jo. 'Don't be so *regular*.' She began to
remove Ruth's peignoir. 'I know Nett's safe with you.' She
made an exaggerated masculine stance. 'Damme, man, I'd

knock you down if you tried to steal her. But I know that you're regular enough.'

By that time, Ruth had not only learned that they lived together as lovers, but had also learned, to her surprise – and to theirs that she should be so innocent of the ways of the world and its many ideals of love – that their passion for one another was not uncommon. Now that she had assimilated the knowledge, she was no longer ill at ease when she went to their room and found them entwined in one another's arms in their shared bed. 'Poor Foxy,' Netty sometimes said in her teasing way. 'Don't want no love till a hairy, hard old fellow can love her.'

'Ah, shame,' Jo had said. 'No soft buzzy for Foxy to lay her head on.'

'Love, love, love here and now, and no counting the days with a furrowed brow,' Netty had said, sing-song. 'I simply could never stand the worry of it all.'

Although Ruth could understand and sympathize with that, she could not imagine what it must be like to lie with another woman as she now knew Netty and Jo to lie. There were many times when her skin prickled and her muscles contracted at the thought of Peter Warren's handsome face above her own and the way that his desire had drawn hers outwards from the centre of her body and the depths of her unconscious.

Eventually, they persuaded Ruth to try Jo's neatly tailored clothes, which, the two of them being of similar build, fitted very well. Her bosom, once it was flattened by binding with a silk scarf and dressed in a tuck-fronted shirt, filled the full-breasted waistcoat fashionably.

'Give her room to breathe, Jo, or she won't be able to sing.'

'She'll sing – you'll see.'

Then the tailored trews and cut-away coat. Her abundant hair was pinned and bound close to her head

before the wig was fixed. Netty had tried to persuade Ruth
to wear a little beard, but as soon as they tried to place it, she
laughed so uncontrollably that they abandoned it and settled
for the full sideburns that were attached to the wig.

They darkened her reddish eyebrows and lashes and
painted her lips to disguise their fullness, handed her a cane
and tall hat, and then uncovered the full-length mirror. As
soon as Ruth saw the masculine reflection, in a most natural
way she tightened the neck-bow and slipped one hand into
the trews pocket.

For once, Netty and Jo had no lightning-flash ironic
comments until Netty said, 'I say, Jo – no nasty hairies
there, but you'd never know.'

'Hands off, Nett,' Jo said a bit sharply.

The three of them walked round to the theatre, Ruth in
her 'disguise'. They had taken her on stage and told her to
sing the ballad 'Come, Come, Come into the Garden'.
Lowering her voice to contralto she sang the passionate plea
of the illicit lovers. 'It's because it isn't *me*. Oh, Netty, you
two are marvels.'

As on the occasion when she had gone with Dolly Warren
to the ready-made dress shop and had not admitted the
reflection in the tan-coloured dress as her own, that same
feeling of manipulating another person allowed Ruth Tylee to
go on stage as 'Rosalie'. Jo had fetched Gustav and Edward
Warren, and Ruth had again sung the ballad with ease.

As she finished, Edward Warren snapped his fingers.
'That's what we will do!'

The following night, she had gone on stage un-named by
the Master of Ceremonies. Netty, Jo, Gustav and Edward
Warren watched from behind the scenes. She had sung
'Come, Come, Come into the Garden' to one of the line
dancers leaning from a scenery balcony, acting as the
sweetheart. At the end of the ballad, Ruth began to walk
towards the walk down-stage as Gustav had instructed her.

Then as the diners began to applaud, she dramatically threw her hat up to the sweetheart in a gesture that appeared to continue the song, then she turned to face the audience and allowed the great tumble of 'Rosalie's' wig to fall about her shoulders.

There had been a moment of silence before the full realization by the diners that the singer was a woman. Then there was such a thundering of fists upon the tables that the glasses and bottles clinked. She took six curtain calls, each time revealing a bit more of herself as a woman until at last, after the quick change Netty and Jo had taught her, she bowed low dressed in a low-cut bodice and hooped skirt.

The place had been in uproar. Men surged forward as they often did when they brought flowers to throw to a singer or dancer they admired. Soon every flower was stripped from the tables and tossed up to Ruth. She was breathless with excitement and laughed and beamed at the extraordinary reception her ruse had gained.

From then on, Edward Warren had fostered her mystery and Gustav trained her in stage-craft.

The fact that Ruth and 'Rosalie' had very different identities enabled Edward Warren to create an even greater mystery about her than he had ever envisaged. By the simple ploy of Ruth going in and out of Bounderby's by way of a back alley, dressed in apron and shawl, none of the admirers who waited to catch a glimpse of 'Rosalie' was ever satisfied. The story had got about that she never left the building, but lived somewhere high up within Bounderby's. On two occasions young men had been discovered sitting outside locked store-rooms in the belief that their patience would be rewarded by the eventual emergence of 'Rosalie'.

The Christmas entertainment for young people contained none of the male-to-female transformations. Everything was circumspect enough for Caroline and Susanna, and every other young person there, to carry back every word and action to their families.

The play ran its predicted course until Cedric Carver had fitted the lost slipper onto Ellie O'Dowd's foot. Then, amid exuberant applause, and to Caroline's and Susanna's extreme delight, 'Rosalie', in being presented centre stage as the foremost member of the cast, kissed the tips of her fingers at them, causing all heads to turn in their direction. Peter Warren stood watching, unseen, from the dim corridor at the back of the gallery and tried to find one thing about the vision on the stage that was Ruth. He could find none and was glad that they had to hurry away to the railway station, with only enough time for a few minutes of thanks and congratulations.

The event fed the three of them long after that Christmas had come and gone. Susanna enjoyed the sweetness of reflected glory repeated to her friends. Caroline experienced the satisfying taste of pride and love of her glorious sister. Peter chewed on the bitter herbs of his longing for the farm-girl he had fallen in love with, and who had been as transformed by his brother Teddy, as had been the princess with the golden slippers.

Selena had primed Auryn so that he made an effort not to dampen his young sister's enthusiasm each time she related an incident. If he lacked enthusiasm, Jack and Ginny certainly did not. 'Tell us again, Carly. About the gentlemen bowing to her in the street,' Ginny would say. Or 'What was that song? La-la-la my fair-air laddie . . .' And Caroline would willingly go over it all again for her aunt and uncle. They, in the warmth and sweet smells of their bakery, told one another again what they already knew of their secret niece. For secret she was, in her role of 'Rosalie'.

During the meal they had eaten together before the performance, Peter Warren had searched for some look, or a gesture of familiarity between Teddy and Ruth, but had found none.

4

PATHETICALLY DROWNING

THE FIRST THING Peter Warren did on his return from London was to go down to the diggings, where he heard of yet another death. In the four years since that other Christmas, when Ruth, Auryn and he had rescued the baby Simeon from the ruins of the broken-backed girl who had carried him, the head of the diggings had moved on miles further. The death-roll of one man per mile of railway had been kept up generously. There had been several outbreaks of typhus, and many children had died of the chicken-pox and the whooping-cough.

After a lifetime together, Dutch and Ollie were together no more. Their idea of a shared income, from the letting out of sleeping-space in the hut, and a shared woman, did not work once Dutch had won both prizes. He developed a taste for extra drinking money and a passion for Kitty. Luckily for Kitty, when he was off the diggings, he was in an almost constant state of drink-induced impotence. Ranting clergymen and parliamentarians who condemned the navvies for their heavy drinking could have had no idea of the extreme harshness of a navvyman's life. Likewise, one would believe that contractors, beer-sellers and railway shareholders could not have known of the awful deprivation and cruelty that many navvy women lived with. How else could they have let the situation continue and profited from it?

But they did know. Of course they knew.

Occasionally a voice was raised and a few concerned people of the likes of Peter Warren tried to do something to change the conditions. But people were in love with the idea of railways. They wanted more and more tracks, leading to and from ever more remote regions of Britain. Engineers and contractors were kings. They reigned over a dunghill that few people cared to know about. Better to believe that navvies were a fearsome race apart, upon which public conscience was wasted. True, they were fearsome when they gathered in great numbers. True, they were a race apart. At fifteen shillings a week for a pickman like Dutch, and only a shilling a week less for a muck-shifter like Ollie, navvies were the highest-paid workers in the country, and the most expensively and extravagantly dressed. And, for the most part, the most exploited as, for all their slogging labour, a great proportion of their wages found its way, via licences, to beer-sellers, shanty tenancies and tommy-shops, back into the pockets of the contractors.

Avoided and ignored by society, the navvies made their own laws. Anarchy and Socialism. Two concepts to cause society beyond the diggings to be fearful. Where navvies tramped, so it was believed, there were the forcing beds of new ideas. There were some very respectable, sober married navvy families, but they were not typical.

More typical were the domestic arrangements of Black Annie and her hutful of lodgers, and of Kitty Fire-Bucket with Dutch and Ollie.

The baby Kitty was now carrying heavily was Ollie's. She made no bones about making the most of telling Dutch how his brother had waylaid her and taken what he thought were as much his rights as his brother's.

The fight had been memorable.

Gangers and local grocers earned good commission on the amount of ale that was brought in once it was learned that Dutch and Ollie were going to have a set-to.

The outcome of it was the first news that reached Peter Warren on his return from London.

Unlike other combatant species of would-be dominant

males, neither would give best even when they were both staggering and dripping blood.

The fight started at the top of an embankment and ended at the bottom after Ollie had lost his footing and crashed down onto a pile of iron rails ready to be laid on the line, taking his brother with him. The brothers, unable to move, were piled into two wooden skips and taken back to the shanty-town, Ollie to Black Annie's, where he had been lodging, and Dutch to Kitty's.

Only Dutch survived, with one blinded eye, broken arm and nose and, unknown to himself or anyone else, a cracked skull. Next day, being pay-out, there was one of the largest burial collections ever made. The diggings were abandoned and two hundred men went off in search of drink to drown their momentary grief at the loss of future entertainment.

When Kitty saw Dutch struggling to get his injured body off the bed, she asked him where in hell he thought he was buggeren off to.

'To see my brother buried decent.'

'You can't go like that, why you'm half dead yourself.'

'Shut your mouth and wash me down.'

When she had done so, she dressed him in his new white trousers, velveteen jacket and embroidered red waistcoat. Then she glossed his high-lace boots, knotted a silk scarf about his neck and brushed his new white felt hat. Although he swayed and listed as he walked, he went off looking as expensively and handsomely turned out as was traditional with navvymen going to a good burial.

As soon as he had gone, Kitty pinned shawls round the children, ready to go out.

The great lumps of meat belonging to the lodgers were netted and tied to their notched identifying sticks, and put into the cauldron to simmer. Not that any of them was likely to be in a state to eat when the burial randy was over, even if they were hungry, but they paid for the service and Kitty had received enough cuffs and blows for her not to invite any. Many of the men would not even be able to stagger home for the amount of drink they would have taken.

Before she left the hut, she went to each of the rowed-up beds and kicked it heartily. The children all did the same, as a matter of course – part of the ritual before going out with her, chanting as she did, 'That's one for you ya bugger. And here's one for you.' One or two receiving a double-kick. When they had done them all, she checked the padlock on the cask cupboard and took the gin-crock away from the hut and hid it under a pile of bavins. Sending the children on ahead, she went back into the hut, hurled Dutch's filthy work-boots hard against the wall, spat into the cauldron and, grinning with satisfaction, closed the door on it all.

'Come on, Maggie, let's get the Vicar's Baby. If they buggers have gone off up the line to bury Ollie, we a go down and see the Vicar.'

Maggie's face fell a mile. 'We don't want teaching no bloody ole reading.'

'No,' supported Agnes.

'It an't nothen to do with you. If I says you goen to read, my ole sonny, then you'm goen to, and if you starts carken me about, I shall stripe your arse, and I shan't tell you no more what Nelly Dean saw.' Spoken with such gentleness, that it is a wonder that her three children ever took account of what she said. But, considering that they lived in a shanty-town under the same roof as a bunch of men who could put fear into the hearts of villagers and estate workers, the three of them were not troublesome to Kitty, as they carried out their allotted work of cleaning, emptying and fetching.

Possibly their behaviour owed something to Kitty's own nature, and something to the rewards they received by way of a few minutes a day, when Kitty read to them from *Wuthering Heights*. If her literal reading of Joseph might have sounded comical to another audience, her children fell under the spell of the drama, if not the language; the three of them sitting poke-necked as she struggled with the tortured dialect: 'May-ister, may-ister he's stallen tee lantern! Hee, G-nasher! Hee dog! hol-lid him hol-lid him!'

The thin years of the early childhood of Maggie and Agnes showed in their bowed legs and knobby elbows, but the Vicar's Baby, Simeon, had grown up sturdier than the girls.

Kitty sometimes had a vaguely uneasy feeling that she ought to like the girls a bit more, but they had the look of their father about them. The Vicar's Baby looked like no one but himself. Fair skin, with eyebrows and hair of a darker hue than the masses of freckles that covered his arms and nose. Although Kitty could not be blamed for any defects such as his speckled complexion, she could take credit for his sturdy legs.

It was his legs, more than anything, that led Kitty to feel obligated to Peter Warren, and to agree to let him teach the children their letters. 'Well, 'tis your baby, Vicar-dear, and I got to admit, for myself, I wasen't never sorry my Mam learnt me to read, but if I'd a know reading had things like Heathcliff, I should a paid more heed to it.'

'You get better at it every time I hear you.'

'Ah, but I want to get as good as you, Vicar-dear, and read anythen that passes in front of my eyes.'

Although Kitty thought much about Heathcliff, she was not in love with him; his surly petulance and selfish, cruel ways were too true in real-life men. Kitty admired Edgar Linton with his grange and servants and lack of contact with anything workaday or soiled. Peter tried to explain his belief that people ought not to try to leave their station in life and climb into another, but to try to improve the conditions of their own station.

If Kitty did not understand all that he said, she saw the

implications for herself. 'Ah well, Vicar-dear, that's all well and good for you, because you can get on out of here any time you wants. If I waits a lifetime, I shan't get out of here, not lest Mr Linton was to come and get me.'

'At least you can see the value of the children learning something.'

'Then 'tis a pity they won't let ours go to the schools like normal childer.'

'In time they will. There are more schools these days that will accept children from the diggings.'

'Not round here, though.'

'In time they will. Till then, we have to do the best we can.'

And so it was that, in a very small way, Peter Warren had begun teaching some of the navvy children to read and count, until they reached the age of about seven or eight years old when they became of an age to work on the diggings.

Kitty liked to take her children to the Mission Hall, because she liked the vicar who was the nearest she ever came to her beloved Mr Linton.

When she reached the ramshackle Mission Hut, there were perhaps a dozen children hanging about waiting to see if Vicar would come and if there would be a bit of bread and soup. There was something particularly attractive about the black pot into which they were allowed to dip lumps of bread as a reward for having stumbled through a line of reading, or correctly summed up some numbers.

As an encouragement to her, as well as an acknowledgement that he trusted and respected her, he had long ago given Kitty a key to the hut. She unlocked it and was swept in on the tide of little children. The place was cold and dark and smelled of earth and of the pipe-tobacco smoke of those men and women who had sat waiting for Vicar to compose a letter or to try to right a wrong, or who had come to ask him to stand up for them when they appeared in court.

For an hour, the children were occupied enough in opening shutters, fetching firewood and generally amusing themselves with flicking, squabbling, wrestling and stone-throwing. Soon their span to boredom was reached.

'Ma'am, where's Vicar?'

'He be here when he gets back from Blackbrook.'

'I be cold.'

'I be hungry.'

'I can't see nothing to eat.'

They all mumbled about the place in a dissatisfied way.

'I an't stopping here.'

'It an't worth it.'

Kitty had seen enough of their fathers on strike to recognize the signs. If they went off dissatisfied, then it would take Vicar a lot of time and trouble to get them back again.

'Tell you what,' Kitty said. 'Maggie, you go up to the tommy-shop and ask for a bag of lentils and a bag of brown sugar in Dutch's name. And some of the others of you can get some water and a pot going so as we can make somethen nice and tushy till Vicar comes.'

The making of the sweet 'tushy' lentil broth took another hour. And still Vicar had not come.

Of all of them, Kitty was the most disappointed. The children had got what they had come for – the dip in the broth-pot – but Kitty had not. She had come to be in the company of the man who spoke gently and who had some regard for her, who spoke nice and said, 'Thank you, Kitty' that sweet and kind. Yet he had never so much as laid a hand on her, ever, even though they sat quite close when he pointed to a difficult word she was trying to read.

Today, she had made up her mind she would ask him if he'd a been disappointed by some girl, for he'd had a look about him these last weeks that was so sad that it made your heart fair ache for him. And, knowing how easy it is for men to be comforted, then she would offer him to come to her place if he wanted, just for to comfort him a bit – he'd been good enough to her, seeing she wasn't out of pocket with his Baby and getting her the Heathcliff book and learning her to read it.

Lately, since the Heathcliff book, she had started to find out about other things, things she had not known existed. Once, Vicar had brought in a map and had shown her how the lines on the paper were equal to roads and which was the Waltham road, which the Blackbrook, and where the diggings were running. Until then, it had never occurred to her that there was anything in reading and writing where letters equalled words that could be thought into pictures inside your head. He had said that there were other things, but 'time enough for all that, Kitty, when you can read anything that passes in front of your eyes'.

Recently, the desire to know about things outside the diggings had become more intense, until she was convinced that if she could only somehow find out what they were, then her own Mr Linton would come and find her.

No nice Mr Linton would ever step foot in no bloody ole diggen, which meant that Kitty would have to find her way out.

5

FUNERAL RITES

IT HAD BEEN IN THE MARCH of that same year that one hundred and fifty navvies had gathered on the outskirts of Blackbrook, which was the nearest place where a grave could be found for Ollie. A few women, including Black Annie, dressed as respectably as any of the Blackbrook burghers' wives in close bonnet and hooped skirt. Although the local clergyman was to conduct the service, Dutch wanted Peter Warren, their 'own Diggings Vicar', to say the words that mattered. In their way, the navvies on the Great Southern diggings had a rough regard for the young man who daily tramped the lines and would listen to them, or write a letter home for them. 'He don't think no less of 'ee, no matter what.'

Neither did he think less of them nor work less hard for them because they were thought to have 'infidel opinions', keep 'unmarried wives' and believe in revolution. Though he hated their casual treatment of the women and children.

What the Reverend Warren wanted was to bring a bit of dignity and decency to their lives, and he saw no gain in abusing them for what, he believed, they could not alter. The very nature of life on the diggings gave them no option but to live in squalid, overcrowded conditions, where it was not uncommon for beer to be imposed in lieu of wages, and forty was a good age for a navvy to reach, and if they rejected his simple prayer services on other occasions, they did not feel that one of their own had a proper introduction to his Maker unless it was made by the Diggings Vicar.

By the time the procession bringing Ollie's boxed corpse on a hand-truck reached the edge of town, there was little sign of people shopping, deliveries being made, or any of the usual active morning life in Blackbrook. 'They're burying a navvy!' Peter Warren knew from experience that the sight of a dozen navvies together was enough to close down that part of town where the burial was to take place. He smiled as he thought of the keepers of alehouses and inns – unwilling to put up the shutters, hoping that lavish drinking money might come their way – busy removing to a safer place anything that was not fixed to the floor or walls.

Although the Diggings Vicar would never have vouched for their behaviour once the burial was over, he knew that, as the men walked into town, the respectable people of Blackbrook need not have looked out from secured houses through blinds, for he could be sure that practically every man had come sober to Ollie's graveside. Even those who had not sobered up from yesterday would be orderly – or kept so by the rest.

He walked with no frightful drunken mob, but an orderly procession of strong men in their expensive, distinctive dress. Silk neckerchiefs fluttered dashingly, white felt hats with turned-up brims at jaunty angles, each of the velveteen and moleskin jackets trimmed with ten or a dozen pearly buttons, and a white favour in every lapel.

On another occasion, the Diggings Vicar might have thought: *If they had decent homes, and employers who saw them as men like themselves . . . if the contractors would stop the flood of ale and gin . . . if the society they live in weren't so rotted away . . . if these strong, skilled men . . . if . . . if . . . then what could they not do? It made no difference whether you approved or no – they, and the thousands who had gone the same way as Ollie was going this morning, were transforming the entire country . . . the entire nation. It was extraordinary when you thought about it being done, shovel by shovelful . . . they had cut through mountains, made tunnels, spanned estuaries, re-directed rivers and controlled*

them to make canals. Now his 'navvies' were daily going
uphill and downhill over the Southern Downs linking the
entire southern part of England with the North.

But on this occasion he was pale-faced and holding on to
his emotions.

A look at the weathered, manly faces and one might
understand how many a trader's wife, and many a sweetheart of a broad-shouldered farm labourer, had so often
been willing to throw her cap over the windmill when she
was sweet-talked by a navigator in his best get-up.

There were third-hand tales of navvy burials where men
were said to have been so drunk that they had forgotten
where they had left the corpse and whose it was, anyhow;
one of the legends that abounded in the world outside the
diggings was of three hundred men who had raised money
for a grave and a wake by raffling the corpse, which, after
being unclaimed for a fortnight, was eventually buried at the
expense of the Parish. But if these stories were true, they
were not typical of the navvyman's respect for the dead.
Especially for a man like Ollie who, in locked holds with
Dutch, had given hours of pleasure and good cause for a
gamble and a bit of a randy.

Still orderly, they waited along the paths of the churchyard whilst Peter Warren went to seek out the Parish
clergyman who was to perform the service.

Now that his sudden fury had subsided, and he had forgiven
Ollie giving Kitty that baby, Dutch realized that he would
miss his brother.

Looking at the coffin on the cart, and in his throbbing
head imagining Ollie laid out inside in a decent shirt, he
mumbled to no one in particular, 'Been with Ollie a bloody
sight longer than I been roostin' in that skinny magpie's
nest.' His voice fell into Black Annie's ear.

'You a miss him, Dutch.'

'And when it comes down to it, you can have as many women as you like . . . Ollie was my brother. We must of work together on the best part of fifty mile of line. If he'd a wanted her that much, he could have come and asked.'

'You never denied nothing to each other as I remember, Dutch.'

'There wasn't never a minute's trouble between us over you, Annie, not in all the time we was with you.'

'That's true, Dutch – then there's a bit more of Black Annie than there is of her.'

'Right up to the night when I jumped the stick with her, me and Ollie was all right with you.'

'Right up to the hour, as you might say.'

'Bugger Kitty Fire-Bucket.'

'I don't know what she ever wanted to tell you for. You and Ollie's like enough that it wouldn't hardly matter who give her the child.'

'It waddn't that, it was the way she said he waylaid her and held her down, and how she tried to call out "Dutch". Ollie done the dirty on me.'

'And you believed her?' 'Billygoat', another of Black Annie's old faithfuls, chimed in. 'I'm surprised at you, Dutchy, me boy, lettin' that little fancy-bag split up you and Ollie. I reckon you been keeping cully there.'

Black Annie said nothing but nodded meaningfully at Billygoat.

Dutch massaged his temples and shook his head. 'What do you mean? Kitty don't like it enough to give it away, it's got to be took from her. Anyway, Ollie tole me he done it.'

'You all right? Where's the bloody Vicar got to?' asked Black Annie.

'I keep gettin' this pain like me head's splitting down the middle, and I can see everything double. She an't been making herself a bit behind my back, have she, Annie? Bugger, I'd give her the same as Ollie if I thought she'd been

. . . Christ, Annie! 'Tis like a steam-hammer in here.' He thwacked the side of his head as though a blockage needed clearing.

'You needs a bit to keep you going till we put Ollie down.' Black Annie drew a flat three-quarter bottle from within her sleeve and Dutch swigged a long pull. 'You don't want to take no notice about that, Dutch, we all knows who birthed that one she calls the Vicar's Baby, and it an't because he give it to her like Ollie did.' She swigged herself and handed the spirit to as many standing close by as the bottle would stand.

The spirits seemed to clear Dutch's head for a minute. The last bit of conversation came back to him. 'Why, I don't reckon he knows what it's for yet, and if he do, he'd say it was fornication and a sin.' He slapped his temple again. 'Christ, if that an't made it worst now than it was before.'

At that point Peter Warren returned, and they fell silent on hearing his news that the open grave they had assumed was Ollie's was for another man. 'Ollie is to go just down the slope there. We're to make our way on down, and the clergyman will follow as soon as we're assembled.'

They found the second grave. A very different affair from the other neatly dug oblong close to the path. Ollie was to be laid to meet his Maker in a shallow irregular hole in a waterlogged out-of-the-way corner. The sort of corner that any soul-gathering angel would not happily want to search for a newcomer.

'Blast and bugger my eyes! Will you just look at that!' Dutch said.

'Why, 'tis a hole for a dead bloody cat dug by a two-year-old.'

'Water! I might be seeing double, but that's bloody water. It'll want a pump going twenty-four hours a day to keep that dry.'

Although the entire one hundred and fifty experts on

excavation could not all inspect the grave at the same time, they at least tried, and the trampling of three hundred boots immediately provided evidence of the boggy nature of the forsaken corner of the churchyard.

'You sure you got it right, Vicar?'

'Yes. Close by the willow. I'm sorry, Dutch, I had no idea . . .'

The air rumbled with voices of one hundred and fifty men who knew that once again they had been slighted by the society they slogged their guts out for.

'Ollie an't going down no rat-hole like that.'

There was support from the mourners as well as from their vicar.

'You sure the sexton or whoever it was got paid?' Black Annie asked.

Peter nodded. 'Everybody's been paid – and over the odds from what I've heard.'

'We don't mind over the odds . . . Egod! My bloody head.' Dutch swayed but was held upright by half a dozen iron fists.

'Listen, friends.' Peter Warren raised himself a head above the crowd by wedging his boot in a low fork of the willow tree. 'Ollie was a hard worker, and although he has – as we have all done – committed sins against God, that is no reason for denying him a decent resting place for his earthly remains. Taking a woman against her will is a vile and terrible sin, may God forgive him.' *For I may not.*

It took Peter Warren a great deal of control to make that short sermon. When he had discovered that the great wrestler had way-laid Kitty and raped her, the most terrible blood-lust for the man had come upon him. Bewildered at his own rank aggression, he had done the only thing he knew to expel his demon – he had run every mile to Winchester where, in a state of near exhaustion, he had gone to his trusted seminary tutor and talked the torment out. Now, to all appearances, he was his calm and normal self.

A murmur of agreement – or perhaps not, but, anyhow, a murmur.

'On the Day of Judgement, Ollie's sins will be weighed as will yours and mine. Only then shall it be decided whether he spend eternity with the sheep or with the goats, and only Our Lord shall decide. Till then, Ollie's bones shall lie with all others.'

Again a loud cheer; but it was the first which had brought both sexton and clergyman from the vestry of the church, since when they had been standing listening and watching from the dark recesses of the porch. After the second cheer, they wisely returned whence they came.

Peter Warren, who had seen them from his vantage point, continued: 'Six of you go to the green shed and get digging tools. Dutch, come with me and we will select a place for your brother.'

By now, it was obvious that Dutch had received worse injuries at the hands of Ollie than he had at first believed. He looked sick and pale, and he constantly shook his head, trying to clear his impaired vision. Black Annie seated him upon a tomb and wiped his forehead with the dregs of the gin-flask.

With the very best skill of the most experienced excavators in the nation to hand, a precise oblong cutting with embankments at correctly sloping angles was soon achieved.

Peter Warren stood at the side with Dutch, as old Billygoat and a couple of others who had known Ollie the longest manhandled the coffin to two men who were in the grave waiting to up-end it and lay it flat. Peter Warren raised his voice: 'What I had to say about Ollie and his life I have already said. May his soul rest here in peace until the Day of Judgement. Amen.'

Somehow, despite his deteriorating condition, Dutch

had seemed to be aware of his role as chief mourner. As pale as a corpse himself, he had nevertheless taken a spade, sliced the earth about six inches above the pile and collapsed beside the grave of his dead brother, with blood trickling from his nose.

When Peter Warren went into the smoky murk of Kitty's hut, the brilliance and glitter of Bounderby's was still in his eye. The last few days of the year were filled with cold mists which blotted out the outline of the South Downs and filled the valleys and raw railway cuttings with dripping wetness.

A lodger was snoring on one of the lower-level row of narrow beds, and the three children were quietly picking over the bones and jelly of some cold pig's feet.

Kitty was sweeping between the lodgers' beds, holding her swollen belly like a bundle of washing with one hand, whilst she pushed the broom with the other. She dropped the broom at once and carried her bundle towards him. His heart was wrenched at the sight of her, renewed after his days of absence. Still a thin, ageless girl, top-heavy with her swollen breasts and her gravity off-centred by her full-time condition. 'Oh, Vicar-dear, I'm that glad to see you, there's some words I just wanted to ask you.'

'And I am glad that I have not come too late – not that a mere man like myself is of any use except to pray for a safe delivery, but I did think that I might be of some comfort.'

'Well, Vicar-dear, I can't say I'm pleased it still haven't come, I'm that weary of it.' She arched her back and rubbed it. 'Still, it an't long now. I have took some vervain, and Maggie have told Mistress "Fairy". She's somewhere else at the moment, but she will come in time.'

Mistress Dowlas, known as 'Fairy' as a tribute to her large bulk, was the conventional wife of 'London' Dowlas, a mason who had 'never touched a drop nor any other woman except Fairy'.

The respectable lives they led in the shanty-town set them apart: London was the only 'near' navvy not to be despised by his fellows, while Fairy's skill as a midwife added to the high regard in which they were held by the entire community. Fairy kept a small horse, and would ride sidesaddle with the regality of a duchess to a confinement, where she would quickly set about massaging and numbing some of the woman's pain with henbane oil. Perhaps it was that while people like the Dowlases existed the entire community felt itself to be not entirely a tribe of wandering outcasts, for there was no family life anywhere in the country better conducted than that inside the Dowlases' wood and tin hut.

Peter Warren looked a little alarmed at the prospect of Fairy's visit. 'Are you so close to your time?'

'Ah, don't you worry, Vicar-dear, I shan't be asken you to cut the cord for me. I got a bit of time to go yet.'

The fact of the two worlds in which he lived, and his two separate selves, was always a source of interest and surprise to Peter Warren. In his mind, Dolly and Kitty represented the two worlds. Had Dolly realized, even to a minute degree, the extent of openness there was between himself and the people he ministered to, she would have been shocked and disgusted. It was bad enough that John should have chosen such an earthy profession as doctoring in a lying-in hospital in London, but to have two brothers who were familiar with such unpleasant facts of life would have been too distasteful for words for Dolly's ever-developing sensibilities.

Peter had seen men and women in every state of nature. How could it be otherwise in the primitive and crowded conditions in which these people lived? He often sat in the company of whores and talked with them in much the same way that he talked with Dolly – young whores needed an older brother to complain to in much the same way as Dolly

complained of her sweethearts or the unfairness of everything: the difference only in that the young whores had
reason to pout and weep.

What would his mother think? Open-minded woman as
she considered herself to be, he could imagine her displeasure if she knew him capable of discussing such a subject
as an imminent birth with a young woman; if she knew that
he had once listened sympathetically to that same young
woman when she had unburdened herself of the story of
how, for the second time in her short life, her pregnancy had
been the result of assault. No – as the result of rape. He
forced himself to acknowledge the word.

Slowly, especially since the night of the explosion when
he had taken on the responsibility with her for keeping the
baby Simeon, he had come to realize that he could no longer
see himself as a student of theology, and that the days of the
idealistic youth with a mission to 'save' were over. When he
had rescued the baby, he had brought it to Kitty's world,
where the word 'rape' took on its meaning. He had never
thought of taking the child to his mother's and Dolly's
world.

When he was here on the diggings, a schism was created
where part of him was sympathetic and understanding
towards the men, with their endless hours of hard labour
alleviated only by their women and whores, fighting, or
drunken stupor.

He felt that he did understand the navvymen.

Before the episode with Ruth, he had been able to
manage his oestrus by submerging his natural desires in
study, work and swimming. Since that time, whenever the
vivid memory of Ruth sprang unexpectedly upon him, he
had frequently visited a discreet woman in Winchester
whose sweet reputation was well-known to many young
men who wore clerical black. Mrs Briggingham was the
youngish widow of an old cleric; her understanding of

young clergymen was more Christian than that of any bishop. At first, although several of his fellow ex-students insisted that hers was an acceptable and ecumenical church, he had been ill-at-ease, until he realized how much better he worked after an hour with her.

His own weaknesses proved an insight into the navvy-men. And, given their lives, who might not take a drink to ease the hardships? But, whilst he could understand the reasons for their behaviour he could not forgive the results of it upon the women.

He understood, and often felt achingly for, the women and the children.

The pathetic young whores, fed and watered like any animal that earns its keep, who were trundled up and down the diggings during working hours and were then usually on duty in the huts and fields at night.

The wives and women, whose costly new bonnets or frocks could never compensate for the bruised eyes and the cracked ribs.

The unwanted babies and the abandoned children whose fathers had sloped off to create more unwanted babies and other abandoned families at the next digging, and at the next . . .

There were times when Peter Warren felt he was pathetically drowning in a flood of human misery and degradation yet, whilst he could do little with his few resources to alleviate the huge problems of such an under-belly society, he could not leave it.

He watched as Kitty swayed and rolled along between the beds with her copy of 'the Heathcliff book' which she had taken from its place of safety where she kept it hidden for fear it might find its way into a pawnshop.

In his usual corner beside the stove, as much of Dutch as Kitty had managed to salvage after he collapsed from his cracked skull, sat with his feet on the hearthstone, grasping a thick walking stick, thinking nothing in his empty mind and seeing nothing with his only good eye.

'How has he been?'

'Same as always. Maggie's as good as gold with him. She treats him like a great baby, tellen him to do this, do that; takes him to the jakes, tells him to eat up his dinner, and he does it all ever so well. He's better with her than with anybody.' She laughed as though telling of the achievement of a real baby.

'Kitty, why don't you . . .'

At the same time as massaging her lower belly, she wagged a finger at him. 'Now then, Vicar-dear, don't start that agen. I'm buggered if I shall chuck him out and take another bloody ole pickman.' She poked Dutch, but it brought no response from him. 'He can stop there, an be the rightful tenant-holder under the company's rules, as long as me and the little'ns needs a roof over our heads.'

He looked at his boots to ask the next question. 'What about the overseer?'

Familiarly, she put a finger under his chin and raised his head. 'Now look at me, Vicar-dear, you knows I'm serious. 'Tis no great thing I do for him. He likes me and he quite a gentleman in his way. If rafty old buggers like Cocky and Dutch and Ollie had rights to take me, then I can give myself to Ainsley Chambers once in a while for the sake of keepen Dutch's name on the tenancy and a roof over the little'ns' heads. You know as well as I do that he could send in a report about Dutch and we should be out tomorrow. 'Tis how we live down here.' She loosened the waist-cord of her skirt and slid her hand inside to massage her belly. 'I needs to go out to the jakey.'

For the five minutes that she was gone, he mused upon the vision of the girl in Ruth's Christmas play, in her stage rags, and upon the reality of a truly poor girl. This led him to think of Ruth. 'Rosalie'. She had lost her prettiness and become beautiful.

It had been many months since he had seen her, and in that time he had seen that it was not only she who had changed; he too had matured. It had been painful to watch and listen as she had sung so beautifully and to remember that earlier Christmas; to sit opposite her conversing politely and to realize that what was happening to transform Ruth into 'Rosalie' could never be reversed.

Kitty returned. 'Lord alive, that vervain do rollick your innards about. I hope Fairy won't be delayed.'

'Would you like me to find her?'

'No, Vicar-dear. She knows I'm ready, and if she's got another birthen, she won't thank you for ferretten her out. She a ride up here in time. You'll see. Ah . . . bugger!' Clutching her knees, she put her head back and closed her eyes for a minute.

Calm again, she continued, 'Now then, Vicar-dear.' She fingered open her 'Heathcliff book'. 'This word. Ee-miss-ry? Tell me what it is.'

Reluctantly, suspicious of what was happening to her, he looked. 'Emissaries. No, Kitty, I shan't tell you.'

'Oh now, come on, Vicar-dear, don't bugger about teasen me. 'Tis what Nelly said she despatched "down this path and that path", and I can't get the picture till I know what it was she despatched. Emiss-a-ries.'

'I shan't tell you, Kitty, because I have brought a book from London so that you can find it for yourself. A dictionary – a book of word meanings.'

'I know what a dictionary is, I an't daft. Is it a present?' Her eyes shone like her children's, who came running when they heard the word 'present'.

'And a little thing for each, all the same so that there shall be no squabbles. They are kaleidoscopes.'

'Tell the Vicar thank you.'

Awkwardly they did so, then soon ran back to their corner where they became totally absorbed in a new world of fantasy, colour and pattern. Then he began to show Kitty how to use the dictionary until she said, 'It isn't no good, Vicar-dear, I shall have to lie down, it's coming quicker now I been out to the jakey. Maggie, run up over the top and see if you can see Fairy; if not go down to the Tunnel End and tell her – nice, mind – that the baby's very low and the pains is close. And if she can't come straight away, then go and fetch Black Annie and I shall have to put up with it.'

'Let me go.'

'Maggie's faster than you. Now go on your way, Vicar-dear, you should ought to get on. It was nice you comen in with all they things. Ah . . . !' Again, to his consternation, she closed her eyes and seemed to disappear inside herself once more.

'I can't leave you like this.'

'Why 'tis only a baby being birthed. There's plenty more comen before the day's out.'

Her face contorted and sweat showed on her brow.

He put his hand in hers and she gripped with more force than he would have ever imagined a woman to possess. Then she released him and grinned. 'You a be getten a bad name comen in here and holden my hand in front of Dutch. Tell you what, Vicar-dear, if you wants to be helpful, take this good mattress off and unroll that straw one. And just move Dutch away a bit so that Fairy can get to the kettles. And put the big one over the fire a bit more. Fairy uses hot water like it come down by stream.'

He did as he was bid, and she continued to order him about, as well as the two children. 'Agnes, if that young guller wakes up, tell him to sling hisself off till it's supper, and keep the Vicar's Baby down there till Fairy's finished.' The two children were so absorbed with their toys that it seemed unlikely that they would cause much interference.

'That's better, Vicar-dear. Lord, I'm sorry to put you about like that, but it has just caught me a bit quick. Why don't you go?'

'I'll go as soon as Fairy gets here.'

She began lashing her head from side to side, then she untied the cord at her waist. 'Go, Vicar-dear . . . ah!' She drew in her breath and he held both her hands as the great muscles in her belly began to labour greatly.

'Tell me what to do.' He removed his jacket and waistcoat.

'You can't.'

'Don't tell me what I can't do.'

She laughed. 'Bugger all, Vicar-dear, you a be the death of me. Go on then, help me get off my skirt and cover me with that ole sheet.'

Deftly and quickly he removed the skirt and covered her exposed white skin. As he did so, he saw her muscles contract and instinctively gave her his hands to grip. 'Tell me what to do, Kitty! Tell me!'

As the pain subsided, she smiled at him. 'It an't you that got to do anythen, it's me and my belly together.'

'Don't treat me like a child, Kitty. I've seen a dozen whelpings and helped at a calving before now. And I was there when young Simeon was born, wasn't I?'

'You'm the queerest vicar I ever came across.'

'Tell me what Fairy would have to do.'

'Same as when you brought the calf. Help en out if he needs it.' She lashed her head again and held on to his hands.

The world shrank until there was nothing except this room, this bed, this woman, this moving, mysterious mound of white flesh, so different from that terrible occasion when he and Auryn Tylee had held the dying girl and Ruth had brought out the baby. Now, he had the sensation of being at the very centre of the universe. Nothing that had gone before, or would come after, could have the significance of these moments. He felt that the answers to all the mysteries of God were about to be revealed.

'Would it help if I rubbed your back? Is that where the pain is?'

She pointed to a bottle of oil she had put to warm on the hearth. 'The lavender.'

He helped her to turn on her side, poured some of the oil into his hands and began massaging her.

'Bless you, Vicar, if you an't got hands like an angel. Would it be all right if you did my belly?'

He warmed his hands and placed them on either side of her belly, momentarily taken aback at the rock-like hardness of it. He had no idea what to do, so began describing an arc upon her, starting at the waist and ending at her groin.

'Is that right, Kitty?'

She closed her eyes. 'Ah, 'tis the most comfort anybody ever give me.' She touched his hair, then ran her hand down his cheek. 'There an't a better man ever stepped foot into a pair of shoes than you.'

'Rubbish, Kitty. I don't even know what to do to help you.'

'Just be-en here. Help isn't only *doing*, it being with people as well. And touchen. Sometimes that all a fretten babe wants – to feel somebody's hands. Ah, Vicar-dear, 'tis the greatest comfort, more even than speaken.'

His hands jerked away from her. 'Something's happening, what is it?'

'That's your other baby trying to get out.'

Gently, as he let his hands rest upon her contraction, the miracle, more awesome than burning bushes or heaven-sent manna, the commonplace miracle was played out for him. All the 'begats' of the Old Testament upon which he had spent many hours of study, and the stories of 'barren women' and women bearing late in life, and the ultimate birth . . . all life since the world began was *this*.

Closely watching Kitty's face, sweat dripping from his own, he let his hands follow the movements going on within her and wondered at his own arrogance. How could any priest who had not laid his hands upon the power of a mother giving life to an unborn child, have *anything* to say to women? How have men come to believe that they are such lords of creation? The Church, the priesthood, every religion about which he knew anything, was entirely centred upon the male. God/He. Jesus/He. Shem begat ... Arphaxad begat ... Salah begat ... Eber begat ... and so on right down to Terah who died in Haran. All stated as though the whole of creation was in the seed of the man, and no woman had ever lain with her belly as hard and round as Kitty's.

'What can I do, Kitty?'

'Don't worry, Vicar-dear.' Another movement. 'Women an't ... no different from ... cattle or horses when ... it comes to this.'

She groaned as she expelled a huge breath. 'You got really nice feelen hands, did you know that? Good hands, warm and dry.'

'What about the water, Kitty? What does Fairy use the water for?'

'Bugger the water, Vicar. I think it's comen. You seen the Vicar's Baby born all right. You don't mind, Vicar-dear, do you?' She spread her legs wide. 'Do you mind haven a look and see how much of its head you can see, I can't hold back no more.'

'Oh dear God ... it's ... I think it's ...'

He never said what it was, for the baby began to emerge. In many ways, she was right in saying that women were no different from animals giving birth. He helped the small bony head slip through the birth-canal, then, as soon as he had eased its shoulders, Kitty pushed her baby forcefully into Peter Warren's hands.

'Kitty, Kitty, Kitty, he's a boy.' Sweat and tears dripping from his face, Peter Warren held up the wet baby for her to see.

He thought that her acknowledging smile was the most beautiful that he had ever seen. 'Well then, it looks like we got another Vicar's Baby in the family.'

'I tell you, London, in all my born years,' said Fairy Dowlas over their shared meat broth that evening, 'my eyes never seen a queerer sight when I opened that door. There was Kitty Fire-Bucket all – you know how – and young Reverend Warren in his best pulpit trousers and shirtsleeves, holding up her baby like he won a prize. And not hardly an arm's length away was that daft Dutch who killed his brother over that very baby, not even knowing what was going on.'

London nodded and continued half-listening to her usual evening recital of the events that occurred on the periphery of her mysterious profession.

'And what do you reckon she's set on naming him?'

London, concentrating on chewing away from his mouth and throat the earthy taste of masonry dust, shook his head so that she could reply.

'Edgar.' She wagged her head at the queerness of people. 'Edgar Linton. So I asked her straight out if Linton was what Dutch and Ollie was called. "No," she says – you know in that soft way she's got of speaking – " 'tis the one I wishes his father was like." Never in all my born days have I heard a navvyman's child called Edgar. Especially not one that got his father killed and his uncle made senseless before he was birthed.'

6

QUEEN OF LONDON

'It is very beautiful.' Ruth fingered the pendant that lay in the division of her bosom.

'Who would think of offering less than perfection to the Queen of all London?' Familiarly, he adjusted the comb that held her knot of red curls in place, watching her reflection as he did so.

She smiled. 'You are as extravagant in your compliments, sir, as you are with your gifts. But you know very well that I cannot accept anything so expensive. My rule has always been that I will accept flowers because they have no value except of the moment.'

'And what of *my* rule – that Rosalie must wear only the latest fashion and the most beautiful adornments?'

Bending to kiss her shoulder gently, he did not see in the mirror how Ruth closed her eyes and momentarily struggled with herself. He did not need to see.

'I wish that you had not done that!'

'The deuce you do, Rosalie. I believe that you desire to have it done near as much as I desire to do it – and as you desire the pendant.'

With a sudden cold expression of outrage on her face, she rose and walked to the door, removing the jewel from her neck as she did so.

'Kindly leave, or I shall be forced to call my Manager. He will forbid you enter Bounderby's again.' She handed him the pendant and flung open the door. 'To be sure, I shall instruct my dresser to see to it that you are not admitted to my dressing-room in future.'

He spread his hands in a gesture of submission. 'Rosalie,

I should die rather.' Suddenly, with a complete change of expression, Edward Warren said, 'Wonderful, my darling girl. I believe that I was ready to be banished.' Coming back into the room, he flung himself onto a chaise-longue and put his feet up. Ruth went back to her dressing-table and sat facing him.

'Truly?'

'Truly. I should not o'erstep the mark twice with Mistress Rosalie in her mood of displeasure.' He kissed her lightly. 'You have a very icy tone, Miss. If I did not know you better I should believe you to be very hard. Two things – you should not have smiled when you rejected his gift, and you had better been a bit swifter moving away when he bent to kiss you.'

She went to the chaise-longue, stood behind him, linked her arms about his neck and buried her face in his side-whiskers. 'Then, my dear, you had best send someone whose kisses I like less than yours to practise me. Let Gustav practise me.'

'Poor Gustav, after all that he has done to teach you to breathe and bring out the quality of your voice.'

Taking her hand, he gently pulled her onto his lap and fastened the garnet-and-diamond-encrusted pendant about her neck. 'Now that the exercise is over, you may as well have these. Comfits for a good girl.' And dropped into her hand long earrings of the same style and jewels.

'Really, Teddy! And I have so many pretty necklaces and lots of earrings – you need not have bought more just for half an hour's exercise.'

'These are not for you – they are for Rosalie. *You* are not permitted to refuse them.'

A secret that he shared only with himself. He smiled. *She is almost entirely innocent of the difference between paste and jewels. Her eye sees the colour, the glitter and the style. She is developing quite an eye for style. Money is still a mystery to her. She's unworldly – I could have nominated any sum for her salary, and she would have accepted it. Riches to her are anything above what it costs to live. Wealth is to have enough to give away. When she sends money to her family, she is wealthy. She has no conception of my own financial standing now that Bounderby's and the omnibuses are successful.*

He recalled the first gift that he had bought her. A fob watch set in scores of small diamonds. Jesting, when she had opened the package, he had said, 'I am sorry about the bits of broken glass, but the watch has very good time.' She had put it to her ear. 'Oh, Teddy, so it has . . . such a delicate tick I should love it whatever was on its case.' And, as he had pinned it upon her jacket, she had said, 'It is so pretty, I don't know why anyone wants the worry of jewels at all. I should be too much afraid to wear them for fear I should be attacked by a thief.'

It had been altogether so delightful an episode that he had wanted to repeat it again and again. It was his assurance that he was not spoiling her, that something still existed of the lovely girl who had been dressed up so appallingly by Dolly the first time he saw her, but who had then been nothing more than the means for him to carry out his fantasy.

Each and every time I do something to create Rosalie, I am changing something of Ruth. Now that 'Rosalie' is almost complete, how can I keep Ruth?

Yet the idea of transformation was close to obsession with him.

It was what made him rise early each morning, eager to begin another day, when he could commence his work of transforming, yet again, the bricks and mortar of a cold, dark building into a sparkling wonderland.

Many people connected with Bounderby's shared something of that obsession – the ice chef, who transformed juice and water into fairy confections; the cook who changed lumps of dead oxen into a dish of rare beef; Harry who could arrange filters in front of lamps and make half the world seem to disappear, and Gustav, who played what was in reality a wooden box containing wire and hammers and made it into a living thing with his music.

A nearby church struck two.

He held her at a short distance from him, his eyes taking in her bare, creamy, sloping shoulders whose skin was lightly dusted with tiny freckles, her vulnerable neck from which sprang tendrils of fine hair, a wonderful neck which under his tuition she had learned to carry erect and imperiously. In the yellow light of shaded oil-lamps, except for her mass of red hair, she looked entirely golden.

Only I know how vulnerable she is.

Only he and Gustav knew of the terror of her dreams that she would find herself on stage without costume and her face unpainted, and of the precipice on whose edge she still occasionally awoke. As Ruth, she would have been stuttering and tongue-tied before the audience. Rosalie, however, swept and flounced. Rosalie was professional, hardworking and ambitious. Rosalie was Ruth's protector.

Impossible not to want them both.

He thought of how totally his she had become. When he and Gustav had begun to coax her talent from her, they had found it to be great, closer to art than talent. So too it had been with passion. Once she had discovered that it was not a thing to be feared, repressed, but was a wholesome part of her nature, so had Ruth come to enjoy the act of love itself – through Rosalie.

Warren's own creation. Not only was Rosalie, with her deep-throated voice like an earthly angel's, his creation, but so also was Ruth, the loving woman with a temperament at one extreme as cool and delicate as her skin, and at the other as fiery and generous as her hair. Except to a very few of her intimates, she did not reveal the passionate side of her nature; it did, however, come swooping into her voice, thrilling the women, exciting the men.

'Mysterious', 'Enigmatic', 'Exotic' were the words that had been attached to both Rosalie and her voice. Now, as Edward Warren looked at her, he too felt this about her. For three years she had been his, to teach, to dress, to mould and, eventually, to love. For three years, beneath the maturing exterior of the idolized Queen of Bounderby's – and consequently of all London's night-life – he had known the unaffected farm-girl still to exist.

But she is growing away. She has only to realize what she is to be entirely independent. But for the present, I shall keep as much of her for myself as I can keep.

He kissed her ear gently, knowing what response he would get.

With closed eyes, she said, 'Now here . . . and here . . . and here.'

'Wanton.'

'No, no. A wanton would say "here and here and here" to *any* man.' She kissed his eyes, his cheeks and, for longer, his mouth. 'But *I* say . . . ' laughing, she playfully repeated her kisses . . . "here and here and here" *only* to my lover.'

She rose from the chaise-longue and drew him to the bedroom where he knew that he would still be when Sunday bells, several streets away from his house in Coram Street, would awaken him.

If I am honest with myself, I know that I have never once slept with Ruth in my arms. It is Rosalie who wears the silk night-gowns I brought from Paris. How tantalizing . . . the thought of awaking just once to find her now as she was when Peter knew her . . . farm-girl in a flannel night-shift . . . awaking to find those arms about me.

They had both drifted off into a light sleep when the sound of the young servant with Ruth's morning coffee aroused him.

*Two cups. Does the girl peep in to see if Ruth is alone
before preparing the tray, or does she always bring two cups
in anticipation of finding me here? Perhaps she always brings
two cups in anticipation of finding* someone *here.*

He stopped his thoughts going along that path. He knew
well enough that there was no one else. Eventually there
would be someone else, he knew that as surely as he knew
many things about Ruth.

Carefully, so as not to disturb her, he drank the coffee.
Several churches announced eight o'clock. Ruth inhaled
deeply, slowly coming from sleep.

Never, of all the women he had known, had he ever been
so entirely overwhelmed as he was by her. Now, as he lay
propped up beside her, half-satiated by their dawn love-
making, half-aroused again by the gentle rise and fall of her
lace-enclosed breasts, he wondered how much longer they
could continue as they were now.

Twice since they had become lovers he had not been able
to control his ardour, and she had not tried, or perhaps not
been able, to stop him. On the last occasion he had caused
her to become pregnant, and they had both hated the days
that followed until she had agreed to submit to the surgeon.

The surgeon was an habitué of Bounderby's as well as an
admirer of Rosalie, and one of a group of medical men – of
whom Edward Warren's brother John was one, and to
whom Edward had known he could turn for help – who
were promoting among the child-laden poor of the city the
unethical idea that a woman might try to protect herself
against the results of love as wisely as she would protect
herself against the results of rain.

It was this same doctor who had later advised her how
she should care for herself, and when she demurred at the
idea of such a practice, had said, 'My dear, it is quite a
respectable and wise thing to do. If I did not entirely believe
so, then I should not put my reputation and livelihood at

risk each time I give such advice. I could only wish that Her
Majesty would be half as sensible as some of her subjects,
then she would not be so much in terror of childbed as she is.
And see . . . what else might such dear little sponges be put
upon earth for?'

She had told him all this straightforwardly, naively – as
Ruth.

As the sun moved round the airy room, Edward Warren
continued to watch her. There were times when she affected
him so greatly, that he would do anything she asked. Even to
the extent, at such moments, of offering to return to the
unfashionable and uncultured backwoods of his hometown,
if that was what she wished. He knew that he was on safe
ground here. Ruth loved the city.

The first time they had made love with one another had
been sudden and unexpected to both of them. *Two years
ago? Probably . . . she was still in the rooms at Coxy's. I had
taken her new costume over. There was no reason why I
should not have sent one of the porters, but I wanted to see
her face when she saw the creation 'made by the best
theatrical costumier in London'.*

Smiling at her reposing face, knowing that she was not as
deeply asleep as she pretended, he teased her by running the
ribbon of her satin and lace bustier over her skin, but she
would not respond.

*She was wearing the same skirt and bodice she had worn
when I first collected her from the railway station.
Vulnerable.* It has always been that quality in her that affects
me. Yet he knew that she must have other, strong qualities,
must be durable and determined. She had defied her brother,
had come alone to London, and had virtually cut herself off
from the isolated little farm in that backwater of a hamlet and
now, except for a few letters, had all but lost contact with her
family.

The smell of food cooking. Savoury. Kidneys frying. A

breakfast for him – Ruth still kept to her old ways and took only a bowl of frumenty which she often made for herself and ate sitting in the tiny kitchen of the rented house.

I still wonder about her and The Church.

That time when Peter brought the young girls to Bounderby's for the Christmas entertainment, he was watching me with Ruth as closely as I watched her with him . . . looking for the signs.

'Was there anything ever between you and The Church?'

She had shaken her head. 'No, never anything between us at all.' A sudden flush upon her cheeks. She was lying. If there was nothing between them at the time she first came to London, then there had been at some time. Around old loves and lovers there is always . . . something – like pollen in the air, unseen, but one will sneeze from its presence.

Now, she half-turned on her side, away from him. He rested his hand lightly upon her hip. It was Sunday, they might stay like this all day if they chose.

Netty and Jo had walked casually in that first time. We were lying together like this . . .

''Od rabbit, Nett! Cast down thine eyes, there's big snoozles going on in Foxy's bed.'

He smiled at the memory of their audaciousness. *It will be good to see them again.*

They had taken their graceful sauciness to some of the large cities of the Midlands, but London was where their talents were most appreciated and Bounderby's in particular.

Ruth's eyelids twitched as she began to wake up.

He leaned over and kissed her, deep in the hollow of her shoulder which he knew caused her to be most defenceless. 'Let us be married, Ruth.' Although she was the first woman he had ever asked that question, it was not the first time he had asked it of Ruth.

Eyes still closed. 'Hush, Teddy . . . don't spoil it.' Whispered.

7

EVENTS AND ACTS

JO AND NETTY had been engaged for a long season at
Bounderby's. There was to be a gala opening evening when
no diner who wanted a place in the main hall would be
admitted unless in fancy costume and wearing a domino.
This, having regard for the ladies who were for the first time
to gain admission to the main hall. Bounderby's had become
such a fashionable place for young society life in London,
that on most evenings the balcony tables were reserved days
ahead.

Ruth had invited them to use her house for a few days
whilst they were rehearsing for the gala night.

'Foxy, dear Foxy!'

They smothered her with kisses. 'I *say*, Nett, just look at
the girl – who'd ever say she was the country maiden now?'

'Is she still snoozling with Teddy?'

'Faith! Nett, do ye not see the colleen's bright and
smiling eye?'

'Oh look, Jo-Jo, an entirely *won-n-derful* Jennens &
Bettridge like the one we said we should have.' She draped
herself in the hollow of the buttoned-velvet shell of an
armchair Ruth had recently installed in her pretty parlour.

Jo flicked the garnet-and-diamond pendant. 'Oh law,
Foxy's getting rich.'

Ruth stood in the midst of their swooping and wooshing
nonsense, holding their Indian silk shawls, and smiling with
great pleasure at the return of her two friends.

A letter from Lidia Toose to Ruth

My Dearest Child,

Your father is dead. I am sorry, but I have been all morning trying to think of a gentler way of breaking this news to you.

Can you understand, dear Ruth, what misery it is to me to find myself in a world where there is no Adam Tylee? Our love was born out of revolt and turbulence, and vengeful reprisal, yet you live because he and I were alive with the spirit of those times. On the day before he died, he said 'The only worthwhile thing to have come out of those times has been the children. Perhaps, in the end, they will prove it to have been all worthwhile.'

He seemed so spirited that I believed the crisis to have passed. 'When you write, Lidi, tell them all to become rich – poor people in revolt cannot make changes.'

You will be pleased to know that he has not been buried amongst the banished murderers and thieves, but on our own land.

Please go to Selena, she will be grievously hurt to hear of Adam's death.

Your affectionate mother,
Lidia Toose

This letter, in spite of having arrived in England weeks ago, had not reached Ruth.

The first delay was when it gathered dust at Mrs Cox's before being put into the hands of Ruth's young serving girl. The letter, together with two others from Cantle, lay unopened, caught up in a bundle of papers that had been pushed into a drawer by Ruth's servant.

Of course, they could not possibly have known this at

Croud Cantle Farm. They had received one of Ruth's short, hastily written letters, enclosing a money draft for the repair of the roof, but she had made no mention of what Auryn had written and, when the news of their father's death came, they still heard nothing from her.

Now, Auryn was preparing to go to London.

'I wish you would let me go with you, Aury.'

'Best not, Carly. If there's anything amiss . . .'

'Goodness, lad,' Selena said, 'you're a real old goody when it come to worriment.'

'Not a question of worriment, Auntie. It's weeks since we heard, I might have to go looking . . .'

'Of course you won't have to go looking.' Caroline was scornful. 'If you had come with me and Susanna, you would have seen how different everything is for somebody like Rosalie. She don't have evenings to sit at home writing.'

'I don't either . . . and for Christ's sake, Carly, stop calling her by that stupid name.'

'And you had better stop behaving like a bull with a sore head trying to gore every word anybody says.'

'Now come on, both of you. Carly, let Auryn get on with it. He can ask Ruth if you can visit her now that she's settled in a place of her own.'

'Can you imagine, Auntie Sel – our Ruthie renting her own place and a servant?'

'And can you imagine what Ma would think about that,' Auryn said.

'Ma wouldn't think anything except that you never wanted Ruth to go in the first place and you've been picking holes in her ever since.'

'You are such a child still, Caroline,' Auryn said, pulling the straps on his overnight pack tighter than necessary.

But a child Caroline Tylee was not. At eighteen she was womanly, and as round-hipped and full-bosomed as she would ever be, and she had inherited the height of her

father's family, some of whom were renowned for their tall
stature. Large mouth and eyes, broad jaw with uneven but
strong teeth, high fine cheekbones, and a straight, bony
brow. Taken individually, none of her features were as
beautiful as Ruth's. Yet there was a striking symmetry and
positiveness about her face that added up to more than
beauty; it was a face that always drew a second look.

It was unlikely that Caroline Tylee would ever go about
the world unnoticed.

'Now come along, Auryn, be off, railway trains aren't
like wagons, they won't stop if you wave them down.'
Although Selena had never been a single mile on the railway,
she was good at giving travel instructions to others. In the
eight or so years since Lidia had left the children in Selena's
care she had grown more easy in her mind than in all the
years since her brother's sentence to be hanged. It was the
presence of Carly and Auryn that had enabled her to deal
with her grief at the news of his death.

At fifty, she was grey-haired and lined. She wanted
nothing more of life now than to live to see 'her' children
with children of their own. But with children such as they
were, having been given so much freedom and independence
from an early age, and having the legacy of such a strange
upbringing in the penal settlement, Selena did not count on
the fulfilment of her dream of babies on the hearth at Croud
Cantle Farm.

Auryn was as edgy as he was unsettled, and Selena
suspected that he would probably not stay much longer in
England. And Caroline had inherited so much of the
characteristics of Lidi and Adam that Selena was sure that,
before very long, she would find some outlet for her
growing sense of conscience. What it might be, Selena could
not imagine, but she had the impression that Caroline was
marking time, looking for a cause into which she might fling
herself. A practical cause – Caroline liked to see the results of

her efforts. Selena's causes – theoretical Socialism, Chartism and the like – were too philosophical for Caroline, and in any case they were the causes of the past generation. For a time, Caroline joined the Methodists, but found them too self-satisfied and sure of themselves. In the meantime, she read everything that came her way.

Selena and Caroline went out into the yard to watch Auryn climb the path over Tradden Raike towards the main road.

He waved to the two tall women in their coarse skirts, working aprons and dairy caps, leaning against the house wall. He strode out, puffing out the steam of his breath as he took the slope over the downs. Far below he heard the chink of traces and the 'whey-y-up!' calls as a ploughman across the valley changed the heavy brown tweed of the winter fields into terracotta-red corduroy. The sun was barely up but, in every knot of bramble, birds were building and setting. He sniffed the damp greenness of Hampshire air. Rotting leaves. Moss. Dampness. Fern. Moss and decay. Suddenly he longed to breathe the air of Toolagarry. Dead-bone dry, or humid. Spicy, medicinal air that could sting your eyes. Clumps of primroses were in bloom; he liked those little flowers, stuck one in his button-hole and remembered the flowers that grew at the fringe of the brush that the settlers called 'primroses'. Toolagarry. Ma was now without a man about the place except for young Barney.

Everything that grew here was predictable. People in this village could go on a certain morning to a certain place and know for sure that they would find mushrooms; another morning they would know for sure that the daffodils had come out or the elderberries would fill and ripen. Nothing in Toolagarry was predictable. By the afternoon he would be in London. His thoughts drifted beyond London, beyond Plymouth, the Azores, the Cape. In only months he could be in Toolagarry.

As he went over the chalkhills, his heart lightened with the combined thoughts of Toolagarry and of seeing Ruth. He was determined to try to see her as Carly did. If she had chosen to do anything but to flaunt herself in public, he would never have forbidden her. If he hadn't always felt less able than her. If she had been willing to consult him instead of laying down the law and just going off as she did . . . then there might not have been the quarrel . . . then they might not each have hurt the other so badly. Carly said it was all respectable and dignified and all that he was objecting to was simply innocent pleasure. He would try to look upon what Ruth did in a different light. It would not be easy. He had set her above ordinary women. He had been angry and hurt for a long time.

Caroline and Selena waved back as he reached the place on Tradden where he would disappear from sight.

'I know Aury's an old fussbugger, Auntie, but you've got to admit that it's queer that we haven't heard from Ruth.'

'People do grow away, Carly. You've got to be prepared for that. I've grown away from my family. It's years since I heard much of any of them, nor them of me – except Adam.'

'That's because people let it happen. I shan't. I shall be like Ma – even if I'm a thousand miles away, I shall let everyone know.' They walked across the yard together.

'Look, Auntie Sel, the white violets are out.'

'Twenty-fifth of March, like clockwork.'

In the dim milking shed, Selena sat with her cheek pressed against the cow's red flank and began the rhythmic chup-chup-chup into the pail. Caroline usually did the scouring work later in the day, but today felt the need to stay with her aunt for a bit longer. The news of Pa's death had come as a shock to them all, but it was as though her aunt had so often prepared herself for it that in the event it was not as hard for her as they had all thought.

When she had read her sister-in-law's letter, Selena had

let out a deep sigh and said, 'It's over at last' as though she had been sitting at the bedside of someone dying. They had sat and wept together, Auryn had poured them each some brandy cup and had blown his nose a few times, and remained masculinely dry-eyed.

Auryn did not reach London in the afternoon as he had intended; he had missed one train and the second had been shunted around because of a breakdown. It was evening when he went in search of Ruth's house, and dark when he found it.

A small house by the standards of the area, one of a long row built in pairs. The low-silled front window jutted out level with a porch entrance up two stone steps. It was very much like a long row of similar houses recently built in Blackbrook. Jack and Ginny had rented one, which everyone thought very smart and modern.

He lifted the shiny brass wreath and knocked. Light footsteps trotted along the passage, and the door was opened, not by Ruth as he had expected, but by a girl of about sixteen, pert, and cheeky-looking, dressed in a dark frock and white cap. After some questioning on both sides, it was established that this was Miss Ruth Tylee's home.

'Madam's gawn to the theatre. She's always gawn by this time.'

'I shall have to go there. Can I leave my bag?'

'Is Madam expecting you, Sir?'

'Madam is my sister. What's your name?'

'Kaff, Sir.'

'Well, Kath, I have written to her twice and there hasn't been any reply. I've got to see her tonight because I've got to get the first train out in the morning.'

She gave him a look as though that was of no interest to her.

'Tell me, if letters had been sent to her old address, would they have been sent round here?'

The girl was about to say something, when she stopped and a deep flush spread over her face, as she remembered the occasion. Mrs Cox's son, in his striped waistcoat, his hat over one eye. He had given her some letters with one hand, and had . . . 'They might be. They might. I don't know.'

Something about the letters. That was obvious to Auryn. The girl had done something. 'Look. Will you let me leave my bag? Tell me which way to get to the theatre, and I will come back for it later.'

'Lawk, Sir, they won't let you in dressed like that.'

'Like what?'

'Full eve'nin' dress tonight, Sir. Gala night. Special.'

'Perhaps if I ask the owner . . . I have met him.'

'They wouldn't even fetch him out front lest you got something to say who you are. Haven't you got no ticket, Sir . . . to get in?'

'I haven't.'

'Tell you what, Sir, you try going to the stage door. Tell the man there who you are. He's me uncle. It was him that got me this place with Madam. Mind you, he just as like won't take no notice . . . well, that's his job, ain't it, keeping people out of the place.'

Having got over whatever it was that had gone amiss about the letters, in a flood of chatter and eagerness to be helpful, the girl gave him directions to Bounderby's.

The idea that this was night-time struck Auryn as very strange as he made his way through the busy streets, where there seemed to be a night-watchman guarding open road-works and piles of pipes and bricks at every turn. The roads thronged with long omnibuses full of passengers, while hackney cabs and shiny crested coaches passed one another's wheels within an inch and tried to out-do one another for a gap in the traffic.

Where are they all going? When do they sleep? An upside-down existence, where girls like Ruth went to their work at a time when the people in Cantle would be douting their fires for the night.

He found Bounderby's, recognizing it at a distance from his visit seven years ago. The place looked even bigger than he remembered it. The front was ablaze with light, and from the corner where he stood gazing at the façade, he saw an enormous head-and-shoulders painting of Ruth.

He flushed like a girl. Why, he did not know. Probably the surprise of seeing his sister larger than life-size, her hand dramatically clutching her breast, smiling at the distant sky with so many white teeth and such abundant golden curls. A vast banner read: 'ROSALIE – QUEEN OF BOUNDERBY'S', across which was the announcement: 'THE GALA NIGHT'.

Well. He had come to find the reason why his sister was so silent about Pa's death, concerned for her welfare, and found her to be the smiling 'Queen of the Gala Night'. He had thought it all to be Carly's vivid imagination and boastful pride. It had been fact. On the way here, he had passed probably eight or nine theatres and supper rooms, each with an announcement of the performers – there had been none so spectacular and so thronging with exotic people as this.

He did not know what to do. Slowly, he walked up and down the street. Several street-sellers thrust coloured pictures in front of his face, offering 'Coloured Rosalies – three poses, all different'. He bought the three. Ruth in a golden wig, shoulders bare to the furrow between her breasts, standing in a bower of roses. Ruth with golden head bowed, jewels hanging from her ears. Ruth, arms held wide, head back in the act of singing, the fingers of one hand entwined in a filmy shawl and a long rope of pearls. He stood staring down at them for some time before he realized that the breathing behind his shoulder was that of someone else looking. 'Gawd, if she don't just stun a bloke. I'd give me left leg to be in there tonight.'

Auryn stuffed the pictures in his pocket and without replying crossed the street. The girl Kath had explained about going up the next side street and along the alley to get to where her uncle guarded the back entrance. He found it without difficulty, but the doorkeeper would have no truck with a broad-speaking bumpkin who could think of nothing cleverer than to say that he was Miss Rosalie's – *brother*?

'I must see her.'

'You and a dozen others. Miss Rosalie don't see nobody.'

'Then tell her that Auryn is here.'

The man peered dubiously over his stable-type door.

'Well then, fetch Mr Warren – he knows me. I've been to his house.'

'Oh, then tell me where he lives.'

'I don't know the name . . .' Without thinking twice, he rushed by the old man and into the building before he could get out of his lair.

The behind-the-scenes employees were used to young men who wagered one another on access backstage of various theatres. Auryn was soon marched off to Edward Warren's office, which suited him very well.

'Faith! My dear fellow,' he said, offering his hand by way of apology. 'Ruth's brother. You are the last person to need to break in to Bounderby's.'

'It must be easier to get into the Queen's palace.'

'You must blame your sister for that, young men wager one another to find her apartment, legend has it that she never leaves the building.'

After hearing why Auryn had come so unexpectedly to London, Edward Warren said, 'I am very sorry to hear such unhappy news. And as to Ruth, I assure you she knows nothing of your father's death. Only yesterday she was berating herself for having left it so long since her last letter to her mother and father, and we had talked about her visiting Cantle for a few days. But listen, my dear fellow, you must excuse me if I appear less than hospitable. You may have gathered that this is a special night.'

'Well . . . a gala? Whatever that is.'

'It is a kind of re-opening of Bounderby's. The hall has been newly decorated with due consideration of the future presence of the ladies. There is a wide, new stage. From tonight Bounderby's is changed from supper-rooms-with-entertainment to entertainment-hall-with-good-food. The acts will be all new – never done in this country before tonight. Ruth has a most wonderful appearance, a real spectacle.'

'You surely won't ask Ruth to do that once she knows about Pa?'

'Lord alive! She must not know, it would throw her out entirely.'

'Of course she must. I must see her as soon as possible. We have not heard from her in weeks. I came here to see if she was well and . . . and . . . well to talk to her about family matters. And for goodness' sake – her Pa's dead! You can't expect her to go singing and smiling in front of people when her Pa's dead.'

For a moment Edward Warren had a vision of disaster because of a possessive and doltish brother.

'Oh, but she can and she will. Performers never let their private lives intrude upon their professional. There are people out there tonight who have come to see your sister. They may have grief of their own, or be at death's door within the week, but for an hour or two it will be Ruth's responsibility, and ours – Bounderby's – to alleviate their unhappiness, give them happy memories. They have paid a great deal of money and will expect to get what they have paid for. Which at Bounderby's means, Rosalie and excellent food.'

If necessary, the older man thought, he would have him

arrested as an intruder or locked away by his own men. But that was to use a sledgehammer to crack a cob . . . the man was handleable, treated in the right way.

'What about Ruth's sorrow to discover afterwards that she has been singing like a lark when she should have been crying?'

'Why should she cry?'

'Why should she *cry*! For her father's death.'

'But until you tell her, she does not know. Auryn, when did your father die?'

Auryn looked grimly at Edward Warren, his view of him as a genial and kindly man was quickly changing.

'February-time.'

'Last year?'

'Well, for sure not this.'

'So, my dear fellow, an evening more will make little difference.'

Auryn looked sullen. He kept telling himself that he was the equal of Edward Warren, there was no reason to defer to him – yet the difference in their dress, the condition of their hands, and the broadness of the one accent and the narrowness of the other, announced labourer and gentleman.

Of habit in the presence of a gentleman, Auryn allowed himself to be treated as of lower status. Of habit, he resented the gentleman-like presumption. He further allowed himself politely to accept a private apartment on the balcony where, it was agreed, he could dine on saddle of mutton baked rare on a bed of rosemary and served with jellied mint and a dish of roasted potatoes or, if preferred, chops and 'jackets'.

'Guest of Bounderby's, my dear fellow. The waiting will be worth it. I guarantee that you will never be sorry that you had just a bit more patience before breaking such bad news.' He lowered his voice and leaned confidentially towards

Auryn. 'I wouldn't dare tell your sister, and not more than half a dozen people know it ... but a vastly wealthy American theatre manager and the heir to one of the oldest thrones in Europe will be in the other private apartments tonight. They have come expressly to see Rosalie. How could we do anything that might spoil her greatest night? From here on she could well receive offers to travel the world.

'Of course, she will not know who it is watching from those boxes, any more than she will that it is you watching from another.' He laughed, ushering Auryn out of the room. 'She would be so nervous, we should have to put a bag on her head to get her onto the stage.'

Not knowing at all the significance of this last remark, Auryn followed silently.

'I promise you, dear fellow, the very second the curtain comes down, I shall tell Ruth that you are here.'

8

GALA NIGHT AT BOUNDERBY'S

FOR DRESSING AND PAINTING their faces, all of the
performers shared two cramped areas, which were called
dressing-rooms for all that there was little space for dressing
and that they were not rooms. Women together, separated
from the men by a partition. In the women's dressing-room
there was a long mirror and a wide mirror, around which
dancers, acrobats, reciters, magician's assistants came to
some sort of acrimonious agreement as to priority of the
moment.

Netty and Jo, needing space for their dresser to coat
them with their chalk-like paint, and to be close to the stage
so as not to spoil it once ready, always had a separate
curtained-off place of their own lit by a naphtha lamp.

Ruth's new act was another one of Teddy's transformation fantasies, and was to be the greatest spectacle he had yet
conceived. In it, in the few seconds it took for her to walk
behind a cardboard tree, the entire scene would change from
winter to summer and Ruth from rags to riches. It was the
last act of the evening, when it was expected that people
would go home from Bounderby's taking that wonderful
image alight in their minds.

The other high point was Netty and Jo's tableau. It would
come earlier and would be a revelation rather than a transformation. Both of these acts were shrouded in secrecy and,
except for the performers themselves, the details were supposed to be known only to their dressers, people immediately
involved in the workings of various devices. Inevitably,
enough details had leaked out to have made expectation crackle
around the supper halls like a dry electric storm.

Backstage seemed chaotic to anyone not knowing what was going on. Although they had rehearsed over and over, and it was ages before her own performance, Ruth kept going back, and back again, to see that her costume and new wig were in place and hanging correctly for the quick change right at the end of her performance.

It was some while before Netty and Jo's tableau, but their making-up was long and complicated; they would already be standing, legs straddled, on their wheeled pedestals with their arms resting in slings whilst two chattering dressers painted them.

Ruth's own make-up was complete – she was always less nervous if she got into costume early in the evening, so she was already dressed in her 'rags' dress and bedraggled golden wig, ready to go on. The opening music had finished, now there were spurts of music and rolling of drums followed by applause, and from the side she watched for a few minutes as the dancers, who interspersed each act, did a kind of marching dance dressed in red and black costumes and little military caps.

Once she was in costume and hiding behind her make-up, Ruth loved this part – the excitement, the anticipation – and would wander about talking to anybody and everybody. Because she was genuinely interested in how everything worked, she had gained an exceptional amount of knowledge about the workings of a theatre from scenery-making to the fixing of spangles.

Tonight it was more thrilling than usual, and there was the added pleasure of Netty and Jo being back. There was to be an on-stage party afterwards for all the artists, and a pie supper for the 'hands' in the kitchens. In contrast to other music-hall directors, who were tight-fisted employers, much of Edward Warren's success came from his treatment of the people who worked for him. He knew from his own experience as a humble young clerk that employees will love, and work harder for, the employer who is generous enough to provide a bit of fun.

Ruth had not seen him all evening, which was not unusual as she knew that he always spent the first part of the evening welcoming some of the patrons as genially as though they had been guests taking supper at his own house. She had just decided to go and sit and watch Netty and Jo being made up, when suddenly there was a shout followed by a piercing scream, a moment of silence, then a muffled hubbub. Ruth ran to Netty and Jo's corner from where the scream had come.

Netty, her top half beautifully painted, lay bleeding profusely from a huge gash in her thigh. On the floor, pieces of a shattered mirror. Jo and the two women were putting her face-down on a blanket. 'The wheels went. The wheels went. I couldn't stop her.'

'Go out front and ask for a doctor,' Ruth ordered one of the dressers. 'Quickly. Quickly, Mildred, and stop wasting time. Tell Harry to stop the show and ask for help.'

'I can't do that, Miss.'

'Oh Lord, Mildred! If you don't I'll do it myself. Jo, you must hold the cut together and press it. The rest of you get out! This isn't part of the show. Somebody go and find Mr Teddy.'

The stopping of the show and request for help revealed the great number of doctors who apparently patronized Bounderby's. In minutes, a distinguished elderly gentleman identified himself as 'a senior surgeon at Saint Bart's' and had come backstage. After he had staunched the bleeding and bound the wound, he whisked his exotic and lovely patient into a cab where she lay limply across the knees of two women whilst he held the wound tight with his own hands.

Frantic, Jo had been forbidden by the genial old man to go with Netty.

'They can make do with one statue, but not without any

statue at all.' He had taken the opportunity of giving the undamaged statue an encouraging, avuncular pat, and said that he hoped that he would be back in time to see the finale and expected a special seat when the statues were back together again.

Whether or not his kindly speed in an emergency meant that he was a good surgeon, those left behind were certainly stunned by it. The two dressers tried to relate what had happened when the wheels which were attached to the plinth, and which were supposed to have been locked, moved causing Netty to crash backwards into the mirror, all the while attending to the distraught Jo. Mildred flashed ammoniac salts under Jo's nose, while the other dresser gave her a swig from the flask of gin she discovered deep in a pocket of her skirt. Revived, Jo began trying to assemble her thoughts on how she could salvage their act. The idea upon which it was based was really not much different from their earlier ones, it was the staging of it that made it what it was.

It was a depiction of carved American Indian totems, around which the dancers created a tableau where they prayed for rain. Then the carved figures would be symbolically transported from the sunny plains of North America to English shores to be presented to the Queen Empress, where the rain-god totems decide to answer the prayers.

Edward Warren had been found, and came backstage. 'Damn, damn and curse it! If that's not a joker in the pack, after I've done my damnedest to see that there are none.'

'Foxy will do it, won't you, Foxy dear?' Jo came and took Ruth's hand.

'Do . . . ? Oh no, I couldn't . . . I couldn't.'

Edward Warren stopped his agitated movements. 'Of course. You know the moves as well as Netty.'

'Teddy! I could never go on stage naked.'

'Oh, Foxy, no one would know it was you. It could be anyone under the paint.'

'You know that I could never stand still. In any case, I should *breathe*.'

'Rubbish, Ruth,' Edward Warren said. 'If you have learned one thing from Gustav, then it is breath control.'

'But the finale – everyone would see me.' She looked horrified at the prospect.

'You could face a little more up-stage, Foxy dear. And in any case, the wig – and the head-dress. Even Teddy would never know you.'

Ruth looked from one to the other. She knew that she was capable of taking Netty's place – but not before the public. Yet she knew that she could do no other than help these two and Netty – people who loved her.

'If I do it, Teddy, then promise me that you will bring down the curtain before anyone can see that it is me and not Netty.'

'Of course. I promise. In fact I will stand with the stage hands myself, to see to the exact second that you are not revealed.'

There was little time to spare as the body painting was more complicated than when the act was based upon the marble statues. Edward Warren helped the dresser by applying the ochre body paint, whilst she applied the pattern of vivid colour. Ruth could see only the top half of her body in the broken mirror, but was fascinated as she saw her own character submerge beneath the mask of paint.

As the totem image grew, so Ruth became silent and withdrawn. The drying paint was irritating, but she turned her mind from it. Gustav came in and instructed her on the minimal and shallow breathing that was necessary to achieve the stillness.

'Wonderful, wonderful. Don't blink! Good. No, don't blink so quickly. Good, keep the breath only at the top of the lung.' If anything gave Ruth assurance that she could go through with it, it was Gustav's same high, excitable voice with which he had eased Rosalie from the shell of Ruth.

She controlled the breathing and blinking, then concentrated upon Netty, trying to pull Netty's character around her. If she could hold on to it, then she felt that she might not fail.

Suddenly the call: 'Indians. Indians. Ten minutes.' Then, immediately, as it seemed, the wooden plinths in which their feet were enclosed ankle-deep were being rolled on stage. The drummer began beating the introduction and the curtains opened, whereupon the sudden revelation of vivid colour and great activity stopped the diners in their eating tracks, and brought loud cheers and applause from them.

It was that sound, coming up over the row of flaring lamps, that daily brought Ruth through her fears and out on to the platform night after night as Rosalie. A tremor went through her – *standing naked before a thousand people* – but she held herself in such control that it did not manifest itself physically.

Ruth concentrated on being Netty and imagining being encased in wood. She stared ahead and discovered that the stage hand had, in turning her towards the wings, put her immediately facing the private apartments of the first-floor dining balcony. The glare of the bright gas-lamps at the foot of the stage made it virtually impossible to see anything beyond, but from deep within the first apartment, her eye was continually caught by a gleam. So to take her mind from thinking of the eyes that she knew were watching her naked body, she concentrated upon watching the gleam.

The first dance on the sunny plains ended without anything untoward happening, she had blinked only twice and her breathing was done without movement. Her confidence grew. She was Netty. Not Ruth who, without the protection of costume and the person of Rosalie, went rigid with fright at the thought of the audience. She was Netty, who could unflinchingly appear naked before hundreds of men, yet who would 'spit in the eye' of any one of them who tried to lay hands upon her. She felt Netty's contempt for them.

Suddenly the plinth was being moved up-stage, closer to the lights. In the movement she could see for a moment into the little dark dining apartment and saw that the gleam came from opera glasses.

Her curiosity was mildly roused. The two apartments, one on either side of the stage, were always kept available for any extremely wealthy or blue-blooded visitor who expected to be welcomed anywhere at a moment's notice. It was always interesting to the performers if there should be an occupant.

The tableau reached the shores of England. Red, white and blue streamed across the scene, Union Jacks were lowered. The audience was delighted. Ruth held herself rigid and tried to look into the wings to see if Teddy was there to keep his promise that the curtain would be lowered quickly at the end. This was the test of her professionalism. It was also a test of Teddy. He had made her a promise.

The two statues were moved centre stage, ready for the presentation to the figure of Britannia. One almost felt the audience crackling with anticipation. The finale of any performance of Annette & Josephine was famous for the unexpected. Often it took the form of an outrageous joke at their own expense. There were other acts in which girls were seen in various states of undress, but these were mostly tasteless and unpleasantly sensational and seen only in low taverns. There was a kind of convention about Annette & Josephine that nothing they did in their act was unacceptable, because their skin was never seen in its natural state.

Then the rain began to fall.

At first the audience did not realize what was happening.

Then the dancers and chorus unfurled umbrellas. Some of the dancers fell onto their knees before the rain-god totems. Then, as the 'rain' became heavier, laughter broke out in the audience. Slowly, the paint on the totems began to dissolve. The laughter grew. The paint merged and began to run, to the accompaniment of loud cheering and the traditional hammering of spoons on the tables as an accolade for an appreciated performance.

This was the crucial point of the act. It was necessary to keep the rain falling to start the paint running, but to allow the curtain to swing over the scene before very much pink flesh could be seen.

Whatever act Teddy allowed to go on stage at Bounderby's, he would see that it was taken as far as he could possibly make it go, pushing the boundaries of each act to hold the anticipation of the audience. It was a kind of tussle between himself and the habitués of Bounderby's.

She trusted him. He would never overstep his own rules of propriety. Although those rules would be frowned upon in provincial places such as Blackbrook's stuffy Assembly Hall, in the sophisticated world of the London supper rooms and music-halls, they were seen as most decorous and rigid. He *would* drop the curtain as he promised. The reputation he most cherished of his establishment was its respectability. Tonight there were ladies sitting with gentlemen. He would surely drop the curtain as he had said.

The rain continued, she watched the paint of the unflinching Jo totem, trickle down into the base of the plinth. Teddy had said that he would lower the curtain five seconds sooner than had been allowed in the timing worked out with Netty and Jo.

Panic rose within her as she clearly saw a patch of Jo's unadorned shoulder appear through the paint. She pushed down the panic, staying rigid as the applause rose like a tide. The area of visible flesh grew. She fought the urge to look down at herself. Rosalie would be destroyed if it were ever revealed that she had appeared naked. The curtain mechanism wasn't working! The rain wouldn't stop! She must jump down and run.

Then, a whoosh and a clatter. The curtain was down and the dressers ran on with brightly coloured wraps. She leapt down from the plinth. Jo hugged her. 'Sweet Foxy, you were won-n-derful! Poor Nett would be quite jealous if she knew.'

'Why didn't the curtain fall?'

The curtain swept back again and they both bowed low.

Teddy was waiting also to tell her that she was won-n-derful!

'Why didn't the curtain fall, Teddy? You promised.'

He raised his eyebrows at Gustav who had come to say that she had been as won-n-derful! as he had said that she would be. 'Dear girl, it went down two seconds earlier than Mr Teddy promised.'

'It seemed much over. I was in such panic.'

'But you did not flinch, Miss Ruth, your apprenticeship has finished. You are entirely the professional performer.'

Hot water was waiting, the dressers soaped and rinsed the two girls, and with scarcely a pause for breath, Ruth had changed back into the rags of her Rosalie costume.

In the apartment of the gleaming opera glasses, a man with bright blue eyes, narrow autocratic nose and tightly curling brown hair, still leaned forward in the direction of the stage. Whilst he was not conventionally handsome, the sad downward line of his eyebrows conflicting with the amused upward turn of his mouth, his was the kind of attractiveness that always drew eyes to him.

'Ah!' he said, and sat back in his chair.

'Well, Alex? Aren't they just as I said?' An older man.

'Yeah. It's good entertainment.'

'Wait till you see the finale.'

'You reckon it's better?' He pronounced it 'beddah'.

'High class, nothing like it in America.' He kissed the tips of his fingers effusively. 'I'll wager you've seen nothing like her.'

'Dollah if she's better than Adah.'

'Sovereign. Your Mr Irving might say the dollar is "almighty", but I'll wager gold on our Rosalie against your Adah.'

The young man laughed and nodded. 'You Europeans are all the same.' He rubbed his hands in a gesture of anticipation. 'Very well – a sovereign, and I'll be glad to pay up.'

In the next apartment, Auryn too was still sitting in much the same position as he had been in when the curtain had fallen. It was his first encounter with any kind of evening entertainment beyond Christmas mummers, barn dances and travelling showmen.

He sat ill at ease. In confusion as much from finding himself in such a fantasy world, as from the spectacle he had just witnessed. He wanted to run away and yet to see it all again. His unease was exacerbated by knowing that he could not run away – the place was vast and he had been led to this little screened box through a labyrinth of passages. He would only make a fool of himself. He imagined losing his way and suddenly finding himself on the platform in the glare of the lamps, and grew hot at the thought of the two women who had proved to have been entirely naked under the decoration.

From below came the roar of people talking and the clatter of drinking glasses and plates. Disturbingly, he wished that he was like them, not in his present bewildered state but as they were, familiar with the place, knowing what to expect next, able to enjoy the spectacle. His own table was littered with the debris of the meal of chops and floury potatoes brought to him by a polite waiter who kept coming back to ask, 'A bit more, sir? Another chop, sir?' and refilling his glass with the sharp, fizzing wine that tasted like a mixture of elderflower and apple.

His mind went back again and again to the act that had just finished, excitement rising again at the memory of the sudden revelation of the statues as living women. Right up to the last seconds before the curtain had come down, he had not realized that these were real women.

His own arousal and the shamelessness of the performance caused him to blush in the semi-darkness as he relived the moment when the paint of the statue with its back to him had been washed clean, revealing a patch of the pink skin on her buttock. How could they? To stand before a crowd of onlookers as naked as the primitive blacks who used sometimes to wander into Toolagarry.

He felt excited at the cleverness, yet tricked by it. It made him feel foolish that he was not in the secret that, as he now realized, the thousand people in the hall were in on – they had known that those were not statues and had expected some sort of surprise.

In his introspection, he had sat through a series of acts and performances and it was not until a hush came over the hall as the Chairman's voice penetrated that he once more became aware of his surroundings.

Suddenly Ruth was there below in the glare of the lamps. He automatically drew himself back into the deepest shadow.

Ruth, dressed in a kind of representation of the clothes that she had worn every day of her working life on the farm, moved about the stage pretending to pick up sticks, then she sank down with feigned tiredness and began to sing. There was absolute silence in the hall. The voice that came from the woman on the stage was nothing like Ruth's. She had always had a pretty voice, right from when they were little, but this voice . . . It was deep and gentle, it made the hairs on the skin rise as she sang a tragic song about hungry children, and empty hearths, and death. Auryn felt the grief of the woman singing. A lump was in his throat. He swallowed and found tears blurring his vision.

He sat enthralled as her series of songs led to her dying in the dark wood, the lights getting dimmer as her life ebbed. For a few seconds the music stopped and the stage was in darkness. A fanfare, and the stage was suddenly ablaze with glittering light. The dark leafless trees that he had scarcely noticed till now were somehow turned on a pivot to reveal masses of white blossom; there was birdsong and a fountain of real water; flowers appeared in profusion everywhere and a flight of doves rose. Then, from behind a tree, Ruth stepped, entirely transformed. She shone from the top of her golden curls to her glittering slippers. Her bodice seemed made of thousands of jewels and her skirt glittered as she moved. She came right down the row of lamps. Over her arm she carried a basket of flowers.

Although the orchestra was playing, it was impossible to hear the music for the cheering and applause. He had thought the painted women had raised a tumult, but that was nothing compared to what greeted his sister when she took the first flower from her basket and cast it out to the crowd where men scrambled for it.

In the neighbouring apartment, the older man held out his hand and clenched in a triumphant fist the gold coin the younger man flicked into it.

As they left, the younger of the two, an American from his accent, shook his head and, smiling, pursed his lips. 'You know somethin', Forbes . . . I reckon Ed Warren is about to lose the most sensational performer I've seen in a long, long time.'

The voices carried to Auryn who sat staring at the spot where Ruth had taken her final bow. The waiter entered.

'Well, Sir? Ain't Miss Rosalie the marvel?'

Auryn turned slightly in the waiter's direction.

'Who else could a done what she done tonight? Get you anything else, sir?' He refilled Auryn's glass, wanting to gossip on about the back-stage excitement. 'There she was as pretty pure as a golden angel, throwing flowers at the beaux and none of them knowing it was her bit of bare they caught a glimpse of when the paint started to run. She's a rare one is our Miss Rosalie, sends the beaux wild. But they reckon you should a seen her when she found Miss Netty.' He wagged his head in admiration. 'If the front-row brandy-faces had half an inkling it was Miss Rosalie doing the statues tonight, they'd a invaded the stage.'

Suddenly the door to the compartment opened a couple of inches. 'Parker, pull the curtains round.'

The waiter jumped to it. 'Yes, Miss. There y'are, Miss. There, Sir, it's quite private for you now. I shan't let anybody in. Just press the bell if you want . . .'

'Parker! Go.' It was Ruth.

As he heard her voice, all of his flooding streams of emotions drained into one pit – Ruth.

The rancour that had stuck in his chest, like a kernel swallowed whole, ever since she left home, began to swell. No wonder she did not write home . . . how could she find anything to tell them? No wonder she sent money.

Parker flung the door open and held it for Ruth, enveloped in a hooded woollen cloak, to enter. She came in quickly, threw off her cloak and sat down opposite. Leaning to be close to Auryn, she took both his hands, grasping them with great emotion. 'Oh, Aury. How dreadful. Teddy told me as soon as I came off stage. It was wonderful of you to come to London to break it to me. I can't believe it's you. Aury, poor Ma. Poor Auntie Sel. How has Carly taken it? Oh Carly . . . she's so young still. I feel so overwhelmed that I can't even cry. Oh, but you're here. Aury, it is so marvellous to see you, but with such terrible news. I can scarcely *believe* that it's you.'

In great agitation, she held her brother's hands tightly as she caressed his knuckles.

The amount of wine that the waiter had poured, which Auryn had been drinking unthinkingly, added to the quick sequence of emotional blows he had received, caused him to look abstracted. He remained silent, frowning as though trying to remember something, as he sat, still and unmoving, his hands limp under her grasp.

'Aury?'

Slowly he withdrew his hands to his side of the table and held them fisted on the edge of the table.

It was only now that Ruth became conscious of his expression.

'When did you hear?'

When he at last spoke, his voice came out low and gruff. 'A few weeks . . .'

'A few *weeks*! Why didn't anyone tell me before this?'

'Because Ma wrote to you at the same time.'

'She didn't.'

'Oh?'

'No . . . well she may have written, but I didn't receive it – else I should have gone to Auntie Sel at once.'

'Would you?'

'What do you mean "Would you?" You know that I would have. Aury, what's wrong, why are you like this? Do you think I would not have come home if I had known that Pa . . . was . . . dead?' Suddenly the realization hit her like a physical blow. With tears in her eyes, she jumped to her feet, and with one hand covering her mouth and with the other held out to her brother she made a move towards him.

He leapt away as though he was thinking that she would attack him.

'Don't come near *me*!' He hardly raised his voice.

'Aury . . . I . . .'

'Don't!'

Alarmed now, and shocked by a terrible transmutation, she stepped back. 'Aury, what's wrong?'

'Wrong? "What's wrong, Aury?" Just what does that word mean to you? Do lewd bitches know about "wrong"?'

The two words spat through closed teeth struck her in the solar plexus and she sucked in a short gasp.

He backed away from her towards the door.

'It don't matter a witch's twat whether you got Ma's letter or no. Can't you just imagine how proud of you Pa would have been if he had seen you baring your arse for a hall full of debauched men . . .'

'Aury, no . . . ! It wasn't like . . .' She knew there was nothing at all that she could say.

He now seemed close to tears. 'I hope you are proud of yourself.'

He snatched up his coat and fumbled at the door latch.

'Don't, Aury . . . don't go. Please. I can't bear it if you go.' She was too bemused by the anguish that twisted his face and the viciousness of his attack.

'I can't bear being in the same room as you . . . nor even in the same country.'

In a second he was gone, leaving her rigid and unmoving, staring at the place where he had been.

A GREEN-PAINTED HUT

BEFORE RUTH LEFT for America she paid a last visit to the village in which she had been born. It was only then, when she was suddenly plunged into the stillness and quiet of Croud Cantle Farm, that she realized how easily she had convinced herself that she could go away with a clear conscience. The large sums of money that had been written into an agreement, and the assurance of her future as a professional singer, had overcome every doubt about leaving Caroline. She had told herself that, by going to Boston, she would be able to keep the farm going in bad times, and give Caroline any security she might need.

'You're only just starting your life, Carly, you don't have to stop here. You could do anything. I could help you in anything you want to do. Pa was right, people can't do anything without money.'

Caroline had smiled at her sister as though Ruth was the younger. 'I don't think Pa meant it like that.'

'Well, you seem so . . . out of things here. Just you and Auntie Sel.'

'I like it here, Ruthie. I love the farm, I love living close to the downs, I can't think of living anywhere but here.'

Ruth sensed a withholding.

'You shouldn't be shut away in this little place, you've grown so pretty.'

She was indeed pretty. In young womanhood, the childhood flame of Caroline Tylee's red hair had darkened deep and rich, its heavy fullness usually under control in a netted snood. Her eyes were wide-set and their serious expression was enhanced by thick, almost straight brows, but absolute seriousness was countered by the upward tilt of her nose and a mouth that smiled easily, revealing her strong ivory-coloured teeth. Taken all together, with her pink, freckled and weathered complexion, her appearance was that of beauty, robust and healthy.

When Ruth was dressed in her London style, it was difficult to tell who might be the taller, for Ruth wore heeled boots and, on the advice of Teddy, she always had her hair dressed high to show its colour, rather than in the fashionable low closely-sculpted style that followed the Queen. But walking shoulder to shoulder, as they were now, on Tradden Raike, it was clear that Caroline was the slightly taller of the two tall, red-headed sisters.

'And you haven't *seen* anywhere else. You haven't tried doing anything except growing vegetables and making stuff for market.'

'Ruthie, you are doing what you want, and I am doing what I want.'

But Ruth was not convinced. In her girlhood, she too had loved the chalk hills, had felt the spirits of her ancestors and had heard the voices of the downs. But that was before she had drunk from the sweet flagon of success and been intoxicated by the heady fumes of recognition and acknowledgement of her worth. That was before she had learned the art of pleasing and being pleased by a lover. That was before flowers had been strewn at her feet and men had called her name in the streets of London, before young girls had dreamed of becoming like her, before women had copied her style of dress.

If she could believe that Caroline was having some pleasure from life, then her own pleasure at the prospect of her new life would not be diminished. Auryn had already cast his blight upon her, she strongly needed not to feel badly about Caroline.

'You might think it is what you want . . .'

'It is what I want now. You may be right, Ruthie, perhaps there will come a time when I shall want other things, but here and now I don't want anything except what I've got.'

'But what have you got? Carly, I feel so guilty leaving you in this place now that Aury's gone back home.'

'Why should you feel guilty?'

For a moment Ruth's sophisticated assurance faltered as the memory of Auryn's unexpected appearance on that night a year ago momentarily broke from its bonds. She could never bring herself to talk to her young sister of the humiliation she had felt when she realized that whilst she had been concentrating upon the 'special' balcony booth, Auryn had been sitting in the next.

It was now spring, and they spontaneously halted at a point where the track flattened out and one could look down upon the Cantle Valley. Mid-morning and the sounds of rural England.

'There's a lot of rooks this year.'

'Auntie Sel says it's a good sign.'

Ruth smiled. 'Auntie Sel is getting a regular old goody these days.'

'She misses Pa really bad.'

'Lord above, Carly – it's thirty years since Pa was transported.'

'That's not the same as him dying. Don't you feel that too, Ruth? I do. It's like Aury – maybe I shan't ever see him again, but I don't feel that he's *gone*, not as if I knew he was dead.'

Ruth felt that too. Being dead meant that you could never make amends for what you had done to people. One day it would be all right again between her and Aury.

'What about Ma?' Ruth asked.

'If there's one thing I *should* like, it's to see her.'

'Perhaps later, when my money comes through, I could . . .'

'No, no, I don't mean that. I could never go back there. I doubt if any of you ever understood what it meant to me, coming here. It was the first time in my life that I ever had a moment's peace from my skin. It's that I have lost her face in my mind.'

'I remember her clearly. Lots of pictures in my mind . . . right back to the day when we sailed from Portsmouth when I was seven.'

They stood in the clear air of the downs, each young woman looking at the furtively nibbling ewes and giddy lambs, yet not seeing them. What Ruth saw was the ocean, less than a hundred miles away, that she would soon cross to her new life and to the acclaim that Alexander Marney promised her.

What Caroline saw was much closer; it was a hut that was being painted green by Isaac Evans and Peter Warren. She took a quick decision.

'Ruth, would you like to see what keeps me here?'

Ruth looked at her quizzically. 'Of course.'

'Don't ask me, then. Just come and see. How are you for walking these days?'

'I haven't lost the use of my legs entirely.'

Wrapping shawls tightly about them, they set off against the blusters of the high part of the downs.

Kitty Fire-Bucket thought that the changes that had taken place in her were because she had decided to be called Kitty Linton. It was the new name that had given her the courage to ask the Vicar if she could help seriously at the Mission Hall.

That was how she had put it to him, but what she had in mind was to make him a bit more business-like. He let them all take advantage of his good nature. Most of the navvies who asked him for help could well have given something more than the odd few pence to keep the place running.

After cutting her teeth on her beloved 'Heathcliff book', she had gone on to read others that the Vicar had loaned her. Reading in every snatched moment, her speed at reading and her understanding of plots and language quickly grew.

At first she judged everything against 'Heathcliff', and took against authors for what their characters did and said. *'That there Missis Austen . . . you'd a thought she wouldn't a let that nasty Emma behave like that to Miss Bates. Miss Bates couldn't help being poor – you'd a thought Missis Austen would a known that – what was wrong with her being proud of her niece? All that that Emma can do is poke fun at them and be spiteful. Ha, but Mr Knightley told her off for behaving so unkind. Then he goes and marries her. He was too nice for her. I'm surprised Missis Austen made him marry her. I woulden't, I'd a made her marry somebody like Mr Collins.'*

Mr Collins was a nasty little snipe, worse than any that Kitty had encountered in all her years living on the diggings. As she scrubbed and cleaned the bare floor and rough benches of the Mission Hall, she talked constantly to Peter Warren of the fictional people who had entered her life. He was the man who brought them to her, she believed that he must know them as intimately as she did herself. As he was bending over his letter-writing for navvies – perhaps to their mothers, or for a navvy's wife who had been left unprovided for – Kitty could become quite irate.

Kitty had strong views on fictional clerics. At the little snipe Collins – *'His blimmen cheek, thinking he was good enough for Lizzy Bennet! And as for that ole Bishop Proudy, the milksop, he should a give his wife a good cuff on the ear.'* She waited eagerly for the next episode of the goings-on of Arthur Vincent for whom she had a soft spot. *'I reckon that your ole sermons was better than his, Vicar-dear,. though you'm both a bit too hopeful of humin nature.'* However, her declared enemy was *'Him! Slope. Why, I tell you, Vicar-dear,*

*I should a only have to a heard his name and I should a know
he was a bad'n. He'd a made a good navvy, ole Slope off.'*

But now, as she walked along the track towards 'By
Privett', Kitty was willing to forgo her half-hour of private
uninterrupted commune with people who lived strange and
remote lives of gowns and balls, intrigue in bishops' palaces
and trivial and mistaken romances, and she thought instead
of how she could put to the Vicar her scheme for the
Mission, so that it sounded sense. *'Look, Vicar-dear, I got
this idea . . . it'd mean you woulden't have to waste so much
of your time . . .'* no, not 'waste', that sounded wrong . . .
*'it'd mean you'd have more time to spend do-en more
important . . .'* no, he'd soon say writen the letters was
important. Perhaps just say it straight out, and put it right if
it came out all wrong . . . perhaps not, better to try to get the
right words in the first place . . .

The old Mission Hall had long since been abandoned,
along with the rest of the growth of dwellings that had
sprung up and become 'Great Hole' during the building of
the main line and long tunnel. The 'hall' that now existed
was situated in a shanty-town that had grown up a few miles
distant from the old. The new agglomeration was known as
'By Privett'. The hamlet of Privett was in fact some miles
from it, but whilst the old shanty-town had still existed in
parallel, 'the place up by Privett' had distinguished it from
Great Hole.

With the aid of Ainsley Chambers, the overseer, Kitty
Linton, formerly Fire-Bucket, had continued to keep the
tenancy of a six-berth hut in the name of Dutch. Maggie had
finished her 'obliged' schooling, but Agnes, Simeon and
Edgar were sent for lessons at the village school. Still very
few navvy children went there, but Kitty told her children
that they were obliged by law to go – seeing as how the Vicar
had kicked up such a stink to get them taken in there.

* * *

Caroline and Ruth approached By Privett.

'Where are we going, Carly? If we keep going we shall be in Alresford.'

Caroline smiled. 'I told you, you'll know when we get there.' Purposely, she had kept up a light-hearted mystery about where she was taking Ruth. She had no faith in Ruth's prejudice about navvies and the way they lived having changed, so she intended a *fait accompli*.

The Mission Hall was set a little apart from the rest of the community, at the fork of two lanes. Ruth was down the incline of a rutted and high-hedged path and upon the place before she realized that they had reached habitation. As the sisters came to the fork, two children rushed from the other lane. A young boy, and an even younger one. Both were bleeding from several nasty cuts on their heads and hands.

Caroline snatched up the younger. 'Linty! What have you done to yourself!'

The boy's extremely dirty, snot-smeared face was channelled with snail-trails of dried tears.

The older boy answered for him. 'He didn't do nothen. It was the boys in the 'tato fields waiten for us 'at did it. And Linty couldn't help apee-en hisself, because he had just stopped to do it, when they jumped out on us.' He showed her his grazed knuckles. 'But I plastered they all right and tole Linty to run offt.'

'Oh, Vic, just look at your hands! Just look at his hands, Ruth.'

The boy held them out to Ruth.

Ruth was taken aback, not so much by the gashed and bloody hands, but by the sudden appearance of the boys and the familiar way her sister had snatched up the small one and now held the dirty little creature close.

Caroline again became aware of Ruth. 'Oh, that is Vic and this is Linty. This lady is my sister, Ruth – Miss Tylee.

Say hello decently to her. Come quick and let's get these cuts washed and greased.'

They had now reached the hut at the fork of the paths. A low hut, about forty feet in length, with clapboard walls and a tin roof with an iron chimney at either end. A workman in a battered hat, sleeves rolled and yorks about the legs of his trousers, was doing the last lap in painting the hut dark green.

At their approach he pushed back his hat and turned in the direction of their voices.

'Peter!' The sight of him caught her unawares. It had never occurred to her for a second that it would be he who was at the end of Caroline's invitation to take this mysterious walk over the downs.

Peter Warren. His hair was now quite streaked with grey, making him look more like Teddy than ever. Thinner, more browned by exposure to weather, and more handsome now than his elder brother, but very like him. Realizing that she was staring, she turned her gaze from him to Caroline who was setting down the small boy.

Peter Warren put down the can and brush. 'Ruth? Why, it's good to see you.'

After wiping his hands down his cord trousers, he held one out to Ruth, and offered the other to the small boy. 'And what are you two doing back from school at this time of day?'

'Leave it for now, Peter.' Caroline's tone was one to take notice of. 'Let's get them cleaned up and see what damage is done. There's no bones broken. Some nasty cuts.' She went to a rainwater butt and baled some water into a stone dish. 'I'll get some clean rags and carbolic.' She disappeared into the hut leaving Ruth and Peter silently regarding one another.

'The boy said some others jumped out on them.' Ruth hoped that she did not sound as disconcerted as she felt.

Peter Warren nodded. 'It's not the first time. It's the village. The village people don't want these children to attend the school. They look upon it as *their* school – it's not, of course, but that doesn't stop them making life so unbearable that they stop going. The girls get only verbally abused, but the boys . . . poor old Vic, that's a nasty one you've got on your head . . . This time it isn't too bad. There have been bones broken in the past.'

'Why, that's terrible.'

'Of course it is. And unfair, illegal and unChristian.'

Caroline came back with a large bottle and some torn sheeting with which she proceeded to clean off the wincing, squirming boys whilst Peter held them still. Ruth stood by feeling excluded and a little foolish, as well as quite bewildered at the transformation of Peter Warren.

'Where's Kitty?' Caroline asked.

'She should be here about now. That's if she hasn't got waylaid by Mr Dobbin or Sir Pitt . . .'

'Oh Lord, Peter, you haven't got her going on another book – we shan't get any sense out of her for a fortnight.'

He shrugged and set the little boy on his feet. 'There, Linty my boy. Now take off your breeks and hang them on the bramble.'

The child sidled a look at Ruth.

'Ah, pull down your shirt-tail. Miss Tylee will have seen plenty of bare ones before today.'

There was a barb there. She felt the challenge. Felt sure of some anger, resentment. Was he still jealous of Teddy because she had chosen him? She felt her colour rising, and when she saw Caroline flash a look at him, knew that she wasn't mistaken.

'There's a pair of cut-offs in the big cupboard. Go put them on, Linty,' Caroline said, saving the situation. 'I didn't expect to find you here this morning, Peter. I wanted to bring Ruth to see what we are trying to do at By Privett.'

'And I didn't expect you; I thought you would be too occupied at home with your sister. Excuse me, but I must finish this.' Re-starting his painting, speaking over his shoulder. 'I've heard all about your good fortune.'

'Thank you.'

'I am sure that you will be very popular with the . . . Bostonians? Or is it Philadelphians?'

He knew where she was bound, she could tell by his tone, but he was trying to appear uninterested and casual.

'I am going first to Boston.'

'I believe that Boston is quite a place of culture.'

Now she did not trust herself to decide whether his tone was ironic or sincere. Neither did she trust herself to remain in his company, for there was no doubt that he was very changed.

It had appeared that Caroline acted upon impulse in asking Ruth to go with her to By Privett, but, if she were honest with herself, she had hoped that she could show, rather than tell, her sister what she was doing with her time. Until Ruth knew, Caroline felt that she was acting under-handedly in letting Ruth contribute to the upkeep of Croud Cantle, whilst she herself was not working there every hour of every day. Auntie Sel said that it was putting Ruth's money to good use, but Caroline wanted Ruth's approval.

However, she had not expected to find Peter here, or she would not have come. She had never known how serious their relationship had been before Ruth had gone away, but it was obvious that, whenever she was mentioned, he was always torn two ways — part of him eager to know everything about her life, part wanting to forget her.

Certainly, Caroline would never have brought them together intentionally. But it had happened, and as a consequence had, perhaps, done something for her to see them together and to judge whether there was anything left of their old romance. Although she had been still a child at the time, she had always thought that there had been one.

Now that she had seen them together, Caroline was certain that there had been, and that perhaps it was not dead. She was equally certain that Ruth's desire to continue to rise in the world as a singer would never be sacrificed to other desires. In a flash of revelation, she realized what had prompted Ruth to take up with Peter's older brother. The two brothers were very alike in appearance – perhaps in nature too – but with Edward Warren Ruth had her fulfilment as a singer as well. The best of both worlds? Not really the best if Edward Warren was not Ruth's first choice as a lover.

'Come and look, Ruth. It is very primitive, but it serves. Better than nothing.'

Ruth looked around the long hut. At one end were one or two rows of benches, at the other a couple of narrow cots. Various wooden cupboards, a long table, a desk and several chairs.

'Can't you tell what it is?'

'Well, that end might be for a . . . church? A school-room?'

Caroline laughed quietly. 'Right, Ruthie! It's both. And that end is a hospital . . . well not a true hospital, but it is somewhere for men to have wounds dressed. Before, there was nothing. There's room for a few men, when they've been weathered off and have been thrown out of their shants, just to sit and have a bit of a smoke without having to drink ale all the time. Most people outside the diggings think that's all navvies want to do, but there's plenty of decent men who'd be content not to take another drop if they weren't pushed into it.'

She knew that she was not making a very good job of explaining herself. Ruth's expression was as noncommittal as her silence. Caroline plunged on. 'What we hope to do eventually is to have a proper separate schoolroom, and a hospital with a place for women lying-in, and a rest-hut with somewhere to sit for single men. It all has to be easily disassembled and transportable on a wagon, so that we could follow the diggings along the line.'

'It sounds . . . really . . . admirable. But from what I know of these people, aren't they rather too . . . well, brutish, to need . . . No, I don't mean brutish, that sounds bad. What I mean is, everybody knows the way navvy people are, they're used to their coarse life . . . aren't there more deserving people, of our own kind, who need these very things?'

Caroline's pink complexion became red, but she withheld herself very well.

'What makes one injured man more deserving than another? Or one woman with a difficult labour – or one child's schooling – more deserving than the next? You're saying it's where they're born . . . who they are. Oh yes, navvy children *are* tough – you've just seen how tough . . . I reckon you wouldn't have kept going to school knowing you'd likely be set upon when you didn't have to. Your school was nice and safe at the kitchen table with Ma – was that because you were more deserving? Of course it wasn't, it was because there wasn't a school and Ma provided what you needed. And that's what *we* want to do – provide a school that these children will want to attend.'

She heaved a breath and became calmer. 'I remember what it was like when we came to Cantle. My way of talking, my scabby sores . . . the *outsider*, the teacher's scapegoat, the children poking and jeering – but at least nobody split open my head. Can you imagine what it's like for poor little Linty? He's only five years old!'

Caroline heard in her own voice indignant echoes of Ma and Pa's voices against something that was unjust, and wondered how far Ruth had retreated from their influence. The flames of her own idealism were constantly fanned by Peter and Auntie Sel, and by daily contact with the poverty

of Cantle neighbours and the degradation of many of the
inhabitants of the diggings.

Ruth did not have a chance to reply to Caroline's
outburst, for suddenly the door opened.

'Mis-an-throp-est. Mis-an – mis-an – don't stop me –
where's that bloody ole dictionary?'

Kitty Fire-Bucket dumped the bundle she had been
carrying by the door, ranted open a cupboard, took out a
thick book and bent over it, quickly flicking the pages.

'Ah, "Misanthrope. A man-hater; one who distrusts
men and avoids them."' She banged the book shut. 'I
couldn't make out from the reading of it what a "young
misanthropist" might be. And I never would a took Becky
Sharp for a man-*hater*.' She gave a short laugh. 'But there
. . . she's a woman, so it an't likely she a be any more trusten
of men than the rest of us.' She laughed again. 'An't that so,
Caroline?' She stopped short as her eye alighted on Ruth.
'Oh. I thought you was on your own, Caroline. Vicar never
said we had company. He said the boys was beat up again,
but you had cleaned them up. They all right?'

'Just a bit shook up. Linty peed himself again.'

'What do you expect, poor little mite, always getting
bullied about.'

'Ruth, this is Kitty Linton . . . Kitty, my sister, Ruth.'

Ruth nodded. 'Mrs Linton.'

Kitty looked Ruth up and down. 'Oh, anybody can see
that, even without the Vicar's picture. You're the one that
sings. Though I never thought you to have the same hair as
Caroline. The picture don't show it, shows you all yellow
curls. Where's the boys gone? I expect Caroline's brought
you to see the lying-in room.'

Caroline indicated that she didn't know where the boys
had gone.

'I had better find them or they'll go slopen off, and if

they an't going to school, then they can do some here. Did Caroline tell you about the school?'

Before Ruth could answer, Kitty had gone back outside, from where her voice calling 'Vic-Vic-Vic' came back through the timber walls.

'Goodness,' said Ruth, 'she is quite a whirlwind.'

'Ruth . . . I'm sorry I took off just now.'

Ruth indicated that it was of no consequence. Caroline continued, 'Kitty's marvellous. Nothing ever gets her down. She seems to have more energy than half a dozen of the rest of us.'

'Do I get the impression that the – the schoolroom is hers?'

'Such as it is at present.'

Ruth smiled. 'I never saw anybody more eager to run to a dictionary.'

'Would you put her among your "deserving people of our own kind"? She's a *woman*.'

Ruth felt a flash of anger at having her own words thrown back to embarrass her. 'I didn't mean it to sound like that.'

'It really doesn't matter what you meant it to sound like – it's that you *think* in phrases like "deserving people" and "our own kind". Kitty is intelligent, hardworking and better read than either you or me and she knows better than either of us the way to use her mind and her wits. I like her very well indeed. In fact, since I have known her, she's been as close to me as anybody in my life. She's not really Mrs Linton, she's the daughter of a navvyman and a navvy woman, and now broomstick-wife of a navvyman. She was born on the diggings and has lived here all her life. She runs a shanty lodging-house and now teaches anybody to read who wants to learn. Man, woman or child, she don't mind. She's one of your brutes, Ruthie – until recently she's been called Kitty Fire-Bucket. She's a navvy woman, Ruth.'

'And is she why you brought me here?'

'Not really, but I am pleased that you've met her. I brought you here to see what I spend some of the time on that I should have to be spending on Croud Cantle work, if it wasn't for what you send us. I hoped in bringing you to see for yourself . . .'

Before Caroline could tell Ruth any more about her reason for bringing her here, the door again burst open and the two boys came through all the faster for a helping hand from Kitty. Behind them Peter came, wiping his hands on a rag.

'Look, Caroline,' Peter said, 'the boy's head wound must have been worse than it first looked.'

The hair at the back of the older boy's head had become matted with blood. Kitty pushed him to sit down, whilst they all peered at the wound. Nobody had said, but Ruth surmised that the woman must be their mother.

More often than not at the centre of attention during the last few years, Ruth now felt ill-at-ease at this inattention to herself; then gradually she realized the forgotten pleasure of not being always at the centre of things.

It seemed to her that everything in the hut, which Peter Warren was painting green, had its own importance. When Caroline had been showing off the 'schoolroom' and the 'treatment-room' and the 'rest-room', each was significant. As too were the boys, and the woman. As she stood apart from them she had a brief time to contemplate.

'Ruth, would you like to see what keeps me here?'

'Here and now I don't want anything except what I've got.'

Obviously what Caroline was prepared to settle for was whatever went on in this green hut.

'I think it needs a stitch,' Caroline said. 'Isaac's the best one to see to it.'

'No!' The boy cupped his hand protectively over his wound.

'Don't be so silly, Vic,' the woman said. 'Isaac don't hurt.'

'He bloody do. What about when they broke my finger?'

'It was them bullies who hurt it, not Isaac – he was making it better.'

The vehemence with which the boy expressed his fear brought a sympathetic smile from Ruth. She spoke quietly to him. 'Not long ago, I saw somebody, a friend of mine, and she had the biggest cut I've ever seen and it wouldn't stop bleeding. And do you know what the surgeon did?'

The boy stared up at her suspiciously.

'He sewed up the cut just like it was a rent in a shirt.'

'And I bet it bloody hurt too.'

'Not so much as having the cut left open.'

For the first time, she saw the boy. The boy named Vic. Beneath the rough haircut and the grimy face, and beyond her own prejudices, she saw the pretty features of a small vulnerable boy with thick hair and a complexion as freckled as Caroline's. Green eyes fringed by long, thick lashes. He looked not at all like the woman. His nose was as well constructed as the rest of his face. Washed and dressed decently, and with his coarse voice silenced, he would make a very presentable child. By the size of him, the boy must have been about ten years of age.

'I think if I were you, I would let Mr Isaac mend it for you, Victor.'

For a second the boy looked blank.

'I an't called Victor – 'tis Vic.'

Ruth saw that the mistake had caused amusement amongst the others.

'Oh, I'm sorry – I thought . . .'

Kitty Linton chuckled. 'That's my fault, he always been called the Vicar's Baby, an't he, Vicar-dear?'

A moment of confusion at the woman's familiarity. And

hot jealousy. And an unthinkable suspicion. Right from the first moment when the boys had gone to him, Peter had treated them exactly as a father would have.

'He's altered since you saw him last, Ruth.' Peter's voice was quiet.

Time went by in halted seconds.

Puzzlement. *Who . . . ? I have never seen any of this navvy family in my life.*

She was aware of Caroline fiddling with the piece of rag she had used for cleaning the boy's wounds; of the woman gradually turning her head to look at Ruth's face; of her own thoughts unwinding and mingling with Peter's words . . .

'Vic, tell Miss Tylee your proper name.'

'Simeon Peter Linton.'

Ruth never knew whether she had said the name aloud, or if it was only the child's voice that seemed to unroll the gruesome picture of the broken-backed girl dangling, as Peter and Auryn held her up so that Ruth could bring out that pathetic baby.

The red flares lighting the walls of Great Hole; the faint roar of moving air as it passed through the tunnel; the drip of water into the rusty pools; the old dank smells of the tunnel and the new smells of tar-smoke, blood and explosives and vomited gin; the chilling coldness and the wet; and the most awful fear that had linked the three of them – linked them so tightly that she had often wondered whether it had eventually been active in cutting them off from one another.

The vision and the thought came in a second of actual time. Ruth could never after understand why it was that she had never till that moment comprehended that a tragedy so terrible and terrifying can only be destructive to those involved in it. Yet not to the baby.

'At this moment he's more yours than mine.'

'Then let him be Simeon, Peter.'

The baby that the woman had said they had called the

Vicar's Baby. No . . . Ruth's baby. Who had ever remembered that it was Ruth's hands he had felt before any others? The first garment that had ever covered him had been her own petticoat; it was Ruth who had carried him back to Croud Cantle, holding him close, next to her bosom to protect him from the December air. Since then, the feel of his warm, soft body had come back to her in a hundred fragmented dreams.

How fast and slow is time at moments of such revelation. It seemed to Ruth that she relived every detail of that evening years ago. It seemed to the others, that it took Ruth a moment or two to collect her thoughts.

Who had remembered? Of the four adults, all of them except Ruth herself.

She gathered her thoughts. 'I like that. "Peter" – that's the same as Mr Warren, isn't it?'

'Simeon Peter,' the boy said. 'Vicar says it means "rock".'

ANGER ON TRADDEN RAIKE

FOR THE FIRST PART of the walk back the two sisters, both deep in thought, did not exchange many words, then Caroline said, 'I wanted to tell you about our plans. I'm sorry it turned out so bad.'

'It wasn't bad, Carly. It was just one of those times when everything comes tumbling down one after another . . . seeing Peter like that, then the woman and the boys. Is it always so . . . ?'

'Chaotic? And me being so strung up, wanting to show you why I'm so happy here, that I say all the wrong things?'

'I didn't mean the place was chaotic . . . perhaps hectic. So much going on, and I have always envisaged you leading a simple, quiet life.'

Caroline smiled. 'This was quite one of our quieter days.'

'Then it must be rather like what goes on back-stage before a performance starts – that *is* chaotic.'

Ruth, stimulated by the longest walk she had taken in years, and again enjoying the feel of springy turf on solid chalk, strode out. As they approached the western face of the downs at Tradden Raike, the wind gusted and took Ruth's head-cloth, whipping and bouncing it over the hummocks. They gave chase until the scarf was caught in a knot of brambles. They puffed and panted exaggeratedly and fell down on the turf to gain their breath, laughing. Instead of replacing the scarf, Ruth removed the pins and combs from her hair, faced into the wind so that her hair streamed out behind her.

'Ah, Carly . . . this is something a woman may not do in London.'

'Not even "Rosalie"? I thought she could do what she would, that where Rosalie leads, the rest follow.'

Ruth nodded her head vaguely and smiled wryly. 'True. I dare say that if she removed her bonnet and unpinned her hair at the Ascot Heath Races or in Hyde Park, there would be twenty women to follow suit before the day was out.'

'That gives her some power. I should be a bit overawed to think that if I took to wearing streamers in my hair others would copy.'

'So should *I* be overawed – but Rosalie knows how to cope.'

Caroline looked sideways at her sister and saw that she was not intending to be amusing, but was seriously speaking of 'Rosalie' as another person.

'It doesn't matter much with ribbons and trivialities, it is how she behaves that must be worthy of being emulated. She appeals so much to the young. We never allow her to accept gifts from her admirers, only flowers.' Casually, absent-mindedly, Ruth unfastened her young sister's hair. Caroline flicked her head and joined in Ruth's wide smile of satisfaction as she indicated the twin streams of foxy hair.

'Is it all right if I ask you something, Ruth?'

'Why ask if you may ask? You never used to be reticent.'

'Quite a few things I would like to know about you.'

Ruth hunched her shoulders noncommittally.

'Something's different from when we were going to By Privett – you seem different, happier, it seems.'

'He's not the Vicar's Baby, you know. I birthed him.'

'I know. But Kitty's his mother right enough.'

'But he was mine first. Peter and Auryn only propped up the girl, I was the one who got him from her – she was about dead, you know.'

'No, I didn't know that. I knew that you were the one

who took him from the mother . . . and that it was you who named him.'

'Did you know that? Peter christened him in a puddle of muddy water. Do you know if he's been christened again since then?'

'I doubt it. Kitty is pretty scathing about anything to do with the Church. Not Peter's kind of ministry.' She laughed generously. 'Since she has discovered some book or other that Peter has given her she has taken against a clergyman in it – she calls anything to do with the Church that she disapproves of "Casaubonning"; you should hear the expression she puts into it. If you ask where Peter's gone and he's off taking Communion or something, she says, "Don't ask me, all I know is he's gone blimmen Casaubonning off to Winchester." So I should think that the puddle christening is the only one.'

Ruth looked satisfied at this answer. 'I shall be quite well off in Boston . . . I thought I might do something for him.'

'I doubt if Kitty would take it.'

'I can only ask – at least get him an apprenticeship or something.

'It's an extraordinary thing, this American offer. I even have a witnessed contract saying that I shall get so much money, for so many years, and a steamship ticket to Europe every other year.'

'You must be really very famous.'

'It's all Teddy's doing, really. He's done what he wanted to do – he said he wanted to create a fantasy. That's what I am. I know it.'

'I thought you were already well off.'

'I shall be even better-off . . . perhaps rich. I had no idea that he was doing so, but Teddy has been putting a large amount of my earnings into shares ever since I started at Bounderby's.'

'Goodness!'

'Shares pay dividends. Did you know that? It's money for nothing.'

'What Ma always reckoned . . .'

'Oh, *Carly*! Never mind what Ma reckoned. Dividends might have everything wrong with them, but it's what is going to pay to get the things you need for your school and lying-in hospital.'

'Are you serious?'

'Of course. It wouldn't be a very funny jest, would it?'

'Oh, Ruth. I hardly know what to say.'

'Just say that you will accept it and never make any fuss about how the money was come by.' She paused, then went on. 'You don't have to tell me what Ma thinks about dividends, and money that's not honestly earned. I have my own conscience to worry about without worrying about anybody else's. You had better spend the money on something decent, or it will all be wasted on a house in London or something else that I don't really need.'

'And I shall have to come to terms with my conscience. And I shall, Ruthie, don't worry . . . I'd do almost anything to make the living conditions in the shanty-towns a bit more decent. Ruth, you are such a generous person.'

'Don't weigh me down with any more flattery, Carly. Just say that you'll take some money, and use it.'

'Don't worry, I will use it.'

'So let that be the end of it; just see that young Simeon Peter gets some sort of schooling where he won't get thrashed for being a navvy boy.'

'At Cantle school, our boys used to go hunting gypsy boys.'

'And at Toolagarry, the soldiers used to go hunting black natives.'

'Like the militia here hunted Pa.'

'It doesn't start with the children, Carly. Children have to be taught to despise, and it is grown people who teach them.'

Caroline suddenly realized that she really did not know her sister very well at all – and wondered, in view of her earlier prejudiced expressions, whether Ruth knew herself.

She had loved her uncritically in childhood, and been in awe of her as 'Rosalie'. Until now, they had never been together as equals. She felt a pang that, just as she was discovering the intelligence and depths that she had not known Ruth to possess, they were to be separated by the Atlantic Ocean.

'Well, what else do you want to ask me before we go back home?'

'Is your . . . will you . . . are you and Edward Warren . . . finished? I thought you might marry.'

'He would like it. But I don't love him, and I'm not sure that he loves me – *me*, Ruth – he is probably in love with the fantasy he created, and would like to be in love with a legend he thinks he can create. I don't believe he loves Ruth, he loves the fantasy of a wife and babies. I don't want to marry.'

'Not if you fall in love?'

'A person doesn't always fall in love with a suitable marriage partner.' Ruth's gaze was directed out over the downs but she was looking inwardly. 'What about you, Carly?'

'Isaac Evans and I are in love – very much.'

Ruth drew her thoughts back. 'Oh Carly! In love? No wonder you said that everything you wanted is here . . . and I thought you meant the green hut. Isaac . . . he's the one who is going to stitch Simeon Peter's head? Is he good? Of course he is. Is he handsome? What does he look like?'

'He's not very handsome, but he's got the sort of face I like – he minds me a lot of Pa. He is very kind and gentle. But, oh lor, he's a most terrible strong Socialist, quite as likely as Pa was to make a speech at the drop of a hat. And he's a trained physician with a university degree in philosophy. Dr Isaac Evans, in fact.'

'A doctor!' Ruth smiled. From the way that they had all referred to him as Isaac, she had surmised that he was some kind of local healer. That he was Dr Isaac Evans was what she needed to know to allow her to go to Boston with a clear conscience. A doctor meant stability for Carly. And if he was a Socialist, then he must be a man of high ideals like Pa. 'Oh, Carly, can't I meet him before I go? Goodness, you'll get married and I shan't be here to see you wed.'

'Ruth, Ruth. You do get carried away. Isaac is not in any way a conventional physician. He and I will jump the stick when I am twenty-one. He won't agree for me to do it before then – that will show you the kind of man he is.' She laughed delightedly. 'But I shall persuade him. Especially now we shall be working together on making a medical clinic and a lying-in place. There is an enormous community attached to railway building – and not a single proper facility in this part of the south. He is training me in nursing – not that you would think it by my performance today. But what he is teaching isn't about cut heads, he's teaching me the theories of a friend of his, Ignaz. Ignaz Semmel, who knows what causes hundreds of women to go into hospital to die of childbed fever. It is a simple idea of cleanness.'

Voluble, gesticulating, eyes sparkling, Caroline poured out her enthusiasm.

'Ignaz is being called a charlatan because he suggests that physicians should simply wash their hands and implements between patients. Isaac so admires Ignaz, and believes that he must be right. Well, when Isaac explained it to me I *knew* that he was right, it made such sense. I mean, Ruth – what happens if things in the dairy don't get scrubbed with hot soda-water? The milk goes off, doesn't it? Bad milk passes its badness on to new milk if the dip isn't scoured . . . so why shouldn't a physician's hands pass the badness from one person to another, or from a cadaver to a person?'

Caroline had told of her conviction many times, and she

always got an immediate response, especially at the mention of cadavers. But there were a few moments' silence before Ruth responded. 'What do you mean that you will jump the stick?'

Now it was Caroline who, at the tone of her sister's voice, paused. 'You know what I mean. That we will marry in the navvy way.'

'And what does Peter Warren have to say about it?'

'Peter Warren? What is it to do with him? It's not him I'm marrying.'

'Jumping the stick is not marrying.'

'To me and Isaac it is. Isaac is a navvy.'

Ruth got to her knees and faced her young sister.

'A navvy? You said he was a trained physician.'

'And he is. He works at navvying on the diggings for the big wages they pay, and puts it into his research work.'

'And this . . . lying-in. Did you mean that you and he work together when women are giving birth?'

'Of course. It's the most wonderful thing you ever saw.'

'Carly, I have seen childbirth! It is terrible and grotesque, and it's not the place for a young girl to be.'

'You saw a dead woman give birth, Ruth. There can't be any comparison with normal birthing.'

'I'm shocked, Carly.'

'At what? I'm a farm-girl, Ruth.'

'At . . . at your whole attitude. How can I leave you to a man who will happily call jumping over a stick a marriage, and who takes a young unmarried girl to work with him on the techniques of childbed – and it is *not* the same as working with calving heifers or helping a midwife. For goodness' sake . . . you're a young girl and the man's not even your husband.'

Caroline jumped to her feet and stood flaring down at her sister. 'Ruth Tylee! You hypocrite! You and your lover have been living "over the stick" for years – or is it Rosalie

who lives with him? And who was the young girl who
delivered a baby in the presence of her brother and a
clergyman?'

She was breathless with emotion and trembling from the
effort of trying to stem her tears. 'And if you're shocked at
me and Isaac delivering babies, then I'm glad you went away
and left Peter, because if there's *really* a Vicar's Baby, then
it's not Vic, but Linty . . . because it was Peter who birthed
him for Kitty.'

If Ruth had felt herself to be a stranger here, she now had
a feeling of total alienation. Her young sister no longer
existed. This extraordinary dragonfly that was Caroline had
grown from Carly the nymph. Ruth felt unable to cope with
the circumstances she discovered, and unwilling because she
had abrogated any right to criticize.

'And that's why he's helping me and Isaac; twice Peter's
been involved in a childbirth and both times there was no
one trained to help the mother. I'm *glad* you didn't get the
best brother. You didn't *deserve* a good man like Peter.' She
snatched up her shawl and ran off downhill.

Ruth left for America aware that in the pursuit of her career,
and her ambition for fame, she had forfeited her place in the
family. She never did meet Isaac Evans, and for all that
Selena fussed about her, and Caroline kissed and apolo-
gized, Ruth knew that those three had wound their lives
about one another, a three-stranded plait which supported
the farm, the market-stall and the work on the diggings. All
that Ruth could offer now was money. Perhaps they needed
it more than they needed her.

* * *

A letter from Auryn to Caroline

Old Marl, Toolagarry, N.S.W., Australia

September 1862

Dear Carly,

We congratulate you heartily on your marriage, though I have to say that when a woman marries a man it is a strange thing that she wishes to retain her old name. I should have thought you would consider it, if not an honour, then a pleasure, to have been given the name of a man such as you have described Isaac to us, and I think that, were I in his boots, I should not take so kindly to such strange notions. I wonder how people will know that you belong to Isaac? I trust your notions don't run as far as not wearing a wedding band.

Is a 'Handclasp Marriage' a legal marriage? Mother says that it is an ancient form of commitment, but I know nothing of its implications – particularly the legal ones. I hope that you are protected by the law.

We are pleased to hear that things are going well for you. However, you do not say much about this work that you are doing. You have to admit that 'charitable' is not a very good description of something that seems to take up so much of your time and thoughts.

What is it you do exactly? Is it teaching children to read? Or is it nursing them? You write of both. Are these sick children who cannot attend regular school? Where do you teach them?

How do you find time for so much charitable work as well as working at Croud Cantle? Is the labour I hired before I left still with you? And are they satisfactory in their work? Mother is particularly eager to know. Carly – I insist that you write more fully. Ma frets so these days if she does not know what her children are doing. I suppose that is because she is ageing, though to see her turn a sheep on its back, no one would think her to be sixty years of age.

She does not hear much of her daughter in America, a letter at Christmas and birthdays. Perhaps you know more, but don't write to me, for I do not wish to hear – you know my feelings in that direction. Perhaps, though, you can prevail upon her to write to Ma more frequently. The rumours of unrest between the North and the South there are disturbing to her.

Here, the unsettlement generally amongst the shearers is getting worse. Rough and ready as the Old Marl bunk-houses are, the men who apply to us for work are many times over the number we need. We get so many because our lodgings are wind-proof, dry and have board floors, and we provide the same food as we eat ourselves.

Barney will make a good sheep-man, he seems to know instinctively what I have to strive to learn about livestock and wool. Recently there have been more and more meetings of shearers protesting at the pay and conditions imposed upon them by their employers. I try to stop Ma hearing of these meetings, for she will travel miles to attend one. She will stand up and speak out on the side of the shearers and has made enemies amongst the other employers, berating them openly for treating their labour in the same way as 'bad landowners in the Old Country'.

I try to make her see that such rough gatherings are no place for a woman. Feelings run so high that I am sure that one day violence will break out. She takes it all as a great jest and says that these meetings are tea-parties compared to those in the old days in the Old Country. So I have taken to going with her.

On two occasions recently, I have been prompted to

speak out in support of the shearers, for without them people like ourselves would not survive. If we at Old Marl can provide dry and decent lodgings for transitory workers, then any sheep station can do so. Employers are so greedy, there is so much here to be had, yet many people do seem to want everything for themselves. I believe that Ma is better pleased at my small protests at meetings, than she is when I fetch her to see a hundred top-class fleece bales ready for wagoning up.

I am just back from registering the purchase of some new land. Can you visualize a single sheep-farm equal in size to Hampshire? With this new land, this is what we shall be, but as you know there are no lush Cantle pastures here. Ma says so often, 'I don't know what your Pa would think – we was for common ownership in the Old Country.' Then I give her back Pa's words about poor people not being in any position to bring about change. Not that we are rich, far from it, we still live no different from the poorest estate labourers in Cantle, but I can see that there is the means for people like us to make a bit of a fortune – with a following wind as one might say. Perhaps if not ourselves, then our children. There is plenty of land going begging. If the woollen markets hold good and we are willing to live on mutton and bread, then we can continue to expand.

Is it possible to hold on to beliefs such as Pa's and Ma's in the face of such opportunity? Equally important, is it possible to educate the next generation in those beliefs if they are heirs to perhaps a million sheep and a farm the size of England?

Vinia, Barney, Martha and Ma send love to you and to Auntie Sel. Our best wishes to your husband.

Your affectionate brother,

Auryn Tylee

PART THREE

Treading New Ground

BOSTON

RUTH'S ARRIVAL IN AMERICA coincided with the beginnings of the troubles between North and South that were to break into civil war. Now, with the country in a state of high emotion, and the economy beginning to rise, its people were ready to be entertained.

Ruth too was affected, both by the buoyant atmosphere that prevailed in the North, and her own feeling of freedom and self-assurance. She no longer felt that she could only perform from behind the cosmetic mask and beneath the wig of 'Rosalie' and, although she still used that name professionally, she dispensed with the golden curls and heightened the natural redness of her own hair.

She would have been amused to learn that people thought her autocratic, but on reflection she would likely have understood why. She consciously held her back straight, shoulders square and her head erect as Teddy had taught her, she was good at smiling and pleasant expressions, but she was hardly ever seen to laugh. She had outgrown prettiness into beauty – 'lovely' was the journalists' favourite adjective:

At the dedication of the great pipe organ in the new Music Hall, Boston, the lovely singer Miss 'Rosalie' was present in company with Mr Alexander Marney the theatre manager, and his father Mr Jarrett O'Mahoney the wealthy Boston businessman and benefactor.

* * *

Although this was her third winter in Boston, Ruth was still overawed at the savagery with which it attacked the city. A girlhood in Australia and Hampshire had not prepared her for the sight of such depths of snow or such lengths of icicles or the severity of the winter months when the temperature frequently dropped far below freezing point.

Yet she revelled in living here. She had a warm house, well insulated against the cold, plenty of fuel and abundant hot water. The snow was dry and puffy, constantly thawing and freezing, making sidewalks and roads impossibly rutted, but not decaying into the quagmires of the Hampshire roads when under snow.

When she first arrived, people had told her that she would feel perfectly at home, because the State was very like England – this usually from people who claimed to have descended from the early settlers and thus had ultimate wisdom on both the Old and the New Englands. Early settlements had been given names to reinforce the idea that they had brought 'Home' with them – Portsmouth, Gloucester, Plymouth, Boston. Although, of the English towns, Ruth had seen only Portsmouth and Plymouth, as far as she could tell there was not much resemblance in the American counterparts, certainly not in climate.

And there was New Hampshire. One of the earliest settlements. She had twice been engaged to sing there, the fact of her having been born in 'old' Hampshire being a point of great interest to the readers of gossip items in newspapers and ladies' magazines.

Part of Alexander Marney's plan was for 'Rosalie' to win over the readers of ladies' magazines by persuading editors to write a series of articles promoting her life. He intended that she should never be classed as a music-hall singer, but that she be integrated into society at a high level; to this end he set out to get the women of Boston to admire her as much as did the Boston men.

From the outset, Alex had endeavoured to foster the image of Ruth's acceptability in 'impeccable' circles. In the past, the ballet and the theatre had a poor image so far as good taste was concerned, and although present-day respectable society might no longer be as affronted as its parents had been at the sight of a French ballerina showing fleshing tights as far as the crotch, they did not yet find the theatre entirely acceptable.

With Ruth's elegant performances, Alex was determined to alter their attitude. Now, three years on, he was proving to be succeeding, and chose only the most high-class venues for her appearances.

'It is my intention to make a beautiful feminine leg as acceptable for public compliment as her complexion, and the woman who bares herself to nakedness in my musical plays shall do it without lewdness and only for the sake of beauty and for dramatic effect,' Alex declared to one newspaper. This caused an outcry, which, of course, stimulated interest as he had intended.

The theatre in which his first musical play written especially for Ruth was performed had seats for 3000 people. It was, as were many theatres at the time, built in a kind of no-man's-land outside the reach of highly moral civic laws. On the first evening, every seat was taken, and on subsequent evenings were over-subscribed.

The scenery and settings were spectacular and the costumes rich and costly. Ruth wore dresses of such fine gossamer that men paid highly for seats close to the stage and argued endlessly as to whether the gossamer covered fleshings or flesh. If the habitués of Bounderby's had supposed that only London or Paris could provide great spectacles of exotic style, then they would have been astonished at the splendour of some of these theatres-in-the-wilderness.

Soon after her arrival she was accompanied on several

train journeys by a journalist and an illustrator so that she might point out features that had evocations of England. But if she were honest – and to the notable people who invited her into their fine houses, she was not (in the interests of politeness) very honest – she could not find much to make her feel nostalgic.

There were too many lakes and ponds and streams to evoke England; there were no rolling downlands with fat flocks, nor ancient hovels. Instead there were mountainous ridges that were sometimes deep with snow; houses such as were never seen in southern England, many wooden and painted, and bearing no resemblance to the cob and thatch, grey flints, red bricks or stone which time had smudged into the true Hampshire landscape; in the city of Boston itself, however, many of the fine buildings did remind her of London. Her statements to the journalist on this fact pleased the Bostonians who were soon persuaded that a woman who considered architecture must be a high class of entertainer.

One street in particular reminded her of home, Chestnut Avenue, and it was there that she rented a small house. And it was there, not long after her arrival, that Ruth and Alexander Marney slid into a happy relationship. A secret life, separated from her exposed public life. From their first meeting, she had known that she would have him for her next lover. She found him intriguing. He had an autocratic appearance and the exuberance of a child, a contradiction that she found so exciting that, had she not been laid low from seasickness, she might have exchanged Edward Warren for Alexander Marney within days. He was not as gentle and relaxed a lover as Teddy Warren, but had an unexpectedly romantic side to his nature that pleased her.

On her voyage out, whilst she was suffering from the movement of the vessel, she had spent a lot of her time thinking about Toolagarry, something she had not done since she had heard that Auryn had returned there. It had been a terrible time of dreaming and awakenings teetering on the precipice. In her low state, she had confessed to Alexander Marney the great fear her dreams put her in. Then, having told him, she began to find herself awakening much before the dangerous edge. 'You are saving me from falling,' she told him, and it had seemed at the time to be a very profound observation. That had been the beginning of their relationship.

In the Boston spring, the green was there, though greener than was ever seen in the Cantle Valley; in summer the sky was bluer. In a Cantle hedgerow there is only one true autumn flame – that of the wayfarer tree – but in the other Hampshire it seemed that every tree and bush was alight, and Ruth loved to drive out to look at the spectacle.

Except for her house, Ruth Tylee did not want reminders of England, did not wish to feel nostalgic. When she came to Massachusetts she fell in love with its vitality and thought that she would never wish to leave.

She and Edward Warren had parted amicably so far as her contract with him was concerned. Quite likely he had already realized that there was a limit to the number of times that they could surprise the Bounderby's clientele with musical spectacles centred upon Ruth. He had fashioned her to perfection, but having completed his work there was a limit to the amount of satisfaction he could get out of admiring his own art. She suspected that he had ideas for a new 'creation'.

After three days of great emotion and passion in Plymouth, he had seen her off, wishing her well, telling her how proud of her he was. 'I love you, Ruth. If you ever change your mind, then you know that I'll be waiting for you.' They both knew that this was not true. He had always desired the company of lovely women and would still, though Ruth was the only one that he had ever asked to marry him.

'I shall miss you, Teddy. If I ever marry anyone, then it

shall be you.' But, by now, they both knew that it was not likely that she ever would marry at all. Ruth knew for sure, and Edward sensed it, for she had always immediately countered any suggestion of marriage. 'Don't spoil it, Teddy.' On her last visit to Cantle, he had sensed that something had happened to change her, but she was evasive when he broached it, saying, 'No, it is nothing, farewells are never happy.' He knew her well enough to know that something else had affected her – and well enough to know that she would keep her own counsel about it.

'I shall have to learn to look after my own affairs in America,' she said when he handed her a case of documents and explained the arrangements he had made with Alexander Marney on her behalf.

'You are perfectly able to look to your own affairs. You're pretty nicely off now and there's no doubt, from what Marney says, that there are excellent prospects in the American cities for entertainers of your calibre.'

It was one of the characteristics that she liked him for – his willingness to recognize her capability, the way he often treated her as an equal, asking her opinion, not speaking down to her.

When he had kissed her for the last time he had said yet again, 'Ah, Ruth, you are *such* a woman, what a waste if you don't marry . . . yet if you won't marry me, then I don't want another man to have you.'

The last words she said to him, other than 'Goodbye, Teddy dear', were 'I know that you will never understand it, Teddy, but not all women think that there is a place for them inside marriage. It is not my place. And I don't know where mine is.'

That moment came back to her now as she walked along the busy harbour silently with Alexander Marney. Silently, enclosed in a glass ball of their own aggrieved tension.

The morning was cold and clear, sunlight reflecting off the newly fallen, thick soft snow gave everything a brightness. She looked across the harbour at the vessel he had brought her to see, its new dark red paintwork gleamed, reflecting on the blue water – the new steam-powered ocean-going yacht in which Alexander Marney planned to sail to Europe in the spring.

The vessel was anchored a short distance off-shore. He had flung his arm in her direction. 'She's designed to average fifteen knots on a cross-Atlantic run. An hotel afloat. She'll skim the rich and famous back and forth to Europe so fast, in such an atmosphere of luxury, and be so tempting to the ambitious bankers' wives that they will fling their dollars at me by the fistful to get aboard.'

'At *you*? Is she yours, then?'

'Seventy-eight per cent of her.' He could scarcely take his eyes from his new acquisition and dollar-getting investment.

'She's very beautiful, Alex.'

'I want to name her *Rosalie*.'

'Goodness!'

'And I want you to come to Europe with me on her maiden voyage.'

'How could I? I have so many engagements, I couldn't be out of the country for so many weeks.'

'Damn to the engagements, Ruth. If you're Mrs Marney, then you'd be engaged in other matters.' He had looked delighted with himself at having sprung this surprise on her.

'Mrs Marney?'

'I want to marry you, Ruth. Marry you in the spring and sail to Europe for the honeymoon.'

So far as she could tell, until that moment, there had been no suggestion that he had such a plan in his head. It was like him to act on an impulse.

'I don't know what to say.'

'Just say that you'll come, and we can begin this very morning to set the thing in motion. Your clothes . . . not many . . . you will want to buy your trousseau in London.'

'No, Alex. No!' She had said it quietly but with great determination.

'Well then, Paris . . . yes, in Paris of course.'

He had turned to face her, his strong good looks alight with eagerness, and clasped both of her hands in his own.

It was obvious that he had not considered the possibility of her refusing him. She withdrew her hands from his clasp. 'No, Alexander . . . no, I do not want to be married.'

'What do you mean? I thought it was understood . . .'

'Understood? That we should be married?'

'Yes. We've been lovers . . .' Said as though he believed that she could not have comprehended his meaning. 'Men are not often free to marry their mistresses, and most of them wouldn't do so, anyway. But I am free and I want you to be my wife.'

'Mistress? I am not your mistress. I don't want to be any man's wife. I don't want to marry. I've been as happy since I've been here as I have any right to be.'

He looked at her as though it was the strangest thing that anyone had ever said to him.

'I don't understand.'

To regain her composure, she turned away from him and looked out across the water to where another vessel graced the harbour – an old three-masted clipper of pure classic beauty, moving gently up and down on the blue water. Fast, beautiful, but with quarters so cramped that, for all her lavishness, the Europe-hungry Bostonian society would certainly abandon her in favour of Alexander Marney's steam-powered hotel. In one respect, Alexander was like Teddy – filled with dreams of the bigger, better, faster, newer and more spectacular. They loved to have people's heads turn in their direction, to stun, to astound.

Which was why they had each proposed marriage to Ruth. If they did not realize this, then she did. She liked them both, enjoyed their free-thinking ideas, their willingness to abandon conventions, their zest and energy, and sensuality. In return, she offered them similar attributes and she gave them the use of her body – as a lover and as a head-turning beauty. She was convinced that Alexander's offer of marriage was prompted by the same need as his investment in the steamship . . . the need to possess something that others would desire to own.

Collar up against the cold of the slight on-shore breeze that carried ice particles, both hands thrust into the deep pockets of his long coat, he also stood looking out across the harbour.

He won't take refusal as reasonably as Teddy. He's still got too much pride, too much poverty-stricken Irish left. He does not know how to take rejection.

She knew him. She knew, because it was that same fear of being rejected which had in the past prevented her from performing as Ruth Tylee – if the public was ever inclined to ridicule or to hostility, then it would be directed at 'Rosalie'.

One needed generations of financial security for rejection not to be too hurtful. Teddy had inherited his security from his mother – but, as Ruth knew, Alexander's poverty, like that of her own family, was ancient, and not even one generation remote. His father and mother had arrived as penniless, in their day, as the thousands of new Irish families who were continuously arriving to create settlements which were particularly their own.

From these areas, such as down-town Southey where the O'Mahoneys once lived, some immigrants – as had Jarrett O'Mahoney – would scramble out by whatever means they could find. And like the O'Mahoneys, would graduate by stages through respectable Roxburgh and Dorchester until

they reached the graciousness of Louisburg Square and
Beacon Hill, from where they would send the next generation out with a name more suited to the New World.

Jarrett O'Mahoney's rise in the world had been initially
through his own harsh labour when Mayor Quincy was
transforming Boston from a colonial town into a cultured,
sanitary, modern city. From pick and shovel, he had gone
on to form his own gangs of Irish labour, then to small sub-
contracting, to main contracting, until, by the time
Alexander came to business age, there was an established
building business, and interests in railways, ship-building
and, recently, the huge operation of land-filling Boston's
Lower Back Bay.

Along the way, his son's name changed from
O'Mahoney to Marney.

If the tough old Jarrett O'Mahoney was displeased with
his only son's ideas for suddenly forming new companies, it
did not show. Ruth had met him and had been charmed by
his rough straight ways and his exaggerated broad Irish
accent when relating a tale.

'So you're the latest notion of this young feller o' mine.'

'I don't know about notion.'

'Ah, I mean theatre notion. Don't tell him I said so, but
he's rare good at business. This theatre affair is something
new, but I've no doubt he'll make his fortune – he has the
nose for it. But it was surprising – after all, O'Mahoneys has
always been building and contracting. "Father," he says.
"Father, I'm going into the entertainment business."

'"Oh, entertainment, is it?" says I. "Are y' going round
the streets with a dancing bear or what then?"

'"No," says me young feller there, "I'm going to
Europe to buy up the best musicians and singers I can find,
and I shall fetch them over the Atlantic and get engagements
in every city in the country. I'm goin' to raise the quality of
the theatre."

'"Oh yes?" says I. "And what kind of business is that when it's at home?"

'"Why, you old skinflint," he says, "what's wrong with a charitable business? I shall do it for the love of music and culture."' The old man had puffed at his pipe and frowned at Alex, though his eyes were smiling at the profligate proof of his own wealth as he took Ruth by the elbow and led her to the supper room.

'"Charity begins on Beacon Hill," I says. "Now tell us what this business is."

'"'Tis a twenty per cent business," he says. "Me new company makes the arrangements, and takes twenty per cent for its trouble."

'"Baloney," I says to him. "Have you not learned a thing from me? 'Tis the main contractor who gets the big potatoes. Contract for the theatre and sub-contract the selling of the tickets."

'"I never thought you had such ideas in you, Father," he says.

'"Why not?" says I. "Do you not think that the O'Mahoneys has got brains then?"

'"I have," he says, "brains enough for two men." (No O'Mahoney was ever backward with praisin' hisself.)

'"Then would you not suppose the one that give you them brains had an abundance of his own before he parted with any to you?"

'"Why, Father, I should never've thought of it that way if you hadn't pointed it out."'

Ruth had laughed spontaneously – a rare happening. He was astute and as honest in business as the system allowed, and while he had no physical feature one could compliment he was warm and likeable. He reminded her very much of her Aunt Ginny.

'So then it is you who are the creator of New English Enterprises that I am contracted to?'

The old man knocked out his pipe in the fireplace and looked up sideways at his handsome son, with a restrained smile of pride as he looked him up and down. 'No – just my joke. I have to admit that I should not be a deal o'use in the hiring of theatres and the selling of tickets, and I have to admit I should be bested when it came to the hiring of performers – buck muscle is Jarrett O'Mahoney's line. Right, me boy?'

Alex returned his father's smile with his eyes. 'No performance without performers,' he said.

The old man nodded. 'Right! So 'tis upon this pretty miss that the New English Enterprises rests then. Pretty delicate shoulders to be supportin' so many bags of silver dollars.'

It had been old Jarrett O'Mahoney's jesting comments that had finally overturned Ruth's view of herself.

Until then she had seen herself at the bottom of the pyramid, with the theatre owners and the managers at the top. *Of course . . . Without the performers, New English Entertainments Enterprises would be nothing. Wasn't this exactly what Ma and Pa had always said about working people? 'Without the likes of us, They would be nothing – no gold for the King's crown unless he went and got it for himself, no coal for the Owners lest they took a pick themselves, no wool, no cloth, no boots, and no food for anybody.'*

Suddenly, she heard her Ma's voice, saw her Ma's face, more clearly than she had for years; saw her with her arms red and lathered from doing the washing, pausing, stabbing a finger into the palm of her hand as she emphasized her points. But, as so often with parental opinion, the realization of its truth came upon hearing it voiced by a stranger.

It was from that evening that the 'Rosalie' carapace began to break up. Ruth had no more use for her. Ruth became proud of her talent to entertain. Not only was she contributing something towards keeping Croud Cantle in repair but, as now became clear to her, she was helping to support the shareholders in the N.E.E.E. Company, and everyone else connected with it, from Alex to the floor-sweepers.

And it was her newly developed pride that enabled her to hold her own before Alexander's strong personality. Particularly now, when he was bringing all his masculine forcefulness to bear upon her to marry him.

He indicated the steam-yacht.

'I had her made for you, Ruth. The finest, fastest, most modern ship that Boston has ever seen, and the twenty-two per cent balance of the holding is in your name. I had planned Boston's most glittering gathering as we sailed off for Europe, and when we returned, it would be to the house that is to be built in Vermont – I thought that you'd like it there, it is most beautiful.' Now that his initial anger had subsided, he brought forth his charm once more. 'I never supposed that you would turn me down. You'll break my heart . . . I can't not have you.'

'How could you suppose that? And to assume so much without consulting me in one detail! You not only decided that we should be married, but where we should go and where we should live. Did you think that, because the O'Mahoneys have dined with the Cabots and Lodges, you could buy me like you bought the ship?'

'You know that is not true.'

'How do I? You say to yourself that you *will* have something, and you *do* have it. I am enormously fond of your father, but he dotes upon you for the way that you have what you *will* have. You start up enterprises and companies and buy businesses almost as the idea enters your head . . . well that is very fine, except that I am not an enterprise.'

'I thought that we were . . . in a sense . . . I thought that we had an understanding that went beyond our contract.'

'I never gave you any intimation that we were anything other than . . . than what we are.'

'And what is that?'

Now that she had to bend her mind to define their relationship, Ruth found it difficult. 'You know what we are.'

'No.'

'We are in business together. We sometimes sleep in the same bed together . . . we suit one another in both.'

'And I am mistaken to think that we have something more? My father assumes it too. He dotes upon you. You are the daughter he has always wanted.'

'Then he has assumed such without foundation.' She paused, allowing her gaze to rest upon the two vessels riding the smooth water of the harbour, the bobbing slender spars of the graceful obsolete clipper, and Alex's ocean-going paddle-wheeler, sturdily built for speed and the manufacture of dollars. *The twenty-two per cent balance of the holding is in your name.* She mentally quartered the vessel. *I suppose that my twenty-two per cent is that with no paddle-wheel.* Amusement warmed her eyes at the knowledge – and the self-knowledge.

'He will be disappointed. He had set his heart on having you in the family.'

For a second, the thought that she should marry the son so as not to hurt the kindly father.

'I'm sorry if you are hurt, but it is probably inbred in me. The women in my family don't much like to be tied down in a marriage.'

Holding her elbow, he guided her away from the harbour towards the town.

'What shall you do?'

'About what?'

'About us . . . about everything.'

He was silent for the next hundred yards. 'I suppose that

if I can't have you as a wife,' he said, 'then I must have you how else I can.' And without a care who should see, he kissed her amidst respectable Bostonian ladies doing their morning marketing in the busy street.

From that morning on, their relationship began to falter. Alexander tried to persuade Ruth to make the expedition to Europe with him, but she refused. He did not tell old Jarrett that his hopes of Ruth as a daughter were dashed, perhaps in the belief that she was bound to come round in the end. He continued with the building of the beautiful house in Vermont, possibly with that same thought in mind. He was a sufficiently good businessman not to allow his emotions to interfere with his money-making, and continued to arrange very good contracts for Ruth throughout the northern states of America. For, by now, Ruth was worth a fortune to whoever held her contract.

Ruth was in New York, where she was appearing as 'Queen of the Nile', when her twenty-two and Alex's seventy-eight per cent of *Cracker* sailed from there. Alex had judged rightly. The bankers' wives and the rich armaments and shipbuilding families of both North and South had dollars to spend – and they loved to spend them in London, Florence and Paris. They were becoming used to fast travel and, having had enough of the vagaries of the arrival dates of the clippers were greatly taken with the idea of speed and luxury combined, and they were prepared to pay highly for it.

Ruth and Alex had spent a very unsatisfactory two weeks together in New York, with Alex busy all day and Ruth's day beginning when his ended. They were irritable with each other, quarrelled, and did not make it up till the night before he sailed, when they spent the hours enjoying one another as they had in the early days of their relationship.

As they walked along the dockside next day, linked-armed and smiling, he said, 'If anything should happen to me . . . '

'Ach no, Alex!' She gently stopped him with her finger-tips.

'Are you afraid the Devil will hear?'

'Nothing *will* happen to you. How could it in that great steaming monster?' Yet, even as she said it, she felt something of the presence of those same shades which she used to sense when out on the Cantle chalkhills; they breathed out a chill sea mist and she shivered and held her fingers crossed.

'Ah, Ruth, there's still a bit of the peasant in you. But listen, you must know. The house is yours, and my share of *Cracker*. And with my shares in N.E.E.E. joined with yours, you will have the majority holding. You have only to place an explosive aboard, and you are quite a rich woman.' His charming grin. 'The rest goes to my father.'

She wanted him not to have said it. She had felt the shade's breath. Her early tuition under Gustav Braun helped her to put on a vivacious face. 'Alex, I couldn't accept . . . '

'It would have been yours anyway. You've been a better wife than many a wife who is married and who else have I to leave anything at all to?'

'No! I've never been a wife!'

'All right, better than a wife then. And in any case, you need not let the inheritance worry you – I intend to return from Europe very soon with another two hundred passengers.'

But he never did.

When the steamer *Belle Marie*, holed and limping, reached her destination seven days overdue, her captain reported a collision in fog between his vessel and *Cracker*. Not one member of *Cracker*'s crew had been saved, nor any of the two hundred wealthy passengers.

Ruth Tylee had become a quite-rich woman by Bostonian standards – and wealthy by many another measure.

As soon as she received the news of the tragedy, Ruth took the fastest train to Boston. Old Jarrett O'Mahoney was grief-stricken beyond anything that Ruth had ever seen, yet he was concerned and protective of her. 'Ah, child, how can ye bear it, your husband that was to be and all the generations of O'Mahoneys to come, all gone, and us not able to touch his face in farewell.'

Ruth felt so distressed at the old man's state of mind that she cancelled all her immediate engagements to stay with him. Soon, however, the time came when she had to leave for a tour of engagements which she had to fulfil across the breadth of America. She was uneasy at the thought of leaving him in his grief.

'Why don't you come on tour with me, Mr O'Mahoney?'

'Travel with the Company? Go West?'

'Yes, why not? It will be good for you to go away.'

She paused before revealing a secret that would commit her and change her future. Once it was out, there was no going back, it would be like surrendering herself to the O'Mahoney empire. In the end, she decided it was the right thing to do.

'Alex would be pleased to know that you had accompanied his unborn child on its first railroad journey.'

Even before she had missed her first cycle, she had known that she was pregnant, recognized from past experience the unmistakable nausea when catching the aroma of tea or tobacco-smoke. She had been preparing herself to undergo once again the misery of abortion when she heard that Alex was lost in the Atlantic. As soon as she knew that, she knew that she could not go through with it.

Jarrett O'Mahoney could not speak when he realized

what it was that Ruth was telling him, but clasped her hands tightly and shook his tear-streamed head again and again as though disbelieving this change of Fate's mind.

When he was once again composed, he said, 'I will come, child, I will . . . yes. I promise I'll not fuss ye like some old hen, but I'll come with ye to see to it that you're not melancholy.' And in seeing to it, he slowly began to accept the fact of the death of Alex.

Often during the weeks that followed, Ruth would look up from her book to find the old man staring in the direction of her waistband, and on being caught he would smile and say unashamedly, 'Ah it's not over, not at all, not at all.'

Not long after the tragedy in the fog, Ruth and Jarrett O'Mahoney took their seats in the plushly upholstered, mahogany-and-crystal travelling compartment of a railroad carriage at the start of her tour that would take her across several states, ending in the silver mines of Nevada.

2

THE BROWN-PAINTED HUT

PETER WARREN SAT on the bank beside the hut, rubbing brown paint from his hands with turpentine, and remembering the time five years ago when he had last put a coat of paint on the place.

It had been his own fault that he had encountered Ruth then. Knowing full well that Caroline was sure to bring Ruth, he had gone on painting the hut all week. He had knowingly put himself right in her path – it was no wonder she had tripped over him. He remembered vividly the moment when he had looked up and she had been there. More delightful than ever. A mature woman, coolly composed and yet physically desirable. Engrossed in his thoughts, he did not hear Kitty come up behind him.

'Poor ole Vicar-dear. Still painten the blimmen hut.'

'I was just thinking about the last time.'

'When She come down here.'

He looked up sharply.

'Lord love you, Vicar-dear, don't look like that . . . anybody could see you was that love-sick for her . . .'

'No!'

'All right then, you wasen't.'

He smiled at her, creasing the corners of his eyes so that for a moment youth flashed over his face. 'Kitty Fire-Bucket, you are as saucy as a girl, and you as easy give me a flea in my ear as you do Linty.'

'Well, you got nothen to worry about then – 'tis when I treats you like the girls that you wants to worry.'

He sat fiddling with the turpentine rag. Kitty, head on one side, followed his movements.

'Summet's botheren you.'

He pulled a paper from his shirt pocket. 'A letter from brother John.'

'That's nice.'

'Not really. It's about Ruth's ... her ...' He felt foolish not being able to articulate such words as 'lover' ... 'the man who persuaded her to go to America. John says, "I met Ted recently. Do you remember the singer that he took up with who went off to America (Ted says that she had been a friend of yours)" ...'

Kitty sat down just behind him a little higher up the bank. He knew her so well, that even though he could not see her, he knew that she would listen with her hand over her mouth, and that an honestly troubled look would invade her face.

'"... It appears that once she was in America she exchanged Ted's patronage for this man's, and became his mistress. It is he who is the subject of this newspaper item. Ted said that you would be interested as it was yourself who introduced her to him (Ted), thus being the prime mover in her creation as a singer. He says that he will enquire as to her situation ..." The rest is about John's meeting with Semmel – Caroline and Isaac will be interested. Here.' He handed her the newspaper cutting.

She read:

London. February 14th 1864. Tragedy at Sea. In thick fog, on January 24th, on her maiden voyage from New York to London the paddle-steamer *Cracker* collided in mid-Atlantic with the steamship *Belle Marie*. Although the *Belle Marie* was holed and listing and in danger herself of sinking, her captain ordered a search of the scene of the tragedy in the hope of rescuing passengers and crew from the tragic passenger ship. After six hours the search was abandoned. The entire

crew and two hundred passengers were lost. Mr
Alexander Patrick Marney, the owner of the vessel,
who was the only son of a wealthy Boston, Mass.
businessman, was travelling as a passenger on the
Cracker's maiden voyage. Mr Marney was unmarried.

Kitty crushed the paper angrily. 'I tell you, Vicar – I
hates your bloody ole God. What sort of a person is He to let
two hundred people and all them worken men set off all
innocent on the sea and then sink them to the bottom? Why,
'tis just plain evel.'

He turned and looked up at her. 'It's not like that, Kitty.
God didn't take those people out and sink them. He doesn't
work like that.'

'It's His world though, isn't it?'

'Yes.'

'And He can run it how He likes?'

'He could if He chose to.'

'Then why don't He?'

'Because he gave us that freedom. We can run His world
exactly as *we* want to.'

'Oh, Vicar!' contemptuously. 'How could those people
have chose? They never knew there was anything to choose
from. If you'm honest, you know that an't true that we got
freedom. The world's run by God and them that has got
most money and fewest brains. If it was run by me and you,
then there would be warm fires for old people, and kindness
to idiots, and women woulden't die of childbed fever when
there's ways of stoppen it. If your ole God is supposed to
have give human be-ens freedom, how come I an't free to
have a school and teach readen?'

'You know why. The Government says that schools
must be run properly and teaching must be done by properly
trained teachers.'

'Then why an't I free to have a say in who is going to be

the Government and make up rules like that! You know I teaches readen better than that ole man over at the National School.'

He felt for her rejection and frustration. He had forebears who had been open-minded and who had had a desire for rightfulness – their blood ran thick in his veins. He saw no reason why an able member of the poor should not be trained to teach in schools, nor even why a woman should not be ordained. Peter Warren was a man who knew himself very well, and had come to realize that it was because he could not bear the established order and yet was not the man to make changes that he had chosen to bury himself in the one community where the grain of a sense of mutual care prevailed. A navvy on the tramp had only to ask for money and food and it was given without question. A kind of security for men who knew that it might be themselves who were penniless and on the tramp tomorrow. He believed that, harsh and brutish as their lives were, he had found in this underbelly society the beginnings of a sense of community among navvymen.

Navvymen.

But not women.

They, once they had thrown in their lot with the itinerant community, were excluded from this sense of mutual care. Yet, as Peter saw daily, there were good ears of corn growing on the dunghill of the shanty-towns, women like Fairy Dowlas, who had spent years comforting women in labour; even Black Annie, who *had* got out and bought a small house far away from the diggings; and Kitty, who he had seen develop from an abused and sluttish sixteen-year-old into a woman who, given the same advantages as himself, could have made an excellent teacher . . . or overseer, or contractor, or clergyman.

'If it were up to me, Kitty, I should give you a certificate tomorrow – and I'd give you a school, and put in it a hundred children who couldn't read and I'd let you loose on them.'

The angry red in her cheeks subsided, and she smiled affectionately at him. 'Ah, Vicar-dear, but you an't no more bloody free to do that than I am, are you?'

She sees through me as clearly as through crystal. She is the best woman I have ever known. I have nothing good enough to give her. Only that I love her. That I have always loved her. That I loved her when I was obsessed with Ruth, and when she was owned by Cocky and by Dutch and Ollie and Chambers.

The matter of Kitty and her desire to teach flared up regularly. After the attack that her boys had suffered five years ago, Kitty had refused any longer to allow her children to attend the National School. This action had started in motion the grinding stones that would not stop until they had tried to crush her grains of rebellion against authority.

First, she appeared before a Board of Governors where she talked so much common sense that they had no answer except 'Rules are rules!' But still she refused to send her children to that school. Next she was called to answer to the Inspectorate, who threatened her with 'The Law'. She asked if it wasn't against The Law for a mother to put her children into such danger as hers faced at the local school. She was told that all boys throve on a bit of honest bullying – makes men of them. Then she received a summons to appear before a local Magistrate who threatened her with the County Court and imprisonment if she did not send her children to school.

'Lissen, Your Honour – if you sends me to prison, who is goen to look after my children?'

'That is another matter.'

'I don't see that – 'tis all part of the same matter. If I am in prison, then they will be took into the Workhouse.'

'Very likely. So you would be well advised to do as you are bid and not put your children in such a situation.'

'Would you send them to the Workhouse?'

'I would. Children must be sent to school – it is the law.'

'But if they was in the Workhouse, they woulden't get no schoolen.'

'That is not so.'

'Lissen . . . don't you tell me Workhouse kids gets sent to school, because I know better!'

He was sure that she did, so offered no rebuttal.

'Mrs . . . ? Your name cannot truly be – ah – *Fire-Bucket*?'

She would not tell him that she had adopted Linton as her name, amused he should feel the discomfort of having to use her old one.

'And I'm not "Mrs"; I'm *Miss* Fire-Bucket. I am a navvy woman. And if you send me to prison and send my children to the Workhouse, then they won't get no schoolen – which is what you would be senden me to prison for. Isn't that it, Your Honour? And anybody can see that is the most stupidest kind of reasonen.'

It was her mention of 'navvy woman' that had given the Magistrate the key to let himself out of this box of rules and laws in which he found he was trapped. He declared that, in his opinion, navvies should be considered as gypsies and there seemed to be no law that said that gypsies must send their children to local schools.

If Kitty had won the day, she felt it a poor victory. And as for the children, there were times when they might have preferred the taunts and blows of the village children to their mother's strict regime when she was force-feeding them with learning.

Maggie had inherited the same slender strength as her mother. She helped clean and cook for Kitty's lodgers and took on casual work on local farms when it was available, breaking the bonds of the shanty-town and the railway makers' community.

Agnes, two years her junior, had grown thin and wiry and clever. She worked as a tipper, running alongside a wagonload of 'muck' and then releasing it at the crucial time to allow the spoil to run down the embankment. It was dangerous and poorly paid work, but it was the traditional work of children of Agnes's age. It lasted until they ended up beneath a load of spoil when the wagon ran wild, or, if they escaped that fate, when the boys sloped off and began pick-and-shovel work, or the girls became pregnant. Kitty had no intention of allowing her daughter to suffer either of those fates, so Agnes was kept out of mischief by Kitty and Peter's watchful eyes.

Vic, who had been a pretty child, was now a youth at the stage of development where he had a man's chin and a child's nose. He was of average height and broad, and had long since outgrown Agnes who had shared Kitty's milk with him fourteen years ago. He no longer lived in the shanty-town, but was apprenticed to a furniture-maker in Alton. This extraordinary escape for a navvy child came about because of Ruth's charity.

Linty, whose scruffy grubbiness belied his intelligence, was Peter's favourite and frequently to be found wherever Peter was.

The children had no real conception of the exceptional education they had received during the five years since they had been categorized as 'children of travelling people'. It was received at odd times and in many places, but theirs was a small class with several teachers.

Kitty fed them a cerebral diet of novels and poetry, which they must read, consider and evaluate. It mattered not whether it was Fielding or Gaskell, Austen or Eliot, the children were all expected to have an opinion about the worth of the characters. To Kitty, the plot was a bonus – her evaluation of a book was based upon the credibility of the characters. She would look in mock astonishment at a child who had not seen a fault. 'You don't reckon no *real* person would do a thing like that, do you, Ag? I don't reckon they would. No, that there captain was just put in because she liked to write about him – I reckon she might a been in love with a real captain at the time she was write-en the book. I haven't never took that captain serious. You just read him again, Agnes, and see if I an't right.'

Isaac Evans taught them arithmetic, crude biology and some bits of Latin, whilst Peter had volunteered to resurrect his history and geography lessons for their sake. He was not very good at the lessons, but the children liked his child-like enjoyment of a game.

For a while, Kitty and Peter sat silently, neither of them feeling that it was necessary to speak. Kitty looked at his familiar face. *A good man. That's the face of a good man. If I wrote a book, it would be about a man like that. Not no rich Mr Darcy nor no Mr Pip. People ought to write about men like him. All the years I know him, and I an't never once told him thank you, or I think you'm a good man . . . nor I haven't told him that I love him and I wishes that I wasen't who I am and he wasen't a vicar. I could tell him anythen at all – excepten that. I wonder what he would say . . .*

She jumped when he suddenly sighed and leaned back against her knees.

'When it's like this, Kitty, I wish that time would stand still. I want it to be like this for ever, I want the sky to be blue, the sun to be warm, and to be with the best companion in the world.'

'That an't true – any best companion would have let you talk about Caroline's sister, and her man getten drowned, instead of attacken your ole God.'

'What is there to say? You are probably right – tragedies like that are inexplicable if we believe in a God of love.'

'Ah, you don't want to take no notice of me when I gets on my high horse – it's all talk. You know more about that kind of thing than I do.'

'Not any more, Kitty. The older I get, the less I know. When I was twenty, my faith was so strong that I could have fought the Devil single-handed.'

'And I reckon you'd a won him too.' She rested her hands upon his shoulders and gave him the same kind of motherly kiss upon his hair as she often gave to her children. Except for the unusual circumstances of Linty's birth, there had never been any physical contact between them. His body gave up the tarry smell of medicated soap and his hair, warmed by the sun, gave out a faintly animal scent: she would have loved to let her face sink into his crisp greying curls as naturally as she did to any of her children.

Men had been invading her body since she was a child; in womanhood, she had bargained with it to keep the peace in the Ollie and Dutch years, and more recently had loaned it out in a business-like way to Ainsley Chambers in order to keep a roof over the heads of Dutch and the children. Seldom had she wanted to give herself as she now wished that she was able to give herself to Peter Warren. And he was the last man to whom such an offer could be made.

If it had just been my luck to a been born a farm-girl like Caroline, then . . .

Used to making the best of things, Kitty knew better than to wish for anything for herself – except that as she grew older, she did think that she would have liked to have been born in a 'proper village family'.

She made a move to get up, but he clasped her hand and held on to it.

'Now then, Vicar, I got a lot to do. There's six men

wants me to read a bit more of Becky Shark to them, and
there's readen lessons for Linton . . .'

In no way did Kitty approach Ruth in looks. Ruth was
beautiful and remote. Kitty was pretty and accessible. Had it
been Kitty who Peter Warren had tried to embrace six years
ago, it was likely that neither of them would have taken
fright and fled from one another.

He continued idly caressing her fingers. 'I was just
thinking of that day when you were going down to see
whether it was Dutch or Ollie who had won the fight.'

'That was the day you got me off the gin and got me on
the Heathcliffs.'

'And now you get drunk on the Heathcliffs. I remember
walking with you; you were carrying Agnes and Vic, and I had
Maggie half asleep on my shoulder. I think if it hadn't been for
the fact that I was taking you to a randy to jump the stick, it
would have been the best moment of my life up till then.'

'And you tried to get me to marry Dutch church-proper,
and I said it wasen't fair for women to get tied legal to a
navvyman.'

'You've always been the wiser of us, Kitty.'

'I never touched a drop of gin since that day. But I've
been tied to Dutch right enough.'

As he spoke, it was as though the plan he suggested to
Kitty had been thought through somewhere beneath
consciousness, for it came out as though he had known for a
long time what he would do.

He pulled her gently down to sit beside him, keeping
hold of her hand, feeling the bones through the rough skin
and warm flesh. His own hands which had touched her in
most intimate places when he was acting as midwife to
Linton, had never felt her strong knuckles, her soft and
generous mound at the base of her thumb or her blunt
fingers. She felt almost shy at the unexpectedness of such
intimacy – as though no man before had ever touched her.

'If I went to work officially on the diggings, then I could ask for a tenancy.' He spoke quietly, almost as though thinking aloud. 'I believe that they wouldn't deny me . . . the engineers know that I make their lives smooth for them. I represent the men in disputes, sort out all the petty problems for them – both sides, men and employers.'

For once, she could find no fictional situation with which to compare his actions and her feelings. As it happened, she knew that they were living a love-scene more affecting than any that she had read of. She fixed every word, every touch as a painter fixes a mural-scene in tempera.

'The overseers' and contractors' go-between in disputes – the labour see them as Company men and don't trust them to be fair. But they trust me now.'

'I know that. If they had any sense they'd pay you money. But there, why should they when you'm fool enough to do their dirty work for nothen?'

He needed to convince himself of his argument. 'And there are the wagon-girls . . . these days they nearly always come to me when there's trouble, instead of setting about one another, as they used to do. I don't think you are right that the contractors have no sense, they know that the school and the medical treatment save them money, what you *are* right to suggest is that I'm foolish to put money into rich pockets when we need it here. It has always gone against the grain of my nature to expect payment for doing the work I was called to do . . . but we could do so much more . . .'

He fell silent. Kitty waited, sensing that he had not finished.

Then, in a changed tone, he said, 'What sort of a husband do you think I should make, Kitty?'

Her mind jumped at once to the newspaper clipping that lay crumpled on the grass behind her.

'Well, you would be pretty handy at painten the house.

Mind you, I don't know what sort of a wife would let you sit around idle-en like this when you should be worken.'

'Would *you* marry me, Kitty?'

'A course I would, Vicar-dear. We could get the Bishop to do it instead of jumpen the stick.' She replied in jest for fear she was mistaken.

He turned fully towards her. 'I am quite serious, Kitty. Would you marry me? Jump the stick, walk down the aisle, marry church-proper, any way you like – but would you marry me?'

'Marry you, Vicar-dear? Well, that's the nicest theng anybody ever asked.'

'But would you?'

Now, from the tone of his voice and the tight way he gripped her hand, she was forced to believe that he was serious, but now that her fantasy was in danger of becoming reality, she hardly knew how to deal with it.

She said, 'Like lightnen, Vicar-dear.'

'Then, will you marry me, Kitty? You're a thousand times too good for me, but if you will, then I shall be more happy than I have any right to be. And I will ask the Company to take me onto their pay-roll and let me have a tenancy.'

'Let's hear this proper. Are you sayen that you wants me and you should get married church-proper, and let Dutch stay on liven with us?'

'Yes.'

'Bugger me, Vicar-dear, I can't hardly think.'

'Marry me church-proper, Kitty. If you say "no" then I shall go roaming all over the embankments calling, "Kitt-ee, Kitt-ee", all wild like Heathcliff.'

'With a gold band too, like Fairy?'

'Yes, with a gold band so that everybody will know that you're my wife.'

'What about you then?'

'You mean a gold band for me?'

'Sauce for the gander . . . I should want everybody to know that you'm my husband.'

'Two gold bands would cost a fair bit of money.'

'Two curtain rings then – or no bands at all.'

He wagged his head and smiled wryly. 'Silver bands, then. I think that I could run to that.'

Kitty felt overwhelmed by the complexity of the emotions that broke over her.

'Vicar-dear, I don't know whether to laugh or cry at the thought of it. For years I loved the ground you walk on. Lord, woulden't that just put the cat among the pigeons. A vicar with a navvy wife . . . it'd be queerer than Isaac and Caroline.'

Clasping both her hands to his face, he said, 'Kitty Fire-Bucket, if you don't give me a straight answer, I don't know what I shall do. Yes? Or no?'

'Well then, yes, Vicar-dear, I should like to be wed to you more than anythen in the world.'

'Lord help us, Kitty, you don't know what you do to a man with your banter.' This time it was he who gave the kiss, gently, firmly on her lips, not a kiss of great passion, rather it was the sealing of an unbreakable contract. 'I will do everything to make you a good husband, Kitty.'

Her hands smoothed his temples and he closed his eyes, leaning back against her warm body.

'Ah, there's times these days when I forget what you really are. You've had a few women, I'll be bound.'

He found himself embarrassed. 'You're nothing if not straight-out, Kitty. Two women. Two, when there should have been none . . . I should have found celibacy impossible.'

'All the years, you never as much as kissed me till today.'

'I've thought about it often enough.'

'Have you? Well. Then why haven't you?'

He shrugged his shoulders.

'Because of her, Caroline's sister? I an't blind, you know.'

'I had a strong kind of obsession for her – I can understand why it is that she is so idolized by people who have never been closer to her than fifty feet. She was the first woman I ever really wanted – before she went away.'

'And woulden't she have you?'

'I don't know. Perhaps we felt nothing stronger than desire. Or perhaps it was me – I have never learned the graces as well as my brothers and sisters. Anyway, she went away straight after. I think it frightened us both . . . the un-expectedness of it.'

'Bugger me if you don't make a fuss about it. 'Tis a natural theng – desire. People have need of one another's bodies. If people wants to give their own selves to some-body, I don't see why there's got to be so much fuss. 'Tis the taken of it forceful and the have-en no choice but to sell it that riles me up.' Then she laughed. 'I tell you what though, there woulden't be half so many stories in readen books if people was always nice to each other and went layen freely with each other without everybody have-en to say "no" before they are allowed to say "yes".'

For years, he had been husband to Kitty and father to her children in everything but the physical act and the name.

Kitty ventured again to put her lips on his hair.

'Certainly we shouldn't be no Cathy and Edgar Linton, should we, Vicar-dear?'

He smiled. 'Rest assured, there's not much of the gentleman in me.'

'Ah, you'm better than him.'

'Kitty Fire-Bucket, I never expected such a compliment . . . better than Edgar Linton?'

'Not so foolish and helpless, Vicar-dear – that's the fault with being a gentleman, most of them needs a kick up the arse, if you asks me.'

He bent his neck right back so that he was looking up at her.

Some of her thick, fair hair was falling from her cap. Her cheeks were red from the winter chill and a hot cooking stove. The top of her bosom too was reddened, but where her bodice fell away as she leaned forward, there was still the plump whiteness that had transfixed him many years ago.

'I love you, Kitty, and I realize now that I've probably always loved you.'

She smiled at him. 'That's all right, then. You're the honestest man in the world, and I know that you won't ever slope off. Only one theng, and I hope you don't mind, but I couldn't ever see myself callen you "Peter".' She laughed. 'See, it sounds that funny when I say it.'

'Could you see yourself calling me "Husband"?'

'Well, you know, Vicar-dear, I wonder if I an't been thinken somethen like that ever since you rubbed oil into me and fetched young Linty out. Not thinken it outward, but inside my mind . . . to myself. Times like when Fairy Dowlas is here and she says, "Like I said to London", or "I must tell London that". Whenever I hears somethen interesten, I finds myself thinken, "I a tell the Vicar that when I see him".'

'Shall we do it, and not tell anybody till it's done?'

'What, marryen?'

'I could arrange it so that the banns aren't called – just get a licence.'

'Don't you want nobody to know?'

'Of course I want them to know. But you realize that my family will not look upon this with any favour. My sister is the worst kind of snob – I couldn't bear you to be hurt by her stupidity.'

She had not lived on the diggings for thirty years without feeling the cuts of the other society – they would be deep if his family were to inflict them. Even deeper for him.

'Well, I can understand that. Navvy women haven't exactly got the best of reputations for making good wives for clergymen. You never know, they might come round in time when they sees I don't go rolling about gin-drunk.'

'"Gin-drunk and cursing like a navvy" is the saying.'

It took a few seconds for his meaning to become clear, then she laughed. 'No, the sayen goes ". . . cursing to all buggery like a bloody navvy" – that's how a navvy would say it. Lord above! I just thought of sometheng – shall I be called "Reverend Warren's wife"?'

He brushed a kiss on her cheek. 'You shall if you are not very careful. But I doubt that the Bishop's lady will trouble you to take tea with her.'

'Oh, that wouldn't be no trouble – I should just like to tell her a few things.'

'Come into the hut, Kitty, where I can kiss you properly before anybody comes for their dose of Becky Sharp.'

'When shall it be – you and me wed?'

'A few weeks, when I've got it all settled with the main contractor that I get work on the diggings and take over Dutch's tenancy.'

They began by kissing lightly, as a token. But soon discovered the exquisite rewards that come when passion and love are found together in the same person, and that same person returns those two same emotions. Twin natures, restrained desires denied fulfilment, until they found it in their mature years, together in the newly painted Navvies' Mission.

'Well, Kitty, do you think at last I shall get a Vicar's-Baby of my own?'

'Love you, my dear man – I reckon you shall have ten. To think when you first came to see me, I used to think that clergymen was not like other men.'

Holding her in the dim, shuttered hut, Peter felt intemperate with the sudden realization of his overwhelming affection for her, and would have made love again had they not heard the deep voice of Isaac and the chatter of Linton in the distance.

'And now you know better.'

'I think that we should wed when the meadow-sweet comes,' said Kitty.

'Ah yes, I was thinking of that earlier.' Peter Warren had long carried a memory of that July day, when he had walked her towards her marriage to Dutch, in a fresh skirt, with her three babies and carrying a sheaf of meadow-sweet. 'You must carry meadow-sweet with you to the church. I shall link that scent with you for ever.'

Kitty pressed his hands to her face and laughed. 'And whenever I smell turpentine, I shall always want you to love me like you just did.'

'Dear Lord, Kitty, then I'd best be careful of you till I've finished putting on the rest of the paint.'

3

ISAAC EVANS

CAROLINE TYLEE AND ISAAC EVANS had lived as husband and wife for two years. They had committed themselves to one another in the manner which had scandalized Ruth, and Caroline had not changed her name to Evans.

They lived at Croud Cantle Farm, Caroline spending some of her time tending the house cow and the crops, and the rest along the ever-extending railway diggings. Isaac took labouring work on the diggings as and when the income from the market was not enough to keep them all. There were now several branch-lines under construction in Hampshire, and because of their distance from Cantle, Caroline and Isaac often had to rise before dawn or drive home after dark.

There had come a point, a while ago when, because of the distance between dressing-station and diggings face, it was not practical for them to walk to By Privett. If they were to do their work properly, they could no longer remain static in the Mission Hut.

Caroline's practical mind soon devised a wagon, in many ways resembling the old travelling brothel, except that the Clinical Wagon had a clean mattress and smelled, not of rancid pomade, gin and tobacco smoke, but of tar-oil and hartshorn solution.

Caroline took great pride in their wagon. She loved to be in it, whether working alongside Isaac or rocking and rumbling along side-roads or over the open downs. Louise had been born in the wagon, and the new baby conceived in it. No matter how late they returned to Croud Cantle, her tall shadow could be seen on the yellow-lit, canvas walls of the wagon as she sluiced down its floor and washed Isaac's dishes and instruments with a cleansing solution, whilst he cleaned the exterior.

Now in her early twenties, with one toddling child and another due in three months, Caroline Tylee was a picture of healthy womanhood. Her intelligent face broke easily into smiles, yet she had a reserve – possibly helped by a long starched linen cook's apron – that kept even the most goatish patients in hand. It is not surprising that Isaac often told her that she was the most desirable woman in the world.

Isaac Evans was in his late twenties. Neither handsome nor plain. A broad-backed, straight-faced young man who was thought to be 'deep'. The truth of it was that he found it difficult to let people close to him. His father, the well-to-do owner of Gelem Hosiery, a stocking factory, had washed his hands of the son who, in embracing the revolutionary idea of a democratic enfranchisement for all adults, had 'turned on his own kind'.

There was nothing that Gelem Evans could do to prevent Isaac getting an inheritance, which came to him at the age of eighteen, so Isaac took it, left Nottingham and went to study medicine in a London hospital. His head full of healing knowledge and his heart even fuller of ideals, and his inheritance gone, he had walked south and found himself hauling muck on the railways.

It was a life that suited him very well until he met Peter Warren – as unusual a clergyman as was Isaac a physician. Isaac might have never found the way of life that was perfect for him had not Peter come across him splinting a complicated fracture of a running-boy's leg. Until then, although Isaac had wanted to, he had had no opportunity to put his healing skill to use, not having any money to buy himself into a practice; besides which, he loved the free and open life of the navvies. Gradually, he fell into the role of physician to the diggings. Then he had met Caroline and found himself the additional role of husband and father. And so, for the first time since leaving home, he was in a static, domestic situation. His reward for giving up his freedom was Caroline's clever mind and her elegant·body – being intelligent and lusty, he wasted neither. Caroline might not have agreed, for his fault was carelessness with her equal needs, and he would not recognize that they might be different from his own. Discussion took place as and when the mood took him – as did their bedding.

It was his thoughts about her that Caroline disturbed as they walked across the downs towards Cantle. The weather had been still and dry for days so that the haymaking in the valley was well under way, and the sounds of jingling harness, haycarts rumbling and men with broad vowels urging horses to 'goo-waan, goo-waan' rose clearly on the evening air.

'Let's sit on the old walls a bit, Isaac.'

At once he became alert with concern. 'There's naught wrong, lass?'

'Don't fuss. I only want to sit and look. It isn't often we have the time.'

'I know, I know. I al'us mean to . . .'

'Isaac, I was not complaining.'

From the ancient walls on Old Winchester Hill, they could see clear across the valley to their home.

'It's a pity your aunt couldn't have been at wedding.'

'I dare say that at sixty she'd rather spend a day with Louise than randying – even though it was quite a sober affair. And in any case, she's not likely to leave the new lad on his own until she's sure of him.'

'Aye, and I reckon I'd a sooner spent a day playing hidey with Louise than that kind of caper.'

'Isaac! After all you said about the wonderful experience of giving a bride in marriage.'

'Lunacy! What else could I say. Who am I to give Kitty to Peter?'

'Ah well, it is what they wanted, and that's what friends are for.'

They sat quietly, watching the darkness on the far side of the valley creep up the side of Beacon, until only the white marker-stone, lit by the last rays of the sun, was visible. As the light went, the moist valley air of the July evening mixed the scents of privet and meadow-sweet, linden flowers and new-mown hay and brought them drifting upwards.

'You're not taking chill from the stones?'

'The stones are still warm.' Caroline had not particularly wanted to sit and rest, only to stretch out a rare evening when there was no one claiming their attention. They had spent a few hours frivolously at the wedding ceremony of Peter and Kitty at Blackbrook, followed by a supper in The Star. They had all had enough barley-wine to release them briefly from their constant worry about mouths to feed and where the next penny was coming from. Of the four, only Isaac and Kitty were earning.

These days, Peter lived more like a beggar than a cleric, trusting that a meal would turn up from somewhere – usually it turned up from Croud Cantle Farm or from the ever-simmering cauldron in Kitty's lodging-hut. Caroline worked long and hard, but her work was unpaid; the sale of farm produce, however, clothed and fed her. Isaac's earnings from muck-shovelling were swallowed up by his career as the navvies' physician.

'They made an odd pair. Peter's coat hadn't seen the light of day for months, and Kitty with her armful of meadow-sweet . . . I could have wept for them.'

'Aye . . . yet well suited.'

'Did you think it odd to see Peter all of a sudden with two grown daughters?'

Isaac laughed. 'Aye. He's got a handful in that Maggie – she's as sharp as a tack.'

'I can't think what will happen to her – or to Agnes, for

that matter. Girls like that – brought up on the diggings in a shanty full of labourers but able to read books and understand bits of Latin – what on earth can they do? Any farm-girl would have been out to service long before she was seventeen, but what household would take an independent girl like Maggie?'

'She'll make some young lad a blessed good wife, and there's naught wrong with having a mother who can read and write.'

'Isaac! It's not every woman who thinks that husbands and babies are life's only blessings.'

'Aye, and there's one not a hundred yards from me.' He laughed as he pulled her to her feet and began walking down towards Cantle.

'What a treat it is when you laugh, Isaac . . . twice in five minutes. You should do it more often.'

'There's not a deal to laugh about, what with the price of feed; and the horse is getting past it, and both axles of the wagon won't do much longer. No wagon could stand up very long to the treatment it gets along the rough tracks.'

The old worry of never enough money clutched at Caroline. She knew very well that their worries would be halved if they gave up their work with the sick and injured, and she put in more hours in making pies and preserves for market or if she helped Auntie Sel to manage more pigs, or another cow . . .

'We can't give up what we are doing, Isaac. I love the work, I would never hoe another row of beans or skin another rabbit if I could spend all my time making sick people well – especially the children, poor little things. I do hate to see a child sick and frightened. I can't stop now that I've learnt such a lot. Baking pies and scrubbing shirts seems so – so petty compared to nursing people.'

'We may have to – likely *shall* have to before too long. We need quite a large sum of money.'

She knew where this was leading yet again, and her spirits sank.

Caroline wanted Isaac to succeed, for in his success lay the fulfilment of her own strong ambition, but she did not want him to press her again to do what was against her conscience to do.

Her ambition was to do what she could to heal, comfort and return to health the scores of sickly fatherless children who lived along the hundreds of miles of the diggings, and to preach her gospel of carbolic acid, hartshorn and creosote, of washed hands and clean water. To keep the children free of the sickness and fevers that went through the shanty communities like wildfire.

Caroline had never revealed to anyone except Kitty Fire-Bucket the extent of that ambition. The two women had come to trust each other with their subversive dreams of fulfilment. Caroline wanted to make children healthy, and Kitty wanted to fill their minds.

The situation of Kitty, whose four children were of assorted parentage, was not at all uncommon in the masculine Rogue Society of the railway builders.

There, the need of virile, male muscle-power to satisfy Bona-fide Society's hunger for railways, over-rode all considerations.

There, virile men with handsome clothes and plenty of money, could enchant or buy women.

There, there were no rules excepting those which men – the contractors and the navvies – chose to make or break.

It was as though both Rogue and Bona-fide Society colluded in producing a situation where there was no bar to a man making a woman pregnant, 'sloping off', adopting another name and disappearing, leaving the woman to fend for herself and her children. The woman, now unacceptable to Bona-fide Society, was trapped into taking another transient husband . . . and another . . . and another . . .

Kitty, however – in the Rogue Society which allowed no place for a woman in its system – had created a niche. As a 'model' shanty-keeper, and a 'friend' of Ainsley Chambers, she had kept her children dry and fed. Often there were hours when navvies were rained-off. They had nowhere to go unless it was to their lodgings to sit on their cots, the charge for which was to spend money on their shanty-keeper's beer.

Kitty's niche was in the Mission Hut. There, reading one of her Heathcliffs, she had become useful to navvies and to contractors who, as a result, had fewer brawls with villagers to deal with. It did not make her popular with those shanty-keepers who earned the most when their lodgers were stupefying themselves with drink, but Kitty understood that. Often it was their only means of trying to get back to the Bona-fide Society.

Since Caroline had come to know Kitty, and more of this other society which was living on her own doorstep, her compassion for the women and the neglected children of the itinerant navvies kept her working early and late with Isaac, for it was only by helping him attend to injured navvies that she was able to do anything for the women and children. Very occasionally, a thought wormed its way into her conscious: *Did I marry Isaac only because I wanted to learn everything that he knew about medicine?* Of course not, Caroline loved her serious husband, he was a good and free-thinking physician and she was glad to have a place beside him.

Isaac had broached the subject before.

She cut him off almost before the suggestion was made. 'I won't ask Ruth.'

'I didn't say that you should.'

'It's where you were leading.'

'Aye, well . . . supposing I were – I can't see why you can't ask your own sister.'

'It's *because* she is my own sister. Can't you see that? I won't ask her because it would put her in the position of not liking to refuse.'

'She used to send you money.'

'And now she doesn't.'

'She's well enough off.'

'That's nothing to do with it. I could just never bring myself to ask Ruth for money.'

'People who have plenty should be willing to share with those who have none.'

Anger tightened Caroline's throat, and tears rose in her eyes. Had she been able to analyse the reason, she would have realized that her anger was at herself. She knew that if she were to ask, then Ruth would help – she had always been generous with gifts if not with her time in letter-writing; it was a long time now since they had had any contact at all with her. Caroline knew that Isaac was right, the amount they needed would hardly be noticed by Ruth.

They walked through the village in prickly silence, a situation they had frequently found themselves in after their first year together. 'Lovers' tiffs,' Selena would say, or 'worry' or 'tired-out . . .' 'You'll settle yourselves into place in time,' she would tell Caroline. But time was passing and the tiffs were becoming more frequent, bitter and long-lasting.

When they reached their gate, Caroline said fiercely, 'If you think that rich people ought to share, and if you think that it's easy to beg for money from your own family – then *you* go and see your father and beg from him!'

Lack of money, or money put to disputed use, was the most frequent cause of trouble between them. They were by no means the first young couple who saw their dreams and ambitions withering for lack of a small bag of coins.

4

A CHURCH-PROPER MARRIAGE

WHEN KITTY AND PETER got back to Kitty's shanty, with
Linty dragging his feet, Kitty's girls had seen to Dutch and
to cooking the lodgers' food.

'No trouble, Mag?'

Always Kitty's first question on returning home. Her
reputation for fair rent and good cooking allowed her to pick
and choose her lodgers. She imposed four rules on them: she
would have no drunkards and no roistering women; she
would have no rotten ole tommy-shop meat in her cauldron;
'and if you was ever consideren layen a hand on any of me or
mine, then I should take it as a sign that you should like me
to cut off yer 'coutrements while you sleep.'

There was seldom any trouble in Kitty's hut. Men got a
better deal for their money from Kitty than from most other
hut-keepers. If they felt like drinking to excess then they
would sleep it off in a ditch rather than risk eviction. And if
they were overcome by a desire to lay a hand on anyone,
then they would not jeopardize their comfortable billet, but
would look elsewhere for that satisfaction.

But Maggie was a young woman, and although Agnes
was still only a bone-thin girl, she was older than Kitty had
been when Cocky Fire-Bucket had forced himself upon her.
Early in their lives, Kitty had schooled her children in the
theory of protecting themselves from predatory navvies.
'Up and under their 'coutrements with the toe of your boot—
don't aim at their front, get them from below. That gives
him summet to think on while you puts some distance
between him and you.' So far, all four of her children had
escaped any forceful sexual attentions from her lodgers.

'Only Dinky Boston,' Maggie answered. 'He was moaning again about his meat was overcooked. But he always do, anyway.'

That night, Kitty and Peter made unsatisfying love amid the snores, mumblings and belches from the tiered cots on one side of a flimsy partition, not helped on Peter's part by his awareness of the children and Dutch on the other side of another partition. Kitty expected something more of their church-wed coupling than she had experienced on the day that he had proposed to her, or when she had occasionally responded to Ainsley Chambers. She had supposed that the fact that they were husband and wife, and felt so affectionately for each other, would enhance her satisfaction. At least he was tender and gentle.

In spite of this unsatisfactory start, each got what they wanted equally – a respected partner, whose presence they enjoyed and who cared about their well-being.

Awkwardly, the next morning, and in spite of being familiar with Kitty's household, Peter tried to fit in with the routine domestic arrangements, slowing Kitty and her three children down in the execution of their chores in his helpfulness.

Eventually Kitty said, 'Look, Vicar-dear, if you wants to have a job of yer own every mornen, why don't you take on Dutch? Usually, we all does a bit each between other things, but it'd be a real help if you was to see to him, then we could get on.'

As Peter was guiding the stumbling Dutch back from where he had just unbuttoned him and pressed him onto one of the seat-holes in the privy, he had his first glimpse of what the past ten years had been like for Kitty.

It is early morning.

Peter feels more aware of himself, and the world in which he has settled himself, than he has for years. July's uniform green foliage, lushly almost blurring the shapes of the trees. Long grasses hardening to razor-sharp edges. Reddening apples, softening peaches, ripening seeds – vetch, henbane, sycamore, holly, thistle, germander, wheat, oats, barley and poppy. July's heavy blue sky is scored by the flight of songless birds, but not of the cuckoo, who has flown. Although sky, trees and flowers do not come close to the By Privett shanties, for the first time in years he feels a sense of communication with Nature and the God whom he had known twenty years ago.

He feels so elated, that had it not been for the fact that Dutch would crumple up without support, Peter might drop to his knees.

'Let us sit on the bank, Dutch. We'll keep out of their way for a bit until we get our instructions.' He smiles at Dutch. 'It would have been more sensible had I gone down and started my new labouring career, but I thought Kitty would be pleased to have me about for a day. Wasn't that a foolish notion?' He speaks normally to the shambling, damaged man, as though Dutch understands him.

It is not the first time that Peter has taken Dutch to the privy, but as, by the rules of the Rogue Society, Kitty is now married to the two of them, the situation is not easy for Peter who, although a rebel against its mores, is a born and bred Bona-fide, and who has only recently entirely given up the wearing of clerical dress.

Dutch sits down, obedient as a docile dog, on the sloping edge of a meadow overlooking the group of huts which have grown haphazardly along the track which leads to the now almost completed cutting. Kitty comes out to the communal pump and slams its handle up and down vigorously until two pails are full.

'Look at her, Dutch, it would take two of each of us to make one of her.' Dutch stares uncomprehendingly with his good eye, his good hand occupied as usual with smoothing his fingertips over anything close by. He smooths the meadow as though it is a green-coated animal.

'Neither of us has made her life any easier – just the reverse. I brought her one baby to add to her troubles, and one of you gave her another. The last thing Kitty needed was more babies. I suppose that I was worse than any; I relied on her good nature to take in young Vic – I knew that if I asked her then she would not send him away. I thought it was enough if I paid her a few shillings for his food and clothes – I never thought beyond the time when she was wet-nursing. Even that bit of money stopped when my income vanished. By then I had begun to think of Vic as hers.'

He lies back and watches the passage of a wisp or two of cloud.

Dutch's eyes close as he slips into his usual half-sleeping state. Peter continues talking as though they have been friends from boyhood. 'Have you ever thought what a phenomenon Kitty is?' His voice is reduced almost to a whisper, so that even if Dutch were able to understand, he would find it difficult to hear. 'She has lived in that mess down there from the day she was born. She has been abused and ill-used in almost every way man can devise. Nobody ever taught her a moral standard nor let her have something for which she did not have to pay dearly.

'And yet ... and yet ... she has brought up four children as bright and clever as you would find. She is more moral than judges and bishops – she doesn't judge in terms of "right or wrong", "without sin, or sinful", "lawful or illegal" – she thinks, "Will that hurt?" "Is that good?"

'Where would you have been if it hadn't been for Kitty? If you had been with Black Annie when it happened, you would have been lucky if she had thrown you scraps like a dog.

'Kitty budgets wonderfully the feeding lodgers, she sees to her children, organizes me, arranges you, barters, cooks, scrubs, brews and mends, yet still makes time to teach children at the Mission their letters. Why, man, if a man in business had so many responsibilities, he would have a wife, a roomful of clerks, and a kitchen full of servants to cosset him.'

He stands up and helps Dutch to his feet. Maggie comes out and bangs dust from a rag mat, Agnes throws out a bucket of dirty water and Kitty hitches the contents of a basket of washing onto a hawthorn hedge.

'It occurred to me one day, Dutch – not that long ago, to be honest – that the world is full of men like me who sit with a cup of tea and a slice of walnut cake being revered as "men of God", and men like you who traipse the world without care or responsibility and a pocket full of silver, and we do our merry morris dance, clacking our staves to show what fine fellows we are . . . yet, there's nothing in your life or mine that we've ever done that's half so worthwhile as what Kitty does every day. The world would manage without the likes of both of us.'

Kitty heard the two men's footsteps, and was standing watching their approach when they neared the shanty.

'Well, there you are then. Dear Lord, I was beginnen to wonder if Dutch hadn't fallen down the hole, and you'd a jumped in to rescue him. Now come on, Vicar-dear, if I an't there when the children gets to the hut, you know what a happen – they little buggers a just go slopen off swimmen in the pond and they won't never learn a theng.'

It was a long walk to the hut, and Dutch was slow, so that, as Kitty had foreseen, most of the children had gone, either to earn a few pence on the cuttings, or to share a dew-pond with some cows and cool their tender skin overheated from being bared to the brazen July sun. Kitty would have rounded them up and laid down the law, but Peter persuaded her to sit with him so that they could talk about their future. She was persuaded, but only on condition that he helped her give the floor a 'good brush and a sluice with some of Isaac's kersote'.

'I don't know if he's right that 'tis better than sand for cleanen proper, but it do surely smell fresh.'

Cleaning the hut floor was not something new to Peter, and he was pleased to be doing anything at all useful after his salutary start to the day.

'Kitty? Listen . . . if I could raise a loan to do something to improve things for the children, what would be the first thing ought to be done?'

'You do say some thengs, Vicar-dear. Was it a loan enough to get a few chairs? Or give it Isaac to mend his wagon? Or was you thenken of borrowen a fortune to give the children their own school, like Town children? Or somewhere better than a sod hut for their mothers to birth them, like Town people? First theng anybody would want to know is how much was you thenken of spenden?'

'Say two thousand pounds. What would you do – take a large house and make it a ragged school? Then nobody could stop you teaching children to read.'

'Ah well, if we are talken fairy stories . . .'

He looked at her, and would have made love to her there in the dimly-lit hut, as he had on the day he proposed, had benches and floor not been awash with Isaac's creosote solution, and had Dutch not been sitting on a bench outside. Instead he put his arms about her and kissed her.

'Kitty Fire-Bucket . . .'

'Mistress Warren, if you please.' With playful archness, pulling away from him. She began to sprinkle sand on the floor.

'Not unless you stop talking to me as you talk to Linty. No other Mistress Warren ever talked to her husband like that. My mother addresses my father as Mister Warren.'

'Well then, happen your father don't talk such Linty kind of nonsense . . . raisen a loan . . . two thousand pound

. . . I haven't even got no idea how much money that is. I never heard Linty talk worst nonsense than that. No good never come out of lenden or borrowen.'

From behind, he folded his arms about her full bosom and kissed her neck.

'Kate Warren, Kate Warren, my family does not know what it is missing by not acknowledging you as a member of it.'

She turned and gave him a brief, tight hug.

'Vicar-dear, what makes me sad is that they have lost you and you have lost them. I don't know how it is that people who couldn't find it in their hearts to come to their own child's wedden could ever have gotten such good a man as you are.' She released him suddenly. 'Now then, if you *was* somehow to come into some money, then you had best ask Caroline – for she has a fantasy that is equal to a fortune.'

Peter Warren guessed that Caroline's ideas were probably no less fantastic than his own. Even so, he decided to act as though the fantastic were no less obtainable than the commonplace, and during the course of the next weeks he wrote a series of letters, one of which was sent to Edward Warren to be forwarded to Ruth.

My Dear Ruth,

My condolences at the death of your manager Alexander Marney. I hope that, in spite of the sad loss, your extraordinarily successful career will not be marred.

I must confess that the above is not my sole reason for writing this letter. At the outset, I will be frank – this is a letter begging for a contribution to a charitable cause.

With the exception of personal comments, the many letters over the signature of The Reverend Peter Warren were in the same vein. They outlined a scheme to provide a small hospital financed by a charitable foundation. It was to put into practice the most advanced theories of hygiene in the treatment of the sick and injured and in the lying-in care of women. There would be a prominent display of the names of every benefactor, and each would have the right to be treated in a special dormitory.

. . . You will have, of course, most probably surmised that this is your sister's and Isaac Evans's scheme. Caroline has no idea that I have included yourself in my list of people to whom I am sending this letter of appeal and I should be in her black books should she know. However, I know that you retain an affection for this part of Hampshire and its people – and it is they who will benefit if this hospital ever comes into being.

I should like you to know that I am now most happily married. My great fortune is in having persuaded dear Kitty, Vic's ('The Vicar's Baby') foster mother, to become my wife. Kitty and I do what we can to provide the hundred and one necessary comforts for families who live in this 'forgotten' society of the railway builders.

By the kind auspices of your good uncle Toose, Kitty is, wisely, soon to put Maggie, her eldest, to an elderly couple of sugar-boilers in Blackbrook in the hope that she will escape the 'unacceptable' society into which she was born. You may not see a comfit and humbug maker as a rise in society, but I assure you that in the eyes of 'acceptable' society, it is indeed a rise. One to which I do not aspire since I am now a paid employee of the contractors building a railway branch-line in Hampshire. This is certainly a novel experiment on the part of the Company, for I do not shovel spoil for them, but I have their agreement that I shall continue to act, as I have long done, as the Navvies' Vicar, and mediator. The Company hopes that in paying me a stipend, it will be refunded through fewer hours lost in disputes. Though you may guess that much of my time at present is spent in such endeavours as writing to possible benefactors . . .

5

THE WILD WHITE HORSE

By THE TIME RUTH reached Virginia City for the final performance of the tour, news of her successes had preceded her. Alex had prepared the details so meticulously that Bret Lauchaise, who had been Alex Marney's able and enthusiastic Assistant Manager, had now taken over Alex's role, and was able to interpret the entire operation with very few hitches.

Newspapers were wild with enthusiasm for 'the golden Venus', with 'divine legs', and breasts 'twin perfect orbs'. Infatuated reporters vied with one another to win the battle of hyperbole. She was 'La Tylee – superb!' 'Tylee the magnificent goddess at whose feet all men fall.' 'Perfect and unattainable.' 'A Deity.'

Her decision gradually to drop 'Rosalie' in favour of her own name had been the right one, done at exactly the right time. She had never received such continuous acclaim and public notice. She now received the accolade of being instantly recognizable as 'La Tylee' or 'Tylee' but mostly as 'The Woman'.

Each town or city was more lavish than the last in the payment of its homage – and each theatre under whose name they were engaged more expansive in the offer of its fees for her return. During the weeks of the tour, Bret secured increases in Ruth's fee from two hundred and fifty dollars a performance, to five hundred dollars – the highest fee ever paid to a single performer. To say nothing of the percentage on every ticket sold.

By the time they arrived in Nevada, a state of such wild excitement had mounted that a local reporter, Mr Mark

Twain of *The Enterprise*, vowed that he should bring this 'circus performer' down to earth – or to the sawdust ring, where he believed she rightly belonged. The fact that Mr Twain had never seen 'The Woman' perform or heard her sing, did not prevent him from making such a vow.

Long ago, Ruth had learned that whilst newspapers had the power to enhance public affection for a performer, they could do little to deflect that affection if the performer was idealized, or idolized. She and Bret discussed – as she had with Alex – her next performance in the light of reports of the last, but seldom made more than minor changes; they were professionals and knew what they were about. Even if they had known *The Enterprise*'s reporter's threat to 'vivisect and show her up as merely a beautiful shape with no histrionic powers', Ruth was by now so confident of her own ability to hold an audience that an entire front row of reporters would not have made her voice tremble on a single note.

It had been good for Jarrett O'Mahoney to get away and be with Ruth. She continued to let him believe that she and Alex were to have been married – it gave the child she was carrying a kind of legitimacy, and herself the status which she felt that her pregnancy required of her. During the course of the journey across the country, he began to drag himself out of the black hole of his grief.

Whereas previously he had taken only a slight interest in his son's business of marketing dazzling enchantment, he now wanted to know all about it. And when he knew, he was for ever retelling of his amazement at the skill and business acumen needed in staging such entertainment, and of Alex's genius as a man of business.

'I never did have any job with completion dates as tight as these. 'Tis like starting on a new building site every few days. Build the sets, take them down, build them again – why those lads could have built Boston a new city hall with the skill and labour that's gone into making that fairyland.'

Although it was becoming usual in the theatre for renowned performers to travel the country taking the lead in a play, they were usually supported by actors and performers engaged locally. The New English Company travelled complete, taking on locally only unskilled labour. They occupied an entire railroad coach, with another for the scenery and Ruth's 'wild' horse.

The performance by Ruth of *The Wild White Horse* came from an idea she had after reading a modern lyric poem. Alex had seen the possibilities for her, and had a version of the tragic poem set to music particularly suited to Ruth's voice range. It was Bret's idea to stage the performance entirely out of doors. The drama called for a rocky terrain and a climate where it could be performed in the open air at night. Where there were no mountains or rises, then they would build a representation with lath and plaster. Ruth and Bret made by their perfect planning, organization and execution of *The Wild White Horse* a memorial to Alex's imagination.

Although her pregnancy was not very far advanced, and was still undetectable, except that 'The Woman's' famous 'twin perfect orbs' were now fuller, Jarrett O'Mahoney had taken to fussing over her. There were so many occasions when he said, in a voice intended to be jovial, 'Rest yourself, m'dear – and if ye'll not rest yourself, then rest me grandson', that Ruth was tempted to tell him that the child was not Alex's, so that she could revert to the state of 'owning herself' as she had once done. But she had grown to like the old Irishman with his rough manners and sentimental nature. She knew that in committing herself to his well-being, she had committed herself to his future.

It was his insistence on his 'grandson' that started Ruth thinking seriously about the future. She would soon be thirty-three, her voice was better than it had ever been, her figure was firm and mature, and her acting ability improving with every performance she made. But in a few months she would be a mother. Could a child so young travel from city to city? Engage a nurse . . . but a child needed stability, a home. The idea of returning to Boston, or of living in the Vermont house, held no attraction for her. Not that she had any real plan, or desire, to settle anywhere, but a woman who expects a child must find a nest for it.

Because of the nature of the dramatic element in the spectacle, there was ever only one performance of *The Wild White Horse* in each city. 'Build up expectation, more than fulfil it, leave the audience gasping and overawed and longing for you to return' – that was their philosophy. It worked: already Bret had been offered engagements for the next five years.

As the Company crossed the continent, excitement at the prospect of this great attraction grew. Consequently, the tour played to huge audiences, who in some towns brought their cushions and shawls and picnic baskets and sat out under the stars. No walls, and simple bench-staging for seats, meant no limit to the size of the audience who paid to pass into the enclosed area. Those who could not afford the high-priced patch of ground, watched from beyond the pale, and the takings from those close to the spectacle were so large that nobody begrudged them their distant view. And, in any case, the opening extravagant fireworks display was free to the entire countryside.

It took three days to set up the scenery which – although there were many other acts before Ruth's finale – was entirely designed to produce most effect at the climax of the evening. The open-air venues were admirable sites for the great spectacle, but when the Company came to the one at the base of a mountain trail in Virginia City, everyone agreed that nothing could be more superb.

Virginia City throve on the mining of silver. When Ruth arrived there, a delegation of mining company and city officials greeted her as though she were a visiting princess. It was a place of high hopes and despair, riches and poverty – and like other gold or silver mining areas, it was a man's town where any woman was welcome. And now they had *The* Woman.

With frontiersmen, gamblers with diamonds set in the buttons of their waistcoats and Madams in sables and rubies, *The Wild White Horse* could not have been more suitable for this place. Here men, who spent their lives alone picking the High Sierras or in isolated camps, were hungry for a bit of glitter and fantasy.

Ruth had expected to feel exhausted by the time she had travelled so far across America and performed her extraordinary exit many times, but she felt well and elated. When Jarrett asked her if she ought not to be resting, she told him not to fuss her and, as she used to when she was a girl in Australia, dressed in trews and jacket and with a large hat to hide her hair, she rode Leucous-Equus, her 'wild' horse, out into a part of the world that appeared untouched by humans. Yet she knew that below the surface of the terrain, thousands of men were blasting and picking at the rock.

Whether it was the brightness of the sun, or the sense of space in every direction, or the rocky terrain, or the sense of walking on land impregnated with silver – or whether it was to do with her condition – she never decided. Whatever it was, on that day she fell in love with this strange, new land.

In the clear air of the high altitude, she looked down upon a river with green fields and cottonwoods along its banks, then beyond to the distant purplish-blue mass of the Humbolts. At the centre of the scene a huge amphitheatre was created by mountains and a bare, white sandy desert. A most sublime view.

Something about the landscape entered her and never left. She knew that if she ever settled anywhere, it would be here. The depth of her feelings quite overwhelmed her.

Never had she felt so emotionally committed – so in *love* –
except . . . except . . . but that was past, she was free of it,
free of such destructive love.

As it had always done when it dropped its guard, her
mind tried to snap shut on that thought, but this time it did
not shut tightly. She let Leuc amble easily and allowed her
mind to open a crack to the image which lived there – a living
likeness kept in the locket of her mind. A profile likeness
. . . fine hair, beautiful jaw, straight forehead . . . the head
turned but she would not let herself look into the image's
loved eyes, even though there was protection for her now
from its destructive love. Her condition protected her.

In the first week or two she had thought of taking
bitter-herb and pennyroyal, and of expensive physicians
whose huge fortunes were made more from their reputation
for discretion, than for their gentleness with women. But,
now that she had dismissed those ideas, she had become one
of the venerated – a woman in a certain condition. She felt as
protected by that condition as the floating child was
protected by its little amniotic sea. Prospective motherhood
defended her against her own defective nature, the presence
of the growing foetus would overwhelm her decadence.

That morning, a letter which had been following her
across several states, reached her. When she recognized
Aury's handwriting, she could scarcely open it for her
fumbling fingers. Aury's writing.

It was getting on for ten years since that disastrous night
when she had stood in for Netty. The night when she heard
that Pa had died – the terrible night when Aury had
discovered the fact she had not wanted him to know. The
fact – that he had 'sat drinking French wine and watched my
own sister . . .' – the fact that she had stood naked on the
stage and allowed the camouflage of cosmetic to be washed
from her naked body before an audience of 'pigs at their
trough drooling at the sight of you'.

What agony it had been to have lost Pa and Aury together. But she had never revealed that to anyone. When, that same night, Alex had offered to buy out her contract with Teddy, it had come as a godsend. A new start, that was how it had seemed. And yet . . . how can one ever get away from years and years of sweet and bitter memories?

His letter was brief to the point of formality, contempt even. Ruth guessed that it was probably her mother who had prompted its sending. *'It is your place, Auryn. Whatever happened is in the past. Blood is thicker than water and she is your sister, and it is her right to know. It is for you to tell her.'*

Dear Ruth

I am shortly to be married. My wife-to-be is the daughter of an immigrant farmer. She was born out here. We shall live here at Marl, so that Ma will have someone when Lavinia goes.

If you can spare ten minutes for Ma, will you please write to her.

Auryn

Not 'Dear Sister', as he would have written to Caroline. And I don't even know where Lavinia is going. Marrying? Probably – she's twenty-three, twenty-four. Disguised barbs – he had not let her know his wife's name, nor what she looked like. Undisguised chides because she did not write home – she deserved these. She never knew what to say in letters except that she was in such-and-such a place, and that she was well. On paper her life appeared ridiculous and worthless, every sentence that she wrote home she examined in the light of how Auryn would interpret it. Nothing would convince him that what she did in giving an hour of pleasure to thousands of people by portraying a fantasy was quite as honourable as providing the raw material for the woollen stockings in which they sat watching her.

She ran her hands down the beautiful, fine white mane of Leucous-Equus, whose performance each night was as memorable as her own, his heavy muscles and thundering hooves a contrast to Rosalie's soft vulnerability as he carried her off stage. Urging him on now, she guided him back towards habitation. Perhaps in future years she could come here and allow herself to open the locket and look fully at the image. But not now. Not yet.

The evening of the final performance of the tour was perfect. After she had been made up and was ready for her performance, Ruth sat at the open door of the travelling-wagon in which she rested and dressed before her appearance. Bret had come in excitedly to say, 'All the newspaper reporters are in the front row,' and she felt elated. In the same way that she had recognized the cold damp breath of peccant spirits on the eve of Alex's departure, she now was aware of a tender presence.

From where she sat she could see the light from the white flares that lit the stage, and hear the rhythmic drumming that indicated the exotic Egyptian tableau that was being created. Half an hour more before the finale.

'Shall you be disturbed if I sit with ye, m'dear?' The old man, as always overawed in the presence of Ruth in her transformed state of half-woman half-goddess.

'If you don't mind my silence.'

He climbed the few steps and sat on the top one. 'Shall you mind if I talk?'

'No.'

'I wanted to put a proposition to ye, but I'm not sure if this is the time. Maybe it'll disturb ye . . . maybe I should wait till . . .'

'It's all right, Mr O'Mahoney, when I am ready to go on there is nothing that would disturb me. Before my face is painted and I am in costume then I am agitated, but now . . .

please, I should be happy to listen to you. Just so long as you don't expect me to join in.'

'If my dear Alex had not been quite so eager . . . I mean, if he'd not have anticipated . . . well, there would have been a marriage, wouldn't there? And the child would have had his name . . .' There was nothing of the wealthy, confident, jovial old Irish immigrant; he was hesitant and unsure. 'Bless us, Ruth, I don't know how to say the first words so that you'll not get my meanin' wrong.' Her silence was unhelpful, but he stumbled on. 'If I was . . . If you was to marry me . . . wait . . . listen, hear me out . . .' Ruth was waiting, limp-wristed and relaxed, listening as though eavesdropping on him speaking to someone other than herself.

'A business arrangement . . . for the child. So that he can inherit . . . so that it is not the last of the O'Mahoneys who will be buried when I die. I've built a small empire, m'dear, and there's none to inherit it closer than Mrs O'Mahoney's cousin's children, who have never sent so much as a card in all the years she was sendin' them things.' He paused, perhaps hoping, in spite of what she had said, that she would respond. She did not.

'Well . . . what I was going to suggest to you, was that you married me . . . in name only . . . I would never come near you . . . you could live as separate as you like. I would make a good settlement on you . . . you would be a wealthy woman. All I want is for Alex's son to bear Alex's name. Nothing else. Only that the O'Mahoney family does not die out.'

From the direction of the performance, the sound of tinkling bells was carried on the still air, followed by cheering. A glittering woman had mysteriously disappeared from a glittering box, and had reappeared, tripping down the mountain track. To the vast audience, a great proportion of which was mining men, it did not matter whether there were two different women dressed in silver, or whether

magic had really been performed before their eyes – they had
come for the spectacle of women dressed in flesh-coloured
tights and sparkling bodices who could dance, and act, and
disappear from a glittering box. And to be entertained
lavishly whilst they waited for the appearance of 'The
Woman' herself.

A youth with a flare came towards the wagon. 'Time,
Miss.'

She stood up, breathed deeply and stretched her arms
wide. 'Coming, Alfy. Is Leuc in a good mood?'

'Yes, Miss, never better. You'd better come.'

She followed the young man with the light to where she
would make her entrance.

Mr Twain and his fellow reporters sit before the
courtyard of the Castle of Laurinski. A mass of buttressed
masonry. Gates and a drawbridge over a moat, and, beyond
them, the rocky terrain leading to the mountains. Nature
has provided a moonless night, so a large replica of a golden
setting moon gives light to the scene. It is ethereal and
mystic. A lithe, young Tartar Prince steps into the scene. He
is superb in velvet cloak and tights that reveal long, slender
legs. Vigorous and graceful he runs to centre stage and hears
the roar of excitement that rises from the audience; it is the
sound of the sea breaking, it is acclaim and La Tylee
responds to it dramatically, open-armed.

So far, she has not uttered a word, yet Mr Twain is at
once ready to defend her against any word that might ever be
written against her. He has not reckoned with her quality of
primitive paganism, nor expected that those elements in her
would have appealed to similar qualities in himself. Mr
Twain is about to join the other reporters who have
witnessed and testified to the divinity of La Tylee. Mr Twain
will not need his notebook, he will never forget the first time
he saw 'The Woman' in the living flesh.

* * *

As she stepped out into the light of the row of white-light flares, Ruth was as usual detached from what was happening, even as at the same time every pore was open and every nerve-end sensitive to the experience. As people were admitted, they had received a copy of the words of the epic work, but Ruth's depiction of it, and the quality of her voice in the tense silence, carried on the still air, made the printed words unnecessary.

As it had been with 'Rosalie', 'The Woman's' professionalism made her word-perfect and sure-footed, whilst Ruth thought about old Jarrett's proposal of marriage.

Years ago, before she ever went to London, Auryn had shouted at her that the music-hall was no place for a woman. He had not recognized that there were some women – like herself – who would shrivel if they were domesticated. Women – like herself perhaps – who live the fullest and most worthwhile part of their lives in full view of thousands of people who had paid to watch. Ruth loved the life, the travelling, the people – without all this there was nothing that stirred her. Aury would never understand why, never see the worth of such loving companions as Netty and Jo, or appreciate the creativity of Teddy or Alex, never appreciate reliable people like Gustav or young Alfy, or the skill of Bret Lauchaise. All that Aury had seen was a display of a woman's body, and he had thought it 'sordid'.

She had a talent to give pleasure, nothing sordid . . . a glittering travelling circus, briefly entering the lives of thousands of people. The world of Bounderby's had been mostly that of men, but the travelling other world that Alex had created was for their wives and children too. There was nothing wrong, nothing disgraceful in what she did. Aury was wrong. This was a place for a woman – a good place – but it was no place for a child.

The Tartar Prince was now running her hands over Leucous-Equus's mane. Ruth snapped her mind shut on the connection that threatened to rise into her consciousness. She glanced into the wings and found the figure of her manager. Withdrawing from her previous dangerous and rambling thoughts and melding safely with the Prince's well-rehearsed lines, she acknowledged a sudden return of desire for the firm, heavy thighs and wide shoulders of Bret Lauchaise.

The Prince fell angrily upon the Count, stabbed him, and he lay still. The sight of blood on the breast of the Count was electrifying to the audience. Pistols were fired and the Prince was apprehended. 'LEAD THE VILE TARTAR HENCE. STRIP HIM OF THAT GARB HE HAS DEGRADED. LEAD OUT THE FIERY, UNTAMED STEED. PREPARE STRONG HEMPEN LASHINGS ROUND THE VILLAIN'S LOINS. LET EVERY BEACON-FIRE ON THE MOUNTAIN-TOP BE LIGHTED AND TORCHES LIKE A BLAZING FOREST CAST THEIR GLARE ACROSS THE NIGHT.'

The curtain fell before the final act.

As it rose again, Leucous-Equus – his white flanks dressed with crystalline powder, his fine mane and beautiful tail dressed as no wild horse, such as he was depicting, ever was dressed – whinnied, nostrils flaring, and tossed his mane and tail as he had been trained to do. A colleague of Mr Twain's whispered confidently, 'They will use a dummy – they will never tie her to that creature.' But as Mr Twain was to see: 'La Tylee's gauzy white loin-cloth, caught in a warm breeze, moved, revealing the whiteness of her elegant thighs. The same breeze caught her long red hair and billowed it around her bare white shoulders. It mattered not that this was a "Prince" who was to be put to death for the assassination of the Count – disbelief was suspended at the door of the temple of This Woman.'

The music reached a dramatic crescendo, broke off suddenly and silence fell.

Leucous-Equus, responding to Ruth's whispered command, reared up, whinnied wildly and galloped off the stage and away up the rocky mountain track with his near-naked rider strapped to his side.

Along the path of the Wild White Horse, the beacons sprang to life. Their bright flames illuminated the animal's eerily glowing flanks, flowing mane and tail. Their fizzing white glow lit the rider's streaming red hair and the movement of her brief garment.

As horse and rider were lost from view there was silence.

Although they had seen the climax many times, the other players, the musicians, the many undefined carriers, transporters and shifters, and Bret Lauçhaise and his staff, were all drawn to see yet again the extraordinary event. They were as stunned by the perfection of Ruth's performance as was the audience.

It was unknown at the end of any performance for a stage to be left open, illuminated and empty. Except in this one. No one to receive flowers tossed in tribute, no smiles and bows, no thrown kisses and low curtseys.

The emptiness of the bright, white stage and scenery was dynamical.

Then the silence was destroyed by tumultuous cheering. Young men and bearded miners ran forward and clambered onto the stage as though to get a last glimpse of horse and rider. Women, tears streaming down their faces at the fate of the 'Prince', held out their arms as though to bring 'him' back, shaking their heads at their neighbours in wonderment at what they had witnessed.

Eventually, reluctantly, they left.

Even before the cheering died down, Leuc had been blanketed and hidden from sight, and Ruth enveloped in a cowled woollen habit and returned to her rooms.

Alex, and now Bret, continued using Edward Warren's idea of creating an air of mystery and remoteness about Ruth, by keeping her away from people after a performance.

While journalists and magazine writers were fostered, her admirers were kept at arm's length as though she were royalty. This suited Ruth, for, although appearing as herself no longer held its former terror for her, she still preferred to keep Ruth as separate from 'La Tylee' and 'The Woman', as she had kept her from 'Rosalie'.

Because Rose Geary, the woman who was her dresser and personal maid, protected her from everyone except, in the past, Alex, Ruth was surprised to hear a tap on her door.

It was Jarrett O'Mahoney. He stood in the doorway looking at his boots like an embarrassed boy. 'I just came to say . . . I shouldn't never for a moment have thought of making such a proposal to ye, m'dear.'

She smiled politely at him. 'Don't stand there, Mr O'Mahoney.'

He came into the room and stood just as awkwardly.

'It's just that I couldn't bear the thought of never having sight of me boy's face again . . . so I got this wild notion, when you said you was carrying his son, that it was because of all the candles I lit for him . . . and the prayers when he was missing . . . and I've been goin' to confession again. I thought, that if . . . ah, but I'm an old fool thinkin' that I can put the clock back. But to get a grandson'd be like Alex'd rise from the ocean and be with me again.' His face was old and crumpled and sagging with sadness. 'But when I saw you there tonight . . . ah, so beautiful, beautiful it made me heart weep at the sight of it . . . I saw what a terrible waste of such a lovely creature, if you was to be bound to me because of Alex and the boy. So I wanted to say that I withdraw and don't expect an answer. It was a thing of the moment and I'm sorry for bein' such a damned old fool.'

Ruth's faint smile was kindly. 'But I don't allow you to withdraw, I intend to accept. I will marry you and the child shall have Alex's name. Alex's name. And on the terms you set out – except that I will never take a financial settlement. In name only, and I shall be free to live as I choose. A business arrangement for the sake of the child's future. He shall inherit the O'Mahoney companies.'

The old man looked quite bewildered for a moment, then said, 'He shall have land, estates ... everything. I should have never thought of any arrangement except in name only – I could never think of you as anything but a daughter. For haven't I already got Mrs O'Mahoney, God rest her soul – I'm married to her for all eternity.' He took her hand and shook it as he had shaken dozens of hands over contracts in the past. 'I would do nothing to harm Alex's son.'

'Nor I . . . Jarrett . . . I must call you that.'

'Yes. And shall you mind being called Ruth O'Mahoney?'

'I am used to playing roles; playing the part of Mrs O'Mahoney won't be difficult.'

'You'll put the face on it very well.' He turned to leave.

'Jarrett, has it never occurred to you that Alex's son might not be a dark-headed O'Mahoney . . . she might be a red-haired daughter?'

She did not see his face. He halted with his hand on the door-handle, nodded slowly and went out.

6

SLOPING OFF

THE EXTENSION OF THE railway network brought no prosperity to Cantle, except to its great Estate.

A halt had been built for the convenience of Sir Eustace, who owned many large parcels of land through which the railway track was laid. Already wealthy from his English estates and great tea and rubber plantations abroad, his payment in its own valuable stock by the railway company created an even greater fortune. Little of this trickled down to revive the life of the dying village.

The final, fatal damage to Cantle village was when the old mansion was converted into a brewery, and brewers were imported from the West Country to brew ... hops grown on Sir Eustace's Hampshire estates. When brewery workers displaced most of the few remaining farm-workers and took over their cottages, the old rancour and enmity rose once more for Cantle people to choke upon. It was not the first time that this had happened.

This time it was too much for them to swallow so, over the course of a few months, with their possessions hung about them and their bedding tied in a bundle, and the one remaining hen safely stowed along with the remedy box in the cauldron, the people of Cantle drifted away.

For a hundred years a boil of animosity between the Estate and the Village had swelled until, in the last generation of Cantle labourers, it had burst and left a still suppurating wound in the tiny community.

For a hundred years the Estate had bled the village, then it had picked its weakened corpse clean of anything worthwhile. Now it swept away its bones, and brought in the already-leached bodies of new labour – men and women made complaisant by other estates. Hungry couples with hungry families, hoping to find better pastures in a new county. Soon they would re-discover what they had always known – as would the lost villagers of Cantle – re-learning the lesson that a hungry family is not likely to elicit any sympathy from a wealthy employer.

But, for much longer than a hundred years, one small corner of Cantle had kept free of the Estate. And even now, with little remaining of Cantle beyond the tenant farms and the brewery, the church and the inn, Croud Cantle Farm still kept its hold on its few acres, which had provided for generations of Caroline's ancestors.

'It's a good offer,' Isaac said. 'If you took it, then we could rent a house and open a clinic in town. I am sure that Selena would prefer the comfort of your Aunt Ginny's nice place right in the centre of Blackbrook.'

'She can go there, of course she can go there. What Aunt Selena wants or does not want has nothing to do with the question. You are clouding the issue.'

'And you are being sentimental and foolish, Caroline. We are poor people who are in no position to refuse such an offer.'

'I am astounded that you could even *think* such a thing . . . *you* who have had so much to say about the death of village life.'

'Of course! But I am realist enough to know when I am defeated. Cantle is already dead.' He changed his aggressive tone. 'Caroline, I admire you for defending what you feel you owe to your family's history; it is honourable, but see it for what it is – sheer stubbornness. You have dug in your heels, but I am sure that you must want to let go. You've had a hard life. Take the offer.'

'No, Isaac. Ruth was born here, and Ma and her Ma, and hers before that. I was looking in that old Family Book . . .

it's over eighty years ago it was started, and the family had
been here for generations before that. Can't you understand, it's not mine to sell. It belongs to those of my family
who have lived and died here, and those in the future. I am
only its temporary keeper.'

'That is merely sentiment. If you look at it logically, this
place is a ramshackle structure of field-stones and wood and
mud and straw . . . Oh, yes, it *is*. Call it bricks and flint, say
it is timber and thatch if you like, the fact remains that it is an
old shelter for human animals that has had its day – no
different from a squirrel's dray or crow's nest when it has
reared its young. All the rest is sentiment, plastered over the
cracks to convince you that it is beyond price.'

Over the two years since the birth of Emily, their
arguments had increased in number and ferocity. Sometimes
he would be the one to make the first move, at other times,
Caroline, but they always kissed and made up, and made
love. And for a week or so they worked amicably together.
Then the cycle of passion, then anger leading to passionate
love, would repeat itself. As in variegated plants the green
leaves will grow strong at the expense of the variegated, so
their anger flourished and the love shrivelled. With Isaac and
Caroline, their resentful anger was the green leaf to the white
tender leaf of their love.

Emily was a grizzling child through the months of
teething. Selena was now very bent and aching from
rheumatics and was often chairbound so that Caroline was
forced to leave her work on the diggings and take on the cow
and the fields again. What with that and the constant worry
about lack of money, their life together began to deteriorate.
Worst of all was the enmity each felt for the other.

Caroline resented his freedom to come and go as he
pleased. He had trained her in many of his own skills, so that
she could staunch and clean the most hideous injuries and
not mind. With fractured bones, she had a better touch than

Isaac the physician, and she was so adept at turning a baby, that there had never been a mother in Caroline's care who had suffered a breech birth.

The argument about the offer made to purchase Croud Cantle by the Berol Estate had been the worst that they had ever had, and it finished when Isaac made a fist and tried to impose his will upon her, and she had shouted and pushed at him.

'But I am not your wife!'

'Aye, if tha' were, there'd be no bloody argument, I tell you that for nowt, woman.'

He had slammed off out, leaving the horse unfed.

It was a month before Caroline faced the certainty that, whilst she had believed that she had taken an educated man with ideals and vision, she had in fact taken a navvy with a navvy's temperament, and that he had, like thousands of others, sloped off and left her with two babies and little else.

It was another month before she faced another certainty.

He had left her with *three* babies.

7

EASY RICHES

RUTH HAD BEEN OVERWHELMED by her warm reception in Virginia City. The spontaneous and kindly gestures, especially from the mining population, plus the liking she had taken for the place itself, caused Ruth to decide that her baby should be born here.

The days immediately following her performance had been extraordinary. Now, when performing in luxurious halls in larger and more sophisticated cities, she was used to receiving after a performance anonymous gifts of rings, clasps, exotic fruit, flowers, and even lengths of silk. In New York, one unknown admirer had sent her a necklace inset with fire opals. She had not expected any such gestures in the unsophisticated mining city.

But, quite apart from the homages in print by Mr Twain and his colleagues, the citizens of Virginia City paid the homage of silver.

A large number of the audience had been silver speculators and miners, hard men, rough, often inarticulate. Their lives were lonely, harsh and dirty, their hunger for the precious ore was achingly obsessive. Hungry also for femininity and softness, they had found a feast in the great glittering event, with its finale of a beautiful bare goddess being borne away on a white horse across their own rocky terrain. The sight of this goddess touched their sentimental hearts.

Goddesses are paid homage to.

Ruth was paid in the form of many bags of silver dust, silver ingots, and certificates of mining stock worth a thousand dollars each. When it was learned that she had bought a house in Virginia City, a tunnel-constructing company and an entire mining district were named La Tylee as a tribute.

Months before October, when the baby was due, Jarrett O'Mahoney's attorney drew up a document which, in effect, made Ruth's child heir to everything Jarrett owned, and if the child should be a girl, there was a clause whereby she must retain the O'Mahoney name on marriage and pass it on to the next generation. Above everything, he wanted the O'Mahoney name to be remembered. It was a simple document which was intended to secure inheritance by Alex's child alone, and not by any that Ruth might conceive at a later date. In the event of this child not surviving, the entire fortune would go to an assortment of cultural charities in Boston.

It was only when Ruth read the document that she realized how wealthy the O'Mahoneys were. Her own inheritance from Alex, which she had thought large, was a mere fraction of the O'Mahoney agglomeration of companies. So, as she did with any problem too frightening for her to confront, she tried to shut her mind to the enormity of what she had done.

She saw that there was a kind of madness in the old man's action, for, when viewed dispassionately, what he was doing was disposing of his fortune to the bastard child of a music-hall singer. And he could not even be certain that the child was Alex's. But then, she thought, to give such a fortune to an unknown child is no more strange than giving it to galleries and churches. He had assured her that, although in the event of his own death she was nominally guardian of the child's inheritance, there were lawyers, accountants and managers to continue running the companies.

Upon having it explained to her, Ruth said, 'It is perfectly agreeable to me,' although she secretly believed that Alex's father was too blinded by the prospect of a grandson to see the possibility of Fate putting a string across his path.

The day of their marriage, he said to her, 'I know what ye said about not wanting anything settled upon you, but never in me life have I had a favour but what I returned it – and there's no favour greater than being given the right to have a say in a child's future. So, I want you to accept something – as a wedding gift, if ye like. There is a nice little parcel of railway stock tucked away, and I want you to have it. Do what you like with it, I really don't care . . . spend it on hats and French boots . . . it is yours to do with as you please.'

'I said no. If I were to take money, it would feel as though I had sold the child to you.'

'You must never say such a thing. You and I have given him a name.'

It was this comment more than any that made her suddenly writhe with guilt. *But it has a name, my name. This baby is a Tylee. I've allowed a Tylee child to be bought by a rich old man because he couldn't bear losing his own child.*

'My Alex was not spared to give you his name as he intended, and so we have done it in our own way. There was never a thing stopping me from leaving everything to Alex's babe if it was only the business of inheritance, but you are giving it a name and a place in the history of the O'Mahoneys. Me dear girl, it's no great thing to accept a marriage gift, is it?'

'Listen, Jarrett, if I needed money then it might be different, but if I never put my foot on a stage again, I have enough money to live in comfort for the rest of my life.'

'Then give it away, m'dear. Have ye no bog-poor family as I have meself?'

From time to time Bret Lauchaise, with a document case full of excuses for his visit, came hurtling on the fastest steam train. Then they would spend a few days that were as idyllic as Ruth had ever experienced.

He was several years younger than Ruth, but experienced with women and sensitive to them. He was in no way like her previous lovers. His flesh was firm and his skin golden-toned and as taut as her own. It was a long time since she had touched a youthful male body. For all that he was as black-haired as Aury was silver, she was reminded of the days when she would rub his back-broken muscles at harvesting. Half-awake, she would watch Bret sleeping and wonder that people who have been close can grow so far apart as she and Aury had and presently Bret too.

Ruth, being already pregnant, was entirely free of that inhibiting concern, free too of any man to dominate her. In taking Bret Lauchaise as her lover, Ruth was giving herself proof that, even on the night of her marriage to Jarrett O'Mahoney, she was a free woman.

She settled into a pretty house close to the edge of town, from where, right into her seventh month, she rode Leuc up into the crystal clear air of Sun Mountain.

But, although he controlled the lives of many hundreds of men, Jarrett O'Mahoney had no control over the vagaries of the womb of one woman. An event which he had not taken into account or planned for, was that Ruth would go into labour much earlier than expected.

A second event, occurring at virtually the same time as the first, and which he had even less opportunity to plan, was a sudden seizure which stopped his heart, thus leaving a situation which he would certainly have rectified had his death not been as premature as his inheritor's birth.

This situation was such that, had he not been already dead, the news might have caused him a seizure: Ruth gave birth to twins.

The first child arrived in the morning. A perfect baby who, in a fit of nostalgia for London days, Ruth named

Annette. Annette O'Mahoney, a five-pound heir to the Boston fortune. Her sibling, of equal weight and perfection, was not born until the afternoon, so that Annette was destined to be always half a day older than her brother Joseph.

The children were legally documented in the name of O'Mahoney. Prior to their birth, Ruth had not expected to have any emotions about the babies sufficient to interfere with her career. In London she had kept a pretty little dog which would bound and greet her and which she had quite missed when she had to leave it – she had imagined this was how it must be to leave a child to a wet-nurse and nannies. But, once they were put to her breast by the midwife, for the first time she fell in love. Her babies were a delight and wonder to her and soon became the centre of her world and her entire purpose for living.

In more than twenty years of womanhood, and ten years of being idealized for her femininity and beauty, she had experienced no love that she could show openly, no love that society permitted. With each of her lovers, there had been a mutual provision of satisfaction for their sexual hungers, and whilst her lovers had been content with the affair, it had been delightful. But each in turn had wanted more of her than she was able to give them – they wanted her to love them.

Before the birth of Anne and Joey, she had had no means of giving full rein to her love for another human being; now she was overwhelmed by her own unconfined emotion. At last she experienced selfless fulfilment, something that had been denied her since the time that she had come to realize that she was not like other women.

In May of the following year, the Cantle bonds that had always been there but slack and unnoticed, began to be felt by Ruth.

During her life with Teddy, then Alex, Ruth's letters to Cantle had slowed down to a trickle. Then, during that eventful year that led up to Alex's death they had stopped altogether. By the October of the twins' birth, she had lost all contact with both the English and the Australian members of her family.

Caroline too contributed to the loosening of their bonds. During that time she never wrote. It was always her intention to do so, but what with Louise and the farm and helping Isaac with the infirm wagon, and then Emily's birth, there was always a more urgent call upon her time.

In the spring, Ruth returned to Boston with the babies, to deal with affairs there. Jarrett had left a letter attached to his will, the expression of understanding and kindness in which surprised her and made her feel even more uneasy at having let him believe that she and Alex were to have been married. She wondered whether he had a premonition of his impending death or a warning spasm, or perhaps it was just that he was aware of his advanced years.

Whatever it was that prompted him to write such a letter, she had been shocked to discover that, although the construction and railway companies were Annette's alone, Ruth inherited the Boston house, some land, and an entire street of small, rented houses which Jarrett had acquired because Alex had been born in one of them. She also had use of much of the profits from his investments. His letter said that he knew that babies could 'play the very devil with a person, worming their way into your life so that you never wanted to be away from them' – therefore, he wanted her to be independent of the theatre if she wished to be. She had never thought him so perceptive a man as that.

In Boston, she grieved for him more than she had ever grieved for Alex – she grieved for not having known him better. For all their great differences, she felt, he and Pa would have got along very well. Even though he had been old enough to be her father, she thought that they might have set up together very happily – he did not want a wife nor she a husband; their common interest would have been the babies. He would have been well satisfied with Joey who, beneath the roundness, showed Alex's fine cheek-bones and wide forehead.

More and more, she realized the strangeness of the situation in which she found herself. Jarrett O'Mahoney had worked to drag himself from the depths of poverty to the heights of wealth, and had put everything into the hands of herself, a virtual stranger, and she had gained his name and his grandchildren. He had made a fortune for his wife and son – a wife who had never seen the peak of her husband's success, and a son who had died in his prime. Then, at the end of his life, just as he might have had some reward, he was gone. The old man had deserved something more than his fortune, but it had been too late.

Too late. Too late. Walking through his house, she felt disturbed. Her nights began to be broken again by dreams in which she was always about to mount horses which galloped away before she had fixed her foot in the stirrup; railway trains left without her, leaving her looking into the black tunnel of Great Hole; ships disappeared over the horizon without her. Always too late.

Her physician said that such a phenomenon was not unusual in newly widowed young women, especially those with babies. Widow? She had almost protested that she was not a widow.

She found it very difficult to see herself as others must see her. A music-hall singer who had trapped a foolish old man? Maybe there were some who said 'good luck to her', perhaps supposing that he was father to the twins.

Much of her time was spent fussing around the babies' room, playing with them, fascinated by each new achievement. Outside their presence, she felt ill at ease, hungry for something but she knew not what. Bret Lauchaise came and went discreetly, leaving her only temporarily at ease. She looked forward to the life that seemed to inhabit the house when he was there – he would whisk her into a polka, behave ridiculously with the babies, call her 'Princess' in the bedroom – but she knew that it was not Bret Lauchaise who could satisfy the deep hunger she felt.

She had made many friends during the years she had lived in America, but most of them were theatrical people, travellers who dropped in and out of her life, so most of the rooms at the Boston house were unused. After a few weeks, she decided to return to Virginia City where she had made several acquaintances during her months living there. It meant seeing less of Bret, but Nevada was hot and dry and welcoming.

One day, as she was giving instructions for the shutting-up of the house, Bret came to discuss future engagements and urge her to start another tour. 'Offers are pouring in from everywhere.'

'Not now, Bret. Let's talk about it when I'm settled down again in Virginia City.'

'You can name your own terms, Princess.'

'The children are too young to be left.'

'Take them with you then.'

For a moment she hesitated at the idea. Was this what she needed to satisfy her?

Bret mistook her hesitation. 'We'll only go to the best places . . . only where there are good railroad services . . . have you heard of the new George Pullman cars? Perhaps we could order one.'

He painted an enticing picture of lavish hotels and the prospect of plush travel which, a little over a year ago, would have put her in the grip of excitement . . . the prospect of travelling with the Company – new scenes, new places.

'No, Bret, it is impossible, I am not ready to go back

yet.' She never really understood what prompted her to say, 'I am going home, I want to show off my babies,' but as the words were created in sound, she realized that it was this that had been at the back of the vague longing – to go to Cantle and to Toolagarry. Before it was too late. Death made lightning visits. Pa's fever. Alex, Mr O'Mahoney . . . and that girl all those years ago, dying in Great Hole Tunnel. Ma must be grey-haired . . . Auntie Sel . . .

No, she would not wait until it was too late.

And she would see Aury – they would make their peace. She would get to know Auryn's wife.

The disturbing dreams stopped as soon as she made the decision to set sail.

PART FOUR

Retracing Steps

A LONG, HOT SUMMER

JULY, THE QUIET MONTH, has come round again. The only birds to send sound across the Cantle Valley are woodpecker and thrush tap-tapping to get at insects and snails. Nightingale and cuckoo have flown, the rest are stripping ripe hedgerow-seed and grain, or are at the strawberry beds in robber-bands.

To look down upon that peaceful valley with its wide acres of ripening wheat and white flocks of sheep on the downs, is to look upon a scene of romantic beauty. A patch of common-land with ancient oaks, a mellow old mansion, a few farmhouses and a mill, a rambling cottage beside the river, and a small church with its small spire suited to so small a community.

Hedgerows brim with dog-roses and wild woodbine, the uncropped sides of the downs are at their most graceful, with patches of rosebay willowherb catching and swaying with every warm breath that rises from the valley; the breath jiggles brizzia grass, puffs away huge bundles of thistledown and starts the firing-off of gorse seed from their dry, black pods.

The last rain has long ago seeped through the chalk and appears almost crystalline in its brilliance as, here and there, it springs out lower down the hill. On the crest of the downs it is dry, the marl that shows the route of ancient footpaths and raikes, is cracked and split; in the dust, pimpernel opens flat from dawn to dusk. Cattle ruminate in any bit of shade, and trout lie deep in the sinuous river-weed.

On Tradden Raike, sit Caroline Tylee and Kitty Warren,

resting from toting large bundles of assorted bedding and clothes.

Caroline Tylee, looking down upon the fruitful valley as she picked savagely at tufts of grass, saw none of it. Instead, she saw the image of her sister as she had last seen her when she still idolized her.

Over the years, that bright image had tarnished. Ruth seldom wrote to them, most of what they heard of her filtered through Edward Warren and then Peter, and that was little better than gossip about her stage triumphs. Then, out of the blue, she had written to say that she was married, widowed and had two children – and was coming home. Behaving in that high-handed way. Not considering whether it was convenient. And it certainly was not. The worst possible time.

Kitty Warren patted her knee affectionately.

'It an't no good you fretten, Caroline. You can't work miracles ... no, that an't really true, I reckon you have done nothen but work miracles this last fortnight. And we'll work some more ... you see, somethen will turn up.'

'Let us hope that you are right. But I wasn't thinking about the children, I was thinking about Ruth.'

'Ah ... was you?'

'There's a letter back home that's come from America; it says "Mrs Jarrett O'Mahoney, to await her arrival". I just looked at it, and thought, I don't know who that person is ... I mean, I knew it was for Ruth, but I suddenly realized that Mrs Jarrett O'Mahoney was somebody I don't know. It's like somebody you never met coming up to you and saying, "I'm your sister".'

'She won't be that much changed, ten years is not that long, and you'll love to see the babies, and hear all about your brothers and sisters and your Ma and your Auryn and his wife and baby and everything.'

'I don't think you're right, Kitty. Perhaps ten years

don't mean much if you stop in the same place and just get ten years older – but Ruth must have changed. That man she married was some sort of Master Builder – that means she must be *somebody*. She owns her own house.'

'Caroline! You an't never been worried about people like that before, and Lord, she's your sister. Treat her like you always have. She's the one who said she wanted to come home to see you, she knows what it's like, she lived there long enough.'

'Oh, it's not that, Kitty. She must take us as she finds us and muck in, we haven't got time to fuss over anybody . . .' Her voice trailed away.

'She won't expect anybody to fuss.'

'There won't be a second to spare . . . she'll come and go, and she'll think that I can't be bothered with my own sister . . . and if she goes away thinking that, then . . .' She felt tears threatening, bit the insides of her mouth and fiercely plucked at the cushion of a scabious flower.

'Caroline. It don't matter if people cry sometimes. I do. There's times when I cry my bloody eyes out.'

'Ach, Kitty, if I was to cry, it would only be for myself. If shedding tears did any good, then I'd cry like rain for all those poor little motherless souls.'

'We'll manage. They a be fine in the old hut till we can find somethen else. Peter says the Company might come up with somethen.'

'Then Peter's got more faith in the Company than I have.'

They gathered up their things and continued their journey to the redundant shanty at By Privett.

'I tell you what I find difficult to swallow, Kitty . . . it's that she never even replied to Peter's letter. Even if she didn't want to do anything, at least she could have said. I think he was a bit hurt over that, wasn't he?'

'No . . . probably a bit embarrassed. I don't think he

minded them other ole buggers refusen . . . but I don't think
he found it easy writen your sister . . . well, you know, I
think there was a time when he was keen on her. I don't
think he knew what to think when she never even wrote
back.'

They trudged on, sweat-marks darkening underarms
and waists. 'Dear sakes, Kitty, I wish I could have kept the
horse and wagon.'

'Ah, but it went in a good cause.' She laughed. 'I did
wonder if it wouldn't have been better if the horse had been
turned into meat instead of shillens.'

'Kitty!'

'You got to be practical, Caroline. He'd a made a good
few stews.'

Imperceptibly, Caroline's mood changed. Nobody
could ever be in Kitty's company for long and not be
brought up from a dark mood. Yet she had said that she
often had a good cry: Caroline found it difficult to imagine –
Kitty could always find a reason for optimism. Even at the
height of the present catastrophe, she would say, 'If we just
keep goen, there a be an end to it, there's always an end to
bad thengs.'

Caroline took a momentary glance at the other woman,
remembering the first time that she had encountered her.
Her first visit to a shanty-town, apprehensive as she had
gone with Peter to help in the Mission Hut, long before Isaac
had come on the scene. She remembered too how astonished
she had been when Peter had entered Kitty's ramshackle
shanty as though he did it every day – which, of course, he
did.

The hut had seemed dim, smoky and chaotic, with every
available bit of space used to hang and store the belongings
of Kitty, her family and the navvies. A row of narrow beds
on either side of the hut, a cauldron steaming, and washing
strung back and forth across the room, and in the midst of all

that, Kitty, on her hands and knees scouring sand into planks
that were laid on the bare earth as a floor – she had looked as
determined as any fussy dairymaid scouring a dairy floor. She
had said, 'Hello, Vicar-dear, you'm a sight for sore eyes,' with
such a light in her eyes, that Caroline wondered at the time it
had taken Peter to get round to marrying her.

'Kitty . . . ?'

'What then, dear?'

'I just wanted to say that I think Peter is the luckiest man
in the world.'

'I don't know about that – he an't that strong a man, and
he has a real hard time of it tryen to do everythen for
everybody at once.'

'I mean, that he is married to you.'

Kitty paused, hefted her bundle to her other shoulder,
and looked, almost shyly, at Caroline.

'All my life I wished that I was born from a farm family,
and now you sayen such a theng as that . . . why 'tis like
getten a citation from the Queen herself . . . no, better than
that – 'tis like I had a sister.'

'You're more to me than my own sister, Kitty.'

'It will turn out all right with her . . . you see if I an't
right.'

At the same time as her sister was trudging over Tradden
Raike, Ruth, with her children and their nurse, was within a
few days of England – many months since she had made the
decision to make the long sea voyages, first to Australia and
now to England. Although she had travelled in the best
available style, on steamships owned by a company in which
her toddling daughter was a shareholder, the time at sea had
been arduous, and the thought of having to make yet
another journey to return home . . . Home? Sitting on the
sheltered observation deck, once again the heavy thought of
where home might be dropped upon her.

Certainly not Australia. For years she had held at the back of her mind a memory of her own freedom as a child, riding out into the empty bush, of life on the Station when there was Ma and Pa, and Aury and Caroline, Vinia and Barney, of a strange feeling of restraint in that freedom. As a girl she had not understood those feelings, but during her visit to Toolagarry she had begun to understand.

It was to do with Ma. Ma, who seldom criticized or made judgements, nevertheless was a constant restraint – *I can never be me when Ma is there. She's too hard to live up to. Idealists are. Such strong views, no half-way. She wants a better, fairer world and has wasted her life trying to change things – and in the end, what has changed?*

Her Ma had known that she had 'done very well' from singing in America – Ma saw nothing wrong with that – but in writing of her planned visit Ruth had not mentioned the wealth that had come to her, as it were, by accident. That wealth had put her beyond the pale. To Ma, she had become one of 'That Lot' – the rich, the landowners. *And yet wasn't that what Aury, with his thousands of sheep and tens of thousands of acres, was becoming?* Although Ma had not spoken of it, Ruth sensed that Aury too had put himself beyond the pale in Ma's eyes. And Ma herself . . . *she lives on land that was handed over to her for next to nothing . . . what is the difference between Jarrett's acquisition of part of Massachusetts and Ma's of a wide expanse of Toolagarry? I've never understood Ma's thinking.*

In a part of her mind into which she deposited unpalatable truths, Ruth consigned that which said she had never understood the beliefs of the family into which she had been born. Silver dust, ingots, land and houses are fine insulation materials against any ethics that may irritate the conscience.

From her lounging seat, warmly clad against the increasingly chillier climate, she watched the rise and fall of the ship against the sea as the fast, modern vessel thrust a

way for itself, unlike the bobbing ship with the huge sails
and mast she still remembered vividly from when Ma had
taken her and Auryn . . . Aury.

I can't think . . . Why do they say that the sea is blue . . .
the months and months of my life I have spent watching
green water . . . how sick I used to feel . . . not now – people
would say that I'm a hardened sea-voyager. Back and forth
across the world . . . thousands of miles, and Auntie Sel has
never travelled further than twenty miles . . . how deep and
green, and Alex – dear God, when I look at the swell and
think of what it must be like below . . . I don't want to think
of Alex. I don't want to think of Jarrett, don't want to think
of Teddy or Netty or Jo, don't want to think of Peter.

Aury. I must think of Aury . . . I have to . . .

How could his appearance have changed so much? He
could be taken for Ma's brother. When he dismounted in
front of Ma's house, I didn't recognize him. She conjured up
a vivid image of the white-bearded, broad, brown man with
only a ring of white hair left around his bare head.
Physically, it was only his voice which had not changed. He
was as disapproving of her now as he had been that night at
Bounderby's when he had looked at her with such disgust,
though at least now he could hide it better.

He was worse than Ma for stopping her being herself. *He*
lets people know that they don't come up to his standards.
And he will never see that they are his standards . . . not mine
but his. This is the way a woman should be – the way that he
ordains. This is how a sister should be – his standards. He has
no right to set standards for me . . . half a glance, and he can
still make me feel shabby. Why can't he accept me as I am? As
I am. This is me. This is my place in the world. Why can't he
like me?

All the years of Ruth's anguish and misery and his sullen
reproach of her had made deep sores that were not much
healed in the few days that he spent visiting. He didn't even

admit that it was a visit – 'I was coming to Ma's, anyway,' he had said. *I think he didn't want me even to meet Tilda and their little boy . . .* that had hurt as much as anything.

And in a few days she would have to face Caroline, possibly meet Peter and probably be disapproved of again – but for her worldly success. *If only Carly was not so proud.* It was years now since Ruth had last offered to help them out and had been politely refused. When Auntie Sel was more in charge, it was easier, but as she handed over the running of Croud Cantle, it had become impossible for Ruth to send money home. Caroline's pride had almost jumped out of her letter and struck Ruth: 'Thank you, Ruth, but we are perfectly capable of keeping the place together.' *The Tylees are all like that, they preach sharing out the wealth of the world, yet are too independent to accept any of it.*

2

THE TERRIBLE SICKNESS

THE DEVASTATION THAT HAD BEEN inflicted upon the shanty community in Peter Warren's 'parish' had been partly as a result of the long, hot summer days of that July. Not that any of its victims, or those who watched helplessly as people suffered and died, knew why such fevers so often came in summer. The sickness came after eating food, but it was never the same sort of food twice. On one occasion it might be cream that was suspect, the next pork. Sometimes each could be eaten with no ill effects. It was truly a case of pot luck.

Not since the Plague had there been so many local deaths in so short a time; never had there been so many children wandering orphaned.

The epidemic had started at the head of the railway cutting. Then, over the course of two or three days, and following the path of a meat-pie seller, it had wended its way, stopping off at hamlets and villages on the way, to the small shanty community at By Privett. Although the invisible sudden killer of scores of healthy people was still ten years off being named, the deadly effect of botulism was well known, although how and where it came from was unknown.

Food poisoning.

It could not be seen, often could not be smelled or tasted. It frequently laid low the healthiest and hungriest. A navvyman might easily consume two large pies at a sitting and, whilst rural labourers seldom had such abundance, what meat there was was traditionally for men. Women, whose labour was not thought to need stoking by the eating of much flesh, would eat what was left by the men, whilst children survived mostly on cereal and potatoes. With the pies, it was different.

Pie-sellers knew how the aroma of meat and herbs could tempt coins from the knot in a woman's shawl, so they made 'bites'. Small, hand-held 'bites' sold for a few ha'pence. A Croud Cantle 'tater and onion bite' had for years been a favourite at Blackbrook and Waltham market. A woman would treat herself to a spicy, succulent delight, eating it standing by the stall. And if the pies were especially delectable, enjoy another.

At Croud Cantle, it had been a tradition of long standing that meat-pie season started on the first day of October and finished on Saint Patrick's Day, and that outside that period, a pie might often just as well have been filled with death caps. Had the death-dealing pie-seller been brought up in such a rural tradition, then a great many lives might have been spared. This pie-seller had been lucky enough to buy a number of chickens which had unaccountably gone off-lay. Chicken, potato and onion pies.

The pie-seller sold dozens.

Not only to navvy women but to village women who, with a few hay-making pence knotted in their kerchiefs, were in a spendthrift mood. The pies, containing their messages of mortality in the chicken-jelly, had brought the two communities to a common point.

Where the two communities merged, with a foot in both camps, were Peter, Kitty and Caroline.

Caroline had worked day and night trying to alleviate some of the suffering. Although some villagers had been taken into one or other of the local hospitals, few navvies or their women attempted to take their sick and dying there.

In very many cases, it was almost over before they even had a chance to try.

From the passage of the pie-seller to the onset of the

sickness was about a day, from then to death was two or three more, so that suddenly and within less than a week, the devastating illness had travelled through the countryside. When a contagious fever swept through the diggings, it was often the case that children would be taken but this time, because of their meatless diet, they survived to be orphaned.

During the worst of the epidemic, the old Mission Hut had become what Peter Warren had once envisaged – a refuge and a hospice. Its failure though, in Christian terms, was that people did not come for his ministrations, but for those of the 'Ginger Lady', the name by which Caroline had become known – whether from her colouring, or from her proclivity for dispensing a compound of the root for simple ailments, is uncertain.

By the time of the outbreak of food-poisoning, the Ginger Lady's reputation had far outstripped that of Fairy Dowlas, but the old midwife felt no antipathy to Caroline, and had long ago adopted her use of hartshorn and creosote solution against childbed infections. She spent days and nights alongside Caroline nursing the victims of the outbreak, but there was little that they could do except try to replace with water the lost body fluids and to administer powerful nostrums to deaden the agonizing pains, and to comfort.

For a week, the four of them, with help from a few women from the old shanty-town, worked in the awful stench, which even creosote solution did not eliminate, and the sounds of the sick and dying men and women. They snatched an hour of sleep in some kind of rotation, but as often as not as soon as they dropped into sleep, the groans of someone in their last agony would arouse Caroline to administer a tincture of opium, and Peter to carry away and burn sodden straw or to trawl for his dim faith as yet another soul gave up the fight against the death that the pie-seller had carried through the beautiful Meon Valley.

Soon, there was another epidemic – one of small wandering children. Often, they had come to the hut with a sick mother seeking a cure from the Ginger Lady, who had then collapsed there. First two or three, then six, then ten and then more.

'I a see to them,' Kitty had said, and had taken them to her shanty which was now too far from the diggings to attract lodgers, and where she and Peter now lived with just Agnes, Linty and Dutch.

At the end of ten days, when the last body had been buried beside a row of other victims from both shanty and village, and there were only two old, dehydrated women left in Caroline's and Fairy's care, Peter at last went home.

It was late evening, and as he walked along the track, he was surprised to discover that it was summer.

Recently, when time and again he had accompanied a gang of navvies who had undertaken the digging of the graves for both communities, Peter had been withdrawn from everything except his own emptiness and sense of failure. Now, suddenly, it was July again and he was going home. The depression that he had lived with for more than a week now – depression at the ineffectiveness of his faith compared with what Caroline had achieved in the saving of life – began to lift at the thought of Kitty. He had not seen her, except briefly, since she had taken the children away from the hut.

He climbed the stony track that had been at the centre of his life for fifteen years. The track that led to and from his old Mission Hut. The track along which he had fled after his physical desire for Ruth had almost got the better of him, and along which she had come before she left for America. The same track that Kitty had trodden on the day when he had asked if she would marry him. The track he had taken on his last visit home when his mother had said, 'If you desire to couple with a savage, you'd as well set up house with a

Hottentot' – that scar was still tender; he had expected execration from Dolly, but had thought his mother to be wider-minded. In recent months, until these tragic occurrences, the track had started to narrow. The head of the diggings had moved miles further on. Now that fewer people came from that direction, wild oats, chamomile, tansy and pimpernel began to take back their old territory.

Soon he reached the meadow that sloped away from his and Kitty's hut. His heart was full, he could hardly bear the emotions that began to take over from depression. There had been a time when he would make a detour to avoid passing beneath the tree where he and Ruth had been within a breath of mutual ravishment ... but perhaps he had always been wrong about that, wrong about Ruth. Later he had bitter-sweet memories of that summer when he had met Kitty with her armful of queen of the meadow going down to the diggings to be claimed by the winner of the wrestle.

Now, from the top of the sloping meadow, with the last of the sun going down behind him, he sat on his hunkers and looked down to where a thin trail of smoke was rising – and he wept as men are supposed not to do.

It was more than an hour later that he reached the shanty at the bottom of the meadow. Kitty, having heard his familiar tread, went to meet him, and kissing him long on the mouth said, 'Bugger me, my dear, if I an't glad to see you.' He had thought she meant something else until he went into the hut. 'Will you just look at that. Caroline and me fetched some great bundles of old blankets and clothes that her auntie had got for us, so me and Agnes soaped every one of the little buggers and washed their hair.'

By the dim lamplight, beyond where Dutch sat in his usual place, Peter saw rows of small children most of whom were fast asleep.

'An't they a pretty sight, Peter?'

Smiling, he nodded and for a few moments he stood silently with his arm about her shoulders.

'You called me "Peter".'

'I know, I don't think "Vicar" suits you no more.'

His unconscious had known for a long time that the God of his youth had gone. It had needed Kitty, with her observant wisdom, to free him and allow him into the adult world where he was responsible for his own actions.

He suddenly felt stronger and more alive than he had been for many years.

3

RETURN TO CANTLE

THE OLD RUIN of grey stones that had once been a Bishop's palace was cool and shadowy. Ruth sat on a broken wall, looked at her boots and smiled. Strange to get such pleasure from such a simple thing as wearing heavy country boots once more. For years now, except for riding boots which her London shoemaker fashioned on her own last, she had worn nothing heavier than fine leathers. As did the feel of her plain woollen skirt and cotton blouse, that of country boots came as a pleasant surprise.

It was fifteen years since she was last in Waltham.

Fifteen years since Ruth Tylee had stood on the market with Selena and sold Croud Cantle produce. The day after she arrived in the town, Ruth had walked to the market-place and tried to bring back the experience of the days before she went away to London. But it was not there . . . the girl was gone. No matter how substantial were the country boots and plain skirt, no matter that she wore her hair in a plain knot, a kerchief tied about it, Ruth O'Mahoney could not resurrect the market girl.

I'll go tomorrow. I will hire a horse and ride over, and let Rose bring the babes next day by the carrier. Annie and Joey will love that. She smoothed the lap of her skirt. *What hands! Nothing will disguise them. They know what I do. Why am I dithering and nervous? I came all this way to see Carly and her children and Auntie Sel.* She turned her hands back and forth, inspecting her polished nails. *Why should I be ashamed? Nobody expects a singer to have farming hands.* And the voice that had chided her since she bought the country boots asked, *Then why disguise yourself as a countrywoman?*

She got up from her seat and tramped a bit more around the edge of the pond, allowing the hem of her skirt to drag and her boots to kick stones and gather mud from the quagmire. Suddenly *If I don't go now, I'll never go.* And having steeled herself to ride over to Cantle she quickly returned to the hotel, gave Rose her instructions and the children rules for good behaviour; she then had a horse saddled and rode northwards from the town.

Instead of taking the Alton road, she went the old way, as the crow flies, across Corhampton Downs until she reached the junction of the main road and the old track down Tradden Raike to Cantle. It was at almost the exact point where Peter Warren had recently sat and cried hot tears of mixed emotions.

Ruth, however, with a sudden jolt of recognition saw not the meadow, but only the crab-apple tree growing at the perimeter. Its shape and form, fixed in her memory, were almost unchanged in the fifteen years since, under its boughs, Peter Warren had asked her to marry him. The same tree into which she had gazed as the sudden urgent desire for Peter spread through her. *Not for Peter . . . desire for a man. It was the surprise . . . seeing his face so close . . . he was so . . . so manly . . . I was so surprised . . . his shirt was open at the neck . . . such black hair for such a fair man . . . not like Aury. A man . . . no longer a priest. A man like the others who have come and gone since then – so many. So many nameless . . . almost faceless . . . except for a few who were important. Teddy, Alex, and now Bret.*

Of all of them, she regretted Bret the most. He was so young, so ardent.

Teddy and Alex were men of the world, older, sophisti-cated and, if the truth be told, using her as she had used them. Unserious attachments. But Bret had begun to talk of love – *was* really in love. Teddy could be philosophical when she told him, *Don't spoil it, Teddy.* And it was only Alex's

pride that had been hurt when she had refused to marry him.
Pique. He had wanted to possess her, own her.

But Bret . . . had begun to talk of love before she left
Boston, and she had known the difference. Young and
vulnerable, for all his experience. He had said, '*I love you, I
love you. Don't go away. If you go away I shall become
shrunken and desiccated.*'

Desiccated – what a strange word. But she had gone,
because she had believed that she would have only ever one
love . . . the one she could not admit to . . . the one in the
locket of her mind whose eyes she could not meet for fear of
them. And now she was sure . . . she could only give her
love to her children.

Of all the lovers she had taken to sublimate the profile in
the locket, it was only the youthful Bret she had felt any true
affection for. But he had said *love* and would find it hard to
settle for less.

She shivered in the July sunshine as a breeze rose up from
the valley. It always blew here, just along this part of the
downs before the path turns down over Tradden. Her heart
palpitating, she kneed the horse to walk on the final mile or
so. She reached the crest of the downs, and there was Cantle.
The scene, with figures moving within it, was a tranquil one,
the only change that she could immediately see was a tall
chimney attached to the side of the old manor-house.

Dear Lord, the place looks like a factory.

And then she saw that it probably was that, for what had
been the walled garden of the old manor-house was now
busy with horses and drays.

She looked down at the foot of Tradden where huddled
Croud Cantle, birthplace to herself and generations of her
family, expecting to feel some strong emotion, but there was
none.

Suddenly she was there. The horse clattered over the
path of cobbles. The porch door was ajar, but no one came

out. Riding through the yard gate, dismounting, leading the horse to the orchard, catching the smells of the yard, outhouses, dairy. Then in the porch the smell particular to that house, that family . . . of woodsmoke, bacon, pickles, of yellow soap and something she hadn't remembered, a new smell – tar-oil.

There was no one in the orchard nor in the house. Although the pine long-case clock, with its twisted door and badly-painted birds was still cock-cock-cocking, it was as though between 1852 when she left and 1867 it had counted no real time. Only Auntie Sel and Caroline would have done that as they pulled at the rope and weight each Sunday night. How many Sunday nights . . .

She called, 'Auntie Sel? Caroline? Are you about?'

A fire was laid on the pad of ash in the hearth . . . yes, of course, she remembered. If the house was to be left empty for the day, then the fire was never bellowed up but allowed to go out and laid ready for their return.

That must be it . . . Blackbrook Market day. Was Auntie Sel still trekking back and forth to market at her age?

So much she did not know about her own family.

So much she had not known about the one in Toolagarry.

Her brown gypsy-like mother, tough and belligerent as any of her prize rams, her hair white with its strange-looking plait of red and more youthful hair. Vinia and Barney physically coarsened by the drying winds and sun, established farmers with worries of roofs collapsing and animals with foot-rot.

And Martha.

Martha. Ruth's sister of Ma's late years, the sister she had not thought of as a real person. Just 'Ma's baby', who had never, in all those years, counted to Ruth as more than a notion. And yet, she had been there, growing up, becoming Martha Tylee, working the sheep with Ma. Martha, at sixteen shockingly like herself at the same age. Ma and Pa's first and last children coming out with the stature of Pa's family and the colouring of Ma's. And Aury, austere as a Calvinist, as judgemental as a Daniel.

It was all too much. She had wanted to show off her babies to her family and had found that her family was hers no longer. Not that they had in any way rejected her. Except Aury, who was no longer Aury Tylee but was now Auryn Draper of Vontobel Sheep Station, Draperstown. Their lives had all been wound around a different spool from her own . . . and it would be the same here.

She lit the fire, pumped water and set the kettle over the fire. In the cold-store she found a knuckle of bacon which she put in the stew-pan with a few vegetables and a handful of barley.

How many years since I cooked a proper meal?

The kettle boiled, she brewed a strong infusion of tea and added sugar. This she took with her when she went to look round the place. Upstairs, there was evidence of children . . . a wooden cot beside the big bed . . . vaguely she recalled that cot . . . Grandpa Toose had made it. Lord . . . fancy it still being in use.

Outside, she went to look in the Dunnock where she and Aury used to fish as children. '*Get back, Ruthie, you're too young . . .*' '*It's too fast for you . . .*' '*I reckon we caught the old pike. You're too little, I will gaff him . . .*' But she hadn't given him the chance. '*Don't you tell me what to do, Auryn Draper!*' She had been too quick for Aury and had flopped in up to her waist just to prove that she wasn't to be told what to do by a brother only a year older than herself. *If it could have stopped there. If only . . . if only . . . wading in the Dunnock to strike trout and hoping for magic so that when they landed it, it would prove to be the old pike.*

For half an hour she wandered all over the farm, marvelling at the amount of produce they were still growing, and the good pig and the row of old bee skeps, busy as they had always been. In a little pasture there was a cow which she took to belong to them. Having stirred the bacon-knuckle stew, she sat out under the grey-barked apple tree. Her very first memory was of being here, picking peas from their pods and being incensed at discovering a maggot.

4

HARD LOVES

SITTING IN THE ORCHARD, Ruth lost count of time. Her reverie was broken into by the sound from the back of the cottage of someone unlatching the scullery door. Only people who had taken a short cut down Tradden came in through the wicket and the scullery door so it wasn't likely to be Caroline and Auntie Sel because that way was too steep coming down with market baskets. She rose.

A voice from the house called, 'Hello. Caroline? Miz Selena?'

Ruth did not recognize the voice.

A woman of about her own age poked her head round the kitchen door. A nice face fringed by fair hair springing from an old-fashioned harvesting bonnet, smiling from behind her hand like a child caught in the act.

'Wey . . . I'm sorry, I shoulden't a come in if I'd known you was here. Only I was took a bit unawares smellen the stew and that – I thought the place was goen to be empty. I knew they'd gone to market today . . . they was go-en to buy some new sheets for the bed.'

Ruth smiled whilst her mind was racing around the reason for the new sheets. *Oh, Lord . . . they probably think I should have decent sheets to sleep in.*

'I had forgotten it was market day.'

'Well, you been away a long time, I dare say there's a lot of thengs you forgot. Tell you what, though, you an't forgot how to make somethen decent to eat by the smells of it.'

Then Ruth remembered the strange dialect, and where she had heard it before.

'You're Simeon's mother aren't you? Vic, I mean. For a

moment I didn't recognize you.' She held out her hand and it was just a second longer than was usual before it was clasped by the woman.

'I recognize you all right – you're Caroline's sister. I met you before.'

'Of course. How is Vic?'

'Vic is do-en ever so well. He's got his papers now. Though 'tis mostly thanks to you, putten him as a 'prentice.'

What was the woman's name . . . something strange.

'Kitty! Am I right? I'm sorry I've entirely forgotten your other name.'

'Warren. Kitty Warren.' She paused as though expecting Ruth to speak. 'I'm married now . . . to Peter.' Caution as she said that.

Now it was Ruth who was a second too slow in her response.

'You're Peter Warren's . . . wife?'

'Didn't you know we was married?'

'No . . . I've been out of touch for a while. I'm not much for writing letters. It's a bad fault of mine.'

Peter's wife! Peter had married a navvy woman? Fire-Bucket! Her name had been Kitty Fire-Bucket.

'Well, I expect you'm like the rest of us, always putten thengs like that off till another day, then the other day don't come, and suddenly it seems such a big theng to have to explain. I was say-en to Caroline, people don't chop off their families of a purpose, it happens by accident I should say.'

Exactly. That was just how it had happened. And Caroline had discussed it with this woman.

'There's a brew of tea on the hearth – shall you have some?'

'Why, I should love it. I come over to collect some bits of ole cut-down clothes Miz Selena have been do-en – for the children.'

'Did you find them?'

'Oh yes, they'm where she said they would be. You don't mind if I stop for a bit of a blow and a beaker of tea? I an't disturben you?'

'No. I rode over on impulse, I hadn't thought about it being market day. I was sitting in the orchard, remembering when I was a child.'

'It must have been lovely, growen up here.'

'I suppose it was. I never thought about it much – I was only seven when we went away.'

Ruth carried the brown pot and beakers out to where she had been seated.

'Well, if this an't a treat. I never thought to be sitten under no apple tree sippen tea. I got a mounten of dirty clouts to wash back home.' She laughed, her breath lifting her full, high bosom, her wide mouth pulling back over her teeth. When she laughed, it was not done out of politeness. 'But you can wager it won't run away – dirty clouts never do. In fact, I reckon they'm more likely to get more when you an't looken.'

There was a moment or two of silence as they drank their tea.

'How is your husband?'

'I don't know, really. You remember he used to be a vicar?'

'Of course I remember. He used to run the Mission for the railway men. What do you mean . . . used to be? Is he no longer a vicar?'

'Well, be-en a vicar an't the kind of theng that you gets sacked from or gives notice of leaven . . . he says as far as the Church goes, once a vicar always a vicar. But he don't have the callen as he used to.'

'I'm sorry about that.'

'Oh, don't be sorry, it's been comen for a long time. But it's not an easy theng for a man like Peter. His vicar-en was the centre of his life. But he got to do a bit of getten used to not being one.' She drank deeply from the large beaker and Ruth saw the woman's eyes withdraw for a moment, then she looked Ruth squarely in the face. 'It fair breaks my heart to see him. Since he admitted it to hisself, he's as happy as I've ever seen him . . . but if he an't a vicar, then he don't know who he is. Do you understand what I mean? He's the sort of person who needs a label on him.'

'Yes . . . I understand. I do understand.'

Very well. 'Rosalie'. 'Queen of London'. Teddy Warren's mistress. Alex Marney's woman. 'The Woman'. Mrs Jarrett O'Mahoney. If there is no label, then how to know who you are? Unless you are brave. Like this woman. She knows who she is.

They fell silent again. Surprisingly, to Ruth, an easy silence. Kitty Warren looked inquisitively about her as though perhaps fixing the detail in her memory.

'Where are your babies? I should a liked to see them.'

'I left them in Waltham. With . . . with a friend who's travelling with me.'

'Perhaps before you go back?'

'Yes. I'm very proud of them. I'll show them off to anyone.'

'Caroline told me you was left a widow. That must be hard, being a widow with two twins like that.'

'Well . . . at least I have a nice home.'

'It's what children needs . . . a roof over their heads, food in their bellies and somebody there when they gets bad dreams.'

How easily we have fallen in with one another. I don't think she's got a sharp bone in her body. I could have come here in my new French gown and embroidered boots and she would have behaved no differently.

Kitty finished her tea and set the mug down with satisfaction. 'Well, I better get go-en.'

'Don't go.' It was out before Ruth realized what she was saying. 'I mean, must you go? It's a long time since I've . . .' She withdrew her eyes in embarrassment.

'I don't mind stay-en.' Kitty laughed. 'Bugger me, who wouldn't? Sitten around in the middle of the day.'

Ruth felt strangely excited at the prospect of eating with the woman, Peter's wife.

'Shall we have some broth? I expect Caroline and Auntie Sel aren't likely to be back for ages.'

The sun moved up to its July apogee, urging on the bees and the larks, silencing the beasts, forcing trout in the River Dunnock into more dense weed and drying out the new wings of great green dragonflies. The low murmur of the two women's voices carried scarcely to the limit of the boughs of the apple tree.

'Your Caroline's a one that don't need no label. I've thought to myself many a time that she knows just what she's about. Isaac was all right, but as long as I've known your Caroline, she haven't needed a man to tell her what's what. A course, it was Isaac that started her off, and he learned her a lot of thengs she'd a probably have to a read a dozen books to find out – but she's the sort that's got backbone and brains together.'

'She was a handful when she was a girl. Always going that bit further than her bounds, always wanting to know everything. They ran out of things to teach her at school. My mother is very clever.'

'You'm a clever family by all accounts. You done well for yourself.'

'Ah . . . that didn't take brains, and my voice came wrapped in my body like a gift.'

'It took bloody guts, though.'

Ruth smiled. 'I never thought of it like that. I've always thought of myself as selfish, going off to do what I wanted.'

'And why shouldn't you? Nobody would a said you

was selfish if you had a been a boy now, would they? Your brother never thought twice when he wanted to go off.'

'But it's different for men.'

'Bugger that for a reason. I tell you, till I met Peter, I'd had enough of men to a drove me to a nunnery.' Her laugh rang out. 'I'm bloody glad I never went, though. My ole vicar's a fair delight to me.' She looked out across the valley towards the brewery, but more likely seeing her husband than the ugly chimney.

Another silence, then Kitty said, 'You ever read a book called *Emma*?'

The woman was full of surprises. The idea of Peter being married to her did not now seem so strange.

'I think so, ages ago.'

'There was a girl called Jane Fairfax? I don't reckon any of them really knew what she was like. She had a' auntie, Miss Bates, who thought the sun shone out of Jane's backside, but nobody else did. The Emma that the story's about never thought one bit of good about Jane Fairfax, and most of the men only saw her as Miss Bates's niece or a pretty pet . . . nobody knew what Jane Fairfax was like inside her.'

'I don't remember all that.'

'Well, it don't matter. It's just that . . . well, you minds me of her – Jane Fairfax. I don't reckon anybody knows you, do they? And I reckon you smiles and smiles, being polite, like she did even when there an't nothen to be polite about.'

If the Lemures of the ancient chalkhills were about in the orchard that afternoon, they might well remember the dark night of Ruth's own urgent conception, when they had breathed their breath into her but a few yards from where, unknowingly, she now sat. Or into the spirit of her mother and grandmother who had dug their toes into the grass and dreamed of some fantastic other life for themselves. If not the Lemures, then perhaps wraiths of people and events a hundred years in the future. Genial spirits, their chalk bones warmed by the sun, their watchfulness lulled by bees. Whatever was at work there, it brought Kitty and Ruth together in a unique situation as when all the planets are aligned for a single rare moment.

For Ruth, it was catharsis.

'I'm glad Peter married you.'

Kitty Warren inspected Ruth's eyes. 'That's the best compliment I had in a long time . . . more so because you said it. I wasen't his first choice. I know he asked you, and for a long time I blamed you for maken him unhappy.'

'I could never have made him happy.'

'I know.' A slight smile. 'I can't bear to think what I would a been now. He would never a stopped on the diggens, and I would never a learnt readen. I dare say I should a been set up with some ole navvy. What should I a done if you hadn't refused to have him?'

'There was never a chance of that.'

'I can see that now.'

A quiver of apprehension went through Ruth. *What does she see?*

'What do you see?'

'Only what used to be in myself. A sort of hatred of the world because I wasen't part of it.'

'I can hardly believe that.'

'There wasen't no reason why I should like myself, nor anybody.' A pause. 'Have a man ever raped you?'

'No . . . never that . . . not quite that . . . only submission.'

'I have . . . more than once. First when I was only just in my teen-years.'

'Perhaps it is like . . . being abortioned? I always thought that to be violation by a man. I know all about that.'

Kitty Warren looked with great compassion at the

woman she had despised for years, then wagged her head.
'It's a bugger of a life for a woman.'

'I'm happy now. You'll see, when my babies come over
from Waltham.'

'Even when I was haten everytheng, I was still happy
with my babies. It never made no difference how they came
to me, it was their selves that I liked to have round me. I
should like for me and Peter to have some . . . but it don't
seem to happen. It an't for the want of what it takes to get
them.'

Her forthrightness reminded Ruth of Netty and Jo . . .
particularly of Jo with her ribald but apt comments.

'Haven't you got anybody?'

'Not really. In America there's a young man – Bret . . .
Dear Lord, why am I telling you this?'

'Because this is the time. Because I was sent here for the
clothes, and Caroline was sent to buy sheets, and you came a
day too soon. It was meant. We was meant. You said, "Have
some tea" – and I said I would. You said, "Don't go" – and I
didn't. I reckon me and you be-en here just now was all
worked out by somebody on the day we was born. I have
that feelen.'

Ruth too knew that Fate had called on them to meet. The
only time in her entire life when she would be able to open
the locket and reveal the face to another human being was
now.

'There has never been any man at all that meant anything
to me . . . not one that I have wanted to live with for ever –
only . . . only my own brother. There's nobody except him.
I can't help it, but it is the truth.'

The gaze of both women was locked. Each was inside
the other, asking and giving understanding.

'For twenty years I have deceived myself and the men I
have been attached to, the men I have lived closest to. I have
had more lovers than I can remember, even the woman who

was my friend's lover when she was lying injured in hospital.
I have a need that stems from loving Auryn that none of
them can fill.'

She took a breath as deep as though coming up for air,
leaned back against the grey bark of the tree and looked up
through its sparse leaves and fruit.

Kitty, her brows pulled together, reached out as though
to touch Ruth, but her hand hovered. 'I'm sorry.'

Ruth nodded. 'I have never admitted that to myself, let
alone to another person. I love my own brother, and I
suppose that it is my punishment that he despises me.'

Kitty now put her hand undramatically on Ruth's.

'Where I was brought up, on the diggens, nobody would
have took much notice of a theng like that, there's more than
that happens. It isn't nothen so terrible, really. Peter
wouldn't see it like that because of the way he was brought
up – but on the diggens people have a different way of
looking at thengs. Like creatures, they don't worry about
nothen like that. Only people – only them who thinks up
thengs like "sinfulness" . . . How can lov-en a person be
bad? People can't choose who they happens to love, now,
can they? It's real bad luck for you that you fell for your
brother and the rules are against it. There's women loves
other women – amongst the wagon-girls they mostly don't
want no men. And men loves other men – you can't grow up
in shanties without learnen that.'

As the woman talked, it felt to Ruth as it did when she
was a girl in Toolagarry. When Pa would bring her up from a
drowning dream with cold, wet hands. And as it did when,
on the creaking vessel on the outward journey, she buried
her head into Aury's back to try to blot out the noises and
the crying coming from the convicts in the bowels of the
ship. Comfort and relief from nameless terrors.

Kitty Warren's broad West Country accent and low
pitch were made for healing a sore mind.

'There was this king in a play that Peter told me about, he lived a long time ago . . . well, he fell in love with his own mother. He couldent help it, he dident even know she was his mother. Well, it could happen to anybody. I think he went mad or sometheng from his feelen bad about it. He couldent help it . . . nor could his mother. When I heard that story, I said it was just not fair that they should come off so bad for sometheng they never asked to happen. Do your brother know?'

'No! He would be disgusted.'

'How do you know that?'

'You don't know Auryn. He's disowned me from the time I refused to obey him and went off to London.'

'Maybe that was because he loved you as much as you love him. Do you think it was because he didn't want to lose you?'

'He saw me on the stage . . . a long time ago. I didn't know that he was there . . . it was a . . . not the sort of thing a girl would do if she knew her brother was watching. He was furious . . . so angry. I was ashamed he saw me like that. It was after that he went away, back home to Australia.'

'Hurt.'

'Yes, hurt. He still is. I saw him a few months ago. It was all still there, every time he looked at me.'

'Because he loves you.'

Ruth traced the lines of her own palm in silence.

'All those years ago and he is still hurt. If he didn't love you, he'd a forgot about it ages ago.'

'It doesn't matter now. It has been hard, but I think I have got over it.'

'It's marvellous how we get over thengs. If people couldn't get over bad thengs, we should all go and jump down a well, shoulden't we?'

'I suppose we should. I'll remember that.'

Kitty wiped the remains of her broth from her bowl with a crust of bread.

'Is it all right if I call you Ruth?'

'Of course.'

'That's all right, then. Only I thought I should go before Caroline gets back. She'll know that we have met, and it'd be queer callen you anytheng else now we got to know each other.'

'And like each other, Kitty?'

'Oh, yes . . . and like. It's a queer theng really, I could never understand why Peter wanted to marry you if you wasen't a nice person . . . bugger me, I thought you wasen't. Just shows . . . you should never judge till you knows.'

5

IN PERPETUITY

THERE HAD BEEN FEW PUBLIC gatherings in the village as unusual as that which occurred in the grounds of Church House, Cantle, almost exactly a year after Ruth O'Mahoney's return there. As well as Ruth, holding the hands of Joey and Anne, there were Caroline and her three children standing grouped around the seated Selena and Jack and Ginny Toose – all arranged before a daguerreotypist and her tripod. With her head bent, she indicated with her fingers '. . . four, three, two, one! Good!' With the tortured vowels of a cultured accent.

The group relaxed their positions and hand-holds and smiled self-consciously at the crowd of people watching the event.

'Now, the family with the administrators, staff and the little ones.'

The group expanded now to include Kitty and her children, and a dozen or so young ones with Peter, Fairy and London Dowlas, and half a dozen young men and women with short stature and weathered rural faces, who stood rigid and staring as the daguerreotypist barked and counted on her fingers again.

'Now, please, in the centre, the celebrated guests.'

Two formally attired gentlemen who had watched the long-drawn-out proceedings with close attention, stood in the midst of the group resting their silk hats on bent forearms.

'Right, ladies and gentlemen . . . and little ones . . . your ordeal is over. Thank you. It has been an honour to be associated with this historic occasion. The plates will be prepared within the week.' Of all the people assembled at Church House on that morning, it was the daguerreotypist herself who attracted the most attention. Her attire was so extraordinary that she cannot have been unaware of the stares she must have attracted in London, let alone in rural Hampshire. Ruth, in thanking her formally, said quietly, 'Your costume. It is wonderful! I should absolutely love to wear it. May I ask . . . ?'

'My dear, I am just back from America. Amelia Bloomer fashion – it is *everywhere*. Little boys laugh at it, men hate it and are wild over it, women adore it. And *you*, my dear, could be the one to give it respectability.'

'*I* could?'

'I am not mistaken? You *are* . . . "The Woman", are you not? The Tartar Prince?'

'Goodness, I thought she wasn't known here!'

'I thought I was not wrong – once seen, never forgotten, "The Woman". I saw her in Phili . . . she was magnificent. I say, you wouldn't let me make some plates of you . . . a marble horse . . . ah, yes.'

Ruth suddenly felt a thrill of anticipation. To be working again. Involved in life. 'Maybe with Leucous-Equus . . . he deserves to be fixed for history.'

'Would he be still? Never mind . . . do let's try. When?'

Ruth's mouth twitched with a smile. 'Not here and now, I think.'

The woman guffawed. 'I say! Yes . . . just the setting. Fair maiden and stallion, village church in the background . . . that kind of thing. The galleries would adore it.' Quieter. 'I'm serious. I should love to do it. Are you going back to America?'

One of those sudden silences that people say happen at twenty minutes past or twenty minutes to the hour, so that when Ruth said, 'I shall be leaving for home next month,' in her normal voice, it sounded as though she had shouted aloud. The rattle of teacups and buzz of conversation started up again immediately.

When the daguerreotypist had packed her trap and left, Caroline came to her sister ostensibly to offer her some tea. 'I couldn't help overhearing what you said, Ru.'

'About leaving?'

'You said, "going home".'

'Yes.'

'I had begun to hope that you were . . . home. The house in Blackbrook . . .'

'It was ever only temporary.'

'You could have stayed at the farm as long as you had wanted.'

'I know. But Rose is an American, a city woman. She's been with me ages, and she's as much a mother to Anne and Joey as I am. You could see that she was a fish out of water on the farm. I never gave her to understand that we should not go back one day. I think it is time. After all, Anne and Joey are Americans.'

'We shall miss you.'

'I'm glad. I don't think I could bear it if you didn't.'

'Shall you ever come again?'

'Of course I shall. I'm quite a well-off woman now.'

'I can see that now.' She indicated the broad expanse of knapped-flint and red brick, interspersed by windows, of Church House. 'Even so, it's very generous of you.'

'No it isn't, Carly. All I have given is money. The rest of you will be giving your lives to it every day.'

'Willingly. If I had been given a magic lamp I would have wished for exactly this.'

'Will you promise that you will see that the farm is kept up?'

'Of course. Peter says that we shall buy as much Croud Cantle dairy food and vegetables as it can produce. I hope that Maggie and her man will go to live with Selena and keep the place going. If they don't, then I shall find some other good couple.'

'So long as it stays in the family.'

'I shall never let it go.'

'You and Kitty will be happy here. I can tell it.'

'And Peter.'

'I thought he might not like living in the shadow of St Peter's . . . oh, how strange, I never thought of that before.'

'I think he is better suited to administering a charity than he was to being a missionary.'

'He did a lot of good work for the navvy people.'

'Those days are nearly over. Not much of this country left without trains running over it.'

'A lot has changed. Can you remember what it was like when we first came, Carly?'

'I remember that first Christmas when you and me and Aury sang a carol in there.' Nodding in the direction of St Peter's church.

Ruth's eyes withdrew as she nodded at the memory.

'I had better go and see to the guests, Ru. We'll talk again later.' Ruth watched her sister walk spring-footed across the ancient turf, and smiled as she thought of how different it would all be from now on.

'You're smiling. It's not something you do often enough.' Peter Warren, coming from behind, rested a hand on her shoulder and pressed it gently. Ruth touched his fingers briefly and patted the seat beside her. Their relationship had grown warm over the months since she and Kitty had each allowed the other to look into her heart and mind. *If only it could have been like this with Aury. If only we could have been at ease with one another.*

He sat down, inspected one of the dainty fairy-cakes and popped it whole into his mouth. 'Nice, but we shall need to have fewer of these and more of sugar buns for filling hungry children.'

'We all need a fairy-cake from time to time. I want you to pledge that they will be served once a month.'

With the palm of his hand held facing her he said, 'The fourth Saturday in every month shall be Founder's Saturday when fairy-cakes shall be served.'

'You make a good father, Peter.'

'Father Peter. Perhaps I chose the wrong Church.'

'You would never have made a Roman Catholic.'

He laughed as he had on the first occasion when they had met, open-mouthed and loud, but lowered his voice to say, 'No. Celibacy was never one of my stronger inclinations.' He ran a hand through his thick greying hair and looked sideways at her. 'How often I should have been at the confessional!'

'Perhaps I should have said you make a good "Pa". You are very good with the children.'

'Because I am childlike, perhaps. Simple and childlike. Opposites do well in a marriage and Kitty is complex and wise. You might not think it . . .'

'Oh, but I do. I believe Kitty is one of the most intelligent people I have known.'

'Doesn't it make you wonder what she might have been . . . you know, if she had had a different start?'

'With a well-to-do family?'

'Yes. Tutored, with access to books early in life.'

'She would have likely turned up here this afternoon dressed in bloomer fashion and ordered us about before she swept off to Timbuctoo to make plates of black people in the jungle.'

His burst of laughter turned heads in their direction.

'Oh, and it is good to see *you* laugh again, Peter.'

Kitty, with two little children barefoot but in striped overalls like shepherds' roundfrocks, came to where Ruth and Peter were sitting.

'Peter, I reckon it's about time you got everything ready for the speech.'

'Oh . . . why can't things happen without speeches?'

'Speeches turn events into special events. If there wasen't a speech people would just go off home and not remember it was a special day.'

Taking the two children by the hand, he raced off across the lawn with them.

'Isn't it nice that the weather holds. It's like having your tea in heaven out here.'

Ruth followed where Kitty's gesture indicated. The lawn, which began at the bottom of shallow, weathered steps leading from a brick terrace in front of the house, sloped very gradually to where it narrowed and became a pathway that led through a brick archway into a small spinney and the churchyard beyond. Round the lawn grew a wide scrambling border of pink and purple phlox, lavender bushes, white and gold lilies, marigolds and cascades of fuchsias dripping with bright red.

'It is lovely. But don't be surprised if Caroline wants to plant it with beans and peas.'

'Do you think she will?'

'If she does, tell her you will tell on her to her big sister.'

'Maybe we could grow the beans in with the flowers, like an ordinary garden.'

'I can see you two are bound to get on together very well.'

'We always have. And now we both got what we wants.'

'I was just saying to Caroline that you will both be getting a lot of hard work.'

'Not harder than we ever had. And 'tis the best sort of work to be do-en what you like do-en.'

They fell silent as they watched Peter place a small table and a few chairs on the terrace, then tie a white ribbon across the house door.

'Ruth? If you don't want to answer it's all right, but are

you going to set up with that young man you was tell-en me about when you gets back to America?'

'I've lived like a nun since I landed in this country. Did Caroline tell you that I'm going back?'

'No. Nobody needed to tell me. I know Caroline hoped you would stay when you got the Blackbrook house, but I always knowed you would go. But you an't go-en back just because you got the itch for a young man.'

'He has sent me a most touching proposal of marriage. Not the kind of thing a woman nearing forty gets after two years' absence from a young man like he is. Young men like Bret Lauchaise get snapped up by rich Roxbury mothers for their daughters, or even by rich Boston widows from Back Bay themselves – a Boston widow who lives along Back Bay means something.'

'Do you live along Back Bay?'

Ruth laughed quite loudly. 'Oh, Kitty . . . me? A rich widow from Back Bay . . . Lord. I never thought of it. No, I live further uptown.' *The Widow O'Mahoney is not rich, she is wealthy. The Widow O'Mahoney lives on Beacon Hill.* 'I have made up my mind to remove from there.'

Peter's voice rang through the still trees, and across the cool green turf on the warm July noon. 'Please gather, ladies and gentlemen.'

The guests were gathered, and Caroline and some of the formal gentlemen were settled at the table.

'I am used to talking too often and for too long. However, on this occasion I am under the admonition of my good wife to "stand up, speak out and say hardly anything at all, because the children will get fiddly".'

The light-hearted tone of his voice sent Ruth suddenly back to the first occasion on which she had heard it. *'Ahoy, there below!'* And he had descended down the golden column of light into their midst. Almost twenty years ago – she had been a girl and Carly a child. *And that was the first*

*time Aury showed his disapproval of me. He knew I wanted
to stop and speak to Peter and he ordered us to leave. I felt
quite ashamed. Peter seemed so gentlemanly. But I went
quite obediently, to please Aury.*

She snapped back at the mention of her name. Ignaz
Semmel, the famous surgeon and Caroline's mentor and
hero, had risen and was holding scissors.

'Zees generous lady, Mistress O'Mahoney, has put a
large sum of money at the disposal of the charity. Zees house
and grounds are secured in perpetuity for za sole purpose as
a refuge for orphaned children and as a lying-in hospital for
mothers who need surgery. Mistress Caroline Tylee is to be
the first woman to be trained in the methods of Ignaz
Semmel, and we vow that not one mother shall ever contract
childbed fever whilst in confinement in these wards. Ladies
and gentlemen – and children – it is my great pleasure and
duty to formally declare Jarrett O'Mahoney House open.'

6

ON THE WATERS OF THE SOLENT

FOR THE THIRD TIME in her life, Ruth set sail on the waters of the Solent. The first time had been as seven-year-old Ruth Draper, sailing with Aury and their mother to the mysterious land they had called Van Dieman's Land. That journey had been on a masted vessel, with sails flapping, boys in the rigging and with the frightening sounds of the chains of transported men and women in the hold. The second journey was as Ruth Tylee and Rosalie, elegant and assured in her twenties, sailing with Alex Marney to America in the most beautiful vessel, a streamlined clipper.

Now, it was as Ruth O'Mahoney, with her adored Anne and Joey and with Rose Geary. This vessel, steam-driven, fast and modern, unaffected by tides and still air.

It was all a far cry from that first creaking wooden ship. In the time span between her childhood and her womanhood, the world had changed out of all recognition.

Now, speed and movement. Nothing static or quiet. Life moved fast. *And I have changed, too, out of all recognition. Twenty years ago I thought I wanted nothing better than to live at Croud Cantle and grow produce for the market. Thirty years ago, I wanted to be the boy who climbed the rigging.*

'Look Joey, look Anne, see those white rocks. They are called the Needles.'

'There's a lighthouse, Mama.'

'Could *we* live in a lighthouse, Mama?' Joey looked hopeful and expectant.

'Silly! People can't live in lighthouses.' Anne, sure of herself.

'Who does live in lighthouses then, Miss, if it is not people? Do the lamps light themselves?' her mother asked and, not for the first time, wondered about the future, when the legacy of Jarrett O'Mahoney would make Anne president of his construction empire.

Joey would need to be an exceptional man to cope with that. *He must learn to be as strong as his sister. He must have a man on which to pattern himself.*

It would be a hard task easing them into such an adulthood as chance had made them heir to. If Joey were to inherit an empire too, then Ruth would need the assistance of Bret Lauchaise to build one. It would be the empire that Alex had dreamed of building. He had talked of using the O'Mahoney construction companies to build a string of theatres and places of entertainment across the length and breadth of America.

Would Bret expect children of his own? She was not far off forty now – he would not expect her to produce a second family. He had said he would settle for anything if she would have him. *Could I bring myself to sail these waters again . . . as Ruth Lauchaise?*

The coast of the Isle of Wight was indistinct in a sea mist. The sea, reflecting the patches of sun and sky, was dead flat and the air hardly moved. Ruth and Rose sat, with the two children, in an observation lounge and watched the Solent gradually expanding to become the English Channel, which within a day or so would become the Atlantic. From the direction of the smoking funnels above them came a farewell salute on the fog-horn.

'See to the children, Rose. I want to go on deck for a minute.'

'Are you all right, Miss Ruth?'

'Never better, Rose. You like the idea of Nevada?'

'Wasn't we happy there! Yes, *Ma'am*! That's the place for us.'

'Yes. I believe it is.' She had a sudden image of the purple mountain range, the bare landscape and rocky terrain not ten minutes on horseback from the house in Virginia City. *Could it be the same with Bret there? Not the same. Bret would be an intrusion. But he was necessary to Joey. And to Anne? Perhaps. Perhaps Anne would take to him. She herself had been seven when she first went to live with Pa. Perhaps it could be like that for Anne. Perhaps Anne needed a father more than Joey. Perhaps that was why she herself . . . No!* She was getting better at stopping herself from thinking of herself in the old way – as unnatural, infected.

'I will just go to see the last of England.' *And leave behind that part of my life.*

Looking out from the observation lounge, Rose Geary was surprised to see her elegant mistress remove her travelling cape and hood and unpin her chignon as though in the privacy of her bedroom.

The first breeze from the open sea as the vessel headed into the Channel blew Ruth's mass of flaming hair, famous in theatres from New York to Virginia City, into a beautiful red spinnaker.

Betty Burton receives letters from many parts of the world from readers interested in her novels. The saga of which this book is part is set in Hampshire and spans the eighteenth, nineteenth and twentieth centuries. Once or twice a year the author sends out a newsletter replying to readers' questions, comments and suggestions and saying a bit about what is coming next.

If you have enjoyed this novel and would like to know more about Betty Burton's other books – both those already in print and those in preparation – you can write to her c/o Grafton Books, 8 Grafton Street, London W1X 3LA.